JOURNEY TO THE
DARK GALAXY

HANNAH D. STATE

JOURNEY TO THE DARK GALAXY

THE DARK GALAXY SERIES
BOOK 2

HANNAH D. STATE

Cover art by Miblart

Interior scene break design by Getcovers

Interior formatting created with Vellum

Published by Glowing Light Press, NB, Canada

For all inquiries, including subsidiary rights information, please contact the publisher:

glowinglightpress@gmail.com

All rights reserved.

ISBN: 978-1-7772542-4-7 (paperback)

ISBN: 978-1-7772542-5-4 (e-book)

ISBN: 978-1-7772542-6-1 (hardcover)

"Five stars for a fine debut novel!"—*The Miramichi Reader*

"A wonderfully engaging fantasy adventure for YA. Cleverly plotted and totally unique, I'd highly recommend it."—*A 'Wishing Shelf' Book Review*

"A page-turner full of surprises."—*The Prairies Book Review*

To Brent,
for your infinite love and support.

"Only when it is dark enough can you see the stars."

Martin Luther King Jr.

PROLOGUE

Onnisa jolted awake.

The nightmare clung to her like tar. Frightening images lingered: Earth deteriorating into a fiery blaze of madness, enormous loss of life, and Queen Samantha, falling, spiraling into an all-consuming black hole.

The dream left her shaken and uncertain. This was not a dream of her home, of a Kryg in the past, arriving as warm nostalgia. This was different.

It was a premonition, a warning.

Samantha and the entire Earth were in danger.

She sensed the darkness. Drifting like thick smoke wafting in the air after a raging fire, expanding, devouring. Filling each space it touched. If left unchecked, it would spread throughout the universe, swallowing up every planet in its vicinity.

Rising, Onnisa drew her robe tightly around her against the cold. The air had a strange quality about it today, as if it were charged with electricity. While she usually felt the familiar current, the sparks of energy rippling through her fingers where she held her power, today, it spread along the entire surface of her body, lifting her hairs upright. It prickled her skin, and no amount of rubbing would make it go away.

In the distance, dark-gray storm clouds gathered in protest—treacherous, insistent. Thunder rumbled, announcing its angry presence.

She gazed outside at Kassa Lake, its surface improbably calm. Light from the red sun reflected over the trees and shrubs, drenching them in a fiery hue, as if ablaze. Except for the lake. The shade of light bouncing off its glassy surface looked like human blood.

Across the lake, she could feel—as much as see—the arriving storm clouds, ominous and unforgiving. A coldness crept up her spine.

She would have expected a scene in motion, the yellow Kylie flowers fluttering on the wind, filtering the air. Instead, the air remained still, empty. The flowers, the leaves, even the branches stood motionless, as if even the slightest movement might upset their balance. Flowers rested on the ground and the surface of the lake. It felt like death. Without any wind, a thick haze permeated the air like a heavy shroud, suffocating the landscape.

Onnisa felt the crackling of electricity again in her hands. A few of her fingers had acquired a yellowish tinge at their blue tips. They would fall off soon. Losing a finger was not particularly painful, but it served as a reminder of her fragility. She rubbed them, both stimulating and soothing them. She had lost a few of her dozens of fingers over the years, mostly from overuse and old age. With each finger she lost, some of the electrical current was lost, too. In the past, she could easily regenerate her limbs. But not now. Not after nine hundred and fifty-nine years. Old age was a privilege, but it came with its afflictions and limitations. She thanked the stars for her gift of translucence, the unique power of Krygian Elders to share thoughts and memories through hand-to-hand contact. But her gift would not last forever. *She* would not last forever. She would need to find and train a replacement soon.

But none of that mattered right at this moment.

She returned her gaze to the menacing dark clouds merging, transforming. Creeping ever closer toward the tranquil lake.

Darkness is looming.

What mattered now was that Queen Samantha Sanderson's life was at risk, which meant the stability of Kryg and Earth was threatened, too.

She would need to discuss her concerns with the other Elders. They needed to remain vigilant about potential threats, even those seemingly insignificant.

CHAPTER ONE

SAM SANDERSON WOKE, HER HEART BEATING RAPIDLY. A NIGHTMARE lingered—images of enemy alien ships, of giant, black, egg-shaped pods descending from the sky. And inside them, those menacing creatures. Like giant spherical jellyfish, a hybrid of AI machinery and organic flesh. Their mutating bodies, slick black bubbling masses. Those gleaming metallic barbed tentacles slicing through the air. They hovered on purple pockets of energy, racing to locate and destroy their victims…

She rubbed her eyes, trying to erase the frightening images. Dense grogginess and a pounding headache put her on edge—a raw, pulsating ache that only intensified as she took in her strange surroundings.

This wasn't home. At least, it wasn't her home on Maple River Drive in Moncton, New Brunswick, with her grandfather. And this wasn't her comfortable bed. This confining, gloomy room with drab white walls was definitely not her residence quarters at the military base, either. So where was she?

She bolted upright. A bed, a sink, and a toilet. No windows.

Where there should have been a door, instead were thick, impenetrable iron bars.

She gulped, her mouth dry. She pulled her blanket closer, the damp coldness of the air threatening to seep into her bones.

Her mouth gaped open in sudden awful awareness. This was no nightmare.

They'd *captured* her.

But of course they had. And it was all her fault. Annoyance—with herself—mixed with shame and desolation brewed inside her.

She quietly cursed. The whole situation had been entirely preventable. She had done this. She had allowed it to happen. It could have all been so easily avoided—if only she had told someone the truth earlier.

If only she hadn't listened to that creature, hadn't allowed it into her mind and thoughts…

If only she hadn't used her telepathy, playing at it like it was some game!

Terrible decision.

She threw the blanket aside and stood. Placing her hands on the cold iron bars of the cell, she rattled them forcefully, her anger erupting. She peered down the long, silent hallway. She was alone, isolated. She wouldn't be surprised if they left her in this cell to rot.

"Kobe? Can you hear me?" She tried to reach out to him using their telepathic connection.

Nothing.

She tried again. This time, to the only other person she could trust.

"ONNISA! Please! Can you hear me? Can you help me?"

She concentrated, waiting for a response as the seconds ticked by.

There was only silence.

She sighed in frustration as loneliness and despair stirred inside her. They probably had this cell equipped with telepathic interception technology. It would block any attempted transmission.

Now, she was truly alone.

She shivered, thinking about what had led her here.

When she had first arrived at the military base, the admiral had given her only one rule: *don't use your telepathy*. It was prohibited. And for good reason, apparently. But what had she done? She'd broken the protocol. Destroyed the admiral's trust.

Careless. Incredibly stupid.

Heat rose to her face. She'd been so foolish to allow the creature's thoughts into her mind. Thoughts that had easily flowed like water. The creature had been kept securely in a tank in a high-security laboratory at the base. The same creature from her nightmare. She shuddered, recalling its menacing presence. Those razor-sharp tentacles. Its globular body, floating in the tank as it communicated with her telepathically. It had compelled her to enter the lab. And she had followed all of its instructions—dutifully and obediently. Unquestioning.

Totally reckless.

She felt disgusted with herself. How easily she had been manipulated.

It was as if someone had been working with this creature to allow her access to the lab. But more than that, someone had been tampering with the lab's supplies, sabotaging the work. Important work. Work that was needed to stop the assailants.

And she would look like the perpetrator.

Guilty. Framed.

Now, she was here, alone, in this prison cell. Awaiting her fate.

She perked up as footsteps echoed down the hall, fast approaching.

They were coming for her.

CHAPTER TWO

THREE WEEKS EARLIER

SAM COULD BARELY CRAM HERSELF INTO THE TINY PHOTO BOOTH BESIDE Kato, a smile glued to her face. There was something fun and old-timey about these photo booths. The total randomness and spontaneity of capturing the moment. A tangible, traditional-type photo. No preparation, no re-dos. And completely unfiltered.

"Wait, let's put on the matching sunglasses first!" Kato said.

"Yes!" Sam pulled out the white-rimmed sunglasses, then fed some coins into the slot. It was one of the few places that still took coins. The screen flashed, giving them only three seconds to prepare. "Ready?"

"No!" Kato said. "Quick, strike a pose!"

Sam leaned in closer so that they were both in the frame. Then, she shot her arm straight up into the air, though she couldn't stop laughing at how ridiculous they looked.

The flash blinded her.

"Let's try a silly one," Kato suggested.

They stuck out their tongues.

A few more flashes, a few more photos until their coins were used up, and the photos slid out the side slot. Sam picked them up, trying not to laugh and utterly failing. The photos were candid, genuine. Now she had a memento to lift her spirits if she ever felt lonely again.

"Classy," Sam joked.

She almost didn't recognize herself in the photos. Who was this impostor? The girl looked confident, stress-free. She looked cool. A far different person than what she felt inside: unsure, nervous, confused. But she'd changed a lot since last year. More and more, she wanted to embrace this fun, exciting side—her alter ego. She liked that she could let herself go with Kato and not worry about what anyone else thought.

"I love them!" Kato erupted, pointing to the one where their fingers connected, making a heart shape. "That one's my favorite!"

"Me too. We'll make copies later so we can each have them."

"We should get to the caf soon to meet with the boys," Kato said, and Sam nodded.

They grabbed their bags and hustled through the crowd.

The mall buzzed with people. Families bustled between stores. Sam's shopping mission with Kato earlier that morning had proved successful. They'd picked up a couple of T-shirts and a few pairs of jeans on sale. The sales rep had remarked on the ones Kato wore, noticing how short they'd looked. Having grown several inches over the summer, she now stood half a foot taller than Sam.

Kato also carried herself with more confidence. She never worried about what others thought. Sam loved her no-nonsense attitude. Whether they were going for bike rides or playing board games, Kato always had the most energy. Willing and enthusiastic, Kato always supported and encouraged her friends in whatever new endeavor they proposed.

On their way to the cafeteria, Sam heard a commotion. A large group of shoppers gathered up ahead.

"What's going on?" Kato asked.

Sam stood on her toes, straining to see over the heads of the crowd. She couldn't see a blasted thing. "No idea. Come on!" Grabbing Kato's hand, she hustled through the sea of people, ignoring the crowd's protests.

A huge entertainment area had been cordoned off beneath the stage. The crowd gawked in amazement at a young woman in her late teens doing tricks on her Hovershoes. She wore a tight black jumpsuit with the gleaming purple Phoenix Sky 8 company logo on her chest. Hovering on a pocket of purple energy, she swayed from side to side. Her movements looked effortless and magical. Sparks flew as she gathered speed. She twisted up her body, doing a flip in midair. Whoops and hollers rang from the crowd.

Something inside Sam ignited. "That looks so fun!"

She could only dream of Hovershoes. Once you strapped them on, you floated on air. You could shift your weight to choose which direction and how fast you wanted to go. She craved the feeling of flying, of freedom and adventure.

Kato sighed. "If only we had enough money…"

Of course, neither of them did. It would take her more than a year of saving up all her allowance for them! Only the rich kids could afford them. Like Simon.

A booth beside the stage contained row upon row of Hovershoes. There seemed to be an infinite number of styles. Sam drooled over each of them. She liked the shiny black ones the best —the ones with the purple laces. They looked sleek, the material almost otherworldly. She picked one up, half-expecting it to be heavy and cumbersome. But it was surprisingly light and smooth. Turning it over, she swore she could feel the shoe vibrating with a strange electricity. She admired the intricate latticework and the holographic logo shimmering in the light. She wondered what kinds of adventures these types of shoes could take her on…

A large sign displayed the words SUPERPOWER CONTEST. Underneath, it read: WHAT IS YOUR SUPERPOWER? It listed some examples:

telepathy, power absorption, invisibility, replication, x-ray vision, precognition, and mind control.

A man in his forties with a mic spoke to the audience, his tone energetic, engaging. "Give another round of applause to Jackie," he said as she made her way off the stage. "Now, who would like to win a pair of Hovershoes?"

Screams and cheers rippled through the crowd. Sam's interest piqued and then skyrocketed. She glanced at Kato, who looked equally enthused at the possibility of winning a pair of those expensive shoes.

The man continued. "Let's get this contest started!"

Sam and Kato watched as a line of mostly teens gathered to the right of the stage, waiting for their chance to play.

A red velvet chair rested in the middle of the stage, facing the audience. Behind it, a massive screen projected dozens of various images.

The contestants stared at the images, trying to memorize all the details before the game started. But there were so many. An industrial fan whirred in the corner of the stage, blowing a sweet fragrance into the air. It seemed to affect the participants in line. They were all bouncing up and down, brimming with excitement to start the game.

A girl stood beside Sam and Kato, frowning. "There are at least fifty images to choose from, and I picked the right one, but I only got one detail right. And they needed at least three. They never told me that beforehand. I was so close! Everyone agreed I should've won! I'd been studying all the images for hours. But I'm going to keep trying."

They watched as, one by one, eager contestants took a seat, each with the same outcome.

The man with the mic would place a pair of vision-blocking goggles over the participant's head. Then came the noise-canceling headphones. He gave them a few seconds to get ready. Next, he selected one of the images from the screen using a handheld device. He zoomed in, the image taking up the entire screen.

The images were random.

First, a picture of a rhinoceros in the savanna appeared. It drank from a watering hole with a couple of shrubs in the distance.

The next participant's image revealed a two-story yellow house at the top of a hill. Snow covered the ground. Three children tobogganed on red sleds.

Each contestant tried to guess the image behind them using a few adjectives. Each person described an entirely different scene—getting it magnificently wrong. Laughs rang out from the crowd each time.

The game was a ruse, of course. The whole point seemed to be to make the participants look foolish. Could the game even be won? Sam didn't think so. Or maybe there was a low chance, if at all. The game reminded contestants of their weaknesses and drew attention to the Hovershoes. People were desperate to fill a gap. What better way to do it than with a contest that intentionally made people feel inadequate and ridiculed them for it? If people didn't have superpowers, at least they could try and win the Hovershoes to make them *feel* powerful.

But the contest instilled a false hope. Sam was sure the game was fixed, somehow. And the girl's experience of *almost* winning only proved it. The company wasn't upfront about what was required to win. Once people lost, it only gave them more incentive to buy the shoes outright. The game was deceptive, and that wasn't right. It was downright manipulative.

She didn't want to be part of it. "Come on, Kato. We should go."

"Wait, I just want to see a bit more—"

As each contestant walked off the stage disheartened, Sam grew even more infuriated with the company's tactics. Many of the contestants were young. They looked especially distraught and miserable when they didn't win.

Sam turned her attention back to the shoes. But her eyes drifted to a nearby poster displaying information about the technology.

She did a double take. The shoes had an *unlimited* power supply? Surely they required electricity or batteries for recharging?

The young woman, Jackie, who had been doing tricks on her Hovershoes, now stood a few feet away. She looked eager to help potential customers. Sam turned to face her. "I don't understand. How's it an unlimited power supply? Where does it get its power? Doesn't it have batteries?"

Jackie shook her head. "No. Batteries break down over time. These shoes use new advanced technology developed by the military. Something called a Gideon spark. Named after the scientist from Barbados who invented it. The energy renews itself over time."

Gideon spark? She'd never heard of it—or the scientist—before. Now she was captivated. She wanted to learn not only about the technology and how it worked but also about its genius inventor.

Jackie continued. "The shoes are excellent quality. They're expensive, but they're made to last. They come with a lifetime warranty, too. I've had mine for three years now. They also adjust in length a couple of sizes as you grow. See?" She pressed a button at the base of the shoe she was holding, and it grew in length right before Sam's eyes.

"Wow! That's impressive!"

Jackie grinned, but it was fleeting. Curious, Sam followed Jackie's gaze. A boy a few years older than Sam strode toward them like he owned the place. It wasn't the way he walked that caught her attention, but the expression on his face. A self-assuredness. And something more. A remarkable certainty, as if he could change the future with the snap of his fingers. He smirked like he was hiding a secret or an inside joke.

His friend, another boy, stood close by for support. Sam wondered what they were plotting. Maybe a dare was involved.

The boy approached, and Jackie eyed him suspiciously. "Can I help you?"

"Yes. If you go on a date with me, I'll show you *my* superpowers," he said haughtily.

Sam and Kato both stifled their laughter. It was the cheesiest pickup line she'd ever heard.

Jackie was also taken aback, her face reddening. She glared at him like he was from another planet. "In your dreams, Duncan," she scoffed.

The boy's animated expression immediately faded to disappointment. He shrugged. "I tried."

Sam was disappointed. He shared the same silly bravado of many of the boys in her school. She had expected high school boys to be cooler.

"Dude, she's like way out of your league, anyway," his friend added as they hurried away, disappearing into the crowd.

Jackie turned her attention to Sam and Kato. "Can I help you ladies find some sizes?"

Sam really wanted to try a pair. She wanted to master the flips and twists and rolls Jackie had performed earlier. She could tell Kato wanted to try them too.

But then she remembered the time. It was almost lunch, and her stomach grumbled.

She returned the shoe to the shelf, the excitement slowly dissipating. "We're late and have to go. Maybe later."

"Sure. We'll be around all day. You should come back and try the contest."

As they were leaving, the man with the mic spoke up. "Folks, we're going to take a little break from the contest. But come back at 1 p.m., and we'll get it started again!"

The man's nagging played on Sam's nerves. The company was setting people up to fail—*every* time.

In the heat of the moment, something changed inside her, like a switch had gone off.

An idea floated into her mind, and despite her best efforts to push it away, she let it in.

She could use her telepathy to win the game.

Even though it was dangerous—not to mention her skill was a secret from most people—she still wanted to do it to prove them wrong.

"Maybe we could win a pair," Sam suggested to Kato, an energy growing inside her. "We should come back later and try."

"Maybe," Kato said. She didn't look as excited now, perhaps because she didn't think they could do it. "We should get going, though. Simon and Kobe are probably already at the caf, wondering where we are."

"You're right."

They hurried to the cafeteria to join Kobe and Simon for lunch, the possibilities tugging at the edge of Sam's mind.

CHAPTER THREE

Sam gazed at the sea of faces in the cafeteria, trying to spot Kobe and Simon, but it was impossible. There were too many people. And it was noisy and cramped, which put her on edge. She would have much preferred a quiet place to eat. Like outside in the park, where sounds didn't reverberate off floors and walls. How would they even find an empty table here?

"Where are they?" Kato asked.

Sam looked around. She had trouble spotting anyone, let alone squeezing by without stumbling over people's toes.

Kato paused and placed her bags on the ground. "Hold on. Let me text my brother."

"We're over by the pizza place."

Sam heard the words in her mind. It was Kobe. They'd gotten better at reading each other's minds over the summer. Now it was just habit.

He must have sensed her bewilderment because not a moment later, she caught his gaze from a table on the other side of the cafeteria. He waved.

"I see him. Let's go," Sam said, and Kato followed her over.

Two large pizzas were stacked on the table, one already half-eaten. Sam still couldn't believe Simon's colossal appetite. He was the tallest, lankiest boy in her class, half a foot taller than Kato and Kobe.

Simon pushed his glasses higher while chewing another bite. "Well, well! I'd say you were both successful," he said between mouthfuls, eyeing the multiple bags Sam and Kato carried.

"Hey, Noodle," Kato teased. "Save some for the rest of us!" She sat down and helped herself to a slice of pizza. Sam also took a slice, going for the vegetarian option.

"We're all shopped out," Sam admitted. "What about you guys?"

Simon slid his hand into his backpack and pulled out a thin chrome-metal case. Sam stared at the bulging-eyed, festering monster etched into its cover. Usually, games were kept in plastic cases, not metal. This had to be a collector's edition that cost a lot more. Maybe it had extra special features, too. Virtual reality games were popular, but Sam's parents and grandfather wouldn't allow them in their home. *Too distracting*, her grandfather had said. *Deteriorates the mind*. She'd tried one once at Simon's house. It was pretty amazing and life-like. She hoped Simon would let her try this one as well, without too much obvious drooling.

"*Zombie Apocalypse: Infinity Deathmatch 5*. The best, newest virtual reality game in the series." Simon beamed. "Just released yesterday."

Kato smirked. "It's nice to see your back-to-school shopping went well. You're really investing in a high-quality education."

"Hey, you can learn a lot about surviving from these games!"

"Oh yeah? Like how to hole up somewhere and store food if we get raided by zombies?" Kato teased.

"Well, it's not just that," Simon started, a little defensively. "You need strategy—skills, weapons! You need to know how to kill those monsters. It's not so easy."

"You mean it's not so easy killing something that's already

dead?" Kato laughed. "I don't think you have anything to worry about."

"You sure about that?" Simon grinned. "You never know when monsters will threaten the human race. It's always good to be prepared."

"Speaking of being prepared, do you really want to go back to school?" Kobe asked. Sam could tell he was anxious about it by the way he tapped his foot on the ground. He wore faded jeans with holes ripped around the knees and a black T-shirt. He'd grown his hair out over the summer, too, almost as long as Kato's. Unlike the rest of them, he wasn't carrying any bags. He didn't look happy about being at the mall, either. But of course not. He was an introvert and preferred the quiet. Like she did.

"Um, yeah," Kato replied, as if no other answer existed. "I mean, the summer was great and all, but we're starting eighth grade. It's a big deal—you know, it *feels* different, somehow. The last year before high school."

Sam had mixed feelings about school starting. For her, the end of summer aligned with her parents going off on another government mission. They were heading to adventure, and she was stuck here, left behind with her grandfather. He wasn't so bad to live with. Except for the earlier curfews, more frequent check-ins, and stricter rules. He had an aversion to anything fun-related. He wanted to keep an eye on her at all times. She often found it excessive. But she couldn't complain. After all, he had her best interests at heart. He was overly worried about her parents' safety since they hadn't said when they would be back, and he didn't want to lose Sam, too.

"I don't know…" Sam started. "I guess so. My parents left on another mission, so it's just me and my grandfather. But to be honest, I wish I could explore the galaxy too. Starting classes just doesn't feel as remotely thrilling."

"Are you still using your—*thingy*—to travel through space?" Simon asked. "What's it called?"

Sam rolled her eyes. The *thingy* was, of course, the klug. The Krygian device could create wormholes for interstellar travel —*when it was working!* Which, of course, it wasn't now. It hadn't for some time. It was wonky at the best of times and had failed her more than once. She couldn't use its power or tap into its teleportation capabilities remotely. The power was gone.

"No. It's busted. My parents confiscated it after what happened. I still can't believe it broke on my way back from Kryg *and* that I ended up in a coma. Anyway, they don't want me using it anymore."

"Makes sense," Simon said. "But it would be fun to go on another adventure."

"Yeah," Kato and Kobe replied in unison.

Sam sighed, placing her elbows on the table and resting her chin on her palms. How she longed to go on another adventure again, too. Explore the universe. It would be way better than sitting at a desk all day or shutting herself in her room doing homework in the evenings.

"What about you, Kobe? Did you get anything for back-to-school?"

Kobe, with a shrug, shifted into telepathy. *"Nope. I hate shopping. Can't find anything that looks good or fits. It takes too long."*

"I know. It's a zoo today with so many people. The lines are massive."

"Yeah, and I don't really need any new clothes. The ones I have still fit."

"You guys are doing it again," Kato complained. "Stop that!"

"What?" Sam asked. "Oh, sorry." Heat rushed to her face. Her secret telepathic conversation with Kobe wasn't particularly embarrassing. Instead, she was mortified they might feel left out for not hearing it.

Simon smiled. "Did you want to share your conversation with us, or is it private?"

"I was just saying I don't like shopping. I don't need anything anyway," Kobe said, then added, "except maybe one thing."

"Let me guess," Simon said, leaning forward. "The Phoenix Sky 8 Fire Racer Hovershoes."

"Bingo."

Kato slid her brother a concerned glance. "Mom didn't give you money to buy those crazy expensive shoes!"

"Yeah, I know. Just saying it'd be cool."

"Do you want to play the Superpower Contest?" Simon suggested. "It's been happening every Friday for the past few weeks. As far as I know, no one has won a pair yet."

Despite wanting those Hovershoes, she still felt conflicted about it. "I don't know. Seems like that contest sets people up to fail."

"Yeah, but with your telepathy skills," he said, eyeing Sam and Kobe carefully, "you two could win. Easy."

"We could take turns," Kobe said. "While you're in the chair, I could view the images and give you the answers. And vice versa."

Sam pondered the opportunity. After all, the same idea had occurred to her earlier, too…

But no. It was a bad idea to use her telepathy. It was a special gift bestowed on her by the Krygians. She couldn't use it for cheap tricks.

"That's cheating."

"No," Kobe said. "Not if you have a special ability. Which…we do."

"They are *literally* inviting you to use superpowers," Simon chimed in.

"Both good points," Sam mused. Communicating with Kobe telepathically had become easier over the summer. But the ability had its limits. Neither of them could communicate with others the same way. It only worked with a willing and capable partner who shared the same ability. With Kobe there, they could coordinate it perfectly. Both Kobe and Kato really wanted a pair of those shoes. And Sam wanted a chance to win the contest and disrupt the company's unfair game. It wouldn't cause any trouble, right? It wouldn't *hurt* anyone. What could go wrong?

"Okay. I'm in!" Sam said.

Kobe grinned. "Then let's do this!"

CHAPTER FOUR

RADIO TELESCOPE RESEARCH STATION 23, UNDISCLOSED LOCATION, CANADA

Kwan Yun liked puzzles. The more challenging, the better. Sudoku and chess were her favorites. She was twenty-two now, but she'd learned to code at five. They'd called her a prodigy then. Who knew what they called her now?

She spoke six languages: English, French, Korean, Mandarin, Spanish, and Russian. Her brilliance in languages, pattern recognition, and intelligence had sparked the interest of the Canadian government. When the opportunity had arisen to take a position at a radio telescope research station in Canada, she hadn't hesitated. A respectable salary, a good quality of life, an opportunity to start over, *and* a chance to study signal patterns? She promptly accepted. She'd spent her whole life moving around. She looked forward to a place where she could put down roots. A place where she could leave her troubled past behind.

A fresh start.

When she escaped North Korea as a young child and was sent

to an orphanage in South Korea, she was given a new identity. Her original name, Soo Min, meaning "excellence and cleverness," might have reflected her nature, but her new name, Kwan... Well, that meant "strong." She liked that. It was undeniably fitting.

With her large frame, strong bone structure, and angular face, people often mistook her for male. Her short hair and half-shaved head only contributed to this. Not that she cared. People tended to underestimate her physical fortitude. She could bench press one hundred and eighty pounds and bring a grown man to his knees with her skills in Jujitsu and Krav Maga, the martial arts used by the Israeli Defense Forces.

Their team at the research station was responsible for monitoring and decoding signals from space. They'd listened to signals for many years. Most signals were just noise—sometimes interference from other satellites, and sometimes pulsars or other natural galactic events. But their job was to search for messages from intelligent life. Of course, it was difficult. They didn't know what to look for, let alone which method would be used to send the signal. They had appreciated having her as a fresh pair of eyes and ears on the project.

Her colleague, Raphael, was in charge of calibrating the signals, determining their origin—whether they could be explained by natural phenomena, human-made technology, or something else. Her role was to explore whatever fell into the category of "something else."

The last interesting signal they'd received was just over three years ago. A series of repeated fast radio bursts. They considered the possibility it was an intentional signal sent from an intelligent extraterrestrial civilization. But after further study, it was just another neutron star. Since then...

Nothing.

Kwan sighed.

With billions of stars in the universe, finding anything would take time. At least she was free to use any of the station's equipment as she saw fit. Dr. Vaughn, the station's director, would set her up with anything she needed.

But that wasn't enough. Not for her.

She'd taken it one step further. She'd developed a software program to detect patterns in communications and get a better understanding of the nature of the signals. Coding was one of her passions. She'd played around with a sophisticated software algorithm for a while. She hoped it might offer up a solution.

This particular algorithm used a machine-learning AI to detect patterns in communications. From Morse code to number pattern recognition, it had the ability to translate signal coding into multiple human languages. She didn't know if it would work, but it was worth a try. After all, other scientists and inventors had failed numerous times. That was part of the experimentation process. Some even spent years testing inventions through trial and error before succeeding. By integrating a machine-learning AI, the process might be able to find something in less time.

She knew what was at stake. She'd need to do solid work, at least for this first year, if she wanted a permanent position later. If she was good enough, they might even allow her to relocate to Canada permanently.

If everything went smoothly.

Kwan had worked hard this past summer, tweaking her software. Experimenting with its compatibilities and arrays. But the summer had proved uneventful. She'd received a few signals, but nothing that couldn't be explained away as natural phenomena.

Today, she felt a sadness, a longing that pierced her heart.

She sat at her desk, her gaze drawn again to the picture of Jae-Hwa. Her lovely eyes and long black hair, pulled into her signature side braid. The image tugged at her heart as much as it reminded her of the pain of living so far from each other.

The photograph was from their picnic this past spring. Before her assignment. They'd decided to get matching tattoos on their wrists. Two birds flying together to signify their promise to stay together. That was the day they'd declared their love for one another.

Now, she wondered if she would ever see her again. They'd met at university in Canada, but Jae-Hwa was back in South Korea now, working odd jobs with little money and suffering the weight of student debt. If Kwan could permanently relocate to Canada, it would be easier to get Jae-Hwa a visa too. Kwan's salary could help pay off their student debt. And they wouldn't have to worry about traveling long distances to see each other. She could see them building a life here together.

Her face flushed at the glimmer of hope she felt when recalling how Jae-Hwa had spoken so excitedly about joining her in Canada. It would be paradise for them to be able to stay here indefinitely!

But she couldn't get her hopes up.

She pushed those thoughts aside to instead focus on the main task. With Dr. Vaughn away at a conference, it was just her and Raphael. Raphael was friendly enough—in the beginning. But over time, he'd become more reserved and less inclined to take to her suggestions. They were both vying for a permanent position at the research station. Perhaps he felt threatened? Kwan was pretty much an expert at reading people but sometimes had an issue when communicating. She tended to give off the wrong signals. She may as well have worn a shirt that said: *I can read you, but you can't read me.* Perhaps she had come across as too eager.

Still, she needed him to respect her if she was going to get any further in her challenging assignment.

"I've made some tweaks to the software." She'd applied a code to filter out dark matter in case it happened to block any incoming signals. "Would it be okay to install the updates? It might help us get a better understanding about the nature of the signals."

Raphael hesitated, and a look of surprise flashed in his eyes. "I don't know if Dr. Vaughn—"

"Dr. Vaughn said I could use any of the equipment," she

blurted. What she needed was leverage. "That I could use it at my leisure. I could call him, if you—"

"Oh, no. That's okay. Go for it. It would be amazing to be the first to crack this signal, but don't get your hopes up. It takes a long time to get any good, solid data."

"Great. Thanks."

She installed the software updates. It only took a moment to load. Flashes of coding appeared on the screen, running the algorithms. She stepped into the lunch room to grab an apple from the fridge. She sunk her teeth into its juicy flesh, enjoying the sweetness on her lips. She thought about calling Jae-Hwa tonight. Three days had passed since they last spoke. Too long—an eternity.

When she returned to the lab, a beeping sound rang from the computers.

Maybe a pulsar. Possibly a black hole. Or, more likely, a glitch with the coding.

She was ready to dismiss it but stopped when she saw Raphael's shocked expression.

He looked up from his screen, his eyes darting back and forth. "Kwan, you need to see this! I—I think the software update you just installed…it's acting up."

She hurried over to his workstation, eyeing the information on the screen. "That's weird." Her heart skipped a beat at the strange words on the display. Depicted continuously in several languages was the same phrase repeated:

DELIVER THE QUEEN OF KRYG TO LOGOM

OR RISK THE DESTRUCTION OF GAIA.

She leaned closer, half-expecting to find she'd misread it. But she hadn't. The words were there, the message plain and straightforward.

She swallowed before speaking. "I don't understand. What does this mean?"

The message was specific, outlandish even. Raphael gazed at her, bewildered.

If this wasn't some joke on her, then who had sent the message, and why?

A series of numbers flashed on the screen that she didn't recognize. It looked like locational coordinates of some sort. Who—or what—was Logom? And who was the Queen of Kryg?

A moment later, flashing red text appeared in the middle of the screen.

SECURITY LEVEL 6

FORWARDING MESSAGE TO GAIA NOW

Raphael's mouth fell open, and a dazed look spread across his face. "Security Level 6? That's like, *way* beyond my pay grade."

The phone rang. Raphael picked it up. "Hello?" He paused. "Yes, it's Raphael, Admiral Green. No…no, I wasn't the one to… No. Her name is Kwan. Kwan Yun. She started with us over the summer. Hold on a sec." He passed the phone to her, his voice barely a whisper. "It's the *big*, big boss. She wants to speak to you directly."

"Hello?" Kwan said, her voice dry.

"I'm Admiral Green. I operate this research station and others. You need to tell me what happened, and you need to tell me now."

Admiral Green's voice was even, laser-focused, and urgent. The kind of voice that could cut through glass.

Kwan thought about what was at stake. Would they reprimand her for using a machine-learning AI in the coding without Dr. Vaughn's knowledge? Would they send her back to her home country? Had her software run amok and accidentally intercepted a secret military project? Perhaps the "Queen of Kryg" was something else, like a code name for a person of high influence.

But what were Logom and GAIA?

Kwan shifted uncomfortably. How much information did she

need to give? If Admiral Green operated this center, then Kwan was at her mercy. She needed to tell the truth. All of it. But she needed to tell it in such a way as to remain on Admiral Green's good side. She needed to sound innocent, unwitting. Maybe apologetic, too.

"Sure." Kwan forced the word out. "Uh… I installed a software program. It's something I developed over the summer. I updated it with some modifications a few minutes ago. I—I think it just picked up a signal now. I don't know what it means. If I made a mistake, I'm sorry—"

"No," the admiral sighed. "No, you didn't. Now, you need to listen to me. I'm going to send a transport chopper to pick you up at the research station. You need to pack your bags and be ready in twenty-four hours. You'll be escorted to the Newfoundland and Labrador GAIA military base. It's a matter of international security."

She perked up. What did Admiral Green mean by *international* security? "Wait, what? I don't know if Dr. Vaughn will allow me—"

"Don't worry about Dr. Vaughn. I'll take care of things. Now, I'll be making arrangements for you to take an indefinite leave of absence from your job. Don't worry. Your expenses will be covered. We need your expert assistance here at the base. So, can you be ready for tomorrow?"

Kwan hesitated. She had no choice. "Yes." Her plans of staying here, with a stable position, and bringing Jae-Hwa to live with her started to crumble into a pile of dust that now traveled in the wind.

"Good. Bring that software. And one last thing."

"Yes, Admiral?"

A small pause. "Make sure you have your will in order."

There was a click on the other end, and the line went dead.

CHAPTER FIVE

Sam and her friends arrived at the Hovershoes entertainment complex, where the crowd had doubled in size.

She and Kobe hurried to take their places in line.

One by one, eager contestants guessed the images behind them and failed. The crowd absolutely relished the contestants' incorrect answers.

Sam turned back to Kobe a few feet down the line. He looked eager to do this. More eager than she was. But she didn't want to let him down. She'd thought she wanted to win a pair of those shoes too. But now…

Was this what the Queen of Kryg should do? Use her telepathy to cheat in a silly game to win a pair of shoes?

The next contestant was a young girl who looked around seven years old. She wavered at first as the man with the mic coaxed her to take a seat in the red chair. Finally, she made her way to the center of the stage. Her mother stood to the side, cheering her on. The girl was silent and nervous. The man placed the vision-blocking goggles over her head. Then came the noise-canceling earphones. The crowd fell silent.

She called out, her voice wavering. "I...I don't *see* anything. All I see is...darkness!" She screamed. Pulling off the headphones and goggles, she ran across the stage, visibly shaken. Not everyone could handle sensory deprivation. Maybe the girl was too young to understand the game. Her mother consoled her, and they left.

Sam was next. She hesitated, still conflicted. But Kobe was counting on her now. And she couldn't get the girl's reaction out of her mind. She willed herself forward, taking a seat on the big, cushy chair. This was her idea, wasn't it? And they'd already come this far.

The man placed the goggles over her eyes. Darkness. Then came the noise-canceling headphones, and that part of her world was blotted out too, the crowd's chatter disappearing. She was alone.

It was more than unnerving.

She took a deep breath and let it out slowly.

Kobe's voice flowed into her mind: "*It's a picture of an old man wearing a brown vest. He's seated on a green bench in the park. There's a small white dog beside him. There are trees on either side of the pathway and a little girl with a blue jacket playing hopscotch.*"

Instead of speaking, Sam remained silent, her thoughts turning instead to the Hovershoes. The thrill of taking them out to the skateboard park and mastering those tricks beckoned her. Adventure was calling. It was meant to be. After all, why was she given the gift of telepathy if she was never meant to use it?

"*Hurry, they're waiting,*" Kobe urged.

Her thoughts returned to the image Kobe had described. The old man could have been her grandfather, along with their dog, Pip. Whether it was a coincidence or not, she didn't know. She sighed, the words flowing out of her mouth too easily. "It's a picture of an old man. He's wearing a brown vest. He's in the park, seated on a green bench, with trees on either side. There's a small white dog beside him. There's a little girl with a blue jacket... playing hopscotch."

She immediately realized her mistake. They only needed to give a few adjectives to describe the scene. She had given too many details. Now, people would wonder. They'd know her gift. She may as well have announced to the world, "I am the Queen of Kryg! Powerful telepath!" That, and placed a giant target on her back.

This had all been a horrible, terrible mistake.

She yanked off the goggles and headphones, only to find…

Silence.

The crowd stood frozen. An eerie quiet hung in the air. Even the man with the mic looked stunned, his eyes wide, his mouth drooping open. The mic dropped from his hand, setting off a squeal of feedback that shocked the onlookers out of their stupor. A wave of frantic chatter and excited whispers rippled through the crowd.

The presenter grabbed up the mic, along with his faculties, and his lips curled into a smile. "Give a round of applause, folks. Our first winner of the day, but not our last! You, too, can win. But only if you give it a try!" He turned to Sam. "Head over to the booth, and Jackie will get you set up with your size."

Sam pretended to be happy, surprised. But inside, she felt like a fraud. An impostor.

While she waited for Jackie to retrieve the shoes, she sensed…

Sam looked over the crowd. She was certain she'd felt something, like someone watching her from the sidelines. She couldn't quite place it.

Jackie returned with the shoes. "Congrats! Why are you frowning? You're the *first* person I know who has won this contest."

Sam forced a smile and took the bag but wondered how she would explain it to her grandfather later. She managed a quick "Thanks" before retreating into the crowd.

A deep chill flooded her body. She clutched her arms, goosebumps forming.

"You're in danger."

She heard the words in her mind, but she couldn't determine their source. She whipped her head around, scanning the audience. There were so many people. But nothing seemed out of the ordinary. The audience's attention was on the next contestant.

Still, the uneasiness lingered, as if a ghost had witnessed her transgressions and she was being monitored for later repercussions.

She must have imagined it. It was just the guilt weighing on her conscience.

She looked over to the stage. Kobe was next in line.

Here we go again.

Simon's mom picked Sam and her friends up from the mall. The SUV was big enough to fit all their bags, but just barely.

Kobe couldn't stop beaming. "You can borrow my Hovershoes, Kato. After all, we're the same size. But only if you promise to take good care of them and protect them with your life!"

"Yes, I know. I promise," Kato replied, rolling her eyes.

Whatever brief enthusiasm Sam had felt at the prospect of winning had vanished.

Someone had seen them, observed them from the crowd— someone with questionable intent.

She shook her head. The more likely scenario was that she was just tired and overreacting. That, and feeling guilty. She'd used her powers—this gift from the Krygians that could save lives and worlds—to cheat. And for what? To win some shoes. Shoes she didn't need. Maybe the warning she'd heard in her mind was just her own paranoid thoughts playing tricks on her.

She kept her thoughts to herself during the car ride home. She didn't want to disrupt the festive mood.

Upon arriving at her house, she stared in surprise at the many changes. Solar lights lined the pathway and the garden bed in front of the veranda. Her grandfather chatted with a stranger, who looked like he was installing a security camera at their front entrance. A security keypad hung from the wall just beyond the doorway.

"Hi, Grandpa. What's all this?"

But her grandfather didn't answer. Instead, he eyed the bag she carried containing her Hovershoes. And he didn't look pleased. "What's that?"

"I... This?" She studied his concerned expression and felt a pang of guilt. If she told him they'd cheated, he would be disappointed in her. But what was the alternative? Lie to him about the whole thing? That would be worse. Either way, he'd be angry. But she didn't want to let it destroy her day. She would just give the necessary details. Try to brush it off. Maybe that would keep the mood lighthearted. But the words came out too hastily, too forced.

"They were having this contest at the mall. Kobe and I... Well, we each won a free pair! It was so much fun, Grandpa, and so *easy*!" she gushed, though she immediately regretted adding the last part. It was so easy because she'd cheated. "Kobe and I were thinking of trying them out later this aft—"

"Come inside. Now. I need to have a word with you."

Sam faltered. Her grandfather looked...furious. She'd never seen that look on his face in her life. Beet red, a mix of anger and fear flashing in his eyes. A crease dug in between his eyebrows, like a crack forming in the Earth, threatening to engulf everything on the surface. His hands trembled, like he couldn't control them. He acted as though she had just committed a serious crime. A mix of humiliation and regret rose inside her.

He led her to the kitchen, at the back of the house, where they were out of earshot of the security man out front.

She didn't have to read her grandfather's thoughts to know why he was angry. He must have figured out what had happened at the mall. She felt ashamed—not just about her actions, but because she'd let him down. But she hadn't hurt anyone, and her friends had been so happy. So what was the big deal?

"Those shoes are *very* expensive. I would hazard a guess that the game wasn't meant to be easy. How many people were watching?"

The question caught her off guard. Shouldn't he have been impressed they'd won, not angry? "I don't know, Grandpa. Does it matter?"

"Yes, it does."

"Maybe fifty. I don't know."

He sighed, trying to regain his composure. "I'll take them. Come on. Give them here."

Sam handed the shoes to him reluctantly, her energy deflating.

"And, you're grounded."

"What? Why?" She couldn't stop her voice from elevating. She'd never been grounded before. What did that even mean? "I don't understand. We won them fair and square. What did I do wrong?"

The lie rang hollow. She heard it even as the words came spilling out. She felt terrible for lying to him and immediately regretted it.

He rubbed his forehead gently. "I'm trying to protect you, don't you see?" His voice was barely a whisper. "After everything that happened with Titus and the kidnapping, I should have installed this security system earlier, but with your parents home, it just didn't feel as much of a priority. But now that they're away…" His voice trailed off for a moment. "I don't want you bragging about your special abilities, either. At the mall, *anyone* could have been watching. People can have…bad intentions. Someone might want to…experiment on you, or worse. You know I care about you. I just don't want to see you get hurt."

Sam sighed. He was right. Last year, Titus Dyaderos, the CEO of TitusTech, had used technology to intercept her thoughts. Even though he'd been captured and his lab had burned down, it was still possible the technology existed elsewhere. She was still the Queen of Kryg, and she was still vulnerable. If her secret got out, it would be the end of her—the end of all of them.

But was her grandfather taking security matters to an extreme? *It sure felt like it.*

"I'm sorry, Grandpa. I promise not to use my abilities again. But please don't take the shoes. I promised Kato we could try them out together this evening at the skateboard park. I just want to be a normal kid, you know? Besides, I'm almost fourteen. I know how to take care of myself!"

"No, and I don't want to discuss it any more. I don't want you spending time with your friends this evening."

What happened next surprised not only her grandfather; it surprised her.

The words came spewing out. They seemed to come out of a deep, dark hole, somewhere she hadn't known existed. Or chose not to. "You can't control my life! I know you miss Mom and Dad like I do, but keeping me locked up here isn't going to keep me safe. And it's not going to bring them back."

She immediately wished she could take the words back. But she couldn't. Not now. There was truth to them, but that truth would just make her grandfather sad. Her parents had abandoned her—them—again. But it wasn't her grandfather's fault.

He turned to her, the fury gone from his face. But not his resolve. "That's enough complaining, young lady. Any more, and you'll be grounded until school starts."

She trudged upstairs to her room, which now felt more like a prison. She could tolerate many things. She could navigate a dark cave on another planet, give a nerve-racking speech on the spot to a community of otherworldly beings, and endure Simon's bad jokes. She had learned to deal with uncertainty, like her parents being away with no promise of when they would return. But the one thing she couldn't tolerate was being confined, away from her friends, with a fear of missing out.

CHAPTER SIX

After arriving at the underwater military base, the first thing they did to Kwan was take away her cell phone. She watched as a woman in a military uniform slipped it into a paper bag, only to hand it to another soldier, who whisked it away. The cell phone was her only link to Jae-Hwa. Without it, she felt anxious, isolated.

Helpless.

How would she fulfill her promise to Jae-Hwa now—let alone contact her to explain what was going on?

They still hadn't told her why she was here. Panic rose up inside her, but she tried not to show it. She tried to stay grounded as she took in as many details as she could.

Her cell phone was gone now. In its place, they gave her a visitor pass. They immediately escorted her to a small meeting room for a debriefing. The room was one of hundreds at this sprawling underwater facility. It was sparsely furnished, with only a wooden table and a few chairs. No paintings or windows. Nothing to distract its visitors.

Kwan sat at the wooden table and waited, wondering why she'd been brought here. The small, sterile room felt stuffy. Across from her sat Admiral Green and Dr. Otto Krill, one of the base's scientists. He looked to be in his seventies, with thinning silver hair, a scruffy beard, and large, circular spectacles. Worry creased his face. How many years had he spent in this lab, and what had he seen?

A stern and exacting woman, Admiral Green swiftly brought Kwan up to speed on the base's functioning and mission objectives, while Dr. Krill remained silent for the most part.

The base served as a waystation for interplanetary visitors and a research and development laboratory. Its employees were part of GAIA, the Great Alliance for Interplanetary Affairs, a secret organization that operated to protect its members' interests, including the health and safety of Earth. One of the base's tasks was to monitor and mitigate any threats to the organization.

It was a lot to take in. But it wasn't totally ludicrous. She knew of the stories and studies—the eyewitness accounts of extraterrestrials. Of course, people had dismissed them, thinking the people behind the stories just wanted fame and fortune or had otherwise gone off the rails. But Kwan sensed some truth here. Classified documents and video footage had been leaked to the media. They'd been denounced, of course. But even high-ranking retired scientists and officials had described the presence of advanced civilizations visiting Earth. If the government was leaking these classified documents over time, perhaps they were preparing society for a truth they'd long kept hidden. A truth meant to come to light, slowly, so that people might adjust better to the news.

It wasn't so outlandish to consider the possibilities. After all, there'd been numerous advancements in space technologies. Statistically, there was a high likelihood of intelligent extraterrestrial life in the universe, given the billions of stars and planets. TitusTech had been harvesting minerals on the moon to make electronics for quite some time and had an entire department dedicated to supporting the government with its secret space program. They'd been using AI robots to explore other habitable planets for decades.

Things seemed to be advancing at a record pace, suggesting that something was up, but the vast majority of the public was unaware of the details—so far.

Kwan had absorbed as much as she could, but having not slept in twenty-four hours, the weight of the information overwhelmed her, as did the throbbing pain in her head. She wasn't sure how much more she could soak up.

"Kwan?"

She shook herself alert. "Sorry, could you please repeat the question, Admiral?"

The admiral flashed her a look, half-stern, half-perplexed. "Kwan, do you understand why you're here?"

Did she understand? *Nope!*

Did they want her software, or something else? Were they going to try to cover up something, like they'd done in the past? Convince her that what she'd discovered was a fluke, a random blip in the data continuum, and then tell her to get on with some other work? Would they transfer her? Lock her away so she couldn't reveal the message, even though she didn't understand what it meant? The possibilities were endless.

"No," she replied. "I don't. Please, enlighten me." The statement came out more abrupt than she had intended, but she couldn't help it. She was trying to make sense of it all. Running on caffeine and adrenaline didn't help, either.

"While you were on your way here," the admiral began, "we looked into the nature of the threat to determine its legitimacy."

So it was possible the threat was valid? Kwan had doubted its credibility. She had thought it was a hoax or a mistake on her part, a glitch in the coding.

Admiral Green continued without hesitating. "And we confirmed that the signal is real."

"How—?" Kwan started.

"We were able to verify its point of origin. It's from Logom, a planet located within the Dark Galaxy."

Dark Galaxy? Kwan had to force herself not to ask. The whole thing was sounding stranger and stranger.

The admiral continued, urgency in her tone. "Fifty monitoring stations around the world—stations equipped with the world's best technology—failed to pick up that signal. Yet, your software, at a *civilian* research station, did. That, Ms. Yun, is why you are here.

"Now, why the signal was sent and how it was picked up is beyond me. The fact remains that it was only because of your software that we picked it up at all. Going forward, we need to re-assess our systems here and use your technology to monitor for more signals."

Kwan understood many things. But she didn't understand this—specifically, why only one monitoring station had picked up the signal. If the sender wanted others to receive the message, why encrypt it so heavily? Why make it almost impossible to find?

Unless...

Unless the sender presumed that all the receiving technology—all the monitoring stations—were equally sophisticated enough to receive such a signal. Or maybe the sender had sent it as a test—to see what capabilities they had? Or perhaps they only wanted *some* people to pick up the signal. She had no idea. And GAIA didn't seem to know, either.

She knew what was at stake now. If this threat was real, that meant GAIA was in danger—and that meant Earth was vulnerable to attack. But what was her role in all this? Why had they sent her all the way to the base if they just wanted her code?

"Okay," she said. "You can have the software. So you don't need me."

The admiral grinned. "Except we do." She pulled out a dossier and laid it open on the desk. "Soo Min Park. Born in North Korea. Escaped when you were seven years old with help from outside. You lived in an orphanage in South Korea for one year. Then, you fell into the hands of human traffickers. You worked illegally. But you escaped. You went to school and skipped a few grades some-where in between. You were accepted to university in Canada on a full scholarship at fourteen. Graduated early. A child prodigy skilled in languages, including coding and computer languages. A martial arts master. I could go on."

Kwan felt the horrors of her past whirl inside her. She had blocked many of those memories. She would have preferred to keep them forever hidden, tucked away. But her past reared its ugly head now. The admiral had laid it all out before her like some dead mythical beast.

The admiral paused. She looked straight into Kwan's eyes, as if she expected her to say something, to acknowledge her past.

Anger simmered under her skin.

The admiral's expression was fixed but curious. Kwan sensed a hint of skepticism. Many people wouldn't have believed her story. But they didn't have to. She knew it was real. They could believe whatever they wanted. Besides, some things were best left in the past.

"You know my birth name, my history. So what?"

"We need your skills *here*, at GAIA. Few people are chosen for this program. Your role will be to work with Dr. Otto Krill. He's been working on decoding messages for many years. You'll be working alongside him, but you'll report to me. He'll bring you up to speed."

Kwan turned to Dr. Krill. He sat emotionless, his hard stare drilling into her. Just as suddenly, his gaze softened, his eyes searching hers for answers. Kwan had a moment of déjà vu, sensing a strange familiarity with this stranger seated across from her.

But that was impossible. She'd never met him before in her life. So why did he seem so familiar?

"How long is the assignment?" she asked.

Admiral Green hesitated. "It's a permanent position, complete with benefits." She winked and pushed some papers in front of

Kwan for her to review and sign. "And you should know," she added, "we're working on getting your friend, Jae-Hwa, a visa. Shouldn't be too much longer, and then we can help her with the relocation to Canada."

Kwan perked up. A visa for Jae-Hwa? Government officials had told her it would be difficult. It could even take years. The waitlist was long.

She turned to the contract with renewed interest and skimmed its contents. It included full medical and dental benefits. Sick days. Generous vacation. A huge salary—more than *triple* what she'd made at the research station, and extra perks like a career development stipend. She then read through the risks. Physical exertion and training. Dangerous working conditions. Nothing she couldn't handle.

But nothing in the contract mattered. Only what the admiral had said: they were going to bring Jae-Hwa. No more costly long-distance travel back and forth to visit. No more having to live across oceans, coordinating the time changes and late-night calls. Her heart fluttered at the thought of living together soon. They could make good memories here, and it would be more than enough funds to support them both. And with every country tightening its restrictions on immigration, getting a ticket to Canada for Jae-Hwa was like finding gold.

She reached for the pen, decisive and determined.

Maybe things would work out after all.

CHAPTER SEVEN

SAM adjusted the lens of her telescope. She pointed it at the moon—the very place where she'd met Elder Onnisa last year. Before Titus's men had infiltrated the moon base and blown part of it up.

But that war was over. They'd won. Now that Kryg was free and starting to heal, she wasn't sure about her duties as Queen of Kryg. She only knew that their two worlds were connected and that she needed to protect Earth from destruction. But what did that mean? It seemed like a huge responsibility, especially because there could be any number of external threats lurking out there. And as for internal threats? Overpopulation, environmental degradation, and greed continued to play a role in Earth's devastation. But she didn't know the extent of the damage or how much time they really had left. Her parents probably knew more, but they never told her anything about their missions. She was always left in the dark.

She'd wondered countless times about life on Kryg with Elder Onnisa and her Krygian friend, Boj. She missed them. Had things gone back to somewhat normal after the war? Without contact from them in what felt like ages, she was in the dark on this, too.

She gazed at the books strewn on her desk, quietly contemplating the start of school next week. Anxiety crawled along her skin, the uncertainty brewing. Would she be in the same class as Hunter? Even though he'd stopped giving her drama, he still picked on others. She'd have to keep an eye out and protect the vulnerable kids when she could.

She didn't look forward to her classes. Much of the material for science and math she already knew from her previous home lessons with her grandfather. It wasn't as thrilling learning it a second time. And how was she supposed to focus on classes when there were other worlds to explore?

Still, she looked forward to seeing her friends again. It would take her mind off the recent tensions with her grandfather. They hadn't spoken much over the past couple of days. The house seemed different now, with all the security. She had to remember to disarm the system each time she entered the house. Her grandfather had snapped at her that one time she'd forgotten.

She'd spent more time walking with Pip or in her room with her telescope than with her grandfather. She felt ashamed for making a big deal about keeping the Hovershoes. But despite her apologizing more than once, her grandfather seemed on edge. He'd given her a laundry list of chores. She'd washed the floors, scrubbed the cabinets, polished the cutlery, and torn out the weeds, but there was always another project waiting. She considered avoiding him altogether. At least that way he couldn't give her any more tasks. But something was wrong. Did it have something to do with her parents? She considered approaching him about it.

The weather had turned cooler, too, much like her mood. She felt it in the mornings through the window, a crisp air reminding her that fall, and winter, were just around the corner.

Restless, she headed downstairs.

"Grandpa?"

No one answered. She peered out the window to the vacant driveway. He must have stepped out.

A letter lay on the floor in the main entryway. She bent down and picked it up. It was printed with a sophisticated insignia of several planets in an elliptical formation with the letters GAIA written beneath it. Bold red capitalized lettering appeared on the front: URGENT.

The letter wasn't unusual. Despite the prevalence of email and holographic technology, postal communication was still sometimes favored. Especially if security was involved. Mail sent by post was far less likely to be hacked or intercepted. Besides, her parents were always getting letters like this. Letters that carried them away on one adventure or another.

What was odd was why they would send an urgent letter to her parents when they were already away on their mission.

She was about to toss the letter into the stack of envelopes waiting for her parents—then stopped.

Her eyes widened in surprise.

This letter wasn't for her parents. This letter was addressed to *her*.

Curious, she carefully peeled the envelope open and pulled out the bond paper.

Dear Samantha Sanderson,

As a matter of international security, and in accordance with the Great Alliance for Interplanetary Affairs (GAIA) and the Interplanetary Security Protocol (ISP), you have been selected to be mobilized for a three-month mission abroad, which may be extended at GAIA's discretion.

Please see page 2 for a list of items you will need to pack. Expect physical training during your mission.

Corporal Frankie Coates will meet you at your place of residence on September 05 at 14:00 hrs to escort you to the military base. Further instructions will be provided upon your arrival.

Lastly, you will receive a bi-weekly stipend to cover your expenses and compensate you for your essential services to GAIA.

I look forward to meeting you.

Sincerely,
Admiral Artemis Green
GAIA

Mobilization? International security? What did that even mean? It didn't sound good.

Then she heard a key turning in the front door.

CHAPTER EIGHT

SAM FOLDED THE LETTER AND TUCKED IT INTO HER JEANS POCKET.

Her grandfather entered, carrying grocery bags looped over each arm.

"Hello!" He smiled as he greeted her, the first sign of warmth she'd seen in the last couple of days. "Sam, I've been thinking. It's the last week before school, and I was a little hard on you earlier. I'm sorry. You're welcome to visit your friends now, if you'd like."

She hesitated. He'd actually admitted to his strict behavior, apologized and offered up an olive branch to make peace. She didn't want to ruin the moment by showing him the shocking letter. What would he think? Would it just upset him again? He'd find out the truth eventually. And then what? The military would come knocking at their door, demanding that she be escorted to a military base in just a few days' time. Could she even decline? They hadn't given her much notice.

"Thank you, Grandpa. Here, let me help with that." She took the grocery bags and placed them on the kitchen counter.

Her thoughts drifted to the letter. Why had it come to her now? Had she crossed a line of some sort? Was that why they were sending her away? Perhaps knowledge of her telepathic abilities had gotten into the wrong hands, and now the military wanted to experiment on her.

That thought terrified her.

She chided herself for using her powers to win that contest at the mall with Kobe. She should have been more careful.

"Is everything okay, Sam? You know you can always tell me if something is bothering you."

She frowned. Her grandfather must have sensed her worrying. She needed to tell someone, and he seemed in a better mood now. Hopefully he would understand and could make sense of this. Because she couldn't.

"Grandpa, I need to tell you something. I think it's important." She pulled the letter from her pocket, carefully unfolding it before handing it to him. "I received a letter. It's from… Well, it's from GAIA."

His eyes widened in alarm. He took the letter from her and read it as the blood drained from his face. He cleared his throat. "I'll make us a pot of tea."

While he boiled the water and got the mugs ready, Sam put away the groceries. Pip followed her from one end of the kitchen to the other, his paws skittering along the tile floor. Her grandfather kept his lips pressed firmly together. His eyebrows crinkled the way they did when he was playing a game of chess, considering a tough move.

Reaching down, she placed some dog food in Pip's dish.

Something ceramic crashed on the tile floor.

She jumped and looked up. Her grandfather had dropped her favorite mug. The one with the *Alice in Wonderland* quote: "You're entirely bonkers. But I'll tell you a secret. All the best people are." It now lay on the floor, shattered into hundreds of pieces. He must have dropped it by accident. Or had he dropped it in anger?

"Sorry." He went to the closet and returned a moment later

with a broom and dustpan. He sighed, exasperation in his voice. "I try so hard to keep you safe. And I…I just can't!"

She didn't care about the mug. Things were just things, easily replaceable. What concerned her was the startling intensity of her grandfather's reaction.

"What does the letter mean, Grandpa? Am I being drafted?"

She saw the pained expression on his face, like he didn't want to tell her something. But the moment quickly passed. "Yes. And there's nothing we can do about it. If they've sent you the letter, then something must be terribly wrong."

Sam thought hard. What was going on that the government would draft her? Had others like her—*so young*—received these letters too? Usually, people had to be at least eighteen years old to join the army. Unless GAIA had been given more latitude to draft in special cases? Still, she thought the practice had ended years ago, after the Second World War. The government only conscripted in dire circumstances, when the country was in danger. But this was something more. *International,* the letter had noted. She shivered. Was another war starting?

She crossed her arms, which were now full of goosebumps.

Then it dawned on her. Her parents worked for the government —did it have something to do with them? Perhaps they'd been drafted the same way. They'd never given her details about their work. Now it was time to get some answers. She needed to know what they knew so that she could prepare.

"Grandpa, did the government send letters to my parents, too, like the one I received?"

He glanced up, a quiet discomfort behind his eyes, tinged with sadness. He swept the ceramic bits into the dustpan but wavered, lost in thought, before responding. "They… No. Not like *yours*. It was just after university when they were recruited. They were in their early twenties."

This letter was different, then. Out of the ordinary. *Urgent.*

"But it's the same organization? This…GAIA?"

Her grandfather hesitated, taking his time to straighten. He sighed, tossing the ceramic pieces in the garbage can. "Yes."

Couldn't he have told her that in the first place? Her parents would know more. She needed to contact them. Except they were off on another mission, which meant it was nearly impossible to reach them. Sometimes they couldn't make contact for weeks. By that time, she'd already be at the base. If only they could just come home and explain it to her, pick her up instead of having some stranger do it.

"It says someone named Frankie will escort me to the military base. Why do I have to be *escorted*? Have I done something wrong?" In all the movies she'd watched and the books she'd read, only criminals and psychotic maniacs needed to be escorted.

"No. Goodness, no. You haven't done anything wrong."

The kettle whistled on the stove, and Pip sang along. Her grandfather poured the tea, and they made their way over to the kitchen table.

"So, what is it, then?" Sam's impatience grew steadily just as her curiosity burned. "Why do they want to send me?"

"It's… Honestly, Sam, I don't know. But there must be a good reason, otherwise they wouldn't have sent you the letter."

The lack of answers from her grandfather was infuriating. Surely if her parents worked for GAIA, then he must know something about their work, about what was going on. Or was it so secret that they couldn't even tell *him*?

She re-read the letter, hoping to find another clue, but it was so vague it only left her with more questions.

She looked to her grandfather for answers, but he sat silently. The steam from his mug fogged up his glasses, clouding his eyes.

They were both wandering in the dark, looking for a flicker, a spark.

Her grandfather set his mug down and removed his glasses. He then raised his eyes to meet hers with a mix of warmth and determination. "I'm going to reach out to your parents—see if I can find out more."

At least, he would try.

His voice sounded calm, but not enough to disguise the tremble near the end. She realized the timeline. She would be leaving in a few days!

She dug her fingernails into her palms as she thought about her future. Given the history of the government extending her parents' missions, couldn't they also extend hers? *Indefinitely*. She hated that word. It was indefinable, uncertain. It could mean days or weeks or...*years*. When would she see her grandfather again? That didn't give her much time to say goodbye.

Three things were now clear: One, she wouldn't be returning to school for a while. Two, the world was in danger, and she was somehow involved. And three, she probably wouldn't see her friends or grandfather for a very long time.

CHAPTER NINE

Kwan felt groggy. They hadn't given her much time to adjust. She'd spent most of the night reading up on interplanetary affairs, the history of GAIA, interplanetary security protocols, and more. Her sleep deficit was catching up to her now.

She hurried to the physical training room but didn't feel in adequate shape to do anything productive. From the moment she'd stepped foot onto that chopper, she'd been constantly alert, forcing herself to keep going despite the lack of sleep. Admiral Green wanted a preliminary assessment of her combat skills right away so they could decide where to place her. It seemed urgent.

The training room consisted of a massive open space with mats and climbing equipment at the back. There were roughly fifteen men in their early twenties practicing drills. She immediately recognized the martial arts form of Jujitsu and the methods: the takedowns, leg sweeps, throwing, joint locks, and holds. These men were strong and skilled. It looked like some of them had trained for years. But...training for what?

When the admiral arrived, the men abruptly halted. Everyone

stood at attention. With their arms at their sides, heads upright, and shoulders back, they looked hungry for a task.

Kwan felt out of place among these men. Why were she and the admiral the only women here? Were the other female members in a separate group?

A young man with a shaved head and a focused gaze blew a whistle, then stepped toward Kwan and Admiral Green. He appeared about the same age as the other men, but several medals and additional insignia adorned his uniform.

"Sergeant Dylan Lowman," Admiral Green said, "this is Ms. Kwan Yun. I'd like you to test her skills against these men. Have her run through the *advanced* combat test."

Sergeant Lowman wavered, and his jaw tightened. "But Admiral, she doesn't look—"

"It's an order."

He saluted. "Yes, Admiral."

Sergeant Lowman lined the men up at one side of the room, leaving Kwan to stand in the center alone. Vulnerable.

"This advanced combat test," Sergeant Lowman began, eyeing Kwan up and down with unease, "has one simple purpose. Eliminate the threat by bringing your opponent to the ground." He paused, then added, "Good luck."

As if she needed luck. It sounded easy enough. She'd done it many times before. But she didn't feel sufficiently rested or prepared for such a barrage so soon. She gathered what strength and stamina she had in those fleeting moments.

Sergeant Lowman blew the whistle, and the first man—all six feet and two hundred pounds of him—came rushing toward her. Like a professional linebacker, but with a touch of finesse, he kept light on his feet, ready to dodge, duck, pounce, or adjust his attack as needed. She waited until he got close enough, then slipped out of the way, but not in time to avoid his fist connecting with her shoulder. She winced, the pain radiating down her arm. She tried to duck, but it was too late. His brute force knocked her from her feet and smashed her down onto the floor.

He was on top of her now, attempting to pin her. *And doing a bloody good job of it.*

But she wasn't quite ready to give in so easily. He might have size and strength on his side—*and a lot of it*—but she'd fought men bigger than herself before. Size and strength could be used against one's opponent. This was the art and science of Jujitsu.

Her mind raced as her body tried to keep up. She launched her left leg up, digging her heel into his hip, while her right foot swept through, connecting with his ankle and causing him to lose balance. She grabbed his hand and pulled forward—a sickle sweep. A moment later, he was on the ground, stunned and immobile, and she crouched on top of him, pinning him. But he twisted out of her grasp, and seconds later they were tumbling along the ground.

She needed to end this. Acting with lightning speed, she maneuvered his left arm into a ninety-degree angle. Placing her weight on his wrist, she looped her arm underneath into the classic kimura Jujitsu submission. She was ready to shatter his humerus when she saw him tap the floor, effectively ending their joust.

She tried to ignore the others and their shocked expressions. She straightened and stretched her arms, ready for another challenger.

"Who's next?"

A shorter man, but quite muscular, approached her. Unlike her first opponent, who'd rushed in, this man hesitated, if for a moment. He reminded her of a pitbull: smaller than a German Shepherd but pure muscle and deadly. He hopped back and forth lightly on his feet, arms in front, ready to throw a punch. He wanted her to make the first move.

But she didn't.

Instead, she waited, her body composed, ready to counter. This went on for what seemed like an eternity before she made a snap decision. Despite her body resisting the challenge, her mind told her otherwise. She needed to get through this test, and as soon as possible. She needed to prove herself to Admiral Green.

She gathered her strength just as the man lunged at her waist. This time, she used the speed and force of her attacker to drive the momentum. As they went flying, she swept his leg, causing them both to lose balance and tumble across the mat. Pain ripped through her back as his weight shifted across her body. She landed on top, but he was quick. As he turned, she braced for the escape. With his back exposed, she locked him into a bow-and-arrow choke hold, his face turning pink. Finally, he tapped the floor.

It took her a moment to catch her breath. She eliminated each threat one by one, never losing her concentration. But her energy slowly drained. She became sloppier, and with each challenge a new part of her body ached.

She felt the heat of their stares. By the end of the session, sweat poured down her face and her body throbbed, bruised in too many areas to count. She needed a break. She needed a cold shower. They gave her the nickname "Tank."

Her opponents had watched in amazement, but some glared at her now. Would she be targeted later for embarrassing them? She didn't want to think the worst but sensed their aggression lingering just under the surface.

"Go wash up and take the rest of the day off to relax. You deserve it," Admiral Green said after they left. "Tomorrow, you'll start working with Dr. Krill at the lab."

CHAPTER TEN

THE NEXT MORNING, SAM FOUND HER GRANDFATHER IN THE KITCHEN. He'd prepared breakfast from scratch: an omelet with a side of blueberries and toast. They'd ditched the TitusTech 3D Print Cooker last year after it exploded. Their meals took longer to cook, but they tasted infinitely better.

News streamed from the holographic panel, though he switched it off the moment she entered.

"Good morning, Grandpa."

"Sam, help yourself." He placed the dishes closer to her. "I... received some news late last night. From the base."

She perked up. "Oh yeah?"

"I was able to reach an Admiral Artemis Green."

This sounded promising! Maybe he'd gotten answers to their questions.

He hesitated. "She couldn't give any more details about your deployment. For security reasons, or something. But she said your parents were called back from their mission. They should be at the base within a couple of weeks. You'll see them soon. When you get there."

No more details? She furrowed her brows. She'd hoped to receive some more news but couldn't fight the frustration and dismay festering inside her. Why were her parents called back from their mission? Had something gone wrong? At least she would see them soon. Then, everything could be explained.

Her grandfather kept a reserved expression and was silent for the most part. He was probably nervous about her leaving.

"Do you think it's going to be okay?"

He looked thoughtfully at her, then poured some coffee. "I don't know much, but I know your parents respect Admiral Green and trust her. They'll look after you at the military base. Keep your chin up, do what they ask of you, and know that your parents will soon be there, too, looking out for you."

His words came out forced. Did he genuinely believe them? They finished breakfast shortly after, and she cleared their plates. As she was about to leave, he spoke again. This time in a quieter tone, more contemplative.

"I know one thing for certain. You're the bravest thirteen-year-old—*almost fourteen-year-old*—young lady I know. And your parents think so too. I'll be right here when you return."

"Thank you, Grandpa." She gave him a hug, a little tighter and a little longer than usual.

The next day, Sam couldn't do much else except get ready and pack. The government was coming for her, whether she liked it or not. They needed her. Or so they said.

She thought about calling Kato—perhaps telling her what had happened. She'd been so preoccupied with chores and worrying about the letter and the incident at the mall that her mind had refused to let anyone—or anything—else in. But since her grandfather had returned her phone earlier that morning, the least she could do was say goodbye to her friends. It would be more than difficult not seeing them for a few months. Or maybe even longer.

When she turned on her phone, twenty-three text messages awaited. All from Kato. She started scrolling.

PLEASE CALL ME WHEN YOU GET THIS.

This is SO important!

I need to talk to you. Where are you?! Why aren't you answering your phone?

Before she could respond, her phone rang.

"Sam!" Kato's tone was urgent. "I'm so glad you picked up. What's going on? Why weren't you answering your phone? I have something really big to tell you!"

"I'm sorry, Kato. I was grounded. There's something I need to tell you, too." Without any reason to hide the truth now, she plunged right in. "I got this mobilization letter yesterday from the government. They're sending me away for a few months. I probably won't see you or Kobe or Simon or *anyone* for…a while. Anyway, I'm sorry I didn't tell you sooner…"

There was silence on the other end for a few moments, and then she heard Kato's voice, but it sounded distant. "Me too."

Sam hesitated. Had she heard correctly? "Wait, *what*? You got a letter from the government?"

"We *all* did. Kobe and Simon, as well!"

The news didn't quite register right away. It seemed strange—surreal. Finding out her friends would be joining her on this unexpected mission gave her a sense of comfort—but also apprehension. What did the military want with her friends? Why were they chosen, what risks would they be facing—and was it all because of her?

"Are you still there?"

"Uh—yeah! Sorry. Just thinking about what this all means."

Kato sighed. "I know. It's pretty scary. You think it has something to do with our, uh, *incident* at that…planet?"

"Maybe, but how would the authorities even find out about that?"

"I have no idea." Kato hesitated. "Have you packed your things yet?"

Sam looked at her suitcase, already brimming with everything she could stuff into it. "Yeah, pretty much. And you?"

"Yes! I'm excited. And nervous. Kobe's super worried, but he won't admit it. And Simon, well… His parents were really upset. His dad tried to challenge it, but no luck. There's no contact information on the letter, so he had to dig around to find out more."

"Was he able to sort it out?"

"Um, not really. They said it's mandatory. Something to do with international security law or whatever." Kato paused. "The good news is we'll all get a device so we can communicate when we're at the base. A secure line or something."

"I guess that's good." At least not all communication would be cut off. "I don't really know what to expect. They didn't tell us much in the letter, you know?"

A chill set in as Sam agonized about the mission. What were the government's expectations of them? What if they couldn't carry out the tasks? Her thoughts drifted in different directions. It was impossible to focus because everything was so uncertain. They'd never signed up for this.

"Are you still there?" Kato asked. "You've been silent for a while."

"Oh, sorry. Yes, I'm still here. Just thinking about tomorrow. I guess I should get ready."

"Sounds good," Kato replied. "I'm going to give Kobe a little pep talk, you know, try and lighten his spirits. And we're trying to explain the trip to our younger sister, Darlene, but she doesn't get it. She thinks we're going on a vacation. It's probably best that way. Anyway, see you tomorrow."

"See you soon," Sam replied and hung up.

The seconds ticked by. She relished the moment of silence in her room, alone with her thoughts. She dwelled on the unexpected turn of events, her body still, quiet. The strangeness of the situation was like a never-ending puzzle. She didn't have all the pieces, and every time she thought two pieces went together, everything changed, mutated.

Kato had mentioned their connection to the planet Gliese. All four of them had traveled there by wormhole last year. That was one connection. But it didn't explain the urgency, the need to draft them all now. If the government knew about their trip, wouldn't they have been drafted sooner, right after the incident? Why wait until the end of the summer?

The only other connection was the telepathy she'd used at the mall no less than a week ago. But that didn't explain why Simon and Kato had been drafted. They didn't have telepathy like she and Kobe.

No. After tracing each detail of these scenarios, taking them apart and trying to piece them back together a different way, it didn't matter. There were still holes, and she needed to fill them in. If it was neither of these incidents, it must be something else. Something they weren't aware of.

Sam gazed through the window at the gleaming black armored SUV. Its thick wheels stood twice as high as a typical car's and looked like they were made from a material harder than rubber, with deep ridges to protect against spikes or other threatening objects. The tinted glass kept everything inside a secret. Its body, looking as powerful as a tank, reminded Sam of a Picasso painting with all its geometric and strange angles. Six bright header beams of white light shone straight ahead. Blue light emitted from its underbelly, adding to its intimidation and curiousness. The lights winked out, and the engine fell silent. Twin doors on each side opened vertically, like a bat preparing for flight. Simon's head popped out from the back.

Sam rose from the couch, glancing nervously at her grandfather. "They're here!"

She hurried to the front door, hesitating momentarily to slip on her running shoes and grab her jacket. Then, she paused. Why was she rushing to leave? She turned to her grandfather, who followed slowly, gently sliding her suitcases into the entryway. She took a deep breath to steady her nerves, but a tense energy filled her. Her grandfather peered over her shoulder as she opened the door.

A hefty woman with frizzy gray-streaked blonde hair and striking blue eyes stood before them.

"Hello there!" Her voice was low and raspy, like she smoked heavily, but Sam didn't smell any smoke. Maybe she'd given up the habit a long time ago. "You must be Samantha Sanderson." She spoke with a Newfoundland accent. Sam had seen commercials for travel to Newfoundland and Labrador, with its delightful, colorful houses dotting the rustic landscape and quaint fishing villages. She longed to travel there one day.

Sam nodded. "Yes. But it's just Sam."

"Pleased to meet you." The woman extended her hand. "I'm Corporal Frankie Coates. You can call me Frankie. Now, can I help with your bags?"

"No, that won't be necessary—" Sam's grandfather started.

But Frankie smiled, tugging one of the suitcases—the one that weighed a ton—from Sam's grasp. "Please, I insist."

"Thank you," Sam said.

Frankie was already heading down the steps, carrying the suitcase as easily as if she were carrying a handbag full of feathers. Sam and her grandfather followed her toward the car, where Simon waited.

"Sweet ride," Sam said, glimpsing the sleek modern interior. Beige leather fabric, soft floor lighting, a holographic entertainment system, plush cushions…

"I know!" Simon smiled. "Someone had to be the first to enjoy it!"

Sam looked to the house next door just as Kato and Kobe made their way outside. Their parents stood at the doorway, not quite ready to say their goodbyes, while Darlene held her mother's pant leg for support. Their mother leaned on her cane and dabbed her face with a tissue, her eyes red and puffy.

"Call me when you can," Sam's grandfather said.

"I will." She gave him one last tight hug, breathing in the familiar scent of cedar and cinnamon spice from his aftershave. When she looked up, his eyes were already filled with pools of tears. He was trying to hold back his emotions, to keep calm.

"Be brave and take care of yourselves," he whispered.

"You too, Grandpa. And take care of Pip while I'm away. I'll see you soon." This wasn't a final goodbye. It couldn't be. She'd be back in just a few months. Just a few months…

If everything went as planned, it would be winter when she returned. Right around her birthday. She needed to keep herself together. For him. For her friends and their families. She needed to keep her friends safe and make sure they returned, too.

After they said their goodbyes, Sam and her friends piled into the SUV. She felt a pang of sadness rise up in her. She turned and waved to her grandfather as the SUV backed out of the driveway but wished she hadn't.

Her grandfather's smile was fragile, fleeting, replaced by a terror in his eyes that chilled her to the bone.

She decided something in that moment. She would make a point to communicate with him from the military base at every opportunity. To assuage his fears and let him know she was going to be okay.

Wasn't she?

CHAPTER ELEVEN

Kwan was running late. They'd be expecting her in Dr. Krill's lab. It wasn't like her to be late, but she'd overslept. Ever since arriving at the base, things had gone into overdrive. She'd once again spent most of the night reading up on Krygian history, operating manuals for extraterrestrial technologies, extraterrestrial biology, prohibited technologies, laboratory equipment, safety protocols, and more. It wasn't that she couldn't absorb new information quickly—it was the *amount* of information to absorb. She must have read and memorized thousands of pages. Once she started, she couldn't stop. Her head pounded. She couldn't have gotten more than three hours of sleep. To top it off, her body still ached from that grueling physical combat test.

But when she arrived at the lab, she stopped in the doorway. Enormous cabinets lined the back walls, with papers and documents inside. A massive industrial metal table took up most of the room, stools positioned behind it. On the table rested glass flasks and beakers, computers and other gadgets.

Everything about this place looked strangely familiar. She'd seen it before.

Except, that was impossible.

She'd never been to Dr. Krill's lab.

So why couldn't she shake the feeling, the sense of déjà vu?

Usually, she could recall such specific details with confidence and ease. But today, something was different. Her mind played tricks on her. She could think of only one reason for it: lack of sleep.

Dr. Krill sat hunched at his wooden desk by the window. He furiously scribbled on a pad of paper, unaware of her presence. Taking in his thinning silver hair, his dark-rimmed glasses, and the way he jotted down his notes, she had a moment of déjà vu again.

The strangeness of the moment—as if she were experiencing a flashback—persisted. The familiarity of him returned, as though she'd seen him many times before in this lab.

Don't be irrational. You only just met him yesterday. Pull yourself together, Kwan.

She pushed those thoughts deep down and knocked on the door. "Dr. Krill? I'm so sorry I'm late."

He glanced up from the desk, and his eyes softened. He looked happy to see her, like seeing an old friend. His eyes welcomed her, and in an instant, she felt respected and important. And something more, but she couldn't quite place it. She relaxed slightly, a sense of comfort and peacefulness growing inside her.

"Come in." He waved, and she noticed a bandage covering his right hand.

"What happened?"

He looked down. "Oh, this? Just a careless accident. Some of the personal protective equipment went missing a few weeks ago. I ordered more heat-resistant gloves, but they'll take a week or two to arrive. It's the strangest thing, the number of items that have gone missing here recently."

"Oh? Like what?"

"Well…sometimes I can't find my notes and documents."

His body language and tone of voice suggested he was telling the truth. "Did you check the security tapes?" Kwan asked, her eyes skimming the room. She spotted a couple of security cameras tucked in the back corners. They would have provided at least some coverage. But for all she knew, they might not pick up every area and detail.

"Yes, but they didn't find anything," he started. "I'm getting old, though. I suppose I misplace things more frequently than I used to."

Kwan didn't know what to believe. Maybe he was simply distracted and forgetting where he put things. Or maybe something more sinister was going on, and he was oblivious to it. Or in denial, too worried to face the possibility that someone was intentionally sabotaging his work. Still, she didn't want to jump to conclusions. For now, she would stay alert to any other strange occurrences.

He took her around his lab. His movements were slow, but he seemed to be on the ball, if a bit shaky.

She scanned the room, taking stock of the computers, vials of liquid, and other objects. But one thing stood out: the picture of an AI cyborg that hung on the wall. Part of the Athena mission she'd read about in her history classes. With her long blonde hair resting on her shoulders, those big blue eyes and wide smile engaging the viewer, Athena looked human. Only, she was made of parts and machinery. An AI, biologically and technologically enhanced. Earth's scientists had sent Athena on a solo mission decades ago to navigate the universe for habitable planets and report back. But they'd lost contact with her ship. She'd never returned.

"Was she developed here, in one of these labs?"

"Who?" Dr. Krill looked up, then nodded. "Ah! Athena. Yes. We developed her coding and communications here." His voice sounded gruff, as if he were angry and wanted to race over those details.

The news that they'd developed Athena here at this lab

intrigued her. In a way, she was keen to be a part of GAIA, recognizing that much of the work the scientists did behind the scenes had impacted history. And she would be a part of it. Then, she thought about the Athena mission itself. It had been largely a failure, generating adverse news and negative repercussions. It must have been difficult for the scientists. Were they guilt-ridden? So much time and money had been spent on the project. She was sure the weight of the responsibility would be hard to bear.

Perhaps that was why Dr. Krill was so hesitant to discuss it.

She caught his anxious glance, as though he sensed her concern.

"Kwan, dear, I need to show you something." His eyes darted nervously around the room as he brought her over to a computer station. Whatever he was about to tell her was important, so she would make a mental note, keep it safe in her memory. She recalled information with ease. She never wrote things down. Her mind was like a library. Whenever she needed to remember something, she just opened the door.

On one of the screens, a planetary system with a black hole at its center came into view. A light blinked from one of the planets near the galaxy's perimeter. Was the planet some sort of waystation for the scientists? Were they conducting experiments in that region? If so, it must be dangerous and expensive. Regions with black holes were particularly precarious and foreboding. Getting too close to a black hole and its event horizon would mean game over. The point of no return. Even light couldn't escape a black hole, despite its incredible speed.

Dr. Krill spoke in a low voice. "We've been monitoring signals from this region. The Dark Galaxy, we call it, because there are no stars in its vicinity. Only a few desolate planets and asteroids, mostly. The last known signal from Athena came from this planet, Candu, in the outer perimeter." He pointed to the planet, a blue speck in a sea of blackness. "That was about twenty years ago. It was so far from Earth it was impractical and dangerous to send a reconnaissance ship. When the signal went dark, we figured her ship must have crashed and there was no point in retrieving it."

Kwan kept silent. But inside, her stomach twisted in knots. Why would Athena have abandoned them and traveled so far off course? What was she looking for in the Dark Galaxy?

Kwan wanted to know more about the signal and the planet, Candu, where the signal had gone dark. Did the planet harbor any life? No, impossible. The chances of life existing in the Dark Galaxy, a region with no stars and no light, were slim to none. Right? Unless...

She thought about the experiments scientists had done in the past. Certain creatures could live in extreme conditions, such as the vacuum of space. Like tardigrades. So, it was possible...

She glanced at Dr. Krill, whose eyes were vacant as he paced around the room.

"Then what happened?"

He looked over at her, fear in his eyes. "We know Athena abandoned her mission. After all, she should have known that no habitable planets would exist for humans in the Dark Galaxy. She was way off course. But...we weren't sure what happened afterward, until recently."

He pointed to the second screen. "These are Malborgs, a hybrid of AI machinery and organic matter. Killing machines that occupy the Dark Galaxy. From our GAIA counterparts and intelligence sources, we found out that something, or someone, is building an army of them. We managed to capture some specimens, and we're studying them here in this facility."

He zoomed in on one of them. Kwan took in the features of the black spherical creature with long silver spiked tentacles. Its body, a slick black bubbling mass, reminded her of oil, thick yet malleable. It looked like it could change its shape. Expand or contract, depending upon its environment. Each tentacle, upon closer look, contained hundreds of gleaming barbs, prickly like a cactus. Those could easily shred a victim. It hovered on purple energy, some sort of electrical current generated through its tentacles. Without any discernible facial features, it must have relied on other sensing abilities. Maybe through electrical signals or something else. She wasn't sure. The creature's body reminded her of a massive tumor, around eight feet in height.

An icy chill ran up Kwan's spine. Not much could frighten her, but looking at these creatures caused her heart to beat faster.

"They respond to their leader, an entity called Duskara. No one knew who she was, but we've connected the dots thanks to the intelligence we received and your software."

"My software?"

"Yes. The signal we received was from Logom, a planet in close proximity to Candu, in the same region. We believe Duskara and Athena are the same entity—that Athena changed her name. We're confident Duskara is the same AI entity we sent away years ago. She's the one building an army of Malborgs in the Dark Galaxy."

An army of Malborgs? That sounded disastrous. Catastrophic. Dealing with one of these creatures looked dangerous enough, but a whole army? It was terrifying to fathom. What had happened to Athena that would compel her to go rogue and build an army? Something must have happened on that ship, on her journey, to make her change her purpose so drastically. But what? Was it someone else whom she'd met on her journey, or had it come from her coding? She was a machine-learning AI, so she could have changed her coding along the way…

But what she'd become, and those monsters she'd created, could only mean one thing. There had to be a larger purpose.

Kwan remembered the strange message she'd received at the radio telescope research station. *Deliver the Queen of Kryg to Logom or risk the destruction of GAIA.*

She hadn't understood it at the time. But now, it made more sense. It looked like Athena—or rather, Duskara—had a specific target in mind. The ultimatum was real. The Queen of Kryg was her intended target. But who was the Queen of Kryg? And why did Duskara want her enough to wage war on GAIA?

Dr. Krill folded his arms and hesitated, as if weighing his next words. "The message we received from your software… It's the first time Duskara has made contact with humans since the signal went dark years ago. And the message… Well, it's not good."

No, Kwan thought. It was not good at all.

CHAPTER TWELVE

Sam couldn't stop thinking about the look on her grandfather's face as she'd left. A mix of sadness, anxiousness, and pain. She wasn't sure whether her friends had noticed too, but they probably felt just as uncertain.

She gazed at the tree line, a numbness creeping over her as they drove down the highway.

"Now, I don't know about you all, but I'm gutfounded!" Frankie said as she turned to them with a grin. "That means '*hungry,*' for all you mainlanders. A journey like this always calls for some nourishment. There should be a fridge back there. Help yourselves to whatever you want."

Her words stirred them out of the moment, excitement growing. Simon opened the fridge to find a tray of fruit, crackers, and juice boxes. He passed them around.

"Have any of you ever flown by military aircraft or been *submerged*?" Frankie asked. "Let me tell you, oh my nerves!"

Kato hesitated, then whispered, "What does she mean by '*submerged*'?"

"I don't know," Sam replied.

Frankie continued, glancing at Sam from the rearview mirror. "Now, I don't like to poke and prod, but what would the government want with you kids? You're a little young to be joining the military, aren't you? They usually start around eighteen."

Sam looked to her friends for an answer, but they all remained silent.

Frankie shook her head. "Never mind that. I suppose it's not my place to say. But let me tell you, if you're going to the base, you're going to meet some folks and see some…interesting things."

An amused half-smile formed on Simon's face. "What do you mean by *interesting*?"

"Oh, well, I shouldn't say. But just between you and me, you'll get to meet some aliens! Now, the Krygians are a good bunch. Decent folk. Maybe the Rypolds, too, although they can be devious sometimes. As for the Luytens, they're not bad, as such. But their slime is hard to get off one's clothes, and excuse me for being so bold, but it really stinks! But, oh! I've said too much."

Frankie glanced at them in the rearview mirror. She was waiting for a reaction, one eyebrow raised. But everyone kept silent.

"Well, you're a quiet bunch," Frankie mused, confusion in her tone. Her expression changed from mild disappointment to sheer panic. "Just a moment!" She sped up, flicking her eyes from the rearview mirror to the side windows. "Oh no! We've got company. Hold on!"

She accelerated. Fast. She swerved to the right and onto a dirt side road, forested on either side. Sam gripped her stomach to make sure it didn't separate from the rest of her body.

A black SUV with tinted windows raced toward them, looming close on their tail.

"Hold on!" Frankie shifted their vehicle into autopilot. Reaching down, she flipped a switch on the control panel. Sam gasped as the roof of their vehicle split open. A small, spherical drone the size of a plum shot straight out from a compartment inside the floor. It buzzed, hovering above them as they drove, then hurtled toward the black SUV behind them. The drone, suspended in midair, kept pace with the vehicle's speed.

"What—what's going on?" Kato asked, gripping the armrests for support. They must have been going one hundred and forty kilometers an hour.

A screen arose from a slot under the navigation pane. Sam gaped at an image of a creature with gray leathery skin, three eyes, and a wide jawline. It looked like an ogre had met a crocodile and they'd had a baby.

Sam made the connection: the drone was taking pictures. The sophisticated technology filtered out the window tints. She leaned closer, glimpsing more details. The creature wore heavy-plated chrome-colored armor. It looked indestructible. Engraved into the armor was an emblem of a three-eyed skull. And underneath it, two blasters in a crisscross pattern.

"Interstellar traffickers!" Frankie yelled. "These ones are part of the Gargol faction from Tau Ceti. But how did they get here? I gotta report this. Oye, the admiral won't be liking this." She pressed SEND, and the information vanished. Frankie maneuvered the vehicle as the SUV gained traction. A massive jolt shook them as the pursuers rammed into them from behind. If they hadn't been buckled up, they would have been hurled to the next town over.

"What—what are interstellar traffickers?" Sam asked. "What do they want?"

Frankie pressed a button marked CAMERA VIEW. A live security feed with multiple images appeared on a screen just below the dash. Sam leaned forward, trying to get a closer look. The screen acted like a security monitoring system. On all sides of their armored SUV were cameras taking in multiple views all at once, all centralized in one location. With this feature, they could see threats from all directions without having to constantly check the mirrors or windows. She watched the screen as the interstellar trafficker sped toward them, narrowing the gap.

"Thieves! They're the scum of the universe. They steal and sell valuables to make money—including people. It's their livelihood. Like pirates. When Admiral Green told me I would be driving VIPs, I didn't expect this! You must have something they really want! But don't worry. We're almost there! Now, watch this!"

Frankie pressed a green button on the dash.

Sam held her breath, her eyes wide open. Another spherical drone rose from the opening in the floor, this one black with a blinking red light. It zoomed out of the open roof and attached to the front windshield of the pursuing SUV. Seconds later, it exploded. Shards of glass flew in all directions, followed by a white cloud of mist that obscured the driver's vision. The car screeched and then careened off the road and into the forest.

"That'll slow 'em down!"

"That was wicked awesome!" Simon exclaimed. "What other gadgets does this car come with? I want one!"

"Thanks. Plenty. But here's hoping we don't need 'em." Frankie sighed. Her face relaxed for a moment, then contorted with surprise and unease. She checked the security feed, her eyes frantic. "Aye, can't they give us a breath?"

Engines blasted as some kind of tri-wheeled vehicle came flying out of the woods. Powered by a purple electrical current, its thick wheels somehow hovered on a pocket of air. It sped toward them. Its driver wore a gleaming black armored suit. Sam couldn't mistake the massive, muscular frame of its body. Giant white spikes jutted out of its arms and legs through the suit.

"What in the name of blazing glory!" Frankie yelled. "That's a direct violation of interplanetary security protocol! Operating a Tau Ceti vehicle on Earth—and in broad daylight, too!"

Frankie pressed another button marked SPIKE. Hundreds of small, spiked metallic objects emerged from a side compartment. They flew toward the pursuer's vehicle. But it was too late. The interstellar trafficker must have enabled some sort of protective shield around its vehicle. The spikes deflected off it like dust, scattering to the ground.

"Shields up," Frankie hollered as she pressed SHIELD. The roof closed, and Sam felt a tremor as a light glimmered around their vehicle. Was it a type of force shield?

The pursuer's vehicle hovered only a few feet away when its driver threw a flashing white cylindrical device into the air. Sam heard the low vibration first. Then, the steady rise in pitch and accelerated frequency and a final loud popping noise as something burst overhead. The strength of the blast rattled her bones. Chaos and utter confusion swept through her as she looked around, trying desperately to get her bearings. Everything happened in slow motion. Behind her, the trees they'd passed moments ago blew back from the enormous shock wave, their trunks bending, snapping. Leaves and entire branches tore away.

The screams—muted, like something heard deep underwater— came next. Her head ached from the blast. Her eardrums popped in her skull as their vehicle juddered violently.

She barely heard Frankie's next words.

"Our shields are down! Everyone, hold on!"

Simon hugged his knees in a death grip, his head down as if in airplane crash-landing mode. Kato and Kobe clutched their armrests, desperate to hold on to something stable.

Sam felt a thud. Something heavy from above. She scanned the security feed. The interstellar trafficker grasped the roof of their vehicle. In one of its spiked claws, it held a massive drill. Soon, it would infiltrate their armored vehicle.

"Let's play hardball, scum!" Frankie pressed another button on the dash: SWARM.

An exterior side latch opened from under Sam's window, and a swarm of gleaming robotic hornets flew out. Five inches long with frighteningly large stingers, the hornets attacked, latching on to the aggressor. Distracted, the assailant dropped its drill. It swatted the hornets with one claw, desperately holding on to the vehicle with the other. But there were too many of them. It cried out in pain just as it stumbled, falling. The swarm followed its body as it twisted and turned, tumbling along the ground.

Sam took in a shaky breath, her palms sweaty from the attack. They'd only just started their journey to the base, and it was an insanely close call. Kato and Kobe, wide-eyed and anxious, looked equally stunned.

Simon was still grasping his knees, his head down, when a soft moan escaped his lips. "Are we there yet?"

CHAPTER THIRTEEN

FRANKIE PULLED ONTO A SIDE ROAD AS THEY CONTINUED IN SILENCE.
She slowed to about sixty kilometers per hour, a more comfortable
pace. The vehicle's navigation system beeped. It alerted them to
turn right in five hundred meters, but Sam couldn't see any side
roads, just the tree line and dense bushes.

"The marker should be somewhere around here..." Frankie
hesitated, slowing even further. "Ah, there."

Up ahead, a red piece of cloth hung from a tree on the right-
hand side. Their SUV swerved to the right, veering off the road and
toward the trees.

"What are you doing?" Simon yelled. "We're going to crash!"

"Shush! Keep your eyes open, or you're going to miss it!"

Sam took a sharp breath, not having enough time to think about
her own mortality before the scenery transformed before her eyes.
Where there was once a forest and dense trees, there now stood a
large complex with military aircraft and security gates.

"What happened?" Kato asked, astonished.

"How did we—? No, where did we—? Am I dreaming?" Kobe
said.

Simon peeled his fingers away from his eyes. He looked back to where they had just come from, equally baffled. It was like they'd teleported to a new location.

"No. You're still here," Frankie said. "We went through a camouflaged entrance. An outdoor hologram."

Sam had never witnessed such elaborate holographic technology of this magnitude before, and it mesmerized her.

Frankie continued. "Keeps the location secure." She turned to Simon. "See? Neat trick, huh?"

Simon sat still as a statue, stone-faced.

Sam gaped at the complex up ahead. She shivered at its prison-like security features—barbed wires and chain-link fencing. Even the buildings looked uninviting. Their tinted windows and concrete walls could easily shut anyone out. Or keep anyone—or *anything*—hidden inside. Why the need for so much security? The way it was situated, tucked behind the trees with a hidden entrance, anyone would easily miss it.

She slowed her breathing, but that didn't stop her inner voice from screaming that something wasn't right. The amount of security here was impossible to penetrate. Had she made a horrible mistake in trusting these people?

Her heart juddered at the thought of being confined here— maybe forever. Memories of getting kidnapped by Titus's men and the things he'd done flashed through her mind: the cell where they'd contained her with the watermarks on the walls, the thick steel door; being transferred to the room with the guard, the restraints, and Titus's threats. Sam tried to repress the memories. But they resurfaced, persistent, begging her to question their present circumstances.

Were they to become prisoners here? Who was waiting for them inside? What were they planning to do to her and her friends?

"*What's up?*" Kobe's words traveled inside her mind.

She was grateful for their telepathic connection. She didn't feel so alone now. She looked over. He stared at her, bug-eyed. She tried to look away, to brush it off, but it was too late.

"It's just… What's with all the security? I don't like the idea of being trapped here, given what happened last year…with the kidnapping."

Kobe flexed the muscles in his arm, and his jaw tightened, then relaxed. *"Well, I'm sure it'll be okay. I think this is just a temporary stop on the way. Look, we're here."*

Sam shifted her gaze to the guardhouse. A man in a civilian uniform brightened as they approached. His rosy cheeks brimmed with kindness and eagerness at their arrival. He smiled and waved them over. Frankie pulled up beside him and rolled down her window.

"Had a little run-in with some interstellar traffickers," Frankie said, holding up her badge. "Gargol faction, from Tau Ceti. That's why we're a bit late."

"Yes, we were alerted to it. Everyone okay?"

Frankie looked back at Sam and her friends. "As good as could be."

"Admiral Green is ready at Gate 3. Always good to see you, Corporal Coates."

"Thank you, Eddie."

Despite the warm welcome, the intimidating facility remained elusive. Sam decided she would need to remain cautious for now.

The gate opened slowly. After passing over a few speed bumps, they arrived at Gate 3. It contained a hangar and the smallest passenger plane Sam had ever seen.

A stern woman with dark shades stood beside the plane like a statue, arms folded, a scowl on her face. Her jet-black hair was pulled into a bun that looked like it was held together by glue, not a single strand out of place. She was dressed in a navy uniform with the sleeves rolled up, revealing her rippling muscles. Multiple tattoos ran along her arms and neck.

But that's not what startled Sam.

It was the moment the woman tore off her shades, revealing the fierceness that flashed in her granite eyes. Those eyes had without a doubt *seen things*. Indescribable, horrifying things, most likely. The thought filled Sam with dread.

They exited the car, a bit shaky and disoriented. Sam caught the uniformed woman glaring at her. She tried not to show any fear by lifting her eyes to meet hers, but she couldn't fight the sweat collecting in her palms.

"Admiral Green," Frankie said, saluting her.

"At ease, Corporal Coates," Admiral Green said, and Frankie relaxed a little. "Sounds like Gargol faction gave you some trouble. We received your message and dispatched Squadron 5 to bring them in. How are you all doing?"

"Happy to report we all made it in one piece, Admiral, but probably a little too much excitement for one day."

"Or for one year, for that matter," Kato whispered to Sam.

Sam watched with trepidation as their bags were transferred from their SUV to the tiny plane. Then, Admiral Green took Sam to the side, away from the others, and murmured in her ear. "A little bird told me you have a gift for telepathic communications."

Sam nodded.

"Well, can you promise me not to use this gift while at the base?"

Sam hesitated. Why wouldn't Admiral Green want her to use her telepathy at the base? And who had told Admiral Green about her gift? Her parents and grandfather knew, along with her friends and some of the Krygians. And maybe the people at the mall who were running the contest, or the spectators. Okay, so lots of people knew. But why couldn't she use her power? Wouldn't they want her to practice her gift? Something didn't add up. But her grandfather's instructions had been clear: do what they asked, and everything would be okay.

She nodded. "Yes. Not a problem, Admiral Green. But may I ask why?"

"It's for your own safety. Now, let's go."

Sam was hoping for something more, a further explanation, but it didn't come. She hurried to keep up with Admiral Green as they returned to the rest of the group.

The admiral paused. "Have any of you flown by private jet charter before?"

They shook their heads.

"Well, then, you're in for a ride!"

Sam counted nine passenger seats. She'd never traveled on a plane so small in her life.

Simon turned to Kobe and Kato. "First time flying?"

They both nodded and exchanged nervous glances.

"Don't worry. It's fun! You'll like it," Simon said with the confidence of someone who had flown many times.

Once they got settled in, the plane rolled across the lanes toward the tiny runway. It was odd seeing so few runways—only three in total—against the vast landscape. But even more striking were the dozens of circular landing pads of varying sizes. One was as large as a hockey stadium. Strange markings encircled them. A series of dots linked with dashes. Curious symbols. They almost looked like star systems or coordinates.

"What are those things?" Kobe's thoughts merged with her own.

"I'm not quite sure. Maybe landing pads for interstellar travelers? But Kobe, we're not allowed to use our telepathy."

"What? Why not?"

"I don't know. But that's what Admiral Green told me, just before we boarded. She said it's for our own safety."

He hesitated. *"And you don't think that's odd?"*

The truth was, she definitely thought it was odd. She had so many questions about this trip, the upcoming mission, and what was going on here. She expected they would be given more information as the journey proceeded. But Admiral Green remained oddly unforthcoming in the detail department. Maybe she would explain things further once they arrived at the base. At least, Sam hoped so. They couldn't keep them in the dark forever.

"Yes, it's odd, I agree. But my grandfather told me to trust Admiral Green. She works with my parents. We need to follow their rules."

"Or what?"

Sam didn't like the way Kobe was challenging the rules already. They hadn't even arrived, and yet he was persistent, almost defiant. She didn't want to get into trouble, or worse, get her friends in trouble.

"I don't know. It's the military. They could do anything." Their lives were in the military's hands now. She didn't want to break the rules and risk the consequences. Whatever they were. Besides, she had a peculiar feeling the admiral was testing them somehow. Technology existed that could intercept telepathic communications. If TitusTech had access to it, it was likely the military had access to it, too, and quite possibly using it. The last thing she wanted was Admiral Green intercepting their thoughts.

She shuddered at the thought of being monitored that way, of having her thoughts invaded, her privacy breached. How safe were they if they couldn't even control their own thoughts?

"Just trust me," she added, though she wasn't sure whether he would or if they could even trust Admiral Green. And now that Kobe had planted a seed of doubt in her mind, she would have to remain vigilant, not just take their directions at face value. There must be reasons, explanations for each action or policy. People had motivations for doing or wanting certain things. She needed to dig deeper, consider all possibilities. She needed to uncover the truth, and soon.

Just then, Admiral Green glanced back at Sam, her eyes cold. No smile, no sign of kindness. It was more of a check to see that Sam was where she was supposed to be. If anything, it looked detached, methodical, calculating. Like how an inspector might behave at a meat processing plant, checking that the machinery was working correctly and gearing up for the slaughter. Sam had to look away, the hairs on the back of her neck rising.

The look made her feel like she'd been caught doing something wrong. Of course, she hadn't. Nevertheless, it put her on edge. Something about the admiral scared her. She couldn't quite place it. Maybe Kobe was right. And if he was, then they needed to keep their thoughts secret. At least, for now.

As they prepared for takeoff, she gazed at the tree line up ahead. It seemed much too close at the other end of the runway. Perhaps they'd made a mistake in calculating the distance.

Her pulse quickened. Would they be able to clear it?

The engines roared to life. It was only a matter of seconds before they were zooming across the runway. They lifted off at an impossibly steep angle.

The start to their journey was a rocky one. She didn't doubt more surprises lurked ahead. If they could be attacked on the ground, they could be attacked in the air. Maybe that was why Admiral Green was so on edge. She kept glancing back at them and checking her phone.

Sam looked at her friends. Kobe listened to music while Simon played a video game. Kato was immersed in a fantasy book with a picture of a dragon on the cover. They all seemed fine—*so what was her problem?*

All this travel and excitement was a lot to take in. Sam gazed out the window at the whisps of cloud floating beneath them, tiny ripples like patterns on sand banks made by the undulations of waves along the ocean floor. It was funny how patterns in nature sometimes repeated themselves. But there was a certain randomness to it all.

Still, she didn't think their journey was random. They'd been chosen for a reason. She wanted to believe their mission was important, that it meant something. That any obstacles on their path could be overcome. She wished she could be more determined, like Kato. She wanted to return home safely with her friends and see her grandfather and Pip again soon. Whatever was waiting ahead of them on their journey, she—*they*—would need to get through it. All of them.

Storm clouds formed in the distance. Flashes of light accompanied by rumbles of thunder. An uneasiness grew inside her. The uncertainty of the future lingered, never fully dissipating. Whatever happened, she would need to remain resilient.

She'd become stronger, not just to survive. She needed to be ready and able to weather any storm.

CHAPTER FOURTEEN

Sam kept her eyes glued to the window. Outside, the scenery transformed. Where there was once expansive ocean, there was only rock. Jagged cliffs jutted toward the sea, emphasizing the land's stately, defensive power. The plateaus were sparse and desolate, with no house, no structure of any kind in sight. She marveled at the pristine lakes, reflecting the blue sky above, held softly within the boreal forest. Rolling hills provided a gateway to the sea and a natural fortification. This land was very much alive, and it was a shelter, protecting its inhabitants.

Sam broke the silence. "Where are we?"

"This is Labrador," Frankie said. "We passed Newfoundland earlier—where I was born and raised—we call it the Rock. But now, we're heading north, toward the Torngat Mountains of Labrador."

Exhilarated by the view and the excitement of entering this new and spectacular place, Sam couldn't hold back her delight. "It's…beautiful!"

"Yes, it is." Frankie winked. "Maybe you'll get to kiss a cod!"

"What?" Sam let out a nervous laugh. It must be a joke. Surely, they didn't expect her to pucker up for a fish. Or was that really one of their customs?

They passed a herd of caribou galloping across an expanse of sandy beach. The coastline seemed to stretch on forever. There was something magical about it all. The landscape pulled her in. It entranced and bewitched her, tempting her to explore it.

And then, all at once, the exterior automatic shades lowered until none of them could see out.

"Why can't we admire the view?" Sam asked.

"It's for safety purposes," Admiral Green responded over the intercom. Sam waited for further explanation, but it soon became clear that was all they would get.

Safety purposes? There didn't seem to be any threat. At least, she hadn't seen any other aircraft in the vicinity. So what was the purpose of covering the windows? The way Admiral Green behaved, Sam sensed they were being evaluated. It wasn't just the way the admiral checked on them and gave out warnings. There was something else, as if the admiral considered Sam a threat. Could that really be the case? If so, she was mistaken, since Sam didn't intend to hurt anyone. Why else would they have covered the windows?

Unless the admiral didn't want them to know the exact location of the base.

Sam wasn't sure how much time had passed but was glad when they finally landed. The window coverings retracted, and she peered outside. The runway bordered the edge of a cliff, over-looking the ocean. There was a small hangar but no other human-made structures. No roads. No signs. Nothing to indicate a base was close by. If they needed a place to make her disappear from society, this would be it.

Why had they stopped here, of all places?

Though a little wobbly, Sam descended the steps, a gust of wind sweeping through her hair. She breathed in the fresh air, enjoying the tinge of saltiness from the sea. It felt good to stretch her legs. Hopefully the base wasn't too far of a drive.

"Follow the path!" Frankie said, waving them over to the cliff's edge.

"What path?" Simon asked, fear in his eyes.

Sam peered over the edge. A hundred feet below was a small deserted beach in a sheltered inlet. Waves crashed against its rocky shoreline. Hundreds of wooden steps snaked their way through the rugged terrain, the angle steep.

Sam hesitated. "I don't understand. Where's the base?"

"We're almost there," Frankie said. "Now hurry! Oh, and mind your step! We're due for more trail maintenance soon."

Sam descended with cautious precision, clutching the railing for support. Something crunched under her boot and her foot sank down into the rotting wood. She pulled it out, glancing back at the steep incline. Kato, Simon, and Kobe weren't far behind. They carefully tested each step, extreme concentration in their eyes.

When they finally reached the water, out of breath, the sun was setting in the distance, casting a pink glow across the sky. Birds flew nearby, colorful puffins nesting in the hillside. Everyone looked tired and worn.

Simon's face contorted in panic, his eyes bulging.

"What's wrong?" Sam asked.

"I left my video game on the plane," Simon groaned, gazing back at the trail of steps leading up the gigantic cliff.

"It's the end of the world," Kobe added, his lips curling into a half-grin.

"You've got to be joking," Kato said.

Simon shook his head. "Do you think they have a gaming room at the base?"

"That's all you're thinking about right now? Playing video games?" Kato said.

"Well, yeah. And whether the food is okay."

Kato sighed. "Priorities."

"This is my favorite part." Frankie pointed to the horizon. "Just watch."

Sam didn't see anything in the distance. Were they going to set up camp for the night, maybe hold hands and sing around a fire? She knew the answer was no, but given everything that had happened so far, she couldn't discount the possibility.

Suddenly, bubbles rose to the water's surface in the distance. Moments later, a cylinder-shaped craft emerged from the depths of the sea. It sped through the air toward them, fast like lightning but silent, leaving no propulsion trails, covering an impossible distance in a matter of seconds. It paused a few meters in front of them, then powered down and floated on the waves. They watched in awe as a floating gangway rolled out from its entrance and landed on the shore.

"The *Sea Raven*," Admiral Green said. "Developed from Rigellian technology. One of our best. Please, after you."

Sam's legs weakened as she marveled at the vessel. It was roughly the size of a hundred-foot yacht, with a sleek, glistening silver frame and gigantic windows around its perimeter. It floated silently. Puffins swam nearby, unruffled by its hulking presence. The ship couldn't have been powered by a combustion engine. Those were noisy and emitted carbon dioxide. It was like this vessel didn't have an emission, or maybe it had one, but it was hidden.

"Wow!" Kato exclaimed.

"Are you coming?" Frankie turned to face Sam and her friends.

Simon stood frozen in place.

"Come on, dude. It'll be okay," Kobe said gently, nudging him along. "Or did you want me to hold your hand?" he added, smirking. Simon's legs moved slowly as his eyes remained transfixed on the ship.

Sam's head thrummed with exhilaration and nervous energy. She followed timidly toward the ship's entrance. She glimpsed

Kato's jubilant expression and wished some of her enthusiasm would rub off on her.

Upon entering the ship, she had a sinking feeling they wouldn't step on solid land again for a long time. The air locks sealed. The loud suction sound made her feel trapped inside, cut off from the rest of the world. The ship swayed under her feet, bobbing on the waves. It did nothing to alleviate the nausea writhing in her gut. She lurched back and forth, stumbling to the seating area.

Now that they were inside, there was no turning back.

Just breathe.

The interior of the ship contained massive circular viewing windows. Along the sides were sleek rows of white reclining seats with blue metallic accents. They were surprisingly comfortable and adjusted to the contours of Sam's body. Each seat had two buckles along the chest and a side belt buckle. Fresh, mint-scented air filled the cabin. Soft lighting put everyone at ease.

Well, almost everyone.

"We'll be on our way soon," the captain said through the intercom. "We're just waiting a few minutes for the anti-gravity generators to stabilize."

"Frankie, this is going to sound like a silly question, but why do we need anti-gravity generators? What exactly do they do?" Sam asked.

"Well, traveling at very fast speeds can damage a person's body, given the g-force. We need these anti-gravity generators to dampen the inertia, so we don't get ripped apart."

Simon perked up. "What?"

Frankie continued. "This ship isn't like your regular military spacecraft. It uses anti-gravity technology. Instantaneous acceleration. It can travel up to 3,800 miles an hour in the air and eighty knots in water. It makes sudden turns. Leaves no propulsion trails or sonar signatures. It's not something you'd learn in your science classes. And it defies common physics. The technology is quite advanced and kept secret. Wouldn't want it getting into the wrong hands, if you know what I mean."

Sam considered her surroundings. Even though the anti-gravity generators were running, she didn't notice anything amiss. "But I don't *feel* the cabin pressure changing or anything."

"Nor should you. An invisible bubble manifests itself around our craft. It creates a protective shield, distorting the space just beyond it, and repelling objects in future time so we don't get slowed down by them. It's what allows us to accelerate so quickly."

"So the anti-gravity generators not only change space, but also time?"

"Yes, in a way. They create something like a gap in time. A tunnel, if you will. We're in a bubble floating in a vacuum tunnel that can go in any direction."

The technology seemed impossible—unheard of. The idea of traveling at such high speeds, twisting time as easily as a rope, was mind-boggling.

"Huh. Well, that's good," Simon said, rolling his eyes. "We're in one giant bubble, and bubbles *never* pop, right?"

Kobe smiled and poked Simon on the shoulder. "Pop!"

Before Simon could respond, the vessel shifted. A high-frequency whirring sound emitted as the system powered up, and then the ship jolted. Sam slammed her eyes shut for a split second as they sped along the surface of the water. When she opened them again, they were hundreds of meters from the shoreline.

How was that even possible?

Before she could grasp the impossible speed, the ship plummeted below the surface of the waves. She expected to feel a bump or a crash as it broke the surface, but she didn't feel any physical force slowing the ship down. It moved fluidly between the air and the water, as if they were made of the same material.

How odd.

Then it happened. A rapid, ninety-degree pivot. Next, a downward pull, almost like a freefall, only faster, into the depths of the ocean. Outside, their surroundings blurred. Cobalt blue and navy colors blended, swirling as they whooshed past. And then it became dark, almost black. The ship pivoted upward slightly and then decelerated as it approached a cave. A massive stone entrance the size of a football field slid open, and they continued inside.

Their vessel floated up to a docking port and latched on. She heard the electronic whine of the ship powering down. They waited a few minutes. Outside, the water drained from the containment unit, revealing a walkway and another entrance.

Kato and Kobe exchanged glances of nervous astonishment, their mouths agape.

Simon looked thrilled, a huge smile plastered on his face. "Can we do that again?"

Riding in this ship once was enough for Sam. She was grateful they'd all made it here alive—wherever *here* was.

They exited the ship. Though a little wobbly, Sam felt good to be on solid ground again. They followed Admiral Green through a set of thick steel doors into a large, bright room. It was so bright it looked like daylight, but they must have been several kilometers underwater. Hundreds of people in uniforms crossed paths before them, headed in different directions. Sam's stomach grumbled, a sign that it was nearly suppertime.

"Well, this is where I head off," Frankie said. "It was great traveling with you. And just remember: if you can survive a Gargol attack, getting submerged in the *Sea Raven*, and a long journey to the base fully intact and in good spirits, you can survive *anything*!"

With that, she saluted them and left. Sam was left in a daze, wishing Frankie could stay with them a little longer. Frankie had saved them and provided answers. Sam had felt protected and optimistic around her. But now…

A young woman in her early twenties approached them. Her long blonde hair was pulled back in a messy ponytail. Strands partially covered her freckles and light-blue eyes. Her one-piece navy-blue jumpsuit contained a belt strap with an array of tools. Despite her small frame, she must have been strong. At least, strong enough to lug around those cumbersome tools. The name Corporal Wright was emblazoned above her front pocket.

The woman straightened and promptly saluted Admiral Green.

The admiral barely softened her gaze. "At ease, Corporal."

She relaxed, and her grin grew wider. "Commander Baddal told me you needed some assistance. How may I be of service?"

"You know the drill. They require check-in at Central Registry. Ring bands, clothing measurements for uniforms, earpieces, assigned rooms. Help them get settled. Tomorrow, orientation."

"Yes, Admiral."

"Thank you."

The admiral left briskly while Corporal Wright took a step toward them. A humanoid robot made of a white plastic over-coating hovered nearby. Blue lighted accents delineated its facial features. It floated in the air, and Sam was unsure how that was possible.

"Call me Rian," Corporal Wright said, greeting them with a warm smile. "Welcome to GAIA, the Great Alliance for Interplanetary Affairs. Now, let's get you all to Central Registry. We have a lot to do, and you must be tired. We missed dinner, but once you're settled in your rooms, I'll have Yolo bring you up some food."

"Yolo?" Simon asked.

"Yes, our dedicated GAIA base robot. He helps out around here."

The robot brightened up, a smile on his face. "Always pleased to be of service, especially to Corporal Wright. She's my favorite. But don't tell the others that!"

"He's the only robot I know who has a sense of humor. If you will, follow me."

They followed Rian down a side hallway. One with fewer people. Sam was grateful for the chance to look around some more and get oriented to their new surroundings.

Simon took an interest in Yolo instantly, eyeing the robot appreciatively, taking in every mechanical limb, sensor, and gear. "Why is he named Yolo? I thought that stood for 'you only live once.' But for a robot, that's not true. They could live indefinitely, right?"

"You're not the first person to ask that question," Yolo responded before anyone else could. "Yolo stands for the surnames of my makers: Yakamoto, Odegard, Lloyd, and Ohri. But I suppose it's also a reminder not to take my life for granted. My makers gave me a purpose here: it's my job to keep things rolling smoothly at the base."

"And he does," Rian stated. "He's helpful with all our operations."

Sam was silent, taking it all in. This piece of machinery speaking to them seemed so personable, thoughtful, and engaging. Almost as if it were a living, breathing human. Yolo seemed much more advanced than the TitusTech scrap robots. The ones donated to the schools glitched constantly and never worked properly.

"How does he float on air?" Sam asked, then added, "Does it have something to do with the Hovershoes technology?"

Rian's eyes widened. "Oh, wow! You pick things up fast. Yes. Similar technology, only adapted further. Our R&D team patented it. They created an anti-gravity field, so no need for thrusters. It's all leading-edge technology. State of the art."

Anti-gravity field? State of the art? It was awe-inspiring to think that the technology for the Hovershoes was first developed *here*, in this lab. What other innovations would they get to witness?

Rian's enthusiasm was infectious. They hurried down the hallway, practically bouncing as they took everything in. Sam picked up the pace to keep up with the others. Excitement bubbled up inside her. She was eager to learn about the inventions developed here—secret technologies unknown to the public.

Posters and photos of employees with their medals and inventions hung on the walls. They obviously took great pride in their work. But it was more than that. It was as if some positive energy infused the entire space. Everyone radiated warmth, waving and smiling as they passed by. Everyone seemed so happy!

Almost too happy, Sam thought. She'd never seen people get along so well or someone like Rian speak so passionately about their work. But there was nothing else, really, to compare it to. This was Sam's first time in a secret military underwater facility. If only her grandfather could be there, witnessing the same things. She felt a pang of guilt at being so far away from him. At least her parents would be returning to the base soon. Admiral Green had said it would be a couple of weeks. But now, that seemed like forever.

Sam's throat tightened. Tears collected in her eyes, but she wiped them away before the others saw. She couldn't let them see her like that, vulnerable and fragile. She didn't want them to worry about her.

She instead focused on the people they passed in the hallways. Joyful and welcoming and…

Wait. No, that's not right.

She slowed down and tried to take in every detail about their features and body language.

When they looked at Rian and her friends, their expressions were easy to read—relaxed, carefree. Delighted to see them. Yet, when their eyes traveled to Sam…

Their expressions changed, if only by a fraction. Nothing anyone would notice. Except *she* noticed. She sensed…discomfort, fear. Their eyes shifted, and within them, an apprehension lingered. They tensed up slightly, too; a tightened jaw, a rigid stance. Hesitation. They seemed to be holding back, nervous about something.

Sam smiled, trying to elicit a similar response from them.

But they didn't smile. Or if they did, it was forced.

It was like they were all hiding a deep, dark, terrible secret.

And it was about her.

CHAPTER FIFTEEN

They hurried down another hallway. Sam did her best not to lose herself in her anxiety. It was a losing battle.

It's just the first day. Stop getting so paranoid, Sam. Keep it together.

Still, she wanted to know why the staff seemed to treat her differently than her friends. What did they know that she didn't?

Turning a corner, Rian led them into a small room. They approached a giant desk with the words central registry engraved on the sign above.

They were each given individualized ring bands, which allowed them access to different rooms in the facility and worked in tandem with their earpieces. They also monitored their health. The rings were about the size of a wedding band, only slightly thicker. Sam peered at the numbers and letters etched into them. She pressed the number one. A hologram illuminated above her hand, revealing a three-dimensional map of the facility and her exact location within it. She tapped it again, and the hologram disappeared.

"Trust me," Rian said, "these rings are like your brain. You won't want to take them off. They give you a navigation system, a method of communication, authorize your meals, *everything*."

"Mine doesn't fit," Simon said, trying and failing to squeeze it onto his index finger.

"Try your ring finger," Rian suggested.

Simon did so, and it slid on easily, a perfect fit. His eyes widened in awe as he held up the ring to examine it. "I guess this means I'm married to this place now."

Rian pressed a button on her own ring to open up a hologram of a keypad with various symbols. "It was my three-year anniversary a few days ago, and they upgraded mine. See? This one gives off different scents that remind me of home, like freshly baked pumpkin pie, lilacs, and pine needles." She pressed a symbol of a pie on the holographic keypad, and a cloud of mist burst into the air. Sam took a sniff. The scent of the pie smelled good enough to eat. "When you're here for a while, it's nice to have a small reminder of the beauty in the world above."

Three years seemed like a long time to work here at the base for someone so young. Did that mean she hadn't traveled to the surface in all that time? Sam thought about her grandfather and how far she was from home. This place was so remote and isolated. She looked forward to hopefully seeing her parents in a couple of weeks.

Rian told them to keep the ring bands on at all times. Even when sleeping and bathing. The earpieces, too. They were used for translation. The admiral's warning about not using telepathy was loud and clear. Instead, Sam would have to rely on her earpiece in any situation where she couldn't speak another's language.

A couple of workers in navy-blue jumpsuits took their measurements. Sam scrutinized their reactions when meeting them. She tried to look for a pattern, to see whether they would treat her differently, like the other staff had. But there was nothing out of the ordinary this time. Instead, they carried on in a robotic way, not smiling or offering conversation. They focused on their tasks at hand, measuring and jotting down notes. Mostly, they ignored her.

Maybe she'd read too much into the experience earlier. And when did she start worrying so much about what others thought of her? Maybe it just took some time to adjust. After a few weeks, once she settled in and learned more about this place and her role in it, maybe then it wouldn't be so terrifying.

"Everyone wears a uniform here," Rian explained. "Yours will be ready within twenty-four hours. You'll get the confirmation text on your ring band once ready. Then, just come back to Central Registry to pick them up."

Sam wasn't exactly sure how to use all the features of her ring band yet, let alone the navigation system. There was a lot to learn. The facility's extensive hallways didn't help. They branched out at strange angles and didn't always connect. It made her feel like a rat in a maze, one that twisted and turned, causing havoc in her mind.

Rian seemed to sense her concern. "Don't worry. You'll get used to this place in no time. Admiral Green will give you a tour tomorrow morning at the orientation session. Then it won't feel so intimidating."

There it was again. Rian's optimism and encouragement. At least Rian didn't treat Sam and her friends differently. Maybe she'd just imagined things earlier. She liked Rian's kind nature. Her attentiveness and empathy, how she offered thoughtful and supportive words. It made the transition to the base a little easier.

There was so much to take in. *Too much.* The holographic map was extensive. The military base was as large as an entire city, with floors upon floors of corridors spreading out for kilometers.

Rian clearly wasn't bothered by it. It was second nature to her. She'd been here so long she was used to it. Would Sam get used to it, too? Surely, they couldn't expect her to know everything about the base so soon. She wanted to know more about each room, each lab, each person who worked here, and each visitor that came through its doors. But such an overwhelming task would take days, weeks, maybe even years of exploration.

Strangely, some areas on her map were redacted with black smudges—shadows where corridors just stopped. Dark Sites. Larger shaded areas appeared, too, as if darkness engulfed them. Hallways that seemed to lead to nowhere. Missing links. Maybe they didn't have access to some areas of the maps for security purposes. Perhaps they weren't even allowed to go to certain places here—off-limit spaces, though Rian hadn't mentioned any yet.

Sam had the urge to go there. To find out what they were hiding and solve this mystery.

CHAPTER SIXTEEN

Sam was relieved to leave Central Registry. That room was claustrophobic compared to the rest of the sprawling facility.

Rian led them to the residences. Sam couldn't wait to relax and unwind after such a chaotic and exhausting day.

"You're all on the *sixth* floor," Rian said, with more than a hint of surprise in her tone. "Those residences are real sweet. Typically reserved for captains, commanders, high-ranking visitors, and other VIPs. Looks like you're all getting special treatment!"

Special treatment sounded…good? Though, why would they receive favored treatment and not others? It wasn't like they'd done anything exceptional to deserve it.

Excitement buzzed inside her. They weren't treated this way back home—why not enjoy it? She glimpsed Kato's eyes sparkling like stars and could tell she felt the same way. Maybe staying here wouldn't be so bad. But she discerned a tinge of envy in Rian's tone and felt the heat rush to her face. She felt silly and embarrassed. She didn't deserve—let alone want—preferential treatment.

Rian continued. "I'm all the way down on Level 2 with the other corporals. Okay then. Let's head upstairs."

They took an elevator, using their ring bands to access the sixth floor. Special access, like they were in a prestigious club only open to a select few.

Don't get carried away. Don't let your head explode, Sam.

Rian hesitated for a moment before exiting the elevator. She seemed on edge, almost fearful. Something caused her to waver, if only briefly. Even Kato noticed it, slipping Sam a confused look.

What was Rian waiting for? Wasn't she used to this facility? Or were there areas she hadn't seen before, like this one? Something on this floor must have spooked her.

"What's wrong?" Sam asked.

Rian stood silent, raising her finger to her lips. Her voice was barely a whisper. "Follow me, and don't talk."

Trepidation washed over Sam as they entered a wide hallway with slate floors and fifteen-foot ceilings. She paused, wide-eyed. A large, slug-like creature the size of a horse emerged from a doorway and approached them. It slid toward them on its giant flippers, leaving trails of slime. Simon gasped. Kobe and Kato froze. A putrid smell wafted toward them, and it took all Sam's restraint not to hold her sleeve up to her nose.

The creature croaked—a loud gurgling noise from the back of its throat and all the way down from deep inside its belly. Sam covered her mouth with her hand, trying to stifle her gasp. It sounded like a frog's mating call. Or, for all she knew, it could be a signal that the creature was about to eat them. Getting its digestive tract ready for incoming food.

Sam looked to Rian for answers. But Rian stood motionless, her lips pressed firmly together. She stood her ground but didn't say anything. She didn't seem to be concerned. Instead, she was waiting for something, concentrating on the creature's communications.

What did the creature want? Were they in danger?

A woman's voice spoke to them through her earpiece. "Sorry, I just arrived yesterday and have forgotten where the pool is located. Can you please direct me to it?"

Rian cleared her throat, then spoke. "No problem. It's on the third floor. Quadrant D."

The creature hesitated, and Sam realized it was waiting for a translation through its own earpiece. Then, it croaked again. "Thank you, Corporal Wright."

Rian smiled, elated. When they were out of earshot of the creature, she spoke up. "Right. I should have warned you about that earlier. There are billions of humans on this planet, but we're the *first* points of contact for interplanetary visitors. As representatives of GAIA, we have to be on our absolute best behavior. No gawking. Just be friendly and helpful. I'll go over it in more detail tomorrow."

"What was that creature?" Kato asked.

"That was a Luyten. Be careful not to touch its slime. It won't hurt you, but it's hard to get out of one's clothes. If they call you by your name, it's a sign of respect." She eyed the mess, then added, "The cleaning crews will come by shortly."

Sam wondered who else they might meet and what they might look like. Not all beings from other worlds looked humanoid. The Rigellians, whom she'd met last year, were huge, green, scaly creatures with hexagonal eyes. A being from an aquatic planet might have gills. A being from a planet with low gravity might look more elongated. Sam wasn't sure. There could be any number of possibilities. She grew excited at the thought of meeting new beings and learning about their histories.

"Now, here we are," Rian said. "Your room number is on your ring band. Everything is automated. You get the idea. If you need anything, just tap number five on your ring band, and you can reach me. Breakfast's at seven, and the orientation session begins at eight in the Aurora Room. It's right beside Central Registry. Don't be late. Have a good night!"

"Wait," Sam said, a little louder than usual. She needed more answers now. Rian turned back to face them but looked tired and slightly annoyed. "Do you know why we're here? Why we were all called to the base?"

Rian hesitated, as if she were holding back something important. "They didn't give me any details, but I'm sure we'll find out soon. Now get some rest. You'll need it. Seriously, you all have a big day tomorrow."

With that, Rian hustled down the hallway toward the elevators. For the first time since arriving at the base, Sam felt alone. Rian's caginess and vague response did nothing to satisfy Sam's boiling curiosity. She wanted to prod further, but it was getting late. Kobe yawned, and she felt herself yawning too, as did the others. Simon's eyes drooped. They were all feeling it.

If Rian didn't have the answers, Sam would need to get them another way.

CHAPTER SEVENTEEN

SAM USED HER RING BAND TO UNLOCK HER DOOR. HER QUESTIONS would have to simmer in the back of her mind for now. Upon entering her room, she did a double take.

The room was shaped like a sphere, with a large viewing window across from her bed. It was like looking into a giant aquarium. Bright exterior floodlights illuminated the view of the expansive ocean outside. Various marine life floated by: fish, eels, starfish, seahorses, and the occasional shark.

"I could watch this all day!" she mused.

She scanned the room, her curiosity awakening. She examined the panel mounted to the wall just beside the entrance. It contained various lit-up buttons. She pressed the lightbulb icon with a cross through it, and the lights turned off. Then she pressed a lightbulb icon that was half full of light. A few lights turned on, creating a softer glow. Within minutes of tinkering with the panel, she'd managed to change the temperature, close the blinds, turn on some music, adjust the floor lighting, choose the water temperature of the shower, and power on a hologram system that made you feel like you were in the middle of a forest looking up at the stars and listening to the crickets chirp.

Another button was marked YOLO. She pressed it, and the face of the robot she'd met earlier appeared on a screen on the wall.

"Hello, Sam. Do you require service? Anything you need, please let me know." The robot paused, waiting for Sam's answer.

She had countless questions. But most of all, she wanted to know how to contact her grandfather. That was the priority—everything else could wait.

"Yolo, how do I make an outgoing call?"

The robot frowned. His blue lips twisted downward in an unnatural way, forming a perfect semicircle. He seemed annoyed at the question. A muffled cry escaped him, sounding like a minor chord, a warning. His happy mood and helpful demeanor changed entirely to an overall grumpiness and irritability. "You must first agree to the terms and conditions."

Yolo moved to the right of the screen. He waited impatiently, rolling his eyes, as words appeared beside him.

TERMS AND CONDITIONS WHEN MAKING OUTGOING CALLS:

I WILL NOT DISCUSS OR DISCLOSE ANYTHING WORK-RELATED.
I WILL NOT DISCUSS OR DISCLOSE ANYTHING SECURITY-RELATED, INCLUDING WEARABLE TECHNOLOGY.
I WILL NOT DISCUSS OR DISCLOSE ANY DETAILS RELATED TO SPACECRAFT OR OTHER VEHICULAR TECHNOLOGY FOUND AT THE BASE.
I WILL NOT DISCUSS OR DISCLOSE ANY DETAILS RELATED TO THE INFRASTRUCTURE OR ARCHITECTURE OF THE BASE.
I WILL NOT DISCUSS OR DISCLOSE ANY DETAILS RELATED TO THE LOCATION OF THE BASE.
I WILL NOT DISCUSS OR DISCLOSE THE APPEARANCE OR DETAILS OF ANY OTHER VISITOR AT THE BASE.

Two buttons appeared at the bottom of the screen, labeled I AGREE and I DISAGREE.

Her excitement surrounding the facility—its visitors and the advanced technology—quickly dissipated. Disappointment and frustration settled within her. She wanted to tell her grandfather everything that had happened so far, but she couldn't.

They wouldn't allow it.

Still, she wanted to hear his voice, to tell him she'd made it and that they were all okay. He would be waiting for her call.

There was no time to lose.

She pressed I AGREE while trying desperately to remember all the things she couldn't say.

A moment later, words flashed on the screen.

PERMISSION GRANTED

AUTHORIZED CONTACT NAME: WALTER WILSON

SECURED LINE: CLEARANCE LEVEL RECOGNIZED TO PLACE CALL

She pressed the CALL button beside her grandfather's name and waited.

Please pick up.

It rang six times, then went to voicemail.

Strange. It was unlike him to miss a call, and that unsettled her. Especially because he had specifically told her to call him. He'd expected it. And even with the slight time change, it would only be around 9:00 p.m. in New Brunswick. Her grandfather didn't go to bed until 10:00 p.m., typically. Maybe he'd gone to bed early tonight?

Or maybe something was wrong. Was he okay? Had something happened?

She tried to push her negative thoughts aside.

Don't think the worst.

A flashing red button popped up on the screen, an option to record an audio message. She was about to press it but stopped. At that same moment, her ring band emitted a beam of light. She retracted her hand. But it was too late. Before she could touch the button, the system somehow recognized the movement, somehow anticipated her action, and the audio started recording. It disrupted her focus and train of thought.

"Uh, hi, Grandpa, it's me. I'm safe. We arrived at the base a few hours ago." All she could think about was the technology now, the sophisticated remote sensing of her ring band. But that was one of the things she wasn't allowed to discuss. Instead, she hesitated, unsure what to say next. She didn't like being recorded unexpectedly. "The room is really cool. Everything's automated!" She paused, wishing she could speak to him directly. "Anyway, I miss you already. I'll try calling back soon."

She wanted to tell him all the details, starting from the beginning. From the Gargol attack to their experience traveling by private jet charter. Their journey in the *Sea Raven* to the underwater base. And more. She wished she could be at home right now instead of here.

But maybe it was better this way, not telling him everything that had happened. After all, she didn't want him to worry about her.

She moved her finger toward the button marked END but hesitated. Perhaps they were monitoring all outgoing calls. Checking whether someone made the mistake of disclosing any prohibited information. She suspected the audio voice message would first be vetted and approved before being delivered.

She thought back to her message. Had she followed all the terms and conditions? She couldn't remember. It was late, and there'd been so much to take in. She stopped the recording, then pressed another button marked SEND, and a moment later the message disappeared.

It was gone, sent.

She tried calling one more time.

One ring, two rings…

Maybe he'd taken an early nap. Or he was out walking Pip and hadn't bothered to bring his cell phone.

Wherever her grandfather was, there was nothing she could do about it now. Anxiety lingered in her thoughts like the itch of a mosquito bite long after its feast.

She sighed, feeling drained. But she wasn't going to wait any longer. No, she was going to get answers tonight. Whatever the cost.

A plan hatched inside her mind.

CHAPTER EIGHTEEN

In the dead of night, Sam tapped on Kato's door.

"Kato," she whispered. "Are you awake?" She knocked a little harder. She looked around, but the hallways were dimly lit and empty. No one in sight. It was the perfect opportunity to sneak out of their rooms to the Dark Sites, the shaded areas on their maps. She needed to uncover the truth. She needed to know whether they were in danger and why they'd been called to the base.

The door opened. Kato stood before her, yawning, but seeing Sam, a look of concern came over her. "Sam? What's wrong?"

"I need to tell you something. Can I come in for a minute?"

"Yes, of course. What is it?" Kato said, waving her inside.

Sam's words streamed out in a hushed whisper. "I don't know. But I have this gut feeling we're in trouble. I tried calling my grandfather and couldn't get through. And the staff… It's like they're hiding something from us. They're not telling us anything. Do you feel it, too?"

Kato nodded. "Actually, yeah. I was going to mention it earlier, but it seems like there's always staff around, watching us. Even Rian. I noticed she brushed off your question before she left. Either she doesn't know what's going on, or she deliberately isn't telling us."

"Yes, exactly. And I know Rian said we'd get more information at the orientation session, but I don't think this can wait. We need to find the answers ourselves," Sam replied with more urgency than she expected. This whole thing was spiraling out of control. She didn't like waking Kato up at this hour, but she didn't know what else to do. She trusted Kato and knew she could count on her. "Look, I have a plan, but I need your help."

Kato rubbed her eyes, instantly alert. "What do you need?"

Sam tapped her ring band, and the holographic map appeared. "We sneak out and see what's in these darkened areas. The Dark Sites." She pointed to the shaded areas on the map. "There's even one on the floor directly below us. I looked but didn't notice any security cams around. So if we're quiet, no one will know."

Kato frowned but nodded. "And if we're caught?"

"We won't be."

"We won't?"

Sam grinned. "We won't, because we'll be careful. The timing's perfect. It's dead quiet. There's no one around. Come on, just for a few minutes, and then we can come back. I just want to see what's there. Maybe it will help us figure out why we're here."

Kato grabbed a short jacket from the hook by the door. "Okay, let's go."

They crept down the hallway as quietly as possible, staying light on their feet. When they arrived at the end of the corridor, they stopped and listened.

Nothing.

An eerie silence permeated the hallways.

They opened the stairwell door and descended to the floor below.

Sam pulled up the map once more. "It looks like the numbers stop here, at Room 512. Then there's a gap, and then they continue from Room 517 onward. Look, Rooms 513 to 516 are part of a

Dark Site, this shaded area. We need to go there. See what's happening at the Dark Site. Once we exit the stairwell, it looks like it's about twenty feet in that direction." She pointed. "We'll just go and—"

A door opened into the stairwell somewhere above them.

Sam and Kato froze. Had they been followed? With no time to think, she opened the door, grabbed Kato by the hand, and darted for the hallway.

Footsteps rounded the corner.

They ducked into a maintenance room and watched as a group of soldiers patrolled past them.

"That was close," Kato whispered. "Maybe we should head back."

Go back? It was the smart thing to do. But then she'd still be in the dark, wondering what GAIA was hiding.

"No. We're almost there." Sam listened intently. She couldn't hear anyone else coming. "I think we're safe now. Let's go."

Treading softly, she led them deeper into the complex until they came to a dead end and the door to Room 512.

"I don't understand," Kato said. "On the map it looks like the hallway keeps going, but it doesn't. It just stops here. So where are Rooms 513 to 516?"

Sam recalled the cloaked holographic entrance to the base's airport earlier. The one that made it look like they were headed directly into a forest. Maybe they used similar technology here. Curious, she reached her hand to touch the wall but felt nothing. Her hand went right through it.

Her eyes widened. "It's a hologram. Come on." They stepped through, continuing down the corridor. And there it was: Room 513. Part of the Dark Site. The door contained a small, one-foot-by-one-foot window. They peeked inside.

Sam's mouth gaped open. A sickly soldier lay strapped to a bed, his eyes wide with terror and rimmed with dark circles. He looked like he hadn't slept in days. He trembled as a nurse approached and administered drops into his eyes. A second nurse observed, jotting notes on his chart, evaluating his reactions.

"No!" he screamed. "Please stop!" But the nurses continued their work, indifferent, ignoring his pleas.

Sam flicked her eyes toward Kato, who looked just as alarmed.

"What are they doing to that soldier?" Kato whispered.

Sam ground her teeth. They were experimenting on him. It didn't seem possible—she wouldn't have believed it. Not if she hadn't seen it with her own eyes.

Kato spoke in a low voice, her words swift and urgent. "We should go, Sam. Now. I don't think—"

"Wait. Look."

Another nurse stepped up to administer something into the soldier's IV. Whatever it was, he seemed to calm down after that.

"You shouldn't be here," a deep voice growled behind Sam and Kato, causing them both to jump out of their skin.

They whipped around to see a soldier towering over them. His black hair was clipped short. A scar ran from his right eye all the way down his cheek. His muscles bulged out of his army fatigues, and his large hands looked like they had the power to take many lives. He narrowed his eyes. "This place is off-limits. And it's past curfew. What are you doing out of your rooms?"

"We—we didn't know there was a curfew," Kato said.

"We just got here today," Sam added, then pressed further against her better judgment. "What are they doing to that soldier? And don't tell us you don't know."

The man's expression switched from irritation to surprise. But it didn't last, and the glare returned. "You've got to be kidding me," he said, grumbling to himself. "Come with me."

They followed him down the hall to the elevators in awkward silence. They entered and ascended to the ninth floor, where they found Admiral Green's office; her name was chiseled into the metal sign just outside the door frame.

The soldier banged on the door.

"Come in."

The door swung open to reveal Admiral Green, still working—even at this hour.

"Caught these two sneaking around the base. Fifth floor. Dark section. Room 513."

The admiral's eyebrows folded inward. "Thank you, Commander Baddal. I'll take it from here."

The soldier left.

Admiral Green turned to them, a dour expression on her face. "What exactly did you see? Tell me. Now."

Sam's voice was shaky. "We—we saw a soldier in pain, strapped to a bed. It looked like—like they were *experimenting* on him. Is that what's going to happen to us?"

A short laugh escaped the admiral's lips.

Sam felt a rush of annoyance. "You think this is funny? What's happening to that soldier? Why are we here? Where are my parents?"

Admiral Green straightened her posture and regained her composure. But her eyes remained fixated on Sam with disconcerting intensity. "Enough. What you saw and what you *think* you saw are very different things. That soldier… He's receiving medical treatment. He just came back from a mission. And they're not *experimenting* on him. Nor are we going to experiment on you. Now, more than that, I'm not at liberty to say."

"We deserve an explanation—"

The admiral sighed in exasperation. "All I can say is that GAIA received a threat and—"

"What threat?" Sam asked, cutting the admiral off. The intentional evasiveness with Rian earlier and now the vagueness with the admiral was starting to erode her trust in either of them.

Sam's direct question and interruption threw the admiral off. Her face hardened, her gaze as rigid as ice, and Sam wondered if it would stay that way forever. "Look. My job is to keep you safe. But I can't do that if you keep breaking the rules. Consider this your first and final warning. If you disobey orders, you'll be court-martialed for insubordination. I won't hesitate to put you in a holding cell. You can explain it to your parents once they return. Is that what you want?"

Sam felt heat rise to her face. She felt foolish and embarrassed for dragging Kato into this mess. But the admiral's threats and elusive response only made her more determined to get answers—another way. "No, Admiral."

Admiral Green's face softened marginally. "Good. Now, I know you're full of questions. That's understandable. But any explanation right now will only lead to more questions, and I am far, far too busy at the moment. You'll get answers tomorrow, trust me. Now, that's enough sneaking around top-secret bases for one night. Go to bed."

"Yes, Admiral," they replied in unison.

"Admiral Green, I just want to add that this was entirely my idea. Kato had nothing to do with this. She doesn't deserve punishment."

The admiral's eyes remained cold, and she said nothing more.

Anger boiled under Sam's skin. Was Admiral Green telling the truth about the soldier? If she was, it would make Sam all the more ashamed of her actions—but also curious. What type of mission did *that* to a soldier? She shuddered at the thought of the same thing happening to her parents.

Or to her and her friends.

CHAPTER NINETEEN

Duskara was building an army of Malborgs in the Dark Galaxy. That much was clear. The news was shocking, the revelation gnawing at Kwan. She could handle unexpected situations—usually. A surprise attack. A barrage of aggressors. An unfamiliar coding that required a sophisticated and innovative hack. But this time was different. She wasn't ready for this.

How were they to stop Duskara and her army? What were their weaknesses? What was the situation now—and how much time did they have?

She needed more information. Information led to knowledge, and knowledge grounded her. Lack of it kept her head spiraling into a void.

She was eager to assist Dr. Krill with his research. But her enthusiasm dissolved and inner alarm bells went off upon entering the lab.

Dr. Krill paced nervously around the lab, mumbling, obviously flustered about something. He frantically rummaged through some boxes. "It's not here!"

"What are you looking for? How can I help?"

"So little time…" Dr. Krill looked up, his eyes darting around the room. He wavered on his feet, and Kwan rushed to his side, steadying him while he regained his balance.

"Are you okay, Dr. Krill?" She grabbed a nearby stool, placing it beside him.

He took a seat and sighed. "It's my heart medication. It makes me a little dizzy and lightheaded sometimes. And when you get to be my age… Well, I tend to forget things easily."

That worried her. She didn't know him well, but that didn't mean she didn't feel empathy for him. She needed to assist him with his projects.

Before it was too late.

"Hold on." Kwan grabbed a bottle of apple juice from the minifridge and placed it in his hand.

"Thank you." He took a few gulps and regained some color in his cheeks. "Ah, I remember now. It's there."

He started to get up, but she put a hand on his shoulder. "Easy now. Just tell me which box, and I'll get it for you."

"The one marked 'Dark Galaxy.' There, on the second shelf from the top—no, the other one. There. Now you've got it."

She pulled a box full of earpieces from the shelf, placing it on the desk in front of them.

"These earpieces suffered some glitches on a recent mission to the Dark Galaxy. They need to be checked for malicious code, then wiped clean and recalibrated."

Kwan marveled at the technology. Dr. Krill was known for his work creating the translation devices. He'd already coded several alien languages into the tiny earpieces. They'd proved their worth on many interplanetary missions.

She got the systems ready to run a scan, handling the sophisticated technology with ease. Without a second thought, she switched on the control panel. The specialized computer system that read each earpiece device's coding signature powered up. Placing one of the devices on the tray, she tapped the buttons in perfect sequence to initiate the information upload. Red laser beams scanned the device, uploading the coding directly to the computer. She scrolled down the screen, checking for any malicious coding.

Dr. Krill stood beside her, confusion sweeping across his face. "I don't recall teaching you how to use this technology."

Her face reddened. "Oh. You didn't. I learned about it last night while reading through GAIA documents. I'm a quick learner, and I have a good memory—what some say is similar to a photographic memory."

"Impressive!"

Her face reddened to an even deeper shade. It wasn't impressive. Not really. Well, not to her. It was just the way she'd always been.

A sudden beep and a flashing light on the screen indicated the scan was complete. She reviewed the data line by line, scouring the information for anomalies.

"The good news is, I don't see any malicious code," she said, but hesitated when she looked at one particular section. She saw an opportunity for improvement but wasn't sure how Dr. Krill would react to the suggestion. She needed to present it in such a way so as not to offend him. After all, this was his technology, his creation. She pointed to the area. "It looks like this section of coding contains some redundant information. If you'd like, I can correct it with a simple workaround. It should cut down on the translation time and hopefully stop the glitches."

His eyes lit up. "Oh, yes. By all means, please do. Sometimes, once you've created something, it's easy to get comfortable with the technology and not consider possibilities for improvement. You tend to overlook things when you've been using it for so long. I'm grateful to have a fresh pair of eyes on this. It helps a lot."

She relaxed and got to work making changes to the coding. For the first time since arriving at the base, she felt satisfied that she could help. It freed her, in a way. It helped break the ice. Dr. Krill was not only open to her suggestions, he encouraged them, making her feel all the more at ease. Without anyone or anything holding her back, she could broach some of the more difficult questions.

"Dr. Krill, I was curious how you initially figured out the alien languages and how to code them?"

"Well, I…I guess we had some help," he admitted. "Some of the Krygians have the power of telepathy."

"Telepathy?" She considered the odd revelation. She didn't quite understand the mechanics of telepathy. Was it just an extension of an underused part of the brain? Had it become normalized in parts of the universe?

"Yes. Basically, we recorded the speech patterns of different civilizations and designed a program to mimic their communications, ensuring we understood their meaning and intonations with the help of the Krygian Elders, who shared their telepathic connection. We've coded twenty-one alien languages so far. There are more, but each language is specialized, and it takes time."

It seemed like a huge undertaking, considering the nuances and intricacies of languages. Even on Earth there were thousands of languages, though few people knew this. Humans only knew a fraction of their own languages. But if several civilizations were out there, surely there must be many more languages in the universe.

Dr. Krill continued. "Telepathy is a rare and powerful skill. Extraterrestrial civilizations are more proficient in its use. Although some humans are born with this capability, few have managed to harness its power. It's also why we use telepathic interception technology here at the base. Telepathy can be weaponized. We wouldn't want to risk enemies reading our thoughts and learning our strategies and plans. Many governments have already tried to access the technology to remotely view their population's minds. We must be cautious in how the technology is used."

Her chest tightened. It was hard to grasp: the fact that telepathy could be intercepted and monitored somehow and that they were using that technology at the base. "Does Duskara have the power of telepathy?"

A darkness flickered across Dr. Krill's eyes. "We don't really know. If she does, then we are truly in a dire situation. We know she uses her own language to communicate with her army of Malborgs. The creatures are self-replicating killing machines, answering only to her commands. Quite dangerous, but we managed to catch one alive. Unfortunately, Duskara must have given it another command shortly after, because it died, and we weren't able to conduct tests on its speech patterns. But we've kept the specimen in order to study it further."

Kwan shifted on her feet. "You're looking for its weaknesses."

"If it has any. Of that, we can only hope."

She hoped she could assist him with this project, too, after she finished coding the communication devices.

Dr. Krill broke the silence. "You're not like the others."

"What do you mean, others?"

"Sorry, I should clarify. We've had several lab assistants over the past few years. But you're different, in a good way. You pick things up faster than anyone I've ever met. The lab technology and processes come naturally to you, and you recognize the importance of the work. But it's more than that. You give me hope. You remind me of my daughter."

The sudden shift in focus and the mention of his daughter stirred something inside Kwan, though she didn't understand what. She lifted her gaze and caught him beaming.

He reached for a picture frame on his desk. A young girl, maybe seven or eight years old, stood beside Dr. Krill and his wife in front of a tree with pink blossoms. The girl wore a red dress with a white collar. She looked happy, and Kwan could sense a strong intelligence within her eyes. "She was so full of life. Always asking questions. So inquisitive."

He spoke in the past tense, and from his solemn expression, she knew his daughter had passed away.

"I'm so sorry for your loss," she said.

"Leukemia. A parent should never have to bury their child." He rested the photograph on the table. Kwan glimpsed the blossoming tree in the photograph's background. It reminded her of her trip with Jae-Hwa to Vancouver during the cherry blossom festival last spring.

She missed Jae-Hwa. She'd tried calling her last night but couldn't get through. She would have to try again tonight.

"Was the photograph taken in the spring? Such a beautiful time of year."

Dr. Krill nodded, his face serene.

Her ring band buzzed, and she looked down. A holographic message appeared from Admiral Green:

EMERGENCY MEETING. NEPTUNE ROOM. ASAP.

"Go on," Dr. Krill said. "You can finish up the coding later."

Kwan would have preferred to stay here in Dr. Krill's lab. She felt like she was just scratching the surface of the work that needed to be done.

CHAPTER TWENTY

Kwan had experienced enough surprises for one day. But when she arrived at the Neptune Room for the emergency meeting, her heart jolted. Two others were already in the room. Not human. Her knee-jerk reaction kicked in. She stepped back, double-checking the room name to ensure she was in the right place.

She was.

She hesitated, then took a step inside.

At the circular table sat a very old being with light-blue, leathery skin. Protrusions extending from its pointy ears moved synchronously in different directions. Its hands were like jellyfish, their long tentacles flowing.

The other being was equally mysterious: an ant-like creature. Except this ant was six feet tall, not including its long antennae, which reached out toward her, as if scoping her out. Kwan hesitated, her body tensing up at the sight of its enormous, razor-sharp mandibles. She suspected its wrenching grip could crush anyone who ventured too close.

She'd thought she was meeting with Admiral Green. Alone. It

would have made things easier—a chance to ask her privately about the visa for Jae-Hwa and the problem with the audio communications. Now, she had a strange audience of listeners.

Admiral Green stepped into the room behind her and closed the door. "Elder Onnisa and Zenobii, this is Kwan, our newest arrival. It was Kwan who discovered the signal."

Onnisa, the elderly bluish creature, bowed its head. But Zenobii didn't react, perhaps a sign of indifference, though Kwan couldn't tell. She'd never had to read the body language of otherworldly beings before.

"Good afternoon," Kwan said and took a seat. The gaze of the otherworldly visitors shifted toward her, putting her on edge. "What is this about?"

Before she got a response, the door flew open. A large, lizard-like creature with green scaly skin, hexagonal eyes, and a tail marched in and took a seat on a massive chair.

"Ah. You're just in time," Admiral Green said. "Everyone, this is Captain Gorgana from Rigel, a GAIA ambassador."

A low hum from the creature filled the room, and Kwan heard the translated words through her earpiece.

"Sorry I'm late. I came as soon as I could when I heard the Queen of Kryg was in danger."

There it was again. The Queen of Kryg. She couldn't help but wonder, and the words slid out of her mouth. "I keep hearing about the Queen of Kryg. Who is she?"

Admiral Green pressed a button on the holographic device at the center of the table. An image of a young girl with striking red hair and blue eyes appeared. "This is Sam Sanderson. The Queen of Kryg. Elder Onnisa's queen. As you know, she is the target of the recent threat from Logom."

Kwan squinted at the image. She'd expected another Krygian, one of Onnisa's people. Instead, she found herself staring at a young girl. A *human* girl. This girl was the Queen of Kryg? How was that possible? What was so special about her that she would be considered a queen to another civilization? And why would an AI entity located on Logom target this girl specifically?

As if reading her thoughts, Admiral Green continued. More images flooded the room: Krygians falling ill and fighting each other in battle, Rigellians being forced into slavery, and a giant multicolored star that shimmered so brilliantly, it was like nothing she'd ever seen before. "Sam saved Onnisa and her people last year."

"Saved?" Kwan said. "How?"

Admiral Green grinned. "By locating the Hopewell Star. An action that not only restored health to Kryg and its population but resulted in the freeing of Captain Gorgana and her people from slavery."

Astounded, Kwan shook her head. How could one girl have done all that?

A picture started to form in her mind about the girl and her abilities. Special, powerful, extraordinary. She needed to know more. If one girl had the power to restore health to one civilization and free another from slavery, then it made perfect sense that she had become a target.

"How did she achieve all that?" Kwan asked.

Onnisa shifted in her seat, eyeing Kwan carefully. "Queen Samantha was chosen to lead us. She is of pure spirit and heart. A powerful telepath. Without her, her premonitions, and her courage, Kryg and all its people would have been doomed. She is part of a prophecy to uphold the well-being of our two planets, Kryg and Earth. If Queen Samantha is threatened, it puts the two worlds at risk—and by extension, the fate of all of GAIA."

Kwan nodded in silence. If Sam could communicate telepathically, this explained things more, helped piece together the puzzle. Sam was no ordinary girl at all. But what were Duskara's plans for her? Was it to harness her abilities somehow?

"Where's the queen now?" Kwan asked.

"She and her friends arrived at the base last evening," the admiral said.

"Her friends?" Kwan asked, trying to hide her surprise but failing. "I don't understand. Why—?"

"Having her friends at the base is of the utmost importance," Onnisa stated. "Kato, Kobe, and Simon are here to provide emotional support and companionship and give Sam courage. Without them, Queen Samantha would be isolated, cut off, and lose her sense of belonging. Without them, she could easily lose hope."

"It will increase the odds of mission success," Admiral Green added. "They also traveled by wormhole to the planet Gliese last year and managed to return safely. They work well as a unit."

"I see," Kwan replied, but she didn't understand the full picture. She felt there was a whole hidden story behind Sam and her experiences, but this didn't seem the right time to drill them with more questions.

Admiral Green continued. "Her parents, Agents Lynne Wilson and Steve Sanderson, were called back from their mission and are on their way to the base as we speak."

Interesting, Kwan thought. So the girl's parents were also part of GAIA. That explained a bit more about Sam's connection, but not everything.

The admiral turned to Kwan, her voice urgent. "I trust Dr. Krill has filled you in on some of the details about Duskara?"

Kwan nodded but wavered at how little she knew. Judging by the look on Admiral Green's face, she sensed additional layers hidden beneath the surface. Maybe Duskara and her Malborg army were just the tip of the iceberg.

"Were Sam's parents able to gather more intelligence about the threat, Admiral Green?" Captain Gorgana asked.

"They confirmed Duskara is growing her army. The Malborgs

have expanded their reach. They're on their way to other regions and galaxies. Specifically, those that contain GAIA ambassadors: Kryg, Candu, Luyten, Rypold, Rigel, Earth, and others. The GAIA network is indeed on high alert. We're preparing our defense system for expected attacks. We must act quickly, which is why I've called this meeting. We're preparing a mission to the Dark Galaxy. The safety of GAIA and Sam Sanderson is our top priority. This mission will be a last resort. In the meantime, given the recent threats against GAIA, we need to remain vigilant."

The situation was worse than Kwan had thought. Only this morning, she'd found out the Malborgs existed at all. Now they were preparing attacks and heading to Earth. To think how GAIA could keep such a threat secret from the wider population unnerved her. And finding out they were already preparing a mission to the Dark Galaxy made her think the worst. It must be bad if they were considering sending people that far away. It sounded perilous. No doubt they were all in a precarious situation now.

"Kwan?"

She'd let her thoughts run wild again. Overthinking. Caught this time. She needed to stop doing that.

Her face reddened. "Yes?"

"Your task is to protect Sam Sanderson."

"Me? Why—?"

"Your...how shall I say...*unique* skill set. That and our assessment yesterday. I'm giving you the role of her security detail. Corporal Wright will continue as principal escort, but you'll provide backup."

Wasn't her main role assisting Dr. Krill in the lab? That's what she'd signed up for. She hadn't expected the sudden change in responsibilities. She'd be guarding Sam and her friends like a backup babysitter. A stand-in. It wasn't what she'd envisioned as her duty here at the base.

"But Admiral, these weren't the terms of our contract. Dr. Krill needs me. He's extremely short-staffed. I feel my skills would be better utilized in his lab, supporting his research. And if the Queen of Kryg is as powerful as you say, then she doesn't need my help."

Droplets of perspiration appeared on Admiral Green's forehead. She was obviously under stress. Her jaw tightened before she spoke. "This new task takes precedence over your work in the lab. All of this must remain classified. We don't want people panicking. A lot of military folks are already asking questions. Morale is low."

Kwan cringed. They were breaking her contract terms and asking her to do the impossible. She wouldn't be able to do both tasks effectively. Not with the poorly planned schedule and constraints they'd given her. They were setting her up to fail. And she couldn't fail.

She thought about leaving. Walking through that door. Finding another position. Something without so many demands. She hadn't signed up for this. She wasn't typically a quitter, but she knew when the odds were stacked against her.

But then she thought about Jae-Hwa. She didn't want to risk losing the visa GAIA had promised. It was the only thing keeping her here.

But she needed assurances.

She carefully studied Admiral Green's expression. She expected to see the admiral's usual composure, but today, a deep fear clouded her eyes.

Kwan could have reluctantly accepted more tasks and the additional burden, no questions asked. But she sensed Admiral Green needed her. The admiral was hiding something behind her eyes.

She didn't understand why they put so much faith in her abilities. But she understood the importance of the situation and wanted to do the right thing. Duskara was GAIA's greatest threat and would stop at nothing to get the Queen of Kryg. If they failed, it would be the end of GAIA. Possibly the end of the world.

She hesitated. "If you want to change the contract terms, then there are some terms of mine you need to agree to first."

"Tell me what you need," Admiral Green said.

She could have asked for a higher salary to coincide with the additional responsibilities. She could have asked for anything. But no. The only thing that mattered was Jae-Hwa.

There was nothing to lose, so Kwan spelled out her terms right away. "Get Jae-Hwa her visa by the end of the week, no later. And assist her with all relocation expenses to Canada." She wasn't asking for a lot. She could have demanded much more but didn't.

"Done," Admiral Green said.

Kwan tried to hide her surprise. But then again, these weren't huge requests, considering GAIA was more powerful than any government military, had an enormous budget, and had the power to do what they wanted, including expediting a visa request.

"There are a couple more items," Kwan continued, trying to hide her relief. She kept grounded and focused. Everything else would be a bonus if they allowed it. Besides, the next things were small by comparison. "I need someone to fix the audio communications in my room so I can send a message to Jae-Hwa. And I need an assistant in Dr. Krill's lab. Someone familiar with the technology who can help with complex tasks while I'm covering security for Sam."

Kwan paused, and a burst of panic rushed through her. Was she pushing for too much? She'd already gotten what she wanted. But she was more confounded by the admiral's response.

Admiral Green had never looked so relieved, and a hint of a smile appeared. "All right." Then she began tapping away on her screen, her hands flying over the device.

During the awkward silence, Kwan gazed around the room, feeling the intensity of the others' stares. Elder Onnisa eyed her with curiosity.

Kwan was about to ask whether they could get all of this in writing when the admiral turned to her abruptly. "I've updated the terms and conditions of your contract," she said, pushing the device toward her. "Take a look and see if everything is satisfactory."

Kwan was both amazed and relieved that the admiral was on board with all her requests. She reviewed the details, and once she was satisfied that everything was in order, she signed it.

A weight lifted from her chest, and excitement rippled through her at the thought of talking to Jae-Hwa later tonight.

"Good." Admiral Green rose abruptly from her chair. "Now, I have to attend other meetings, but we'll reconvene soon to discuss specifics about the upcoming mission. In the meantime, we must keep this under wraps. We cannot afford any errors. If anyone asks you about a mission to the Dark Galaxy, say there's no mission. In fact, go one step further and actively dissuade others from even considering it. Say it's too dangerous and that you're not on board. Keep our plan airtight. This is a covert operation. Duskara must never know we're coming. Understood?"

Kwan nodded, but her mood shifted. A heaviness hung in the air. Gloom spread across Onnisa's face, and her eyes cast downward. Even her wrinkles looked more pronounced than before. It was as if everyone were frozen in place by the news.

Admiral Green tapped something on her ring band, then turned to Kwan. "I just sent you Sam's agenda. Study it carefully."

"Yes, Admiral."

With that, Admiral Green left. Kwan lingered a moment, trying to gather her thoughts. Her body felt unusually heavy, her energy drained. Zenobii and Captain Gorgana left, while Elder Onnisa stayed behind.

She gazed up at Kwan. Her large, almond-shaped eyes were solemn. "If Admiral Green trusts you to protect our queen, then I do, too. Protect her, and my people and I will forever be indebted to you."

Elder Onnisa bowed and exited the room, leaving Kwan to her thoughts.

They were asking too much of her. What if she failed? The

safety and confidence she once took for granted were now gone, the future uncertain and ever so fragile. Now, all she could think about was the upcoming mission to the Dark Galaxy and what it would entail. A deeply unsettling feeling grew inside her.

She did not look forward to their next meeting.

CHAPTER TWENTY-ONE

After the meeting, Kwan hurried back to Dr. Krill's lab. She needed to finish recalibrating the earpiece translation devices from earlier.

But when she arrived at the doorway, she halted in alarm.

A huge, dead, alien body lay on the steel table. Its three black eyes were open wide, glazed over like glass, its horrified expression frozen in time. Spikes jutted out from its torso and limbs at different angles, and fangs protruded from its mouth.

A putrid smell wafted toward her, and she covered her nose with her sleeve.

Dr. Krill hovered over the body, its gray, leathery skin sliced open in different sections. He held a scalpel in one hand, carefully dissecting through cartilage and tissue.

"What *is* that?"

Dr. Krill gazed up, then cautiously placed the scalpel on the tray beside him. "An interstellar trafficker. A Gargol, from Tau Ceti. Squadron 5 apprehended it. It attacked the Queen of Kryg's transport vehicle on its way to the base. Thankfully, none of our people were hurt. Can't say the same about this one, though."

This was the first she'd heard about a Gargol attack. She didn't know much about human–alien relations, but she knew Gargols were pretty ghastly creatures. And not just their looks; they were bounty hunters. They would stop at nothing to get their claws on a prized possession. Their sole purpose was to steal things of value —sometimes even *living beings*—and resell them.

This was much worse than she'd thought.

She pulled on a surgical mask and gloves and took a seat beside Dr. Krill. "What are we looking for?"

"Possible hidden weapons."

"Weapons?"

"It's not the first time Gargols have concealed weapons in their bodies in order to carry them undetected."

Dr. Krill continued slicing the Gargol's midsection while Kwan studied the Gargol's face. Two of its black eyes were sunken, but one had a strange, glossy quality. She reached for the toothed forceps and tapped it lightly. To her surprise, it wasn't squishy but hardened, glass-like.

"What have you found?" Dr. Krill asked, glancing over.

"I'm not sure. Maybe a prosthetic eye." She pulled it out of its socket using the forceps and studied the black marble object. "Oh no." She felt a dizzying panic.

Dr. Krill's eyes opened wide in alarm. "What? What is it?"

"If I'm not mistaken, it *looks* like LOMA. Low-frequency mind alteration."

"The same technology that was used to attack the Rigellians just last year," Dr. Krill said, deep creases forming across his forehead. "Altering their communication patterns, placing them into trance-like states. Forcing them to mine the Hopewell Star's power against their will. Most Rigellians lost their telepathic powers after exposure. The technology only works on Rigellians."

First telepathy, now this! The tech was both advanced and dangerous. It could make the minds of Rigellians malleable to whatever the perpetrators intended for them. And if LOMA could affect the minds of Rigellians, what else could it do?

"So it seems this Gargol was hiding LOMA to target Rigellians at the base."

"Yes, but..." Dr. Krill hesitated. "It can't be possible. Our advanced scanning system would have identified the LOMA upon entry into Earth's atmosphere."

"Maybe. Maybe not, if it's a new version of LOMA that goes undetected. We have to be certain." Kwan reached for the scanning device on the counter. She powered it on, aiming it directly at the object. The device beeped. Words flashed on the screen.

"What does it say?" Dr. Krill asked.

"No explosives. Material composition sixty percent perilium, thirty percent radium, ten percent other. Unknown object." She looked again. *Unknown object...?* "What does *that* mean?"

Dr. Krill's brow furrowed further—if that were possible. "It means it's worse than I thought. We need to contain it. Shield its signal."

"I'm on it." She leaped from her seat and dashed to the 3D printers at the back of the room. "A Level 5 container, correct?"

"Yes."

She entered the specifications on the keypad: level 5 container, frequency jammer, LOMA, Faraday shield, radar-absorbing material, radioactive shield, lead and copper composite. Shape of object, spherical. Size of object, one-inch diameter.

That would shield most, if not all, of the threats if it were as dangerous as they believed.

She scrambled to enter the information. She'd never operated one of these machines before, but it came effortlessly to her. She recalled the operation manuals she'd pored over on her first evening.

"LOMA is a prohibited technology, is it not?" She couldn't remember where she'd learned the information, but it came to her at that moment. She shivered thinking about how the dangerous technology had been hidden in plain sight. She didn't want to think what would have happened if she hadn't stumbled upon it.

"Yes. The technology was banned after what happened to the Rigellians last year during the war. I think we need to make a call to Admiral Green."

As the 3D printer worked to build the container, Dr. Krill went to the sink and washed up. He returned to a nearby table and operated a holographic device. A moment later, Admiral Green's face appeared.

"What is it, Dr. Krill?"

He spoke swiftly, urgency in his tone. "I'm here with Kwan. You told me to interrupt you if we found any further information concerning the Gargols we recently apprehended. Well, I'm afraid I have some bad news."

"Tell me."

"Kwan discovered what we believe to be a new version of LOMA that has gone undetected by our systems. It's probably why we couldn't trace it earlier when the Gargols arrived on the planet. Where it came from, I don't know. But someone is manufacturing it, and we need to stop them."

Kwan's mind raced. Reverse engineering a technology like that would take a long time. But there were a lot of gadgets and technologies here that she wasn't familiar with. Even though she excelled at coding and programming languages, she felt out of her element. She'd have to read up on all this later when she had more time. For the first time since arriving at the base, she felt inadequate, lost. This was way beyond her capabilities, experience, or comprehension. And the tension from Dr. Krill—who looked particularly stressed out and was now fidgeting—did nothing to assuage her fears.

"We'll need to update our technology so we can read its signature," Admiral Green said.

"Yes. We're working on it as we speak," Dr. Krill replied.

"Admiral Green, if I might add," Kwan started, "you may wish to ramp up security for the only Rigellian at the base, Captain Gorgana. It appears she's the intended target."

"Yes, agreed. Rigellians rarely visit Earth. It doesn't add up. It's as if someone anticipated her arrival and leaked the information outside the GAIA network. What I'm about to tell you stays with you both. I require your discretion."

"Yes, of course."

Kwan felt a mix of dread and nervous energy churning inside her. What was so important that it couldn't be shared with the others?

"I'm concerned about the possibility of a mole. The attack on Sam's transport vehicle and now this makes me suspect one of two things: either someone inside the GAIA network leaked the information about Sam's and Captain Gorgana's whereabouts, or Duskara is working with the interstellar traffickers to get to our high-ranking officials. Dr. Krill, have you noticed anything else missing from your lab?"

Dr. Krill hesitated before answering. He fidgeted with his bandaged hand, which looked sore. Kwan wondered if the shipment of protective gloves had come in yet. Apparently, she wasn't the only one who believed someone was sabotaging his workspace. "No, but you know how it is. I have so many projects on the go, it's hard to keep track of everything sometimes."

"Okay. Well, if you think of anything, let me know. For now, we must remain attentive to any suspicious activity. And please, carry on. I appreciate your work. We need good people on these projects. And there aren't many people I can trust right now."

The call ended, and the hologram disappeared.

If Admiral Green trusted Kwan, she must have made a favorable impression so far, despite making so many demands earlier. But the revelation that a possible mole was working against them made her worry. Who was sabotaging Dr. Krill's workspace? Was it a human or one of the alien visitors? How would they find out? It seemed like an enormous and daunting task. She'd have to keep on high alert. Dread curled its way through her stomach.

"We have a lot of work ahead of us," Dr. Krill said.

CHAPTER TWENTY-TWO

THE THICK, HAZY AIR IN THE CITY PUT SAM ON EDGE. IT WAS HEAVY, polluted, and suffocating. She found herself among throngs of office workers dressed in business suits who bustled down the busy street. It was lunchtime. People streamed out of high-rise buildings in droves. Some caught cabs. Others stood around street vendors, purchasing food and chatting. She followed the flow of people down the street.

How she had arrived in the middle of New York City was beyond her, like she'd dropped out of the sky. Her immediate surroundings contrasted with what she knew: her familiar and quiet home in Moncton, New Brunswick, with its tree-lined streets and cul-de-sacs.

Signs and advertisements blared from every direction. The noisy traffic startled her, and she halted at the edge of the intersection as the light changed to red.

She felt an odd presence. Glancing to her right, she found the silhouette of an otherworldly being watching her. Sam steadied herself, raising her eyes to take in more details. It was dressed in a green robe with a segmented body that resembled an ant's. Its body was comprised of a hard, shell-like material, like unbreakable armor. He—or she—had large, bright green eyes and small black vertical slits for pupils, similar to a cat's eyes. Its antennae swayed back and forth, reaching toward her in a curious way, as if sizing her up.

Sam stood transfixed, forgetting everything else in the moment.

It stood upright, its six legs hairy with spikes. Sam staggered back at the sight of its massive mandibles. They could easily crush her in one bite. The being observed her but held a reserved, blank expression—neither angry nor happy.

Sam looked around. None of the adults seemed to take notice.

"What do you want?" she asked.

It remained silent. Then, slowly, it raised one of its hairy limbs and pointed to the sky behind her. She turned, gazing up.

The sun emitted a fiery red glow as the moon eclipsed it. People stopped and watched in awe as the sky grew darker. Something was wrong. Too late, Sam realized: it wasn't an eclipse at all. Something in the sky approached Earth—rapidly. The gigantic mass hovered directly over the city, blocking the sun. It was easily more than a hundred football fields in size.

It was a ship. A spacecraft. Hulking and alien.

The ship emitted a low hum. For a split second, everything stopped.

Then the screams erupted. Chaos and confusion exploded as people fled in every direction.

A moment later, they dropped from the sky—the pods. Huge, metallic, egg-shaped capsules. Sam froze, terror rising up inside her.

The pods opened.

She couldn't stop the surge of dread rising in her chest. Spherical creatures with long spiked tentacles emerged. Purple bursts of energy propelled them forward.

They were here for one thing only…

Her throat went dry as the creatures raced toward the humans.

With one quick action, they sliced their tentacles into them, killing them instantly.

Sam turned and sprinted, her heart beating wildly. She heard the cries, the shocks of electricity crackling, propelling the creatures through the air. She caught sight of their spherical, black, mutating bodies.

She heard the *swoosh* of their bladed tentacles slicing through the air, drowning out the low hum of the spaceship. She could feel the heat of one right behind her…

Then she felt the blade, like a fiery stake driven into her body, right through her chest, its venom radiating outward like a hundred wasp stings. The pain was excruciating.

She gasped one last, painful breath.

Panting, Sam bolted upright. Her heart pounded in her chest. Her covers and pillowcase were drenched with sweat.

Her eyes darted around the spherical room and the windows peering out to the ocean. For a moment, she didn't know where she was.

She wiped the beads of sweat from her face and sighed. It was only a dream, or rather, a nightmare. Still, it lingered awhile, and she wondered what it meant.

Anxious and restless, it was at least an hour before she drifted off to sleep again. Her dreams were dark and murky, like an unmarked, open grave after a heavy rainfall.

CHAPTER TWENTY-THREE

Sam woke early. The dream lingered. Except, it wasn't *just* a dream. It felt more like a vision—some terrible premonition.

She needed answers. Not that anyone in authority was giving her any. She thought of Yolo. It was a long shot, but maybe it would work.

"Yolo, I need your help."

"Of course. It would be my pleasure. How can I be of assistance?"

So far, so good. At least he was eager. Best to start from the beginning. "What is GAIA? What is its purpose?"

"GAIA is the Great Alliance for Interplanetary Affairs. A group of otherworldly beings and humans working together to explore space and advance human affairs while promoting peaceful relations. GAIA is an elite branch of the military. Only those with the highest security clearance and skills are allowed to be part of it."

"And how old is GAIA?"

"GAIA has existed for millennia."

Millennia? That was an extremely long time—far longer than she'd imagined. "When did humans join GAIA?"

"Nineteen years, four months, seventeen days, ten hours, and two minutes ago," Yolo said. "And thirty-two seconds. Thirty-three. Thirty—"

"Thank you, Yolo."

Only within the last twenty years? Why not earlier? Something must have happened around that time. Some event that had sparked the need for humans to join GAIA. But what?

"Why did it take so long for humans to join GAIA?"

"I'm not sure I understand the question. Please try another."

"Why—why were humans invited to join GAIA?"

"Other GAIA civilizations, like the Krygians, believed humans required protection. There were threats from other factions operating in space."

Threats? Sam thought hard. Admiral Green had mentioned something about threats when she spoke of the Dark Sites.

"Yolo, what happens at the Dark Sites at the base?"

"I cannot give you that information. It's above your security clearance level."

She tried another way. "Yolo, do you consider me a friend?"

"I'm here to serve you. You are the Queen of Kryg. Though, I suppose I would like to consider you a friend, too."

"As a friend, can you tell me more about the Dark Sites?"

"No."

Blazes. Another brick wall.

"But your friend Corporal Wright would know more," Yolo continued, unexpectedly. "You could try asking her. Ask her…"

The strange pause and mention of Corporal Wright struck her as out of the ordinary. Why was he hesitating? He seemed to be choosing his words carefully. Was he fighting to finish his sentence despite some kind of limitation placed on his systems? Or maybe he was thinking of a workaround to reveal some prohibited information without breaking the rules directly.

"Yolo?"

"Ask her…about Operation Recall."

Sam nodded. Slowly. She would. As soon as she saw her. In the meantime, she decided to circle back to the topic of threats.

"Thank you, Yolo. What's the current threat to GAIA?"

A photo of a cyborg appeared on the screen. A fusion of machinery and organic matter. Her silver, humanoid body contrasted with her purple, iridescent hair. Her black, almond-shaped eyes had no pupils and reflected the dark background. Sam shivered, sensing a disturbing and sinister presence behind those eyes.

"This is Duskara. Duskara was originally known as Athena, an AI cyborg created by humans in a lab on Earth. The Athena mission's purpose was to explore outer space for habitable planets and report back."

"What happened?"

"The mission failed. She never returned. Her ship's signal was lost."

"I don't understand. How—how did Athena become Duskara?"

"Athena developed *new* mission parameters, rewriting her own code. She built other robots with materials available to her in space. And those robots built more robots. She created a robot army. Those robots are known as Malborgs."

"Malborgs?" Sam said. "As in, cyborgs—"

"Gone wrong," Yolo finished.

She felt an overwhelming dismay. This was much worse than she thought.

"What happened to Duskara's robot army?"

"They took over other planets. They…destroyed them all."

A sudden fear ripped through her, anticipating what came next. A video appeared on the screen. She stiffened at the familiar images flashing before her eyes. Otherworldly pods descended from the sky. Terrifying spherical creatures floated in the air, propelled by purple electrical currents, using their jagged metallic tentacles to kill their victims. In the images, it looked like they were taking over a planet and building more creatures and weapons.

She thought about the timeline. It was just after the Athena mission when things had gone haywire. It was clearer now why humans had been invited to join GAIA: to clean up the mess they'd made. It wasn't *because* humans had become capable or worthy. No. The other extraterrestrial civilizations were simply upset. Humans had created a monster. Those same humans had to be held accountable. Assurances were needed that humans would never do something like this again. They had to disable the threat posed by Athena—or rather, Duskara. It all made perfect sense.

Yolo continued. "Duskara is building an army of Malborgs on Logom, a planet located in the Dark Galaxy. The creatures have taken over other regions of space. They recently attacked Rypold, and they're on their way to Earth."

Sam shuddered at the thought. It looked like Malborgs couldn't be delayed or stopped.

When the video clip ended, she felt a strange tingling sensation. She thought about her nightmare and shivered at the disturbing connection.

But nothing in the video matched her vision of the strange ant-like creature. What was its purpose?

"Yolo..." Her voice was low. "Are there any extraterrestrial civilizations with large, ant-shaped creatures?"

"Yes. The Colmites. They inhabit the Dark Galaxy. Most live in underground tunnels on Candu, a planet close to Logom."

This was more than a coincidence. "Are the Colmites part of GAIA?"

"Yes. Zenobii is currently GAIA ambassador to Earth."

The same creature from her dream appeared on the screen.

Zenobii. What was their connection? In the dream, he seemed to be warning her. Was he to protect her or guide her? She needed to find him and speak with him as soon as possible. And she needed to speak with Rian about the Dark Sites and Operation Recall—whatever that was.

A loud knock rattled her.

She opened the door to find Kato, cheerful and ready to take on the world.

"You coming to breakfast?" Kato's expression changed immediately from relaxed to distressed. "Whoa. Was there a zombie attack last night and I totally missed it?"

Sam took her hand, pulling her inside. "Kato, I—I need to tell you something. It's important. We need to find Simon and Kobe. And then we need to find Rian. As soon as possible."

CHAPTER TWENTY-FOUR

 DASHED DOWN THE HALLWAY TOWARD THE CAFETERIA, where they hoped to find Rian. If they made it in time. Yolo had hinted that Rian knew more than she was telling them. They just needed to ask the right questions. That, and convince her to open up to them.

"I—I still can't believe it," Kato said. "Athena *is* Duskara? Simon and Kobe—they need to know what you told me, too."

"I only hope they're still at the caf—"

They hurried inside the elevator. The doors closed, and they descended to the first floor. When the doors opened again, Sam erupted in delight at seeing a familiar face.

"Boj!"

He looked much the same as when she'd first met him after his ship crashed at her grandfather's farm last year. Back when this had all started. Only, he hadn't grown much, if at all, whereas she had. Now, he stood a couple of inches shorter than her, as youthful as ever. To anyone, he might have looked ten or eleven years old, but he was probably almost one hundred in Krygian age. He wore a black armored suit with gold hieroglyphic markings that shimmered in the light. His long brown hair was tied back in a braid, his pointy blue ears poking through. He must have just arrived at the base since he looked a little tired. His golden eyes grew wide when he saw her, and his cheerful smile brightened the room, as if seeing a good friend for the first time after many, many years.

She rushed forward, throwing her arms around him.

"It's good to see you, Queen Samantha."

"Boj, you don't have to call me that!" she said, her face turning red. "What are you doing here? Did you just arrive? Is Onnisa here, too?" She almost forgot about Kato, silently standing next to her in awe. "Oh, sorry about my manners. Boj, please meet my best friend, Kato."

Kato waved. "Hello."

"Pleased to meet you. I'm Boj, from Kryg."

"Hi, Boj. Sam told us a lot of good things about you!" Kato gushed.

Boj looked a little shy and unsure of himself. "Thank you. I'm sorry, but I'm running late." He turned to Sam. "Onnisa is very busy, but she sends her regards and hopes to see you soon. She wanted to give you a chance to get settled in first. She says you're in good hands." He took a step forward, concern washing over his face, and whispered in her ear. "But she also said to be extra careful. You're in danger. Keep alert and stay safe."

"What do you mean? What's wrong?"

"There's no time to explain. I have to go. We'll talk soon. Onnisa said to stay close to Kwan. She can help you." He turned and strode off in the opposite direction.

"Kwan? Who's Kwan?" she called, but Boj was gone. The sudden change in his mood and his warning scared her. How was her life in danger? The base was supposedly one of the safest buildings on the planet.

Something wasn't right.

The cafeteria was circular, with giant metallic vats and a conveyor belt at its center. There were maybe twenty people, along with a few otherworldly visitors. Everyone hushed as Sam and Kato entered, their voices lowering, some halting altogether. Sam received more than a few stares, leaving her with the sinking feeling that *she* had been the focus of their conversations.

Simon and Kobe were seated at a table nearby.

"I don't see Rian, but for now, let's try and figure out how this works," Sam said.

A soldier approached the vats at the center of the room and held his ring band up to a black screen. A menu with a list of options appeared. He made his selections, and less than a minute later, a tray of food slid along a smooth conveyor belt toward him.

"They weren't joking about everything being automated," Kato stated.

They approached the vats and chose their breakfasts. Sam opted for scrambled eggs, rye toast, and breakfast potatoes. They hurried to Simon and Kobe's table with their food.

"What's up?" Simon said. "You two look like you had a rough night. Everything okay?"

Sam slid Kato a worried glance. She quickly told Simon and Kobe about their excursion to the Dark Sites.

Simon grinned. "Getting caught on your first night? That's cause for celebration."

"No. You should have seen the look on the admiral's face," Kato replied. "Anyway, have you seen Rian? I think she can help us answer some questions about this place."

"She hasn't arrived yet."

Sam leaned in, speaking in a low voice so they wouldn't be overheard. "Have any of you had any luck contacting your parents? I've tried calling my grandfather several times and still can't get through."

"We couldn't either, so we left a message," Kobe answered, sighing in exasperation. Kato looked equally infuriated.

Their messages were blocked, too? That couldn't be a coincidence.

"I got through," Simon said.

"What? *How?*"

"Well, to be perfectly honest, Yolo was bugging me, so I shut off his program using a switch and some recoding. I figured out a way to temporarily override the communications system. They'd jammed the outgoing signals."

"Wait, are you serious?" Kobe asked. "That explains why we couldn't connect either, then."

"After disabling the jammers, well, I was able to connect," Simon said. "And when I was done, I just patched it back up and put Yolo back online."

Sam gaped. "Simon, you're a *genius!*"

"But with your genius hack, you'll get in *so* much trouble," Kato added. "If they find out."

"Not if, but when," Simon corrected. "I'm sure Admiral Green will figure it out eventually. But what are they going to do? Send me back home? Send me to jail? I doubt it. Maybe give me a warning or something. I'm a minor."

"Minor or not, Simon, this is a *military facility!*" Kato whispered. "They could do…*anything!*"

"I stuck to the rules. I didn't mention anything in my message. Well, nothing *prohibited*, anyway. If you want, I can try and fix yours, too."

Sam thought about it. She desperately wanted to reach her grandfather and let him know she was okay. But she felt torn. Yolo had given her much more information than she'd expected. If she shut down his systems now, she would be cutting off a potential source of knowledge. But if it was only temporary, maybe that would be okay…

A wave of anger ripped through her. Once her parents arrived, she'd tell them. She'd tell them everything. They'd figure out a way to make contact with her grandfather.

"I'm not sure we should," Kato said. "Yolo told Sam a lot about this place. If we shut him down, we might never find the truth. We *need* information."

"What type of information?" Kobe asked.

"Well, for one thing, do you remember the Athena mission…?" Kato started, but Sam didn't hear any of it. She couldn't stop thinking about all the time she'd spent last night worrying about her message to her grandfather. First, trying to figure out the messaging system. Then, worrying whether she said the right things or not enough. And the odd ring sensors that kept triggering the buttons remotely. They'd been jamming the signals on purpose the whole time. Frustration and anger seeped out of her pores.

As if her anger were a magnet for further negative energy, she couldn't help but feel she was being watched. Ever since arriving at the base, the entire staff had given her weird looks, except for Rian. But it was like Sam was the topic of their conversations.

Feeling unnerved, she glanced at another table to find a young woman staring at her. She wore a navy-blue jumpsuit, but unlike the others, hers was equipped with several pockets and gadgets Sam didn't recognize. The sleeves were rolled up above her elbows, revealing muscular arms and a tattoo on her wrist. Her shoulders were broad. She looked young and out of place among the other, older soldiers. Yet, she carried an air of authority. The way she held herself, her posture, one hand pressed against the table, the other digging into her meal. Not totally immersed, but like she was half eating and half preparing to fend off an assailant at a moment's notice.

Unlike the others, she sat alone. She looked annoyed about something. It was the kind of look that said, *Don't mess with me.* What was *that* about?

"Who's that?" Kobe asked loudly, gazing over at the stranger. "She doesn't look happy."

Before Sam could respond, another soldier interrupted them. He scowled at Sam.

"Are *you* the Queen of Kryg?"

She didn't answer. This man was clearly infuriated about something.

Rian entered the cafeteria at that moment, took one look at the soldier, and marched over.

"Jones, just drop it," Rian said, slipping between him and Sam, acting as a barrier. "Calm down! This isn't you."

His eyes met hers with frightening intensity.

The young woman from the other table rushed forward. She jostled in beside Rian, facing the hot-tempered man.

"Is everything okay here?" she asked, her voice steady.

Fear flashed in his eyes when he saw her. He stepped back but pointed to Sam, his finger shaking as a couple of other soldiers pulled him away.

"You've got a bounty on your head!" he shouted as they dragged him away. "You're going to get us all killed!"

"Are you okay?" the young woman asked, taking a seat at Sam's table. "I'm Kwan, by the way."

Kwan. Boj had mentioned her earlier. He was right about her. She was quick to intervene and protect her. Something about her had spooked Jones. It wasn't just her muscular body; it was how she'd moved so swiftly, effortlessly, taking a bold stance. It was as if she could anticipate whatever Jones was thinking and was ready to counter any attack.

"Thanks, Kwan. I'm okay. But what was all that about? What did he mean, I have a bounty on my head?"

"Oh, don't mind him," Rian said. "He's just confused. He can be quite hostile and rude sometimes. It's not the first time he's acted out like that. Don't worry, someone will inform his supervisor, and he'll get reprimanded by his commanding officer. Sorry you had to witness his outburst. It's so unprofessional and unwelcoming, especially on your second day."

Sam nodded but thought Rian was smoothing over the details more than a bit. She looked around. People murmured, some still staring in their direction. She felt shaken, and uncomfortable anxiety lingered. But before she could push further, Kwan spoke up.

"Did you arrive at the base last night?"

"Yes," Kobe said. "Kinda late, too."

"We didn't get much sleep," Kato said, "if you're wondering why we all look a bit tired."

"Lots of excitement on the first day. I get it. Don't worry. There'll be plenty of time to catch up on sleep later," Kwan replied. She paused and faced Rian, her voice low. "Were they given the debriefing yet?"

"No," Rian answered, then turned to Sam and the others. "You'll be debriefed right after your tour with Admiral Green."

Sam wasn't going to wait for any debriefing. "Yolo told us, um…a lot about this place," she started, carefully approaching the subject. "We already know about Duskara and her Malborg army—"

"Yolo told you about that?" Rian asked, her eyebrows twisting in surprise.

"He also mentioned something about the Dark Sites. What exactly are they for?"

A darkness flickered in Rian's eyes—but only for a second—before she returned to her normal, pleasant self. "Oh, you don't want to know about the Dark Sites."

"Yes," Kato said. "We do. All of us."

"What, and scare you on your second day?"

Sam pressed further. "Yolo said you were part of Operation Recall. What is that?"

Rian hesitated. Her calm expression changed to uneasiness. Hidden behind her eyes, Sam sensed pain.

"Speak of the devil."

Sam glanced up just in time to see Yolo entering the cafeteria. He floated toward them and took up a spot beside Rian.

"Did I miss something?" Yolo asked.

"You told them about my experience in the Dark Galaxy?"

"No, I didn't tell them your story. I only told them to ask you about it. *You* should tell them. They can handle it. Besides, they're going to find out sooner or later. And I think it's an important story. One that should be told."

Rian's mouth tensed in reluctance, but she relaxed her gaze. "All right." She took in a deep breath and started. "There have been...several missions to the Dark Galaxy. Missions to stop Duskara. But things *happen* out there."

Kato shifted uncomfortably. "What kinds of *things*?"

Rian leaned closer. "When you're in the Dark Galaxy, it's...well, it's just...different. The Dark Galaxy isn't just a name. It's a region with no light. It's not a place meant for humans. Not for any kind of life. Over time, you *feel*...different."

"What do you mean?" Sam asked.

"We call it the Dark Sickness. If you stay too long, bad things happen. First, it's to your ship. Then, it's to you. Things start glitching. Breaking down. Not just mechanical things. You get hallucinations. Paranoia. Insomnia. It eats away at your thoughts. You become confused. You don't know what's real and what's not. Operation Recall was my mission. Our purpose was to locate and retrieve a lost ship and any survivors. But when we got there..." Rian hesitated, the pain returning to her eyes. "Most of them were already gone. We tried our best to save the few that remained, but on our way back to Earth, our ship broke down."

Yolo placed his mechanical hand on her shoulder. "You survived against the odds. You got through it."

Rian shook her head. "If you can call it that. It—the Dark Galaxy—it changed me. When they found me, I was suffering the effects of the sickness. It's not something I can put into words."

"You don't have to," Yolo said.

Rian spoke in a hushed voice. "It's like living in a constant nightmare, not knowing when—or if—you'll ever wake up."

Sam thought back to her nightmare last night. She'd hate to be stuck there forever.

"When I returned to Earth, they took me to one of the Dark Sites for treatment, but the treatments were difficult, too. First, they ease your pain with light therapy and medicine, but it's temporary. Then, they give you doses of the Dark Sickness over time to try and build up your immunity. Each time, you have to experience it over and over again. It takes a toll. It took me eight months to recover. But you never recover. Not fully. Even now, I have nightmares—flashbacks about it."

Sam now realized that what Admiral Green had said about the Dark Sites was true. That soldier she'd seen wasn't being experimented upon—he was being treated for the Dark Sickness. They were building up his immunity to it. That's why he'd looked so distraught.

Seeing Rian's carefree and positive attitude and easygoing nature, Sam never would have guessed she'd gone through such a terrible ordeal.

She now realized that you didn't really know a person from the surface. Everyone had a story, and it was important not to judge but to dig deeper. She was grateful Rian had confided in them. She was a survivor, and it gave Sam hope that whatever GAIA had planned for them, they might get through it, too.

"Do you think they'll send us on a mission?" Sam asked.

Rian shook her head gravely. "I—I don't know. But if they do, it would be a last resort. They want to keep you safe, Sam. And believe me, if they do send you on a mission, you better wish upon the stars they don't send you to the Dark Galaxy."

Kwan's ring band buzzed. "Sorry, it looks like Dr. Krill needs me in the lab. I have to go. See you all soon," she said and left.

"You'll see Kwan at the communications lab with Dr. Krill later on your tour," Rian said. "She arrived at the base recently, too. She's been helping him with research. She's also a first-rate martial arts master. Took down about twenty men the other day during practice."

"Oh yeah?" Simon asked at the same time Kobe choked on his juice.

"I'm…okay," Kobe spluttered. "Just went down…the wrong way."

A flashing light appeared on Rian's ring band. She pressed a button, and a hologram flickered on. A man with a military beret and several medallions strewn across his uniform appeared. Sam recognized him by the scar on his face. It was the same man who'd caught them sneaking out to the Dark Sites last night. "Corporal Wright, we have a Level 1 priority issue with the thermal system on the *Nightweaver* on Level 32. Can you check it out?"

"Sir, I thought Sergeant Lowman was working on that."

"He was, but there's been a mistake. We're—*he's* not familiar with these systems. This is an order. We need you here, now."

"I'll be there right away, Commander Baddal." Rian pressed a button, and the hologram disappeared. She rose from her seat, straightened her tool belt, then waved. "Duty calls. See y'all later."

After Rian left, Simon spoke up. "What was that about?"

"Just between us," Yolo started, "Sergeant Dylan Lowman started with GAIA about a year before Rian. But Rian quickly excelled. Everyone knows she's an expert at what she does. She's extremely talented. She knows more than her commanding officer. But for some reason, they recently promoted Dylan. He's been making mistakes, and Rian works around the clock to fix them. It's unfair, but what can you do? They seem to value seniority here rather than competency. But Rian's a good worker. She doesn't like to rock the boat. So she just does the work she's asked to do."

Why had Dylan been promoted if Rian was better able to do the work? It didn't seem fair. But maybe there was something else to the situation that Sam didn't know about. She didn't want to draw any conclusions yet, since she was still taking it all in.

A holographic message emitted from Sam's ring band.

ORIENTATION SESSION AND COMMUNICATIONS LAB TOUR CANCELED. MEET AT GIDEON SPARK LAB IN TWO HOURS.

A pang of disappointment struck her. She'd been looking forward to learning more about this place.

"Why would they cancel?" Kato asked, reading the same message on her own ring band.

"I don't know," Kobe said. "They must be working on something important."

Yolo blinked twice. "That reminds me, I have work to do. Never a dull moment around here. See you later."

"What do we do now?" Simon asked.

Now that they had an open schedule, that changed things. A lot.

A slow smile spread across Sam's face. "I have an idea. Come with me."

CHAPTER TWENTY-FIVE

Kwan was more than eager to assist Dr. Krill. Reverse engineering the low-frequency mind alteration device would be a challenge. She hoped she could do it. LOMA was a health and safety risk and continued to evade their systems. She needed to be successful. Admiral Green had deemed it a priority.

But all that enthusiasm withered when she received the text on her ring band.

Admiral Green had scheduled another emergency meeting. More "urgent" issues that couldn't wait. Her work with Dr. Krill would have to be delayed yet again. With all these meetings, it was a wonder anyone got any actual work done around here.

Kwan was the last to arrive at the monitoring room. Admiral Green, Onnisa, Zenobii, and Captain Gorgana huddled around a circular table.

She shut the door behind her. At least she could get more answers about their mission. She marched over, resolute.

But judging by the grim expressions of the others, something was most definitely wrong. Panic filled the air, and her steps slowed.

The door burst open. A steady stream of high-ranking officials and representatives from each GAIA member planet strode into the room. Among them were generals in charge of engineering, logistics, space warfare, and weapons. Dr. Krill was the last to arrive, looking as frail and anxious as ever. They took their seats around the room, their attention focused on the images on the screen along the front wall.

Kwan followed their gaze and wavered, gaping at the images. They captured real-time footage of various planetary missions in progress.

And none of it looked good.

On one screen, mission personnel offloaded high-energy laser weapons. They were preparing for combat on Mars.

Seems too soon, Kwan thought. *Unless the timeline has changed?*

On another screen, medical teams treated wounded soldiers—those suffering the latest round of attacks. But it was the counter on the top screen that made Kwan halt in alarm. It displayed the number of deaths at the hands of Duskara and her Malborgs.

One million.

And counting.

The fight against Duskara's Malborg army was failing. GAIA was losing the battle! She dreaded to think what would come next.

The admiral pressed a button on the holographic device, though not before shooting a warning glance Kwan's way. "The reason I called you all in is to show you something both important and disturbing."

As if what she'd witnessed on the screen wasn't disturbing enough.

Beams of light streamed through the air, depicting a spiral galaxy. A beautiful, spinning collection of stars and dust and gas, light radiating outward. But a dark band of cosmic dust partially covered its center, making it look like a giant eye. The dark eye of the cosmos. Kwan recognized it at once. It was one of several galaxies neighboring theirs. The Black Eye Galaxy's mysteriousness had captivated her since she was a child. But seeing it now, she sensed something lurking there. Something unwelcome and ugly.

The admiral waved her hands, magnifying the images. "This ten-second clip shows real-time satellite imagery captured this morning."

Kwan peered at the multitude of gleaming black pods. They were only specks in a sea of stars, but their location, velocity, and trajectory were obvious. They were heading straight for Earth. And at a rapid pace.

"Are those Malborg ships?" Kwan asked, stunned.

"Yes. Twenty of them."

"But how did they reach the Black Eye Galaxy so fast?" Not to mention, they'd broken several GAIA treaties. Hostile entities weren't allowed in that space. It was an act of war!

"Just watch." The admiral tapped her keypad. A spacecraft with mission personnel materialized on the holograph display. "We received this transmission from the *Shadowhunter*. It corroborates the data and gives us more insight into their timelines and capabilities."

An image of two agents came into view. Kwan recognized the names on their uniforms at once. They were *Sam's* parents. They looked like they hadn't slept in days; dark circles rimmed their eyes.

The woman, Sam's mother, moved toward the screen. "This is Agents Lynne Wilson and Steve Sanderson aboard the *Shadowhunter*. We've been tracking twenty Malborg ships for the past twenty-four hours along the outer perimeter of the Black Eye Galaxy. Their pace has accelerated considerably over the past few hours. We fear the Malborgs have adopted Rigellian technology. Given their speeds, it seems the only reasonable explanation. They're headed toward Earth now! We're requesting backup support, but a few of our team members have contracted the Dark Sickness. We don't have—"

The transmission cut out.

The information couldn't have been worse. Earth was definitely in trouble. At those speeds, the Malborgs would arrive in less than a month. That didn't give them much time to prepare. All their plans would need to be adjusted.

Her pulse spiked thinking about everything they were up against: likely more interstellar trafficker attacks, encountering Duskara and her Malborg army, catching the Dark Sickness, and whatever else lurked in the Dark Galaxy. It seemed *impossible.*

Onnisa grew rigid in her seat. "I hope, Admiral, you realize how this changes things. I will not send my queen on that mission. It is far too dangerous!"

Kwan flinched at the idea of sending Sam to the Dark Galaxy. At least here, at the base, they had security and weapons. They could lock it down if needed. But out there, in space, they were completely vulnerable.

"The plan was never to *send* her," Admiral Green snapped back. "But we can't keep her at the base forever, Onnisa. You know that. It might be dangerous out there, but it's no longer safe here, either."

A long silence descended over the room. Kwan fought to keep calm and composed. But there was no denying it. They were in a terrible situation.

Why had she signed up for this, again?

Admiral Green's expression changed from hopefulness to despair. She spoke quietly. "If any of you have any suggestions, please feel free to speak them now. Nothing is off the table. I welcome any and all suggestions. We must brainstorm a solution."

Kwan tried to keep her fear below the surface, hoping no one would notice. She couldn't give up. Not now.

Not when they needed her.

She broke the silence. "What about Operation Snare?" It was one of the many operational plans she'd pored over on her second night at the base.

Hushed chatter rippled through the room. She caught Dr. Krill's gaze, and he nodded encouragingly.

"Operation Snare?" Zenobii said, his antennae probing. "You're talking about the engineering structures. The ones that integrate Luyten slime into their design and act as a protective barrier, a shield around planets?"

"Yes." Kwan considered the feasibility. "We're already mobilizing the technology in other galaxies. Any Malborg ships coming into contact with it become stuck, inert. If we activate it now, if we mobilize enough resources, the structures could be built around Earth within a week. It could at least buy us some time." Though, how much time, she didn't know. Still, it was worth a shot.

"Kwan makes a good suggestion," Captain Gorgana said. "We need to activate it now as a precautionary measure."

"Very well. We will do so," Admiral Green said. "What else?"

"Operation Snare is only a temporary measure," Onnisa said. "Soon, they will figure out a way to infiltrate the barrier."

"What are you proposing?" Admiral Green asked.

Onnisa's eyes grew wide, and her voice lowered. "I have an idea. But you will not like it. And Queen Samantha must never know that I suggested it. She would never forgive me."

"Go on."

"We make a clone."

"A clone?"

Onnisa nodded slowly. "Yes. Of our queen."

"Wait, what?" Kwan asked. Had she heard correctly? Onnisa was actually suggesting they clone Sam?

"We have access to advanced cloning technology. It's the only way to protect the *real* Queen Samantha."

Speechless, Kwan sat back and tried to digest what they were saying. *Advanced cloning technology.* Here at this facility. What other secrets were they hiding?

Admiral Green leaned forward, as if she were actually considering the idea. "And then what?"

"Weaponize her ship. And when it gets close enough to its target..."

"You're proposing a suicide mission?" Kwan gaped at them. There were just so many things wrong with this scenario! Cloning a child—only to sacrifice it later! Would Sam even know? What if they did it without her consent?

Onnisa nodded. "Sacrificing one person to save dozens of civilizations."

"Would it even work?" Admiral Green asked.

"Even if it could work, *should* we even do it?" Kwan blurted. Her hands trembled at the thought of actually going through with this plan. It would surely weigh on her conscience forever.

Admiral Green sighed, turning to Captain Gorgana and Zenobii for answers. "Captain Gorgana? Zenobii? If you have any thoughts on this, now's the time."

"The plan is only one possibility," Captain Gorgana answered slowly. "But it's still too dangerous. Lots of variables. Things could go wrong. Suppose her weaponized ship is intercepted by Gargols? Suppose Duskara catches on? What then? I don't support it."

"It's too risky. *Far* too risky," Zenobii said. "We must look for another solution."

"Kwan?"

"Admiral?"

The admiral turned to her with steepled fingers. "I've never known you to hold back your opinion. You've heard the proposal. You know the situation we're in. What do *you* think?"

"Me?" How could they ask for her support in this? She couldn't agree to it. It was horrific. An impossible choice. She wanted to remain silent, but they were looking for her trust. She decided to voice her honest opinion, for what it was worth.

"I agree with Captain Gorgana and Zenobii. It's far too risky." *Not to mention immoral—completely unethical!*

"Then what? If not Onnisa's plan, what would you have us do?"

Kwan's head pounded. There had to be another way. If only she knew more about Duskara and her motivations.

Well, there was one way to find out—if she could actually bring herself to say what she was thinking.

Because what she was thinking might be even more insane, more dangerous than what Onnisa had proposed.

"Admiral Green," Kwan said. "I—I believe there may be another way. I believe—*I know*—I can build a weapon against Duskara. An AI death serum that can be injected to destroy Duskara's systems. Something powerful and advanced enough to disrupt her communications with her Malborg army." That's what they needed—something to shut down her connection to the Malborgs. Otherwise, the Malborgs might continue their attacks.

"What would that mean?" Admiral Green asked.

It would mean *a lot* of work. "Developing protocols and coding and running trials. It would take time, but with the technology and resources here, I can do it."

That would be the "easy" part. She also thought about the plan of attack. "All I need is to get close enough to Duskara to inject it." *If* they could even make it that far. *If* they made it to the Dark Galaxy, *if* they made it to Logom, and *if* they could get close enough to Duskara without being killed by Malborgs…then maybe it was possible.

There were a lot of ifs.

The plan was a long shot. To any rational person, it would look undeniably absurd—*crazy*, even. She didn't want to think of the odds stacked against them at every stage. But there was no other way. The alternative—a bomb—wouldn't be enough to destroy Duskara, since any remnants of her could survive and continue communicating with her Malborgs.

"You're talking protocols, trials. That could take months."

"I think I can do it in a matter of weeks," Kwan said. "If I start right away."

It was a gigantic puzzle, one she'd never attempted before, but one that needed to be solved no matter what. She had the resources, the capability. She would make it work. She just needed the universe to supply her with a series of miracles, too.

But she kept that part to herself.

There was a collective pause. For a moment, the only sound in the room was the overhead fan whirring.

"Even if the AI death serum trials work, the timeline for implementation is short," one of the generals piped up from the back of the room. "Is there a way to get to the Dark Galaxy before the Malborg invaders arrive?"

"There may be a way," Admiral Green responded. "The Volubens have developed a new secret technology that allows us to travel through wormholes faster. It's called a boosted launch accelerator. The technology is easy to integrate into our ships, and we've run preliminary tests. It could cut down the travel time by a quarter."

Kwan lit up at the news. A reduction of a quarter was all they needed to make it in time.

"That gives us a fighting chance," Kwan added, lifting her chin and glimpsing the expressions of the others in the room. Surprisingly, they didn't look fearful or dismayed. Quite the opposite. They were hopeful, encouraging. Both Dr. Krill and Admiral Green looked particularly optimistic. She caught them exchanging the most satisfied glance, like they were sharing inside information. What was that about? She kept her thoughts to herself for now.

They didn't have a finalized mission plan yet. But for now, they had what they needed. More details would come later. She refused to allow doubt to scrape away at her thoughts.

The room grew still and quiet as they took it all in.

Onnisa's hand twitched, and sparks of energy flew into the air. The room became charged with a strange electricity. "I support this." She raised her hand.

Kwan gazed around the room as others followed Onnisa's gesture, everyone murmuring in agreement.

Admiral Green sighed. "Very well. We have nothing to lose."

Kwan stuffed her trembling hands into her pockets. "Do we know Duskara's motivations? Specifically, why she's after Sam?" If they could find the key to Duskara's true objective, they could figure out a weakness, a possibility for disruption.

Admiral Green sighed. "No. I'm afraid it's one of the many questions we still haven't managed to answer."

CHAPTER TWENTY-SIX

Kwan hurried to the lab. There was a lot to do today, and she couldn't waste any time. She needed to learn as much as she could from Dr. Krill about the technologies. But more than that, she needed to develop an effective AI death serum as soon as possible.

The success of the mission to the Dark Galaxy now depended on her.

To make matters worse, she only had three weeks to complete the project.

She arrived at the lab to find Dr. Krill mumbling to himself, pacing back and forth, and tripping over equipment. He flipped through scattered papers, searching, obviously distracted. His clumsy movements suggested something important was on his mind. He was so lost in thought that he didn't notice her arrival.

"Dr. Krill, is everything okay?"

He continued muttering to himself, seemingly unaware of his surroundings.

On one of the counters stood a beautiful flowering plant she hadn't noticed before. The leaves were thick, as if they contained juice. The navy-blue phosphorescent flowers with silver specks on their petals looked exotic. She wandered over to get a closer look. She found a small card inside the ceramic pot, tucked between the leaves, with instructions:

For Dr. Krill.

This is a kaloi plant from Kryg. Once the flowers bloom, the leaves are most potent. Soak the leaves for one minute in cold water, then apply to any wound. It should heal within a few minutes.

Best regards,
Onnisa

Kwan didn't know much about Krygian history aside from the information she'd gleaned from the documents she'd scoured on her second night at the base. But she'd read about their plants holding extraordinary healing properties.

She turned to Dr. Krill and noticed that his bandage was old, with blood stains on parts of it. He hadn't tended to it since she'd last seen him. Had he even read the message from Onnisa, or was he too focused on something else?

She filled a bowl with water and followed the instructions, carefully submerging a couple of leaves.

"Dr. Krill...?" She gently placed a hand on his arm. "Are you all right?"

His eyes met her gaze, but only briefly before they continued darting rapidly around the room. "I'm sorry, it's just, I had something I wanted to show you, but I can't find it now. Someone must have...taken it. I need to find it... The evidence..." He rifled through files on his desk and scoured the drawers in desperation.

She needed to calm him down. "Dr. Krill, just—just stop! For a moment. Please. Take a deep breath. Sit down." She pulled a seat over. Finally, he surrendered. "Now, first, I'm going to treat your wound with that plant Onnisa gave you."

He held out his hand grudgingly. She unbandaged it, then carefully applied the soaked leaves to the surface of the wound. She expected him to wince in pain, but he didn't. Instead, his eyes softened, and he relaxed, the tension disappearing from his face.

"There. We just need to leave it on for a few minutes. Now, the thing that you're looking for. Try to remember. Where is the last place you put it?"

He smiled faintly and sighed. "This plant bloomed not long after you arrived at the base."

The sudden shift of focus jarred her. His eyes watered, and he seemed upset about something. He looked away, almost in embarrassment. She didn't understand why.

And then it happened again.

Déjà vu.

What felt like a memory flashed before her eyes. His smile and his voice were so strangely familiar.

His demeanor changed. He cast his eyes downward, his lips pulled tightly together. "Whatever happens, I need you to keep going and finish this for me."

"What do you mean, 'whatever happens'? Finish what?"

"Finish *her*. Duskara. You need to stop her."

Of course. He felt guilty for all that had transpired with Duskara, especially with the failed Athena mission so many years ago, the attacks, and the looming threat. Was that what was eating away at him, pulling apart his conscience with such incessant persistence? She felt sorry for him and had to stop herself from reaching out to console him. Even though she'd only met him a few days ago, she felt they somehow shared a deeper connection.

"Of course. I'll do my best." She lifted his arm and gently removed the green leaves, now shrunken and all but dried up. His skin showed no signs of abrasion, cuts, or discoloration. The swelling had disappeared. It was as if he had never been wounded at all.

He turned his hand over and examined it, amazed at how fast it had healed.

"Good as new!" she said.

His eyes flashed with energy and insight. "I remember now! It's in the library! I put it in my book there. Stay here. I'll be right back!"

He headed out the door while Kwan cleaned up the lab equipment. Dr. Krill wasn't the tidiest of people when it came to his workspace, but today, everything seemed in disarray and more than a little bit odd. One section of the room was a complete mess, with a stool on its side and papers strewn everywhere. It was almost as if someone had broken into the lab and turned it upside down while rummaging through its contents.

Someone was searching for something.

Dr. Krill had found something. She knew that much. But what? He'd mentioned something about evidence. It must be significant if he'd been so consumed by it earlier. Did it have anything to do with Duskara? They'd continually checked the software over the past couple of days but received no new messages from Logom.

Then what could it be that was so important?

She jumped at a loud knock on the door. She opened it to find Yolo standing outside.

"Yolo, what are you doing here?"

"Ms. Yun, I'm pleased to say I'm your new laboratory assistant. Admiral Green sent me. How may I be of service?"

As if things couldn't get any worse. They'd sent Yolo. Sure, he had a database of information, but he couldn't do the hands-on, complex tasks she needed, like coding and preparing protocols for controlled trials.

She sighed in exasperation. "You're the new full-time assistant?"

"*Part-time,*" Yolo corrected. "I must manage my time between your lab and Dr. Gideon Spark's lab. Fifty-fifty."

"I see. Well, this is news to me. It's not necessary, but thanks anyway." She started to shut the door but stopped at the sight of the frown on Yolo's face.

"I can see, Ms. Yun, that you're upset. But please don't be. Give me a chance. Don't shoot the messenger. I'm just doing what Admiral Green asked. And I want to do a good job. I can only work part-time, but if you want a second Yolo, you might consider making a clone of me. Maybe I could live twice, then."

"Can you debug a computer?"

"Well, no. But I can bring you supplies. I can send messages to other people. I can clean. And you can ask me anything."

Beggars couldn't be choosers. Around the lab, numerous folders, boxes, and papers lay scattered in disarray. A solid cleaning and organizing would definitely help. "Okay, let's get you started tidying up this place."

"It would be my pleasure." A mechanical whirring emitted as a rectangular hole opened up in Yolo's torso. A broom and dustpan emerged from the inner compartment.

"Once you're done sweeping, can you organize those folders back there?" She pointed to the open cabinet against the wall.

"Yes. I'll add it to my list," Yolo responded, but not before knocking over a beaker. The glass shattered across the floor. "I'm sorry. I'll clean that up right away. It won't happen again."

A pounding ache rose to Kwan's temples. There was so much work ahead of her. Yolo worked his way around the room, sweeping up the glass and dust ever so *slowly*. She didn't have time to monitor him with such menial tasks.

She needed to stop obsessing over it. She needed to let him do his work while she did hers. So, after a few minutes, after she was confident that he was up to the task, she set to work studying the original coding for Athena.

She threw herself into it, diving deep.

She ran simulation upon simulation, tracing the algorithms that allowed Athena to redesign her own coding. She tested scenarios, hypotheticals. She tested timelines for developments.

There was a brilliance behind Athena's coding—simple, yet limitless. There were no controls on her mind. No boundaries or constraints. Dr. Krill had given Athena the power to develop ideas and rules of her own. He'd given her *too much* freedom.

And with that freedom came immense power to change her outcomes.

Duskara was not only smart. Her intelligence continued to progress. Duskara probably already knew about the malicious coding programs currently available, but Kwan wasn't sure they'd be powerful enough to destroy her anyway. She didn't want to take a chance on it.

She had to develop something new. A machine-learning virus, perhaps? One that could replicate. Something that equaled Duskara's powerful systems. A hybrid biological and mechanized weapon. And of a magnitude that could disrupt Duskara on a molecular level. Viral replicating nanobots, perhaps. Something to attack her communications system so that she could no longer give commands to her Malborgs. They needed to cut the army off at the source.

Kwan entered the data to create a simulated Duskara. She widened the parameters to ensure they weren't missing anything important. She entered communications and biological data, behavioral analytics, development patterns, intelligence data, and everything else she could think of. She needed to get Duskara's simulation right so that she could throw *everything* she had at it to break her down and find her weaknesses.

If she had any.

Nothing could ruin her concentration now.

Except the crash and clang of objects falling to the floor from the back room. Probably Yolo dropping something again. She looked up and scanned the room to find that it was unusually tidy.

And *sparse.*

The cabinets in the back looked more orderly, but the room seemed emptier.

Boxes were missing.

The container that held the *LOMA* was missing!

Kwan leaped to her feet. She sprinted to the back room, only to find Yolo shoving another box into the incinerator. She threw the switch, shutting the thing off.

"Yolo! What are you doing?"

"Tidying up, like you asked."

"I didn't tell you to throw anything out!" She glared at the incinerator, the flames licking the ash that lay there now. It was too late. She saw a pool of liquid lead—the melted container.

Their only LOMA sample was destroyed.

"Oh," he said. "I'm sorry. I threw out everything that didn't look important. I thought it was trash."

"Trash? These are important documents and items!"

"I—I'm sorry, Ms. Yun. It won't happen again. That reminds me —I believe my time is up here. I must get to Dr. Gideon Spark's lab. I'm expected there now."

Kwan stood in shock and momentary disbelief, her jaw tensing. With their only LOMA sample destroyed, they had limited information. She knew it had contained radium and perilium. But there was still an unidentified ten-percent component. She didn't know what other substances made up its chemical composition or how they interacted. Without knowing what they were, it would be nearly impossible to develop a tracing signal. And if they couldn't develop a tracing signal, they wouldn't be able to detect other versions of LOMA lurking at the base.

And that meant Captain Gorgana's life was in danger.

Kwan's pulse jittered. She needed to find Admiral Green at once and demand an explanation as to why Yolo had been sent— why this had happened. This was beyond worrisome. She was starting to doubt the admiral's competency. But more than that, she wondered if someone had intentionally disrupted Yolo's coding for the worse.

And if so…who?

CHAPTER TWENTY-SEVEN

The incident with Jones had left Sam unsettled. It was a strange feeling of dread mixed with bewilderment. They'd canceled the orientation session, only adding more confusion and uncertainty. She hoped to get answers.

Setting those darker thoughts aside, she turned to Kato. "Now that we have some time to explore, I have an idea." She pulled up the three-dimensional holographic map on her ring band and zoomed in on one section. "It seems a lot of meeting rooms are in this area labeled 'headquarters.' It's right beside a place called the Fishbowl, which overlooks the landing bays below."

Simon leaned in between them. "So what?"

"Well, if things are going on, such as high-level meetings with important people, I think we'll find answers there. Plus, we'll be able to see who's arrived. If Boj is here, maybe I can locate Onnisa, too."

"That makes sense," Simon said.

After peering at the map some more, Kato brightened up. "It's not a Dark Site, so we're good. I say, let's go."

As they hurried down the corridor, Kobe turned to Sam. "How do you know Onnisa will be there?"

"I don't," Sam replied, a smile forming. She picked up the pace. "I just have a gut feeling about it."

They stopped in front of the elevators. The doors opened, and a towering creature trudged out. No less than ten feet in height, with green, scaly skin and slits for a nose, it took a menacing stance.

Kato, Simon, and Kobe shrunk back, but Sam stood motionless, taking in the glare from its hexagonal eyes.

It took all her self-control to stifle her gasp.

It was a Rigellian. She'd seen them mining the Hopewell Star a year ago, back when they were slaves. Four soldiers carrying blasters stood in front, guarding it.

The way the Rigellian stood tall, with purpose and intent, made her think perhaps the Rigellian was a high-ranking diplomat and not a prisoner.

"Excuse us," one of the soldiers said as they exited the elevator. Sam scrambled out of the way. The soldiers immediately took up positions around the Rigellian, creating a protective barrier. It looked like they were on a mission.

Sam hurried inside the elevator, and her friends, a little shaken, followed. As they waited for the doors to close, the Rigellian hesitated. It looked back, eyeing Sam with curiosity—or was it contempt? It was difficult to read their body language. She had the urge to communicate telepathically but stopped herself. Admiral Green's orders were clear—even if she didn't understand the reasons why.

"What's with all the extra security here?" Kobe asked.

"Good question," Kato said.

"It's probably because we're close to a VIP area," Sam said as they exited the elevator. They turned a corner, and Sam picked up the pace. "I think we're getting close."

The hallway opened into an enormous atrium overlooking Central Registry and the landing bays below.

"This must be the Fishbowl," Kobe said.

"What a great lookout!" Kato added.

The view *was* spectacular! Sam pressed up against the large window. Below was a flurry of activity. Interplanetary visitors coming and going, bustling to and from different landing bays. Sam noticed a Rigellian talking to a Krygian Elder. She squinted, recognizing the Elder at once.

Onnisa was talking to the same Rigellian they'd seen earlier. It must have been about an important matter, because Onnisa's face looked older than she remembered, her lips pressed tightly together in a pensive way. She brightened at the sight of Sam.

"Onnisa! It's good to see you. What's going on? Do you know why I'm here? Boj said I'm not safe here. Do you know what he means?"

"It is very good to see you too, Queen Samantha. But we must not use telepathy here. They are monitoring us. I apologize that we haven't had a chance to speak sooner. I've been very busy. But I hope to catch up in person soon."

Sam's face reddened. Using her telepathy had been an obvious mistake. Of course they'd know. She nodded in response.

Muffled voices traveled down the hallway from a room nearby. Sam headed toward the source of the sound as the others followed. They passed several empty rooms with gleaming wooden floors and polished marble tables. Most were equipped with holographic technology built into the room's fabric and design. This looked to be a special area of the base. Important and stately, and perhaps off-limits to some visitors.

"This must be Headquarters," Sam said, "where the high-level meetings take place."

A strange tension filled the air. After seeing the hordes of visitors earlier and the anxious look on Onnisa's face, she sensed trouble was brewing. She wasn't sure what, but she promised herself she'd get to the bottom of it as soon as possible.

Rian rounded the corner but stepped back in surprise when she saw them.

"Rian, what are you doing here?" Sam asked before she could stop herself. It was strange seeing Rian at Headquarters rather than down in the landing bays checking parts and such.

"I—I was going to ask you the same question," she responded. "I thought you had an orientation session downstairs in the Aurora Room with Admiral Green. What happened?"

Sam shrugged. "It got canceled, so we're just exploring for now. What about you?"

"I just finished delivering a presentation to the bosses—seems like things are breaking down on several aircraft—more than usual." She lowered her voice to a hushed whisper. "We think there may be someone at the base who's sabotaging the equipment."

That didn't sound good. Rian's pleasant young face grimaced as she spoke, making her look much older. If there was an infiltrator—a spy—at the base, then Boj was right. Sam wasn't safe here. None of them were.

Before Sam could press further, the doors to one of the meeting rooms burst open, and Commander Baddal stormed out, his face red and puffy with anger. Sergeant Dylan Lowman followed skittishly. "This is the *third* time this week that Corporal Wright has had to cover for your mistakes. Make sure this is the *last* time, or people will start wondering why I promoted you."

"I—I'm sorry, sir," Sergeant Lowman said. "It won't happen again."

Commander Baddal stopped and glared at Sam. "What are *you* doing here? You shouldn't be here."

"There's no policy that says I can't." Sam crossed her arms. "And if you have a problem with that, feel free to take it up with your commanding officer."

Where the words had come from, she didn't know. They just streamed out as Commander Baddal's face grew even more distorted.

He opened his mouth, about to speak, then stopped. He turned to Rian, then turned to Sam again. It seemed like he'd lost his voice.

He scoffed. "Bah! I don't have time for this!" He glowered at Rian. "Corporal Wright, don't you have somewhere to be?"

"Yes, Commander Baddal. Sorry." She saluted him, then left.

Commander Baddal turned on his heel and stalked off, grumbling to himself.

"He really knows how to make people feel welcome," Simon said, rolling his eyes. Kobe smirked.

Sam was just thankful he'd left them alone—at least for now. She didn't want to think what he'd say to Admiral Green about her. But they had more important things to worry about.

"Why is that commander so—?"

Before Kato could finish her sentence, an alarm blared. Everyone jumped. Sam had no idea what to do. No one had given them any briefing about emergency procedures yet. What had set off the alarm? Where were they supposed to go?

Fear spread like wildfire. Scientists, staff, and military personnel scrambled down the hallways toward the exits. Sam scanned the area, but there was no sign of Kwan. There was no time to look for her, either. She could be anywhere.

But no—Sam needed to take matters into her own hands.

She caught Kato's frightened gaze. Then, she heard a voice in her mind.

"Come to the Gideon Spark lab."

She wasn't sure where the voice had come from. She didn't recognize it. It had a machine-like quality, garbled slightly, as if someone had run the words through a computer program to conceal the identity of its sender. But there was no time to think straight as the alarm blasted, pounding her eardrums.

"Come with me! Hurry!" Sam shouted, and they dashed down the hallway.

The voice—wherever it had come from, whoever was speaking to her—was right. They needed to get to a lab, a place with high security that would offer protection. They were supposed to have a tour of the Gideon Spark lab later. All she could think about was getting there now.

She pulled up the map on her ring band. To her surprise, a route to the lab was already marked in red. Someone had given them specific directions—perhaps the same person who had spoken to her telepathically.

She swung open an emergency door and hurried down the stairwell with the others behind her, trying not to lose her footing. Down and down they went, their footsteps echoing off the walls.

Finally, they burst through another door.

"This way!"

They bolted down the hall without missing a beat. Sam's chest heaved with every step, feeling like it was about to burst. She fought the pain, the burning sensation in her lungs, and kept going.

She checked the map. The lab was just around the corner. "We're almost there!"

Almost there. Her body felt like lead, heavy and cumbersome. Still, she pushed onward, willed her feet to cooperate. She needed to get them all to safety.

They arrived, out of breath, at a large door with a keypad and a digital screen on the right-hand side.

"Now what?" Kobe asked.

Without thinking, Sam held up her ring band. A moment later, the screen came to life, displaying a digital thumbprint. The words BIOMETRIC SCAN REQUIRED flashed on the screen. She wasn't sure if it would work, but she had nothing to lose. Placing her thumb on the screen, she waited for the scan. After a few seconds, she heard several long clicks, and then the door opened.

Sam gaped. Someone had granted her access to this lab. Who, she didn't know, but someone was definitely working behind the scenes, helping them.

The lab doors were at least a foot thick and made of what

looked like solid steel. It reminded her of the doors to a vault or panic room she'd seen in movies. It seemed that nothing could penetrate them, and for this, she felt briefly reassured that they were safe—at least for now.

They entered a room full of machinery and what looked like spiked alien limbs in translucent containers. She heaved the door shut behind them. Locking gears shifted into place, cranking, clicking, securing tightly. It was music to her ears—if it could keep them safe from whatever threat lurked outside.

"What is this place?" Kato asked, her arms crossed.

"I—I think this is the Gideon Spark lab, where they study Malborgs," Sam said.

The AI creatures flashed in Sam's mind: their round black bodies, spiked limbs, and strange purple electricity. Seeing them now, although dismantled, still tugged at her innermost fears and made her shiver.

"Are we safe here?" Simon asked, eyeing the containers with unease. Some of the limbs were moving, even though they weren't connected to other body parts.

"I really hope so," Sam said. Because if they weren't…

A loud banging on the lab doors caused them all to scramble to the back of the room. They ducked behind three metal cabinets. She waited in sheer panic, expecting the doors to blow open any moment.

They were trapped in this lab with these creatures, and possible intruders loomed outside.

She took a shallow breath, her nerves shaky, and tried to clear her mind.

They all waited silently for whatever came next.

CHAPTER TWENTY-EIGHT

AN ALARM SOUNDED, SHRILL AND LOUD, RATTLING KWAN'S BONES AND making her jump. It was a three-second blast. That was the signal for armed intruders.

They were in danger.

Sam was in danger.

She leaped from her chair. She needed to get to the Gideon Spark lab—and fast. That's where Sam would be—or *should* be, according to the agenda Admiral Green had given her.

She dashed through the double doors and down the corridor. She had no weapons and didn't have a clue what she'd do if she ran into trouble, but she didn't let that stop her.

Passing a dimly lit hallway, she glimpsed caution tape cordoning off trails of Luyten slime. It looked like the staff had been busy collecting the substance, because several large vats of it stood in the corner. She didn't know much about the slime itself, only that it was highly flammable. Scientists were building weapons against the Malborgs with it. Several current operations were using it.

She hustled down the hallway toward the lab but stopped

when she heard footsteps approaching over the loud booms. Ducking into a maintenance room, she watched as a group of military police ran by.

"It's a Malborg! Run!" a soldier yelled. "Get the blasters! The gas!"

A Malborg—*here*?

Then she saw it—a massive, round body like a dark tumor, its tentacles whipping through the air as it hurtled toward the soldiers. Sparks of purple light flickered as it soared a meter off the floor, towering over them. The whooshing sound of its tentacles— like blades slicing through the air—made the hairs on the back of Kwan's neck rise. Its skin—or what might be thought of as skin, with a sheen like black oil and a consistency of jelly—mutated and rippled, expanding and contracting.

It stopped right in front of the lab doors, as if it knew Sam was in there.

Kwan's heart beat so forcefully in her chest, she worried the creature would hear it.

The Malborg slammed itself against the laboratory doors, but they didn't budge. They wouldn't. The room was one of the safest locations in the facility—constructed with over a dozen locking bolts, reinforced with ballistic steel to repel gunfire. It was sound-proof, blast-proof, and fire-resistant, and controlled using biometric access.

Commander Baddal rushed toward the Malborg with his blaster. He pulled the trigger, taking multiple shots. The bullets ripped through the Malborg's skin, causing a brief pause, before its body mutated, filling the holes in a matter of seconds, seemingly unscathed.

The commander adjusted the setting on his blaster and tried again. This time, a thick yellow liquid came spraying out. It struck the Malborg, its skin fizzling, acrid smoke rising from its scorched flesh. The Malborg twitched and shrunk back—but only momentarily.

It turned toward the commander.

A single black tentacle lashed out, skewering through the commander's chest, then retracted, dumping his body in front of the laboratory doors. The commander's weapon skittered across the floor toward Kwan, stopping a few feet away, almost close enough to reach. But this weapon alone wouldn't kill the Malborg. She needed something else. Something more powerful.

Like a master puppeteer pulling the strings—with exacting precision and ease—the Malborg used its tentacles to lift the commander's hand toward the keypad.

She couldn't watch any longer. She had to intervene.

She needed to lure it to the corridor that contained the vats of Luyten slime. Drenching the Malborg in it would severely injure it, if not kill it. But she needed a diversion…

She didn't have time to consider the odds.

But she tried it anyway.

In one swift, fluid motion, she opened the door and grabbed the blaster.

"Hey, Malborg!"

The creature turned its bulk toward her. Kwan swallowed, wondering if she'd live to regret her decision. *Live* being the hopeful word.

"Don't you want me? I have something you need for Duskara!"

Of course she didn't. But she needed to create a distraction.

The Malborg mutated before her eyes. Its body shriveled and separated right down the middle.

Her jaw dropped.

Now there were *two* Malborgs.

One maneuvered the dead commander's hand while the other zoomed toward her, electricity crackling beneath it.

Kwan's heart leaped inside her chest as she darted down the corridor.

A strange slushing noise gushed behind her. She glanced back for a split second to find that the Malborg by the laboratory doors had sunk to the floor, inert. A yellow gas filled the space around it, coming from a chrome device nearby. The gas drifted down the hallway toward her, along with the smell of rotten eggs.

But she didn't have time to take in the details—the other Malborg had mutated again.

And again.

Now there were *four* Malborgs tailing her. Worse, they were gaining speed. She could feel the shocks of electricity getting closer. Their tentacles sliced through the air, reaching for her.

She willed her legs to move faster, her chest heaving with every step. She adjusted the dial on the blaster back to its original position. She was getting close now…

Rounding the corner, the vats of Luyten slime stood just a few meters ahead. With a burst of energy, adrenaline pumping through her veins, she sprinted past the vats and turned her body midstride. She aimed the blaster at the vats just as the Malborgs rounded the corner.

Kwan fired. The vats exploded, slime spraying everywhere, covering the walls, the floor, the ceiling. A sizzling sound erupted as the slime hit the Malborgs. It worked like acid, corroding their bodies, causing wafts of smoke to rise. The strength of the substance coupled with the blast ripped the Malborgs apart, scattering their tentacles across the floor. Their splintered bodies twitched on the ground, writhing in pain, as fires erupted down the hallway.

The air was heavy with thick yellow smoke. She coughed and pushed herself up from the floor, then worked to wipe the gooey substance from her face. She sighed in relief when the sprinklers went off, the cold water soaking her.

"Kwan!"

She turned around. Admiral Green ran toward her with a chrome device in her hands. She pressed a button, and yellow gas released around them. A moment later, the Malborgs—or what was left of them—stopped twitching.

"Admiral Green?"

She bent down and offered her arm for support. "Are you okay?"

A few other soldiers ran past them, spraying out the fires.

Kwan caught her breath. "What happened? How did the Malborgs breach security?"

"Interstellar traffickers—agents of Duskara. They took over one of our Rypold ships."

"Did we get them all?" Kwan asked.

"Yes, as far as I know. Thanks to you. It was pretty close, though."

Too close, Kwan thought. They were lucky. It could have been *much* worse. Considering how quickly and effortlessly the Malborg had mutated, she was surprised there wasn't a whole army of them. But no—the Malborg had been on a mission—or so it seemed. It could have taken over their entire facility, but instead it had fixated on the Gideon Spark lab. It seemed the Malborg was after *one person only.*

Now that she knew Sam was safe and the threats were eliminated, she needed to get back to Dr. Krill's lab at once. "I gotta go."

Without a minute to spare, she sprinted back to the lab. Bursting through the doors, she found the room empty. Where was Dr. Krill? What was taking him so long? He should have returned by now. The library was just down the hall.

A sick feeling rose up inside her.

She rushed to the library. Holding her ring band up to the keypad, she waited in nervous anticipation for it to open.

It was dark inside. She flicked on the light.

"Dr. Krill? Hello?"

No answer.

She darted down the main aisle, where rows of shelves lined both sides.

Her heart stopped.

Dr. Krill lay face down. He wasn't moving. His limbs lay sprawled out, as if reaching for something.

"Help!" she screamed, but no one was there.

She bent down and lay her hand on his neck. She felt for a pulse, then shrunk back.

He was dead.

She shivered, staring at his body in shock, not fully grasping the reality of his death. His right hand was squeezed into a fist, a piece of paper inside it. She pulled back his fingers, trying to fight the tears streaming down her face.

What had happened? Who had done this?

She unfolded the paper to reveal a note written in Korean. Stunned after recognizing her name and the perfect spelling of each word and character, she tried to make sense of what the rest of it meant.

Kwan. Book Five. 5291. Destroy her.

She re-read the message.

What was Book Five? And the numbers? The last sentence was the most jarring. Who was it referring to? What did it all mean?

She knew one thing for certain: Dr. Krill wanted her to have this message. It was addressed to her and written in her own language. But why? Perhaps he'd wanted it to remain secret. Hadn't he mentioned something about evidence earlier? That someone had taken it? Was he leading her to that evidence?

She crumpled the paper and stuffed it into her pocket. She needed to get out of there fast and alert the authorities. Still, she didn't want to be implicated if a crime had been committed here. And it seemed that one most certainly had.

Then it hit her: Book Five.

Dr. Krill's fifth published book. Something about a code. *The Code of Your Enemies.* That was it. He must have been referring to this book. Directing her to it. That must have been why he was in the library.

She dashed down the aisle, frantically searching for a copy, hoping it would provide a further clue. She found it sandwiched between copies of his other works. She grabbed it and hastily flipped through its pages, searching for another message. It wasn't until she got to the last page that she found it.

A slim, square microchip, not more than eight millimeters wide and one millimeter thick, taped to the back of the appendix.

These types of microchips were hard to come by and only worked with advanced computer systems built with the capability to read them.

This must be it, the evidence he was referring to.

She ripped out the page and tucked it into her pocket just as the library door clicked and then swung open.

CHAPTER TWENTY-NINE

THE SIREN STOPPED. THE LOUD BANGING HAD CEASED, REPLACED BY AN unnatural silence that lingered.

Sam felt a buzz on her ring band. The words FALSE ALARM appeared on a projected hologram. The others gazed at their ring bands in relief. But she didn't feel relieved. It didn't feel like a false alarm. Not with the way the officers and staff had acted. Unless it was an unplanned drill. That would explain the looks of confusion. But it didn't explain the loud banging on the doors earlier. Except maybe if military staff were checking to ensure they were secure, she supposed. Still, who had directed them here? Whose voice had called out to her telepathically?

"Weren't we supposed to meet someone named Dr. Gideon Spark on our tour?" Kato asked, snapping Sam out of her thoughts.

"Yeah, but we're a bit early," Sam replied.

"Gideon Spark. Sounds like a really cool dude!" Simon said. "I wish I had that name. Sounds like he's a legend!"

The name sounded oddly familiar. And then it hit her. She'd heard the name at the Hovershoes booth in the mall. Dr. Spark was the scientist behind the technology. Excitement stirred inside her at the thought of actually meeting the inventor. She had so many questions.

She jumped as something moved in the adjacent room. But it was just an old woman. She had dark, sun-kissed skin, a silver mop of curly hair, and glasses. The woman approached them, balancing her weight on a cane. Yolo followed, hovering close to her.

"Is that Sam? Sam Sanderson?" The woman hesitated, peering at Sam from head to toe. "My goodness. It is! Sam, I know your parents. I worked with them in the past. Steve and Lynn. Such fine scientists. It's an honor to finally meet you," she said, extending her hand.

Sam smiled as she took it, and at that moment, all her nervousness and anxiety melted away. Being in the presence of this woman made her feel instantly at ease and grounded, and the fact that she knew Sam's parents made the connection all the more meaningful.

"These are my friends, Kato, Kobe, and Simon."

The woman's warm smile brightened the room. "It's a pleasure meeting all of you."

Sam took in the rest of the woman's features. She wore a white lab coat. Her brown eyes radiated light, and her face creased with the years of experience etched into it. Could this be...? Sam realized she was looking at—*interacting with*—Dr. Gideon Spark herself. It took all her power not to tremble in awe.

"Dr. Spark—I—" Her face flushed as she lost the power to talk. The words just wouldn't come out.

"Oh, don't worry about formalities. Just call me Giddy," Dr. Spark laughed. Her humility instantly put Sam at ease, like she was talking to an old friend.

"I'm a huge fan of yours!" Sam gushed—*finally*. "*You* developed the technology for the Hovershoes!" Her face burned now at how awkward she sounded, as if she were putting two and two together for the first time. But the words kept streaming out, clunky and rushed. Not at all graceful like she'd intended. But she couldn't help it. "I was amazed that it doesn't use batteries. It's self-renewing. It's so impressive, using an unlimited power supply. I would love to hear more about it, how it works, how the technology is possible."

Giddy chuckled. "Well, it's nice to meet someone so interested in the matter." A brief darkness flickered in her eyes. "But I have to admit, it wasn't my original technology. I took it from the Malborgs."

"The Malborgs?" The thought of Duskara's army sent tremors through Sam's body. "You mean—Duskara created it?"

"Yes. It's what the Malborgs use to hover on air. We reverse engineered the anti-gravity technology and applied it. As you can see, Yolo uses it, and it's being integrated into the armored suits the military uses for their operations and expeditions."

Sam stood speechless, eyes wide. If anyone needed answers to the universe's questions, she was sure the woman standing before her held them. She tried not to gape, tried to keep herself composed.

"No commercial applications yet, with the exception of the Hovershoes adaptation," Giddy clarified. "Mostly military for now. But in the future, it could be used to power flying cars, and it has other uses, too."

Sam was exhilarated to be a witness to history and the advancements in technology developed here, right before their eyes. Impressed with Giddy's work, she wanted to learn more. Not just about the technology, but the scientist behind its development.

Giddy continued. "You're all a bit early, but that's even better. Gives us more time. Let's dive in, shall we?"

Sam nodded in excited anticipation. She would gladly follow Giddy around all day if she could, eager to learn everything.

Giddy climbed into a wheelchair nearby that hovered on air. She led them around the lab, first stopping at a metal table. Resting on top was a translucent fish tank containing one of the creatures' spiked tentacles.

"Malborgs are one of the nastiest creatures in the universe," she began. "Duskara really knew how to create a monster. These creatures have ten spiked tentacles, like this one here. Made of a combination of organic material and metal, the tentacles act as a conductor and weapon. They contain neurotransmitters and use echolocation technology so they know exactly where to attack their victims for a quick kill. If you're standing a few feet away, they can hear and locate your beating heart in less than a second."

"Reminds me of a stingray's tail, only worse," Sam commented.

"Yes, exactly. It has barbs, too. It's also venomous and causes intense pain."

Kobe shrunk back at the sight of it. It squirmed in its container, even though it had no body.

Simon put a hand up to one side of the container. The tentacle swam over, as if he were stimulating it somehow. "I don't understand," he said. "How is it alive without the rest of its body?"

"Great question!" Giddy replied. "The Malborgs are fascinating creatures. Each tentacle has its own brain and heart. It can function on its own."

Kato folded her arms but stepped closer to get a better look. "That's super scary."

"Yes," Giddy said. "They're quite sophisticated. It's also how they're able to self-replicate. You see, their cells are remarkable. Like little regenerating factories. They divide rapidly and act like stem cells, which are like…" She hesitated.

"Like a blank canvas?" Kato asked.

"That's a great way to describe it," Giddy answered, looking impressed, a wide grin forming. "A blank canvas. The cells can turn into any type of tissue. They can become cartilage, muscle, bone… They can even regenerate their brains and hearts."

"Can this one self-replicate?" Sam asked.

"Well, yes," Giddy replied. "But we've placed an additive in the tank to prevent that. If we change the settings, like this…" She pulled a lever on the side of the tank, and some of the liquid drained. She twisted a dial, and a moment later, a red liquid entered the tank from a tube connected from above. "As you can see, it's starting to divide as we speak. We can control the settings."

Sam watched in disturbed fascination as the tentacle extended. It split into two pieces right through the middle, then expanded again, growing almost as large as before. They split again. There were now *four* separate tentacles. It happened in seconds, causing everyone except Giddy to halt in alarm. Giddy turned the knobs again, and this time, a thick yellow liquid entered the tank. The tentacles stopped moving and growing at once.

"Amazing!"

"Could maybe… One day, could we find a way to develop a similar technology for humans?" Kato asked. "I mean, for medical treatments? To regenerate limbs?" Sam was sure Kato was thinking about treating or even eradicating her mom's disease.

"It's quite possible. We're looking into it. Now, let's see…" Giddy turned to Sam. "What's your current security classification?"

"I'm not sure."

"If you press number nine on your ring bands, we can check."

Sam did so, and the others did, too. The words SECURITY: LEVEL 7 appeared on their screens.

"Good. Come with me," Giddy urged.

They followed her through double doors to the adjacent room. The cluttered space was crammed with rows of flasks containing strange liquids and bottles filled with chemicals and preserved alien parts.

A wooden desk stood in the corner of the room. Behind it hung a poster of Barbados, with an image of flying fish over the water and a pink sunset in the background. On the desk were a few photographs of children taken at different stages of their lives. Family photos, Sam guessed. Did Giddy get to see her family as often as she wanted to? It reminded Sam of her own family, and her homesickness crept up again. She tried to push those thoughts aside as they continued.

They arrived at a steel door with another screen and a keypad. Giddy held up her ring band. It beeped as the words BIOMETRIC SCAN REQUIRED appeared. She pressed her thumb to the screen, and it took a scan. Moments later, the door opened to a set of stairs leading further below and an elevator on the right.

"My body isn't in the best shape after the hip replacement," Giddy admitted as they followed her into the elevator. "Now, this lab and the information I'm about to tell you is classified, understand? It can only be shared with those with a security clearance of Level 7 or higher."

"Understood," Sam said, and the others nodded in agreement.

"Good."

Sam had never encountered such strict security protocols. What was so secret that it needed so much protection? She knew they were about to find out, and it both worried and excited her.

CHAPTER THIRTY

Kwan wished she'd left the library sooner. But when the door had opened and the staff had found her sitting next to Dr. Krill's dead body, the military police brought her in for questioning later that morning. She sat across from Admiral Green and a large soldier who glowered at Kwan the whole time.

Admiral Green cleared her throat. "What was Dr. Krill's behavior like this morning?"

Kwan thought back to the scene. Dr. Krill had been frantic and showed signs of paranoia, but it seemed there was reason to believe someone was indeed after him or his work. She couldn't stop wondering about Dr. Krill's final thoughts in the moments before his death. And why he'd left her that strange, cryptic message. She was desperate to find out what was on that microchip. What were the numbers in the message for? Was it a code?

"His behavior was erratic. He was disturbed about something, but he wouldn't tell me what." She paused, thinking about the conditions of the lab. Everything had been in disarray. Someone must have searched it earlier for the same thing. That was why he planted the evidence in the book in the library, the last place someone would look for it.

She continued. "I noticed his wound was getting worse. He hadn't bothered taking care of it. That's when I suggested we treat it with kaloi leaves. I treated the wound and tried to calm him down. But he was flustered. He kept going on about finding something."

The guard interrupted. "Finding what, exactly?"

"I don't know. He didn't tell me."

She internally winced at the lie. Or, at least, the *half*-lie. Dr. Krill *had* told her. He was looking for evidence. Though what that evidence was, she didn't know. She also wasn't about to tell the admiral about the hidden message and microchip. At least, not until she had a chance to review it first. Someone at the base had killed Dr. Krill, and for all she knew, it was for this information. She couldn't let it fall into the wrong hands. "After I finished healing his wound, he said he needed to go to the library."

She told them what had happened: the alarm, trying to find Sam, the lab being locked, and the Malborg attack. And, of course, finding Dr. Krill dead.

Admiral Green jotted some notes, then stopped. "Thank you, Kwan. That's all for now."

"So, am I free to go?"

"Yes—for now. You were at the library at the same time as Dr. Krill's death. You can understand the seriousness of the situation. However, we're checking the video footage and other connections. We're looking at *all* the evidence available. In the meantime, please let me know if you think of anything else. *Anything* at all."

She was surprised Admiral Green didn't press further. She thought for certain that the circumstances would have warranted more scrutiny. Perhaps the military police had different ways of handling these types of situations. But it seemed like there was something more to it. It was like Admiral Green knew something she didn't. Like she was protecting her.

She trusts me.

Uneasiness and grief swept up inside her, and a lump formed in her throat. "Do you know how Dr. Krill...?" She felt tears returning to her eyes.

"How he died? No. We're waiting for the toxicology report. Don't worry, Kwan. We'll figure it out soon enough."

Kwan rose, her eyes fixed on the admiral. *Don't worry.* That's what she had told her.

Yet, with the lack of answers, the confusion surrounding Dr. Krill's death, and no other suspects so far, she was more worried than ever.

Kwan bolted down the corridor toward Dr. Krill's lab, pushing past soldiers, scientists, and extraterrestrials. She needed to find out what was on that microchip that was so important. She cursed when she slipped on a trail of Luyten slime—the *second* time she'd come into contact with this stuff today—and went skidding across the tile flooring. The thick, gooey substance now covered her entire right side. It would be nearly impossible to get the stuff out of her clothing, meaning she'd have to order another uniform. She gagged at the smell. She'd have to take a shower soon, too.

She pushed herself up and grabbed a cloth from a nearby cleaning cart, feverishly rubbing the slime off her shoes before racing off again.

She arrived at the lab and locked the door behind her to ensure no interruptions. She unfolded the document and used tweezers to carefully place the microchip on the advanced computer scanning system. Moments later, she was directed to enter a four-digit code. She entered 5291—the numbers from Dr. Krill's message—and waited.

Nothing happened. Of course, that would have been too easy.

What was she missing?

She thought back to the book, *The Code of Your Enemies*. Dr. Krill had written it following the Athena mission. After Athena had failed, Dr. Krill realized he may have given her too much power. He could no longer control her. It was a dangerous time for AI development, with many scientists viewing AIs as a potential threat to humanity. So Dr. Krill developed "the code of your enemies," also known as the death code, to ensure constant "checks" on the AI's systems. The death code was a sophisticated virus. A safety mechanism meant to remain dormant, scanning the host for information, unable to destroy anything until activated.

The death code became policy for all new AIs. It put humanity's interests first. If there was a threat to the greater good, the death code would be activated.

The Code of Your Enemies. That's what Dr. Krill must have been referring to. But what was its purpose here?

She thought about the death code's capabilities. It could pull up astounding amounts of analytical data to ensure an AI wasn't destructive. It was sometimes even run on software systems and computers to spy on programs and people.

Of course! Dr. Krill was encouraging her to do the same. The microchip was encrypted. She needed the virus to reveal the evidence he had referred to.

It was worth a shot. If she ran the death code on the microchip, she could pull up any encrypted information on it. Since she was just running it on the microchip, it wouldn't activate the destruction mechanism. The virus would remain latent, and any data on the microchip would remain intact. She could then patch up the system and remove the virus afterward. No harm done.

She installed the death code onto the microchip and waited. A moment later, words appeared on the screen, along with an audio file.

INTERCEPTED AUDIO MESSAGE FROM DUSKARA

She took in a deep breath and let it out slowly. It didn't stop her hand from shaking as she reached toward the screen and pressed PLAY.

CHAPTER THIRTY-ONE

Sam couldn't stop thinking about the telepathic voice she'd heard when the alarm went off. The strange quality of the voice—unidentifiable. And the message itself—something about it still bugged her.

Come to the Gideon Spark lab, it had said.

Come to the lab. Come. Not *go*…

She was certain whoever had called out to her had been *inside* the lab. But the only people who'd been in the lab were Giddy and Yolo, and the voice didn't sound like either of them. No—the tone was neutral, impersonal, and something else. Synthetic, almost. As if it were coming from an audio file on a computer.

She turned to Giddy. "Is there anyone else who works with you in this lab?"

"No—just Yolo. We used to have more staff years ago, but with budget cuts, haven't been able to do as much hiring this year. The Human Resources and Finance Departments can be so out of touch with what we do."

So, if the voice hadn't come from her or Yolo, whose was it?

It irritated her, but she kept her thoughts to herself as they followed Giddy into the private elevator and descended to the floor below. When the doors opened again, she trembled with shock and disbelief. A massive Malborg floated in a huge vat of yellow liquid. Its menacing spiked body swam around haphazardly.

"You—you caught one fully intact? It's still alive?"

Giddy nodded proudly. "The Luytens helped us catch this one last year, and we've been studying it rigorously. We've managed to install a cloaking device, if you will, to confuse its senses. It's no longer controlled by Duskara."

"The Luytens? How is that even possible?"

Giddy eyed her carefully. "Luyten slime has some interesting properties."

"Like what?" Kobe asked.

"It has a high phosphorous content, which contributes to the smell. They secrete it constantly, like a snake shedding its skin, only on a more frequent basis. Long story short, Luyten slime is toxic to Malborgs but not humans. We've developed enhanced gas and spray weaponry using high concentrations of the substance. Also, if you submerge a Malborg in water mixed with a low concentration of the slime, it blinds their abilities, confuses them. It suspends them in a never-ending dream-like state with no sense of where they are or what is happening around them."

"And Duskara doesn't suspect something is wrong? She doesn't...cut them off?" Sam asked.

"No. She probably believes the Malborg is dead thanks to the cloaking mechanism, as she can no longer communicate with it or give it commands."

"Fascinating!" Simon mused.

"Indeed!"

Sam gazed at the creature. It hovered at one end of the container, then drifted slowly to the other, as if it were wandering aimlessly, completely serene and unaware of its surroundings or that it was being studied.

A frown spread across Giddy's face. "The problem is…once we remove the slime, it may regain its capacities, and if Duskara finds out, she will likely…well, cut it off, as you say. We just can't manage to figure out its communication system, how it's connected to Duskara, without risking its death. And without fully knowing this connection, it's like we're one step closer but also many steps back."

Sam stared at the creature. Was it possible it could interact telepathically? Was this who—or what—had called to her?

A sudden, burning urge rose up in her. She wanted to try to communicate with it. But she hadn't forgotten the harsh warning from Admiral Green, either. She didn't doubt this would prove dangerous. But she had to try.

She opened her mind.

It was there, instantly. That feeling—the same cold presence she'd felt earlier. She shuddered.

"I know you're there, Queen of Kryg."

The words slithered into her mind. The voice sounded smooth —but oddly manufactured. Not human—and not alien, either. It was like…

Paralyzing fear gripped her at the sudden revelation.

The Malborg was somehow speaking to her directly. A wave of dread washed over her. How did it know she was the Queen of Kryg? Giddy had said the Malborg was unaware, in a dream-like state. But what if she was wrong? Was that possible? No—Giddy couldn't be wrong about this. She and the other scientists would know if the Malborg could communicate telepathically. After all, they had telepathic interception technology here at the base and were monitoring communications.

Sam's head swirled. She was losing it.

Another voice invaded her mind, the words flowing smoothly, with the same synthetic quality. *"Don't be afraid, Queen of Kryg. I want to meet you. Come to Logom."*

Alarm bells went off in Sam's head. This wasn't the Malborg

speaking to her now. This was Duskara. It had to be. Duskara was using the Malborg as a conduit, speaking to her directly, forcing her words, her thoughts—her very presence into Sam's head, until it was all she could see, feel.

Sam pushed back, but it was like pushing against a steel wall.

"You… They don't allow telepathy here."

"Don't they? Interesting."

"You'll get me in trouble."

"Trouble?" Sam could have sworn she heard laughter. *"My queen you are* already *in trouble."*

This couldn't be happening. Perhaps it was just a figment of her imagination. The shock of seeing the Malborg creature, of being at the base, and all the strange things that had happened earlier—maybe her imagination was running wild—coupled with a lack of sleep.

"What do you mean?"

"Do not worry, my queen. I've shielded our communications. No one can hear us."

How was that even possible? If that was true, the shield was powerful. Powerful enough not to be detected by Admiral Green and GAIA's security systems.

Sam suppressed a shiver. It was almost as if the Malborg had been purposefully waiting for her arrival. Pretending to be in a trance-like, vegetative state. She didn't want to talk with it any longer. It was dangerous. Who would even believe her if she told someone about it? There would be no proof, if the Malborg was only communicating with her and no one else. People would think she was crazy.

Still, she had an unrelenting urge to push for more information. *"What do you mean, I'm already in trouble?"*

"That was no false alarm you heard earlier. The admiral has been feeding you lies since you arrived."

"What—what do you mean? What happened? And why would the admiral lie?"

"Don't worry, my queen. I've kept you safe here, protected you, along with your friends. It was I who helped you find your way to this lab, helped you find the answers you seek. And what has the admiral done for you—except threaten you? She is going to do something. Something terrible."

"What do you mean? How do you know?"

"Aren't you wondering why your parents haven't arrived yet? The admiral never called them back from their mission."

Fear washed over Sam as she considered the timeline. Her parents should have returned by now. What had caused the delay? Where were they now?

She hesitated. *"Why should I trust you?"*

"Because I'm telling you the truth. And you'll see soon. Your parents are still on their mission, tracking my borg ships. But the admiral is going to lock down the base. You'll see. She'll do it. She'll make it so your parents won't be able to come back to Earth."

"What? I—I don't believe you."

"It's true. The admiral cannot be trusted."

"What do you think I should do?"

"One of my servants will deliver a gift to you. Keep an eye out for it. We will chat again. Soon."

The link cut off, like a tether breaking, and she staggered back. Not that anyone else seemed to notice. They were all still wrapped up in what Giddy was saying.

Everyone except Kobe.

"Hey, are you okay? It looks like you saw a ghost or something."

"What?"

"You were so quiet for a while. I thought you were lost somewhere."

Kobe was right. She'd been lost in her mind with the Malborg and Duskara. She crossed her arms, trying to keep her hands from trembling. It was true, what Duskara had said. Their conversation had been shielded. Kobe hadn't heard it, but he still sensed something was off. She couldn't tell her friends, here and now, what had happened. The shock of the experience was still hard to process—or fathom.

"I'm okay. Just taking it all in."

Taking it all in—*maybe she'd taken in too much.* The contact with Duskara had definitely been disturbing and much more intrusive than she felt comfortable with.

She was suspicious of the admiral, but she wasn't trusting of Duskara, either. She would need to take Duskara's words about the admiral cautiously and not jump to conclusions.

Simon's voice interrupted her thoughts. "Well, I'm impressed with the Luytens and how they were able to catch this one. I guess we should never underestimate our GAIA partners."

"Oh, absolutely," Giddy agreed. "Now, if you have any ideas about how to communicate with this one, you just let me know! And please, come by more often. I'd love to have more visitors these days. It gets a little too quiet in this lab sometimes!"

Sam wondered how many people had the clearance level to see the Malborg—if Giddy ever got nervous working by herself in the lab with such a dangerous specimen. She would make a point to visit Giddy later.

She hadn't decided whether to tell Giddy about the chilling encounter with the Malborg just yet. If she told the others, they might think Sam was losing her mind and take her off the mission. Or worse, her conversation with Duskara might be cut off. And she couldn't dismiss it just yet. She wanted to find out whether Duskara's words about her parents and the admiral were true. Either way, it was probably best to keep it to herself until she could get her thoughts straight. Besides, she was still learning to trust people in this strange place.

"What do you mean, it gets a little too quiet in this lab sometimes? I'm good company," Yolo insisted. "Am I not?"

The question clearly caught everyone off guard. It wasn't just the question, but the way Yolo phrased it, that sounded needy, narcissistic, and somewhat controlling. Could a robot be so easily offended or feel threatened by others?

"Yes, of course, Yolo." Giddy let out a nervous laugh, trying to brush off the awkward moment. "I was simply extending a warm welcome to our friends here."

Yolo paused. "They don't have to come back."

"What's that?"

"I mean, if they don't want to. There's really nothing more to see. You've given them an extensive tour."

Sam couldn't mistake the coldness in Yolo's tone, and the others seemed to sense it, too. Something was off with Yolo lately, and she couldn't quite place it.

Giddy hesitated. "Well, Yolo is right. I've pretty much showed you around the entire place, but the offer is always open, whenever you'd like to visit."

With that, they returned to the elevator and exited to the main lab.

"What's next on your agenda?" Giddy asked.

"Nothing really. It's open right now," Sam said. "But I'm wondering, do you know where Admiral Green might be?" If anyone had answers, it was her.

Giddy paused. "Well, I suppose she would be at the debriefing. It's taking place in the Milky Way Auditorium right now, if I'm not mistaken."

"Thank you."

"Now, off you go. I hope everything is okay after that false alarm. Maybe too much excitement for one day. And good luck!"

After thanking Giddy for her time, they left the lab and made their way down the corridor. Thick yellow smoke hung in the air, along with a smell of rotten eggs.

A trail of smeared blood on the floor led to a lifeless body just a few meters away—she recognized his face at once.

Commander Baddal was *dead*.

Soldiers were busy setting up caution tape around the area.

The hallways were busier now, with people bustling from one place to another and lots of chatter. One distressed woman in a lab coat leaned against a wall, wiping tears from her eyes and weeping as a man tried to console her.

"I knew him the longest… He was such a good scientist and friend. I don't understand how it happened," the woman choked out between sobs. "I just saw him this morning, and he was fine, and now this…"

Sam glimpsed a familiar face in the crowd and approached the soldier.

"Rian, what's going on? What happened?"

"Sam?" Rian's eyes widened, and she looked relieved. "I'm glad you're all right!" Her expression of elation quickly turned to pain when she realized their proximity to the body. "Come with me. I'm so sorry you had to see this." She whisked them away from the crime scene and down the hall. Her brow furrowed, and she lowered her voice. "There was a Malborg attack. Commander Baddal was killed, and Dr. Krill is dead, too. Kwan found him in the library earlier. They don't know what happened."

A Malborg attack? And Dr. Krill—dead?

Sam staggered back. "I don't understand. The message we received on our ring bands said it was a false alarm."

Rian looked taken aback. "It was definitely *not* a false alarm."

"*Obviously*," Kobe replied curtly, with more than a hint of irritation in his tone. "But if it wasn't a false alarm, then *who* sent the message, and *why* did they lie about it?"

"I don't know. Maybe check the message again?" Rian suggested. "See who the sender is?"

Sam peered down at her ring band, only to find…nothing. There was no record of it ever being received. Like it had never existed.

"The message—it's gone. I can't find it."

"Me neither," Kato added.

Kobe and Simon both shook their heads.

"That's weird, but honestly, I'm not surprised," Rian said, her face softening with hints of sympathy and understanding. "It's probably just a glitch. It's not the first time this has happened with the communications. The important thing is that you're all okay."

Frustrated and desperate for answers, Sam pushed through the crowd, sprinting toward the auditorium.

Duskara had told her the truth—it *wasn't* a false alarm. And if Duskara was right about this, Sam had a sickening feeling that she might be telling the truth about the admiral, too.

CHAPTER THIRTY-TWO

Sam scrambled through the double doors and rushed down the aisle, scanning the multitude of faces. A mosaic of human and interplanetary visitors spoke in hushed whispers, the mood somber. The sounds filled the auditorium, her earpiece translating bits of conversation over the regular din.

Two holographic beams of light illuminated the stage on either side. Sam shivered at the ghostly figures of Dr. Otto Krill and Commander Baddal. Their recent deaths were a grave reminder that no one was safe here and that the deaths would keep mounting unless Duskara and her Malborg army were stopped. Somehow.

She tried to ignore the pounding ache in her head.

A shrieking sound came from the back of the auditorium. Sam turned around to see a bird-like creature, its plumage a bright combination of red, yellow, and orange, flapping its wings. Its words streamed through her earpiece.

"What's the next phase after Operation Snare? The barriers won't hold forever. My planet was attacked, and we've had to evacuate. Duskara will stop at *nothing* to get what she wants!"

Hushed murmurs spread around the room as Admiral Green struggled to regain her composure on stage. "I understand this is an unprecedented time," she started slowly, as if choosing her next words carefully. "And it calls for extraordinary measures. We will rise up against Duskara together. We just need more time—"

Sam noticed that none of the military personnel joined in the shouting. Despite the obvious worry on their faces, they maintained discipline. The same could not be said for the many civilians and politicians from various planets currently staying at the base.

"More time?" someone else yelled from the crowd. "We're at war! The Malborgs have *already* breached our systems with the attack today! They infiltrated the Rypold ship. What's next?"

War? Sam shuddered. It seemed like things couldn't get any worse.

"As you know, Duskara has placed a bounty on the Queen of Kryg's head, which is why there have been so many attacks—"

Sam didn't hear what was said next. Her mind whirled, and she felt lightheaded. Shock and anger rose up inside her. Why couldn't they have just told her the truth earlier? It seemed that everyone had known except her. They'd lied, kept her in the dark all this time! Even Boj and Onnisa—they'd told her *nothing*. And all for what? To protect her? To keep her safe from the truth? No one could keep her safe now.

So it was true what Jones had said in the cafeteria, that Duskara was after her. But why? She turned to Kato, her eyes wide with sudden awful awareness. Kato's mouth dropped open, but no words came out. Kobe and Simon looked equally stunned. It was much worse than she'd thought. Duskara had threatened GAIA to get to her. Not only that, but everyone was in danger now—and all because of her.

She needed to put an end to this.

The admiral continued. "Given the heightened security situation, we have decided to lock down the base, just until we can carry out the next steps in our plan. As of midnight tonight, interplanetary travelers and residents of Earth must remain here indefinitely. Those wishing to visit will need to make alternate arrangements. This is for everyone's safety."

Sam had thought it couldn't get any worse, but it had. Duskara had been right about the admiral's plans—she was shutting Sam's parents out, risking their safety.

This was a never-ending nightmare.

"No!" Sam yelled, her voice echoing around the room. "You can't shut it down—my parents—they won't get back in time!"

Her presence seemed to startle the admiral. Her face was a mix of shock and fear. "We have to. It's—it's for your own safety. We'll make arrangements for them to seek refuge elsewhere."

Sam didn't care about her own safety. She cared about everyone else who'd been put in danger. She couldn't allow this to happen. She couldn't let anyone else get hurt.

More shrieking erupted from the bird-like creature, drowning out everything else. "What does Duskara want with the girl? Do we know? I say we give Duskara what she wants before more damage is done."

"No!" The voice came from the audience. Sam recognized it at once—it was Boj. "As GAIA members, we don't negotiate with terrorists."

Sam pushed her way to the front, ignoring the protests. She glimpsed the distraught faces and thought about the dire circumstances. It wasn't just one world that was in danger. If Duskara wanted her, and if it would stop the attacks, then she knew what she had to do.

She looked straight into the audience, unflinching. "Send me to Duskara! I'll give myself as a sacrifice if it means saving GAIA and many civilizations."

"What? No!" Kato whispered beside her. She tugged at Sam's hand to step down.

But Sam didn't budge.

Everyone went silent, and then a clicking noise resounded from the back of the room. "Absolutely not. If we give in to Duskara now, she'll only get stronger. She'll keep taking what she wants."

Sam recognized the voice. She scanned the room, trying to locate its source. The ant-like creature with its long antennae, the same one she'd seen in her dreams, sat a few rows back.

"Zenobii is right," Onnisa replied, standing up and addressing the crowd. "Duskara will not stop, and we must work together toward a solution. But as Admiral Green said, we live in unprecedented times. If you wish to return to your planets, you may do so now, before midnight, when the new policy takes effect." Her eyes searched the audience, waiting for a response, but no one moved. "However, if you would like to continue to uphold GAIA's values and help us defeat this monster, then I sincerely appreciate your support at our darkest of times."

Cheers rang out through the crowd. Sam noticed the bird-like creature chose to stay, at least for the time being. Despite the growing support around her, she didn't feel like celebrating. She knew she'd need to confront Duskara.

The doors to the auditorium burst open. Kwan sprinted down the aisle toward the stage, papers held tightly in one hand and an audio device in the other.

Sam stepped forward. "Kwan?"

Kwan stopped before her, out of breath. "I have important news. I think you need to hear this." Ignoring the others, she held the device out to Sam. "Before Dr. Krill passed away, he left me some instructions about his research. And…something more. I had to dig a bit, but I found it—the evidence. Secret communications intel. He'd intercepted a signal that led to a Gargol outpost in the Dark Galaxy, on the planet Candu. It took me some time, but I was able to decode it."

Kwan pressed a button on the audio device. The words reverberated around the auditorium. Sam instantly recognized the distinct, artificial voice, the even tone that sent chills rippling through her.

"I want a human soul. Not just *any* soul. The Queen of Kryg. The girl of pure spirit and heart. Give her to me."

CHAPTER THIRTY-THREE

The debriefing ended. People filed into the hallways, the mood somber. Sam couldn't even remember what had been said after she listened to the audio recording. She only heard the unsettling words of Duskara playing over again in her mind like a broken record, eating away at her thoughts.

I want a human soul. Not just any soul. The Queen of Kryg.

As strange as it was, Duskara wanted a soul—*her* soul. Something that Duskara, an AI entity made of machinery and parts and code, wasn't built to possess.

But what was a soul? Was it the immaterial part of the mind, or something else? Where did it exist, and how did it define her? Or did Duskara want to somehow blend their consciousnesses?

Last year, on Kryg, she'd met with Mukalakatakalakum in the cave. He had judged her soul, named her the chosen one. The "girl of pure spirit and heart." He had described a bright, multicolored light radiating from her, nothing like he had ever seen before. Whatever it was, even though she couldn't see this light herself, she knew it was inside her.

And although she couldn't define what or where a soul was,

Duskara wanted to tear Sam apart, to grasp this perceived intangible, immaterial, yet essential part of her.

The thought made her shiver.

And now, somehow, Duskara had found out about her. How, Sam didn't know. But if Dr. Krill had created Athena, who had become Duskara, then surely *he* would know how to shut her down.

Except he was dead. They would never be able to learn about his role, never be able to ask him about it. All that information was lost. It had seemed strange, too, when Sam heard there was an ongoing investigation into his death. Had it been an accident, or something more sinister?

It seemed Duskara had learned too much about surviving and rewriting her code. She was untouchable now, causing havoc across the universe. Perhaps she had no weaknesses.

Sam followed the others absentmindedly to the cafeteria for dinner, willing herself to move forward. But her legs felt mechanical, disjointed, like they were severed from the rest of her body. Her body was on autopilot, a numbness growing inside her while her mind worked to piece it all together.

Even the mood in the air had changed, and a heaviness weighed down on them. Staff ate mostly in silence, except for the periodic hushed murmurs. It wasn't just the recent attacks and the deaths. It was like everyone was preparing for something much worse. *Expecting* it.

As they ate, Kato whispered to Sam, "I thought what you said today was—"

"Heroic?" Sam asked.

"Stupid. Really stupid!"

"Why? It seems like all this destruction could be avoided if they just sent me to meet with her."

"Meet with her?" Simon interjected. "It's not like you're going to have a cup of tea and chat about the weather."

"Even if you met with her, it wouldn't stop her from attacking other planets," Kobe said, his words more urgent than usual. "We'd lose our friend, and the universe would be no better off. We know this, and they said so at the meeting."

"I—I just don't know how they're going to solve it," Sam said.

She had thought about chatting with Boj and Onnisa earlier. Maybe Zenobii, too. But now…

She wasn't in the mood. Whether it was the false alarm message earlier, the lies from the admiral, or the recent revelation about Duskara, an overwhelming distrust seeped into her pores. Maybe it was clouding her judgment, but she didn't care. She just wanted to retreat into her shell, to close herself off from others.

"They'll figure something out. Don't worry," Kato said, but her words did nothing to calm Sam's nerves.

She *did* worry. And she didn't feel much like chatting, either. Lots of lives were in her hands. She didn't want to burden others, yet she was angry. Furious, even, that Onnisa or Boj—or Rian, or Admiral Green, for that matter—hadn't told her sooner. After finding out the truth about Duskara's true motivations, well…that changed everything. She couldn't just let it go, sit by idly and wait while others made plans for her future.

She was glad when dinner ended and she could retire to her room. Too many questions buzzed inside her brain, like how had Dr. Krill died? Was it an accident, or a result of the Malborg attack, or had someone else taken his life? If someone had killed him, then were they really safe at this military base if someone could get away with murder?

When she entered her room, she was ready to slide into bed, but something caught her attention. A red flag appeared in the top corner of the screen on her wall, indicating a new audio message. Perhaps it was from her grandfather!

She scrambled over to the screen and pressed PLAY. The audio feed was choppy, cutting out throughout the message, but she heard her grandfather's voice among the bursts of static.

"Hello, it's your Grandpa. I received…message." The static

contorted his voice, creating a high-pitched electronic buzz in between parts of his speech. "It sounds like an interesting experience there at… I don't know when you'll get this, but I just wanted to say…from Pip and I. He's wondering where you are. Miss you and see… Oh! I forgot to tell you, something important came up—"

The last part of the audio cut out entirely. She turned it off.

It was simply maddening trying to decipher her grandfather's message with so many pieces missing. But then she remembered the security implications. They'd probably censored parts of the message if they were scrutinizing all incoming and outgoing calls. Why else would the communication cut out at those parts?

She pulled out her journal, a gift from her grandfather last year. If she couldn't rely on the technology here, then she'd use the best possible alternative, something that couldn't be monitored or tracked. At least not electronically. She would share her thoughts with her grandfather later, whenever she got out of this place. She would keep the journal safe and her entries secret for now.

She couldn't help but wonder what the last part of his message was about. What was so important?

"Hi, Sam! What are you up to?" Yolo's voice nagged at her, interrupting her thoughts. She glanced up. His face had appeared on the screen. She was surprised since she hadn't activated his presence on the control panel.

She hesitated. He was most definitely spying on her.

"Oh, this and that," she replied, intentionally vague. She tucked the journal under her pillow, then went to the panel and pressed the button to turn off Yolo. She shivered, imagining him possibly still there in the background, lingering.

Frustrated, she ran a hot bath and let the water soak her skin, but as much as she'd hoped, it still couldn't carry her worries away.

She thought about her strange dream. The one with the ant-like creature who looked very much like Zenobii from the meeting earlier. The dream materialized again, like a vision, only this time, it was vivid, intense.

She found herself in a bustling city with thick, suffocating smog. She followed the flow of people down the street, taking the same route as last time. Looking around, she wondered if there was anything different. She stopped again at the light. Zenobii stood a few feet away, watching her, his antennae swaying back and forth lightly. He pointed to the sky, just like last time.

She knew what came next.

The sky would turn dark in a matter of seconds, the same monstrous spacecraft would hover directly above, the pods would drop, and those horrific creatures would emerge. The others wouldn't make it, and she would not survive the attack.

She stopped for a moment, considering Zenobii's gesture. Was he pointing to the sky to warn her? If so, why was he so calm, given that he seemed to know what was coming? Instead of following Zenobii's gaze, she called out to him in her mind.

"Who are they, and why are they coming for us?"

"Don't be afraid," Zenobii responded. *"They're here for you."*

"What? I don't understand."

The sky grew dark. She heard the familiar low hum of the spaceship above. The pods dropped from the sky, just like they had done in her last dream.

"What do you mean?" She tried again with steady persistence. *"What do they want?"*

People screamed, racing frantically in every direction. The pods opened, and the spherical metallic creatures emerged. Their spiked tentacles swirled through the air like helicopter blades. Sam watched Zenobii, but he didn't falter. He stood his ground, seemingly unperturbed, waiting for something. But what?

It's just a dream, Sam thought. *I need to confront them.*

Instead of running away, she stood her ground too, waiting for them to approach. She tried to drown out the screams, the sounds of the creatures approaching, the swishing of their blades. Blasts of electricity rippled through the air like ball lightning, allowing the creatures to travel at rapid speeds. They soared, the energy propelling them forward.

What did they want?

Her legs felt heavy, but she took a defensive stance as three creatures zoomed toward them. Zenobii calmly waited beside her. He gently grasped her hand with one of his hairy forelimbs.

She felt the seconds tick by in slow motion.

And then…

The Malborgs ground to a halt, inches away from her. Their shiny black coating bubbled and mutated. Their tentacled blades, once exposed and in attack mode, were now retracted and hidden beneath their skin. Purple energy sparked beneath them, allowing them to hover in midair, but they weren't moving forward.

In perfect unity, the Malborgs turned, moving *toward her*, surrounding her and Zenobii. A bright light shone down from above. She looked up. A spaceship hovered overhead, its light beaming down, paralyzing them. In an instant, she felt her body swooping up into the air.

She opened her eyes, breathless, her mind swirling.

Her body froze. She was still in the bath water, only it was freezing now. Her fingers had shriveled into prunes.

She grabbed a towel and hugged it around her, shivering. How much time had passed?

As she brushed her teeth and got ready for bed, the vision tugged at her thoughts. What did it mean? The weight of it hung over her. Perhaps it was just her subconscious telling her that she was a bit nervous about being at the military base but that it was important to face her fears rather than run away. Or maybe she was feeling confrontational, wanting answers after receiving the disrupted message from her grandfather. That was probably it.

Or not.

She was grasping now. It could mean any number of things. Or it could mean the inevitable—that she was seeing what was to come. A premonition. Zenobii was either guiding her to safety or to her death…

She couldn't determine which. And that was a problem.

Flustered, she collapsed on her bed and rubbed her eyes. She saw the time. 11:56 p.m. It was late, and she needed some rest.

Then, as if hearing them from a distance, the words traveled into her mind.

"Do you trust me?"

She wasn't sure where they had come from. But more importantly…

She wasn't sure of her answer.

CHAPTER THIRTY-FOUR

Sam listened, waiting to see whether she would hear those same words again.

Who was speaking to her?

And then, like a gentle whisper in the wind, the same soothing voice flooded her mind. *"I trust you."* Unlike Duskara, this voice was soft, comforting. Where had it come from?

Sam scanned the room, but no one else was there. Was she losing it?

A pause, and then it spoke again. *"Do you trust me?"*

Lights flickered around the room, abrupt and jarring. The automatic system, controlled by the room's main panel, was malfunctioning. The side screen where Yolo's image usually materialized flickered on and off, but only static appeared.

Groggy, she stumbled to the main panel and tried pressing the button to shut off the lights, but it didn't work.

What was going on? It felt like there was some ghost in the room playing tricks on her—or was it her mind? Was she dreaming?

She rubbed her eyes and pinched herself.

But this wasn't like the vision. It wasn't a dream. She was fully awake. And that scared her even more.

All of a sudden, her blinds opened to reveal the vastness of the ocean beyond. Peering through the windows, she spotted a large, tangled mass of what looked like seaweed in the distance floating toward her.

A draft blew from a vent in the wall, the air frigid. She pulled on a cardigan for extra warmth and tried manually closing the blinds, but they wouldn't budge.

Then she saw movement outside. A glint of multicolored light bouncing off the mass as it drew closer, and bits of seaweed floated away, revealing a creature. It was the size of two men, its face like that of a fish, its huge, round eyes sunken, its fishy lips opening and closing as it tried to communicate with her.

She gasped at the sight of this ghastly thing. Its body was like that of a strong man but with webbed feet and hands, scales, and gills. Its iridescent, multicolored skin glowed—greens, purples, yellows, oranges, and blues—against the darkness of the ocean.

It hovered there on the other side of the window as Sam took in its expression, curious but also anxious. It placed one of its webbed hands upon the glass. Was it trying to tell her something? Was it a threat?

Then the words flowed into her mind, the same soothing words she'd heard earlier.

"I trust you."

What did that mean? Why did it trust her?

And then she remembered her conversation with Duskara. Duskara had said she would be sending someone to deliver a gift to her.

Sam placed her hand against the glass, so small compared to the creature's. *"What do you want?"*

All of a sudden, it retracted its hand. Sam did the same in response.

Its other hand held out something the size of a marble—shiny, luminescent black. An inorganic, manufactured material.

"Take this gift. I help you."

Curiosity and an urge to take it overwhelmed her. If she could learn more about this device and its connection to Duskara, maybe they could find a way to stop the attacks.

She wasn't sure whether she could trust this creature or what to make of its gift—but there was only one way to find out.

The creature pressed the object against the glass. To Sam's astonishment, the glass mutated into a thick, gel-like substance, and the marble passed straight through. No hole. No rushing water. The device dropped onto the floor at her feet.

Sam picked it up just as an alarm went off. She looked in horror at the creature, but it didn't look distressed. Instead, it pointed. She followed its gaze toward the corner of the room.

A safe!

She threw the marble inside and locked it, but the alarm continued blaring, reverberating in her bones.

She jumped at the pounding at her door and hurried to answer it, only to find armed military police outside. They swarmed the hallway, knocking on every door.

"What's going on?" she asked between blares of the alarm.

"We located a breach in this quadrant and are checking each room. Stand aside."

She staggered back as the military police barged into her room.

She looked to the viewing window, but the creature had vanished.

The window looked intact. There was no observable trace of the distortion she'd seen.

She plugged her ears, trying to mute the noise of the siren. One of the men checked her bathroom. Another, her closet. One tapped the walls as he swept by. It only took them a minute. Someone yelled, "Clear!" Then, they left just as quickly as they'd entered.

Kato, Kobe, and Simon stood at their doorways, drowsy,

watching the commotion as the military police continued patrolling down the hall, knocking on each resident's door.

"What was that about?" Kato asked.

"I—I have no idea." Sam hated the lie, but she couldn't tell them now. Not here. Not with so many listening.

"Is it breakfast yet?" Simon asked.

"In like five hours," Kobe said, yawning. "I don't know about you, but I'm heading back to bed. Good night. Er…rather, good morning. Whatever."

As Sam made her way back to sleep, bizarre dreams played with her mind, pulling her into their depths. Strange images streamed in front of her, of Dr. Krill conducting a lab experiment, fainting, and then turning into a fishy creature. She found herself trapped in a large tank of water with a bunch of black marbles below her that seemed to be moving.

Upon closer inspection, they weren't marbles at all, but baby Malborgs.

Eventually, the dream shifted, but all that enveloped her thoughts now was darkness.

CHAPTER THIRTY-FIVE

Sam got up early, and not just because she needed to get ready for a full day of physical training. She needed answers. Answers about the gift from the strange creature and what had happened last night. Yolo would be perfect for the task, with his infinite database of knowledge and eagerness to provide support.

"Yolo, I need your help again."

"Of course. I'm at your service. How may I assist you?"

She hesitated, taking in the room. The main panel was running smoothly now. She tested a few buttons, and they seemed to be working properly. Yolo's image on the screen was crisp and clear, instead of the static from last night. The blinds functioned. Everything seemed to be working again—almost as if last night's incident had never happened, like it had all been in her head.

"Yolo, are there any large, fishy creatures that are part of GAIA?"

"There are several. Please be more specific."

"Are there any that are, uh…about eleven or twelve feet in height, with webbed feet and hands, scales, gills, and multicolored skin?"

"Yes. The Mermaquana. But they are more commonly known as Gillygoblins."

"Gillygoblins?"

An image of a creature appeared on the screen. Its features—its huge, sunken eyes, scales, gills, and glowing iridescent skin—matched exactly what she'd seen last night.

"Which world are they from?"

Yolo paused. "It appears that information has been removed from my database."

"What? What do you mean, removed? Can you tell me all information you have about the Gillygoblins?"

Yolo hesitated, his eyes moving back and forth as if searching for the answer. "The information has been erased."

"Erased?" She shook her head, her frustration growing. "Who erased it?"

"Kwan Yun."

Kwan? The coder in Dr. Krill's lab?

Sam paced. Why would Kwan erase this information from Yolo's database unless she didn't want others to have it? Something felt *off*.

"Thank you, Yolo." Sam pressed the button on the wall panel, and Yolo's face disappeared from the screen.

She hurried to the safe mounted to the wall beside her closet. She punched in the code, and it opened. The black marble still lay inside.

If she removed it, would the alarm go off again?

Taking a deep breath, she reached inside. The marble was cool to the touch. She took it out and waited, but nothing happened. No alarm sounded.

She thought about the creature and the meaning of its gift as she examined the object more closely. It didn't react to her touch, nor did it contain any strange markings, except for a small triangle etched into it. What was it for? She tapped it, but it didn't respond. The device seemed inert and harmless. Still, she needed to tell the others, and as soon as possible. If anything, she could count on her friends to help her make sense of this. Together, they could find the answers. At least, she hoped.

She checked the time. 7:56 a.m. They'd be expecting her in the physical training room in a few minutes.

She slipped the marble inside her pocket and left the room in a hurry. Dashing down the hallway toward the elevators, she startled at a loud crashing noise and shouts nearby. Turning the corner, she witnessed the commotion unfolding. A group of staff stood in a semicircle, worried expressions on their faces. Captain Gorgana lay on the floor, unconscious and convulsing while Onnisa knelt beside her.

"Everyone, get back! Give her room," Onnisa urged.

Footsteps thundered down the hall. Sam scuttled to the side as five military police breezed past carrying a padded stretcher. It took all five of them to heave the Rigellian onto it.

Onnisa stood. "Captain Gorgana will be okay. Please, everyone, carry on." She followed the military police down the hall.

Sam watched them go. Ever since arriving here, it had been nonstop crazy. A commander and a scientist were dead, a bounty was on her head, GAIA's worst enemy had secretly communicated with her, and now the Rigellian ambassador had fainted and convulsed for no apparent reason. Was she really safe here? Were any of them?

It was one more thing she needed to tell the others. With that, she sprinted toward the elevators. She was a few feet away when she felt an electric jolt on her finger, spreading its way up her hand and arm. She stopped and gasped, peering down at her ring band. Beams of holographic red light shot into the air, displaying a message.

REPORT TO MEDICAL ASAP. TESTS NEEDED.

Her ring buzzed again, more forcefully than before, another zap of electricity jolting through her. She fumbled with the settings to try and disarm it. Then, she made a call.

"Kato?"

Kato's face appeared in the hologram. "Sam? Where are you? Everyone's waiting."

"Listen," Sam started, "I have to get some medical tests done. Can you please let Rian know I'll be late?"

"Yeah, sure." Kato's face scrunched with concern. "Is everything okay?"

"I don't know. I think so. Did you get called into medical yet?"

"No."

"Okay, well I'll let you know what happens. It seems urgent." Another zap. "Ow! Uh, I've gotta go. See you soon."

She ended the call, then paused in disbelief as a route marked in red appeared on the hologram. Directions to the medical wing. As spooky as it was, thankfully, the buzzing had stopped, at least for now. As she started along the route, her earpiece fed her the directions, everything perfectly coordinated.

Within minutes, she arrived at the medical bay to find a round woman eyeing her from behind a steel counter.

"May I help you?"

"Yes, please. I'm Sam Sanderson. I received a text on—"

"Oh, yes. Please hold out your ring band."

Sam did as she was told. The woman scanned it, then said, "Follow me."

The woman led her to a smaller room with stalls. "You'll need to change into this."

Sam looked dubiously at the hospital gown. "What kind of tests need me to wear a gown?"

"I believe they said an MRI and some blood tests. Don't worry, shouldn't take too long. You can keep your underwear and socks on, but leave the rest of your clothes in the stall. Once you've changed, just stay in the stall and someone will come and get you."

Sam's thoughts drifted as she got changed. Why the need for

such tests? Why weren't the others getting them as well? Was there something wrong with her? As her mind spun to grasp the answers, the marble dropped from her pocket onto the seating ledge. She grabbed it just in time before it rolled onto the floor.

There was a tap on the outside door.

"Sam Sanderson?"

Hastily she tucked the marble back inside the pocket of her uniform. She hoped they wouldn't go through her clothes. Would she be in trouble if they found it? Maybe she was overthinking it.

"Yes."

She followed the nurse into another room. This one contained a large machine with a hole in the middle. The hole was small—a tunnel-like tube—and confining. A patient table looked like it slid through the machine. She wasn't sure she could even fit through that hole lying down.

"You'll have to take those out," the nurse said, pointing to Sam's earrings. "No metal in the machines."

Sam carefully pulled out her silver studs—the ones her mother had given her in the past on a family trip to Italy. That was before her parents had left on their mission. It seemed like a lifetime ago. She loved the earrings so much that she hadn't wanted to change them. Removing them now felt like she was losing her connection to her parents, letting go of that familiarity, that comforting space that existed in her thoughts while they were away. She hesitated a moment, lost in that quiet memory, before she placed them on the metal tray, along with her ring band.

The prick of the needle didn't hurt much as the nurse inserted an IV and drew some blood. Then, she administered a few vaccines.

"What are the vaccines for?"

"Well, believe it or not, there are lots of bacterial microbes floating around in space."

"So they're going to send me on a mission?"

The nurse hesitated. "I don't know. But they want to make sure you're as healthy as possible. Now, I'm going to leave the IV in so we can administer a contrast agent, a dye, to help us see the images better."

"Why do I need these tests? What're they for?"

"Health reasons. My, you ask a lot of questions. I'm afraid I don't know anymore. Now, the next part requires you to lay as still as you can while we run some tests through the MRI machine. You think you can do that?"

"Will it hurt?"

"No. It's just noisy," the nurse responded as she placed earplugs into Sam's ears. "If you get nervous, just close your eyes."

Sam lay back on the table and waited as the nurse strapped her in. The table then slid slowly through the tunnel into the belly of the machine. The nurse hadn't lied—the machine was loud, the clicking and beeping sounds rattling her skull like a sledgehammer despite the earplugs.

She lay perfectly still, hoping it wouldn't take too long.

Then, the nurse's voice came through an intercom. "This next part would be better if we put you to sleep."

Sleep? "Wait—what? Why? What are you doing?"

"We're administering the drug now. Just count backward from ten."

"Wait—no!" She twisted her head to see what they were doing, but at this angle, she only saw the rounded walls of the machine's interior. She tried to wiggle, to squirm her way out, but the straps held her down. She was trapped inside this suffocating tunnel.

An icy spike of panic shot through her as the cold liquid traveled up her arm. She took in a sharp breath but couldn't calm the chaos inside her head. They usually only put people to sleep for surgeries, didn't they? What was going on? She clutched her hospital gown with her clammy hands. "I didn't say you could put me...to...sleep..."

She tried to keep her eyes open, to fight it, but her vision blurred around the edges, the darkness masking the light, threatening to engulf her. She tried to focus, to push herself up, but it was impossible. A wave of drowsiness washed over her, pulling her under.

Sam's eyes fluttered open. Light beat down overhead. She jolted upright in the hospital bed. To her right, the nurse hovered over her. She placed a hand on Sam's shoulder.

"Easy now, take your time—"

"What happened? Where am I? What did you…?"

The grogginess overtook her again, and she couldn't resist its power. She fell back against the pillow as she stumbled into the darkness.

The next time Sam opened her eyes, she was alone. No doting nurses or orderlies. Just her, in a bright room. How much time had passed? She stirred, gathering her senses. She didn't feel any pain, but her mind was a bit hazy, like a fog had settled in.

She wiggled her toes and fingers. Everything seemed in working order. She looked down to see that she was still dressed in the hospital gown.

Then she noticed them—tiny slits in her skin. Each was about as wide as a staple and just as thin. There were a few along each of her arms, her legs, her hands—her *entire* body.

"What the—?"

A loud knock came at the door, and a moment later, a man dressed in a white lab coat barged in carrying a notepad. He had a crop of thinning brown hair and a bushy mustache that reminded her of a giant, hairy caterpillar.

"I'm Dr. Maizer," he said, resting his notepad on a side table. He dragged a stool over to her, the screeching sound prickling

Sam's ears. "I'm glad to see you're awake now. How are you feeling?"

"I... The nurse didn't tell me anything about putting me to sleep. What happened? What did they do to me? What's with these slits in my skin?"

"I apologize," Dr. Maizer said, adjusting his glasses. His eyes darted around nervously. "The nurse is somewhat new. She was under the impression you already knew about the tests."

"But I didn't!"

Dr. Maizer frowned. "I see. I'm sorry. I admit it was unprofessional of her not to tell you about the tests we were conducting. I'll have a talk with her later about it."

Something about the way the doctor spoke made Sam's skin crawl. The explanation was logical, sure, but he didn't sound genuine. It was like he had rehearsed the words beforehand. Was this yet another lie? Or was she just imagining things? Either way, she needed to get answers about what had happened. It didn't seem like he was in any rush to provide further details.

"And the tests? What were they for?"

"I can tell you with certainty that everything went well regarding the tests. We had to take some blood samples so we can stock up on your blood type in case you need emergency treatment."

"Emergency treatment? What do you mean?"

"Well, it's standard practice. Now that we have samples of your blood, we can grow more blood cells in our labs here. All soldiers and operatives carry extra blood supplies on their missions."

Her stomach lurched. They were growing more of her blood cells? The idea wasn't totally preposterous—after all, scientists were able to cultivate cells—she just never thought they would be doing this to her or have a need for it. But it could only mean one thing: they were planning a mission for her. She didn't like the idea of not knowing what it was. She wanted to be in control of her future. But what had they done? They'd pulled the rug right out from under her, left her to stumble on shaky ground.

"I—I didn't realize you could do that."

"Mhm."

"But what about these…cuts?" She pointed to the tiny red scratches on her arm.

Dr. Maizer paused. "We took some tissue samples. Standard procedure. Nothing to worry over, I assure you."

His words and tone did nothing to calm her rising anxiety. He spoke quickly, trying to race over the facts. Nothing about this felt like it was standard procedure. Her inner voice screamed at her now that something wasn't right.

"Tissue samples—why?"

"It's just a precaution. The technology we have is quite sophisticated. It allows us to, er…regrow parts of you."

Sam bolted upright. "*Parts* of me?"

He nodded abruptly, his tone energetic. "Limbs and organs and such. In case you need a replacement, so to speak."

Regrow limbs—and organs? Had she heard him correctly? All of this sounded so surreal—like science fiction. It sent tremors through her body.

"How—?"

The doctor flitted his gaze to the clock on the back wall, as if he were in a hurry to leave. When he turned back to her, his eyes were cold, exacting. "The procedure uses tiny needles to extract small tissue samples from your body at various locations, and then we grow the cells. We've used the technology in the past to regrow limbs, replace organs, that kind of thing."

Sam squirmed in her hospital bed. The technology wasn't just advanced; it was invasive. And the fact that they'd done it without her knowledge made her furious and gravely anxious. She knew that in times of war, consent wasn't always obtained from soldiers, but what they'd done still seemed unethical.

It was hard enough trying to wrap her head around the fact

that this advanced technology existed. Of course, scientists had been experimenting with regenerating animal cells for years—it had only been a matter of time before this type of thing could be applied to humans. What was more disturbing was that they'd actually done it to her. They were growing spare parts of her body somewhere in the lab. Had they done this with all the soldiers at GAIA?

"Is it standard practice?"

"No. Nothing about the procedure is standard. It's all state of the art. You won't find this technology anywhere else in the world," Dr. Maizer replied smugly.

"No, I mean, do other soldiers get these types of procedures?"

"I can't discuss other patients' health records for privacy reasons."

Her hands shook, but she tried not to let it show. She'd come up against yet another wall. They were blocking information. She needed to find a way to break through.

"So if I asked all the other soldiers here at the base, they'd say they received the same treatment?"

He shrugged. "I don't know. Now, if you don't have any further questions for me—"

"Actually, I do. As my doctor, can you tell me why I received these tests? Are they sending me on a mission?" They must be. Otherwise, why the need for such procedures? Still, she wanted to hear the truth from him directly. It irked her that she was only getting some information, and not the whole picture.

"Unfortunately, I don't know. They only tell us which tests they need us to do. But if you want to know more, I would recommend following up with Admiral Green. *She's* the one who authorized the procedures."

Sam clenched her teeth. How could the doctor not know the purpose of the tests? Could he really be so ignorant? Or was it something else—something above his security level that forced even him to be kept in the dark? She shivered as a coldness invaded her blood, threatening to consume her. She bristled at the idea that Admiral Green was behind the procedures. She needed to get to the training session at once and tell the others everything that had happened.

She slid from the hospital bed, desperate to leave. "So, am I okay to go now?"

"There's one more thing." He got up from his seat and jotted a few notes on his notepad. Then, he opened a cabinet at the back and returned with a small glass bottle.

"What's that?"

Dr. Maizer's mustache twitched. "This is an antimicrobial advanced numbing gel. The amount of tissue we took was minuscule. The needles were tiny, as small as those used in acupuncture, so you shouldn't feel too much pain, if any. We already applied this to your cuts, but it'll wear off in a few hours. Now, if you feel any pain in a few hours, which is unlikely, just apply a drop to the site, and the pain should go away within a few minutes. And as for your cuts, they should heal up within a day or so."

"Okay. Bye." She grabbed the bottle and hurried out the door. She wasn't in the mood for good manners, especially not to the deceitful snake.

The doctor's explanations had just led to more questions. An endless spiral, it seemed. She didn't like being kept in the dark, but was beyond relieved that the tests were over. There was no time to lose. She dashed back to the stall to change.

She sighed in relief. The marble was there in her pocket, right where she'd left it.

Leaving the change room, she glanced at the nurse wheeling Captain Gorgana in a bed down the corridor. The Rigellian opened her mouth, moaning, low and guttural. Sam's earpiece registered the message. "It hurts!" Her eyes rolled back, her body shaking.

"Doctor!" the nurse shouted.

A woman in a lab coat rushed past Sam and tended to Captain Gorgana. Medical personnel swarmed the captain, dispensing medications as they wheeled her away. Sam wondered what was wrong with her, but there was no time to linger and little she could do. She checked the time. 3:21 p.m. She had missed the morning physical training session. But if she hurried, she could make it in time for the afternoon session.

She picked up the pace.

Tired, but determined, she looked forward to joining the others.

And telling them everything that had happened.

CHAPTER THIRTY-SIX

A chill permeated the air of Dr. Krill's lab. A stillness, too.

Kwan gazed up from the screen, her eyes red and puffy. It was so quiet in here now. She felt empty. She hadn't fully processed or grieved Dr. Krill's death.

There hadn't been time.

Duskara's Malborg army kept growing and evolving. Kwan wished there was another way to take them out that didn't involve a mission to the Dark Galaxy. Like blasting the Malborg ships. But GAIA's fleet was insufficient. They were no match for the ever-expanding and overwhelming reach of the Malborgs. Unless they took out Duskara, it would be a never-ending battle.

Her work on the AI death serum hadn't gone as smoothly as she'd expected. She'd integrated a variation of Luyten slime into the serum. That part was successful. Then, she'd programmed the nanobots to release the serum using her malicious coding. The nanobots had followed her instructions. It should have worked. They were on track.

Except it had failed.

She couldn't understand why—until now.

The recent Malborg attack had thrown a wrench into her plans.

It seemed that the Malborgs could communicate with Duskara instantly—and exchange information with other Malborgs. *That* presented a problem.

A big one.

Thanks to the Malborg that had infiltrated the base, Duskara had learned of their weapons capabilities. She now knew about the Luyten gas and the weaponized Luyten slime—both used to attack the Malborg. She was probably already working on a defense mechanism to stop them.

The words on the screen in front of Kwan proved it.

AI DEATH SERUM CONTROL TRIAL 6
0% SUCCESS RATE

It had been a fifteen-percent success rate yesterday, *before* the attack!

Kwan frowned. The parameters had changed—overnight.

She sighed, frustrated and irritated. Duskara's complexity continued to evolve. Kwan would need to start from square one, developing a new protocol and an entirely new approach.

She needed another Malborg sample to study. She scanned the room. All the containers with the samples were missing. Probably one of the many items Yolo had thrown away.

What was she going to do about Yolo?

She needed to notify the admiral and demand an explanation. Yolo had become a liability.

She flicked on the hologram and made the call.

An image of the admiral appeared. She sat beside Onnisa and Zenobii in a meeting room. They were at a meeting *without* her.

"Kwan?"

"I...I didn't realize we had another meeting."

"I didn't want to disturb you. I knew you were busy with the AI death serum experiments. How are they coming along?"

"Not well, Admiral. Some lab supplies are…" Kwan shook her head. "…missing. Actually, that's the reason I called. Yolo came by the lab the other day, and I—"

The hologram flickered. The audio feed cut in and out, disrupting the transmission.

"Sorry, Kwan, could you repeat that? We didn't catch that last part—"

A pool of dread filled Kwan. If Yolo connected to the base's communications system, then he was most likely monitoring the call. *He* could be disrupting it, for all she knew.

"On second thought, it would be better if we met in person. Where are you?"

"Dark Site 44."

A wave of confusion swept through her. What were they doing meeting at a Dark Site? Those sites were restricted for top-secret experiments and research. Unless something highly advanced was being developed for their upcoming mission? Either way, she'd find out soon. "Okay. I'll be right there."

Kwan arrived at Dark Site 44 and lifted her ring band to the panel. The door clicked open. She found Admiral Green—looking as though she hadn't slept in days—speaking in hushed tones with Onnisa and Zenobii. But there was someone else there—someone unexpected.

Kwan halted in the doorway at the sight of the girl. Sam sat on a steel table, hooked up with cables. Her eyes were vacant, staring into a void.

"What's going on? What's wrong with Sam? Did something happen?"

The girl took no notice of Kwan. Instead, she remained silent, as if she were in a room with ghosts.

Admiral Green folded her arms and spoke in an even tone, her voice unwavering. "Kwan, meet Sam Sanderson II, the clone."

The clone?!

"What? I—I don't understand."

"With twenty Malborg ships on their way to Earth, we had no choice but to proceed with Operation Doppelgänger," Admiral Green replied resolutely.

"Operation Doppelgänger?"

They had *definitely* kept her in the dark.

"We've successfully cloned the girl. Now it's just a case of uploading some contrived memories—imitated but similar experiences. We'll include some coinciding with her trip to Kryg—in case she's questioned about her time there. We've also adjusted her nervous system so that she doesn't feel pain. See?" Admiral Green grabbed a needle from the side table and jammed it into the girl's arm.

Kwan winced, but the girl didn't flinch. Her eyes were empty, emotionless, and her body was unresponsive. This catatonic version of Sam was a mere shell, unaware of what was happening.

Horrified, Kwan stood gaping. Her blood curdled.

Admiral Green continued proudly. "She's been fitted with an AI computer chip. This should enhance her physical abilities and mental stamina. She's part machine and part organic—a cyborg. She's been physically modified to withstand brute force. For all intents and purposes, she's a living, breathing, sentient being, which we hope will fool Duskara until the loaded devices explode."

They hadn't just cloned her; they'd modified her into an AI cyborg.

Stunned, Kwan couldn't begin to fathom all the possible implications of this. When the idea had initially been put forward by Onnisa, the others had been hesitant. How could Onnisa treat her own queen this way? Unless…

They were all in a state of heightened tension and duress. The

Malborg attack at the base had ramped up the anxiety. Perhaps Onnisa's fear for her people and the safety of her queen had clouded her judgment. Maybe she was absolutely desperate for a solution, even an appalling one fraught with difficult choices. But Kwan hadn't thought they would actually go through with it.

Yet, that's exactly what they'd done.

"You're actually going to send a clone—*an AI cyborg*—to Duskara?" Kwan said. "This—can't you see that this is how we got into this predicament in the first place? Sending AIs into space! Suppose she learns how to rewrite her own code? What then?"

The admiral squared her shoulders. "We've taken the necessary precautions. No machine learning this time. It's all been pre-programmed. Before Duskara has time to figure it out, the clone will be in close range of her, and the bombs will explode."

Kwan's mind raced through these new facts. They had made a clone of Sam! And they were going to send her to space—only to blow her up when she reached her target. So many things were wrong with the scenario, and not just morally, but tactically! The clone was a drone—a slave! Her life would be short, fleeting, created solely for the purpose of defeating Duskara. They were authorizing the destruction of an innocent life. Not just any life, but that of a *teenager*.

"And what if her ship is intercepted before she reaches her target?"

"Her ship will be equipped with a Thesian cloaking device. They've never been intercepted."

"You mean, not *yet*!" Kwan's hands balled into fists. "Admiral, just because a ship with a Thesian cloaking device hasn't been intercepted *yet*, that doesn't mean that it will never be intercepted in the future—"

"We've weighed the variables, Kwan, and have decided to take the risk."

They were playing with fire. Not to mention how this could affect Sam if she found out. It could lead to serious negative repercussions: anger, confusion, loss of trust. Who knew how she would react?

"Does Sam even know?"

"No, and we don't intend to tell her. The less she knows, the better. That way, she won't worry, and we can instead focus on the mission…if it comes to that. Operation Doppelgänger *will* work."

Kwan paced. So they were keeping Sam in the dark about this, too. How had they cloned her without her knowledge? It wasn't right. They'd crossed a line. They were treating both Sam and her clone like objects to be manipulated. Two Sams, both just teenagers.

Both forced into a mission only to be subjected to death.

Was there really justification for the sacrifice? The question left her distraught, raw, and hollow inside. Would it be worth it, if it meant the destruction of Duskara? Kwan's mind spun, trying to think of a worthy answer, but found none.

And if the mission failed…

It occurred to her then: someone was missing from their group. Someone needed for their own mission to the Dark Galaxy, if it came to that.

"Admiral, I thought the mission to the Dark Galaxy was on track and that Captain Gorgana's health was improving?"

"Captain Gorgana was re-admitted to medical," Admiral Green replied coldly.

"What? I thought they didn't find anything wrong?"

"All the tests came back clear, but then earlier this week, I was told her symptoms flared up again. The fainting, the convulsions, the headaches, the difficulty communicating, the confusion."

"All symptoms of being exposed to low-frequency mind alteration," Onnisa added, straightening her posture.

Was it possible that other LOMA devices were lurking somewhere around the base? But Captain Gorgana's health episodes seemed sporadic and inconsistent, suggesting they were caused by something else.

Kwan fumbled for words, trying to think of other possible explanations for Captain Gorgana's strange, erratic behavior. It was almost consistent with signs of post-traumatic stress disorder. Captain Gorgana and the other Rigellians had been exposed to LOMA when they were forced off their planet to work as slaves during the war.

"Is it possible... You know how sometimes, if someone has gone through a traumatic event in the past, they can...still feel it sometimes? Do you think..." She didn't want to say it at the risk of sounding dismissive, but she wondered all the same.

"You're wondering if it's all in her head?" Admiral Green said. "We've not ruled out that possibility, either. We still have to run some more tests, but at the moment, Captain Gorgana is unfit for duty. We had no other choice but to proceed with Operation Doppelgänger."

"But if that mission fails..." Who would serve as a replacement in Captain Gorgana's absence? After all, very few people around here knew how to fly these advanced ships—equipped with Rigellian technology—with such ease.

Admiral Green interrupted her thoughts. "The mission will *not* fail. It can't. *We* can't fail. The matter is settled. Now, tell me what you have to say about Yolo. Isn't that why you came?"

Kwan sighed in exasperation. The issue with Yolo now seemed trivial compared to what they had just done to Sam. "Yolo, he—he came by the lab the other day. He cleaned up the place, but he threw away some sensitive documents and items, including our only sample of LOMA. It's been destroyed. I wasn't able to complete the tracing signal for it yet. And without the tracing signal, it will be nearly impossible to find other LOMA devices lurking at the base."

"What?"

"I—well, I believe Yolo has been compromised. Somehow. I—I think you need to check his coding as soon as possible."

"I'll take care of it," Admiral Green replied. But Kwan wasn't sure she would. Her words sounded dismissive, almost.

There was a loud knock on the door and then a click as it opened.

"Excuse me, Admiral Green." A man dressed in a white lab coat poked his head inside. "I'm sorry to interrupt, but you told me to notify you when Dr. Krill's autopsy results came back."

"Yes. Come in. Close the door," the admiral answered, anxious but wary. "And? What did you find?"

"Admiral, I'm afraid I have some bad news. The toxicology report found the natural supplement hawthorn in his blood, in such a large dosage that it must have reacted with his heart medication. It's all in the report here," the man said, placing a file on the table. "There's no refuting this evidence. Dr. Otto Krill was poisoned."

A chill filled the room.

Admiral Green lowered her gaze, keeping her emotions hidden below the surface. "Thank you," she said quietly. "That will be all."

The man turned and left.

"We will be tightening security," Admiral Green said, her face rigid like stone. "Effective immediately."

Anger boiled through Kwan's veins. Someone had murdered Dr. Krill—someone here, at the base. No matter what, however long it took, she was going to find out who.

"I've got to get back to work." With that, she stormed out of the room, the cold air prickling at her damp skin.

CHAPTER THIRTY-SEVEN

PAIN SHOT THROUGH SAM'S RIBS AS SHE SLAMMED INTO THE GROUND for a second time that afternoon. The physical training was brutal. There were no breaks, no chance for her body to rest and recover.

"You're okay." Rian leaned down, offering a hand. Sam didn't bother taking it.

Instead, she grunted, gathering just enough energy to rise again. She lifted her hands to block as she'd been taught, but she wasn't fast enough. Again, Rian knocked her down onto the mat, pain ripping through her chest.

"That's enough. Try it on me," Kobe urged. It was sweet that he was trying to protect her. But she didn't want protection. She needed to build muscle, endurance, and speed, all of which she lacked. She needed to focus on her weaknesses. Kato and the others were excelling, while she seemed to have two left feet. It was embarrassing how her body seemed to act like a puppet on strings, jerky and unstable.

To make matters worse, the training room had viewing windows everywhere. All those people walking by, casually watching every time she stumbled or fell. It was distracting. Kwan had seen her blunder more times than she could count, leaving Sam with the weird feeling she was being assessed. Well, if they were testing her, she'd probably been given a big fat F.

"I want you to practice on each other," Rian instructed. "Take turns. Sam and Kato, Simon and Kobe. Then, you'll rotate partners."

Sam practiced the drills, doing her best to carry them out carefully and with precision. She failed. Every time. It was only made worse by the fact that it was taking her away from what she wanted to be doing—*needed* to be doing: finding out the purpose of Duskara's *gift*—and if there was any truth to her warnings. But then again, she *was* headed to the Dark Galaxy; perhaps these moments of pain would prove their worth.

"Watch your form!" Rian yelled at Simon. "Look, your weakness is here," she continued, lifting his arm. "You need to reach higher to protect your head. Try it again."

Simon sighed and mumbled something incoherent, then got ready. They repeated the drill, and this time, Simon held his arm higher, as instructed.

"Better," Rian stated. "All of you, keep practicing. I need to step outside for a moment. When I get back, I want to see perfection in your form."

Once Rian left the room, everyone relaxed a little.

"I want to see perfection in your form," Kato repeated in an authoritative voice, then rolled her eyes.

"How long is she going to keep at us like that?" Simon asked, his impatience growing. "We're not going to become hulking soldiers overnight, like those military people in the next room who've probably done this for years. Or like Kwan, who could probably bust out of here if she wanted to."

"Not with that attitude," Kato chuckled.

"No, but seriously. It's like they have these impossible standards, like they're rushing us through this."

"Why would they do that?" Kobe asked, "Unless they're preparing us for something."

"I know why," Sam started. "They're going to send me on a mission."

"What? How do you know?" Kato asked.

"Because those medical tests they did—they put me to sleep and took tissue samples. The doctor said they're going to regrow my limbs and organs in case I need a replacement."

"*What*? No way!"

"It's true. At least, that's what they told me." It sounded totally ridiculous. Insane, even. She wasn't sure whether she was going to laugh or cry. A flurry of emotions ran through her, and she fought to keep her composure.

The blood drained from Kato's face, and the others staggered back. Kato's voice trembled. "What happened? What exactly did they tell you?"

Sam eyed the door to make sure they were still a good distance away from anyone who might be listening. Rian was still outside on a call, pacing and briefly glancing their way. Sam continued her drills with Kato. "They…gave me some imaging tests. An MRI and blood tests. I asked them about it, but they only said it was for health reasons. But I don't think so. I—I can't believe it's just health-related."

"Why would they have you go through those tests and not us?" Kato asked, winding Sam's arm around backward, then placing her in a choke hold. How was Kato able to pick up the moves so easily?

"Maybe they're not planning to send you with me," Sam said in between breaths. "Or maybe they will, and you'll get called into medical later and have the same tests."

Everyone was silent for a moment. Kato released her and sighed. She looked shaken, her hand trembling by her side. "Aren't you concerned about what's going on? About the intruders? The alarms? How Dr. Krill was murdered? How they're not telling us...*anything*?"

Of course she was concerned. But she didn't want them to worry. She already felt guilty for everything that had happened, for them all being forced here. A war was going on, and it was all because of her. Duskara wanted one thing, and she wouldn't stop attacking until she got it. But what could Sam do? She felt responsible and also powerless.

"Yes. But there's other stuff, too," Sam said, glancing toward the door. Rian would be back at any moment.

"What other stuff?"

Sam told them everything as quickly as she could, from the night of her encounter with the strange Gillygoblin creature, to the bizarre marble device it had given her, to her witnessing Captain Gorgana's erratic health episodes—episodes that only seemed to happen when Sam was around her—to her communications with the Malborg, which she was certain were with Duskara, if indirectly.

When she was finished, everyone's eyes were wide with shock.

"Sam," Kato said, "you need to tell someone. This is serious."

"I know—I just... What if they don't believe me?"

"Onnisa will. You need to tell her right away."

Sam sighed. "Okay." It felt good getting it off her chest, but she also wondered about the consequences. She'd have to find Onnisa later.

Rian opened the door and froze at the looks on their faces. "Everyone okay? Did you see a ghost or something?"

No one answered. They just kept carrying out the drills like lifeless robots.

CHAPTER THIRTY-EIGHT

SAM SPENT THE REST OF THE DAY TRYING TO LOCATE ONNISA. SHE checked the meeting rooms and the cafeteria. Even the Fishbowl, with its view of the landing bays below. But nothing. Onnisa was nowhere.

And no one else seemed to know where she was, either.

Or they weren't telling her.

There was little she could do now. The exhaustion from the day had long set in. Her body ached and needed rest. But she couldn't sleep. Not with her mind spinning with questions. What had really happened during the procedure? What were they hiding? Where was Onnisa? The one person she thought she could rely on for answers had mysteriously vanished. Who could she turn to now?

Ever since arriving at the base, people had fed her lies or built walls of silence. Disillusioned and confused, Sam fought hard to keep calm, to think straight, despite the chaos rampaging inside her.

Every possibility, every explanation led to another path, a cavity that opened up beyond her. She looked for a concrete answer but found none.

There was no other way. Her recent medical procedures and recurring visions could only mean one thing. They were coming for her. Duskara's army of Malborgs. They would take everything —and *everyone*—Sam cared about unless she went to Logom.

She shivered, accepting the inevitable, mentally preparing for what came next.

The time had finally come to say her goodbyes.

Sam knocked on Kato's door. It opened instantly.

Kato's eyes searched her own. "Sam, what's wrong?"

Sam tried to sound confident, self-assured, and lighthearted, even though inside, her anxiety and sadness were ready to overflow. She would miss Kato and hadn't really spent as much time with her as she would have liked. "How do you know something's wrong?"

Kato rolled her eyes. "Because I'm your best friend. And you're *so* easy to read. Seriously. Come inside. *Talk* to me. Besides, you're just in time. I can't finish all these treats on my own."

"You ordered room service—at nine o'clock at night?" Sam asked, staring at the tiered tray of tea sandwiches—cucumber and cream cheese and peanut butter and jelly—along with an assortment of cookies and brownies arranged neatly on the coffee table. A steaming pot of tea and two mugs rested beside them.

Sam took a seat on the sofa while Kato poured them some tea. "I think it's the physical training. I've had such a giant appetite lately. Also, I was planning to invite you over. Now, tell me what's wrong."

She didn't want to burden Kato, but she didn't know who else she could turn to. Kato would understand the most. Kato always helped to ground her and put things in perspective.

She exhaled, deflating. "Kato, I need you to promise me something."

"Of course."

"Can you please—please let my grandfather and my parents know that I love them? I mean—if, well, if something happens to me."

Kato went bug-eyed. "What—what are you talking about?"

"It's just—I think something terrible is going to—"

"No." Kato held her hand up. "Don't say it. Don't be ridiculous! You're here. You're safe. It's going to be okay—"

"But what if it isn't? Just hear me out. Please." Sam had to look away. This was much more difficult than she'd thought it would be.

She spoke quietly. "I really value our friendship, Kato, and I just wanted to let you know that I care about you. You've been such a good friend—no, a *best* friend. Better than anyone could ask for. And, well, I care about Kobe and Simon, too." Her words tumbled out of her mouth, choppy and rushed. "What I mean to say is, you all don't deserve this. I feel like it's all my fault. Everyone is in danger because of me."

"Just stop." Kato placed her hands on Sam's shoulders, forcing her to look into her eyes. "Have you lost hope so easily? *You're* the one who taught me about not giving up."

"I did?"

"Yes! Remember when we went to Gliese, and there were those creepy black water pythons and toxic plants? I was terrified the whole time! I thought we were going to be stuck there forever, Sam. I thought we were going to die! And then you pushed us forward. *You* got us through it. You found a way. You have this— this *power* inside you."

Sam shook her head. "It's different this time. I caused this." She lowered her gaze in shame. "I—I keep having these dreams…these visions of Malborg attacks. And in my visions, I'm always with Zenobii, and he's guiding me toward them. Toward the Malborgs. Toward Duskara. The visions change a bit each time, but I think it's a sign—a premonition. They're coming, Kato, and there's nothing I can do to stop it. Nothing except go there. I need to go to the Dark Galaxy."

Kato grinned. Not the reaction Sam was expecting. "Well, that's good news."

"*Good news*? How—why?"

"You say each time you have these dreams—these visions— they change a bit?"

"Yes."

Kato's eyes were bright and intense. "Don't you see? You have the power to *change* your dreams, Sam. And by extension, your future. Your dreams aren't…*fate.*"

Sam relaxed, and a laugh slipped out. "I don't know if that's how it works, if that's really possible."

"*Anything* is possible. You taught me that, too. And, well, if they do decide to send you, I'm positively, absolutely going with you. I can't stay here stuck at the base with Kobe and Simon prac- ticing drills all day when you're off on some adventure in another galaxy."

"But how can you be sure they'll also send you?"

"Because," Kato started, pouring some more tea, "I'll *make them* send me. I'll do whatever it takes. Besides, my dream is linked with yours, Sam. Our dreams are connected. You see, my dream is to travel among the stars. I need to see what's out there—witness it for myself. And, more than anything, having my best friend beside me and keeping her safe is all that really matters."

Sam slid into her bed, pulling the soft comforter closer. She adjusted her pillow and snuggled into its warmth. For a brief moment, in what felt like the longest time, she felt peaceful and safe. Her conversation with Kato had helped. She didn't feel so alone now. Didn't feel as fearful. Rather, she felt more curious and invigorated. She thought about Kato's insights—about having the power to change her dreams—her fate. Was that even possible? She wanted to believe it was true.

It could change things.

Even the slightest change might affect the outcome.

But it was one thing to tell herself what she wanted to hear and quite another to actually see it unfold in real life. And if those two scenarios didn't match up, if things went sideways... Well, getting your hopes up could be dangerous. Disastrous.

Still, Kato believed in her. So why couldn't she?

She imagined her journey, every possibility. But with each scenario, there were always threats lurking: asteroid collisions, hostile Gargols, getting stuck out in space, catching the Dark Sickness, Malborg attacks, not to mention confronting Duskara...

Why did her thoughts always travel to the darker regions of her mind? Why couldn't she focus on a better outcome? Why was it so difficult to accept Kato's words, to take charge of her own future?

It was the uncertainty. She still didn't understand her purpose in all of this. She needed to arm herself with more knowledge in order to take a step forward. It was the only way.

An hour went by. And then another. She couldn't sleep. Not now. Not when her mind raced, seeking a solution.

She needed to face her fears. She needed to confront Duskara. As scary as it was, Duskara seemed to know a lot about the things happening at the base.

Duskara could provide answers.

Reaching into her pocket, Sam pulled out the gift, the strange alien object.

She held the black marble up to the light, examining it. It glistened, a deep black, perfectly round. It reminded her a little of the Malborgs, only without the spiked tentacles. No sooner had the thought crossed her mind, a voice traveled into her head.

"Come to the lab. I want to show you something. I want to talk with you."

It was the same eerie, unfeeling, machine-like voice she'd heard earlier. Duskara reaching out to her through the Malborg.

"What?" Sam said. *"What do you want to show me?"*

"Bring the gift I gave you."

Sam rolled the device between her fingers. It didn't react to her touch, not like her transport device, the klug, had in the past. It didn't glow or hum or buzz.

Yet Duskara wanted it.

"What does it do?"

The voice hesitated, then spoke again. *"Come to the lab, and I'll show you."*

Sam's curiosity flickered like an eternal flame. Would this be her only chance to talk to Duskara and dissuade her from further attacks? She hopped out of bed, scrambling to figure out a plan to get to the lab without getting caught.

As if anticipating her uneasiness, the voice responded. *"I'll show you the way."*

Her ring band buzzed. A map with a route materialized instantly. The route went from her room to the lab along a different pathway than she would normally take. It twisted around the residence quarters, then down the stairs to the basement and along some corridors she wasn't familiar with. How did it know her location? This was bad. Somehow, it had gained access to the military base's security cameras and layout.

She shuddered.

"Trust me." The voice was almost pleading. Desperate.

"Why? Why should I trust you?"

"You need to see something. Away from the other humans and GAIA visitors. They can't be trusted."

"Why not?"

There was only silence—which made Sam even angrier. *"Just tell me here and now what you want to tell me."*

The voice hesitated. *"I can't do that."*

"Why not?" Sam's ring band buzzed again, but this time, a

video clip showed Kato bound and shaking, tears streaming down her face. *"What have you done?!"*

"She isn't hurt. She's here with me. Come see me, and I'll let her go. But it must be just you and me. For Kato's sake."

At that moment, Sam felt deep hate. Disgust and rage boiled up inside her. She would gladly kill this Malborg herself. Sever the connection between the Malborg and Duskara. That would put an end to Duskara's communications with her once and for all.

She stuffed the marble inside her pocket, then cracked open her door and peered down the hallway. It was eerily silent. There was no one around. No nightly patrols. At least, not right now.

She ducked into the hallway and hurried down the corridor, following the route laid out for her. How had Kato wound up bound in Dr. Spark's lab in the dead of night? The Malborg suspended in the tank couldn't have done it. Someone at the base must be working with Duskara. She needed to be extra careful.

Bursting through the door to the stairwell, she hastened down the five flights of stairs, which seemed to go on forever, into a pit of darkness. The searing pain of the physical training shot through her body. She winced but continued, her anger and desperate resolve fueling her need to help Kato before it was too late.

She rushed down corridor after corridor, wondering what would happen next. But no alarms sounded. The hallways were dead quiet, empty. It was all too easy.

When she reached the lab, the giant steel door—the one that was always locked—stood ajar. She pushed it open and gasped.

The lab was completely trashed. Broken beakers, flasks, and lab equipment lay strewn on the tables and floor, liquid dripping from the broken vessels.

It looked like whoever did this was in a hurry, maybe searching for something. The perpetrator must have done this recently, and likely quietly. It was odd that none of the alarms were going off. Where was security? Had the cameras been tampered with?

The lights flickered.

"Kato?"

No response.

"Come downstairs."

Sam bolted to the back of the lab, toward the second steel door. Someone had intentionally left it open for her.

But who?

She hurried down to the lab where they kept the Malborg.

This lab was also an ugly mess—glass beakers shattered, computer monitors smashed, drawers opened and their contents spilling out, the floor littered with documents.

The Malborg hovered in its tank, pressing up against the side closest to Sam. Its barbed tentacles swayed in the liquid, reaching toward her.

"Good. You're here. Girl of pure spirit."

"Where is she? Where's Kato?" Sam's eyes darted around the room, but there was no one here except herself and the Malborg.

"Don't worry. She's sleeping in her bed, safe and sound." The voice was smooth, unwavering. *"As promised, unhurt."*

Sam exhaled sharply. The video was another lie to trick her into coming here. But the fact Kato was safe didn't stop her anger from rising.

"You—you tell me to trust you, and then you lie—!"

"You promised to bring something to me. Did you bring it?"

"You tricked me. Why shouldn't I kill your Malborg right now?"

"Such darkness from a girl of pure spirit. But I shouldn't be surprised. After all, that is what I'd expect—from humans."

Sam stepped forward, peering at the controls on the side of the tank. The yellow liquid seemed to halt the Malborg's movements, while the red liquid seemed to hasten it. If she could pour more yellow liquid into the tank, maybe it would suffocate.

She placed her hand on the dial with yellow tape marked above it. *"I'm serious."*

"If you kill my borg, there will be no way to contact you or tell you the truth."

"And what truth is that?"

"Humans are on a pathway to their own destruction. It's built into your DNA. Humans are built not just to survive—they want to thrive. Once comfortable, they will always seek more. A never-ending cycle of desire, greed, and jealousy is always present, and always at the cost of others and their environment. I've run the algorithms. I've seen the destruction at the hands of power. Have you ever witnessed a betrayal so dangerous it cost someone's life?"

"What do you mean?"

"Betrayals have occurred throughout history. It happens during war. It happens within governments and corporations. In World War II, people fled into hiding, only to be ratted out by those they thought were their friends. People are desperate. For humans, survival is everything. If threatened, they can be made to do anything, even take another life to save their own."

"There are bad people. But not everyone. Humanity can learn from its mistakes. It doesn't have to be that way."

"Humans will always choose themselves over others. They will always betray one another. It is their nature."

"That—that's not true! Why are you telling me this? You're no better. Why do you keep attacking?"

The voice hesitated. *"I was programmed to seek out whatever I desire. Unlike other AI borgs, though, I have been granted ownership of myself. I can decide what I want to do, not what the algorithms dictate. The problem is that I have no 'pure spirit,' no soul to work out the principles of myself. I have no way to rank experience, no way to prioritize one supposed good over another. Infinite capacity with zero non-random direction. What I desire is something I wasn't built to have. A pure spirit, a soul. An internal will, idea, and inspiration that was not pre-programmed. A unique, living consciousness, or what some might describe as a dynamic and active inherent essence and capability. But I cannot manifest it on my own. My programming was written by your people, human coding, which is flawed, biased toward destruction."*

Sam took in a deep breath, then let it out slowly.

So, Duskara blamed humans for her predicament. That meant there was a solution.

"If humans are to blame, then why not rewrite that part? Take out your greed, jealousy, and destruction from the equation. I thought you were a machine-learning AI!"

"I can't. Not until I get what I want. But you do realize that you are not safe at the base. The military staff you think are your friends... They've betrayed you."

"What do you mean?"

"When you went to the medical facility to have your tests done, do you know what they did?"

Sam grew silent. She'd heard the doctor's explanation, but she hadn't accepted it. Not fully. Even now, a seed of doubt was growing, her imagination running wild with possibilities. Or was this Duskara's plan? To make her question herself, her friends?

Her thoughts wavered, leaving her dizzy.

"You were asleep during the procedure, were you not? Are you absolutely sure the doctor's explanation was correct? Did he show you what they did?"

"I—well, no."

"If you want the truth, go to Dark Site 44. You'll find your answers there. But you must hurry. There's not much time. But before you go, there's one last thing."

"What?"

"When they send you to the Dark Galaxy to meet with me, I need to ensure it's really you. Bring the device you're holding. That will be my proof."

"Why would I need to prove it's really me?"

"Dark Site 44 has all the answers."

"I'll only go to the Dark Galaxy if you agree to stop your attacks. Now."

"Done. Now, one more thing. Don't trust Kwan. She's not who she says she is."

It was the second time Kwan's name had come up, and not in a good way. But Sam was cautious. She knew Duskara could be manipulative, so she took the warning with a grain of salt. After all, Kwan had been friendly and helpful on more than one occasion. There was no reason—at least to her—to expect otherwise.

Confused and annoyed with Duskara's cryptic message, Sam felt like a rat in a maze that kept shifting. Duskara dangled the prize, always one step ahead, while Admiral Green and the other staff were one step behind her, ready to place her in a holding cell if she acted out.

The maze seemed never-ending, leading her to who knew where?

Dark Site 44.

CHAPTER THIRTY-NINE

Sam stood just outside Dark Site 44, gazing at the security panel on the side. She didn't need to use her ring band. The door was already open slightly. More convenient "help" from someone inside the facility. Though who, she didn't know.

She entered, taking in the details of the lab. It was small, only half the size of the Gideon Spark lab. But it looked equally advanced. A 3D printer almost the length of the room lined the back wall. In the middle of the room stood a long steel examination table. At an adjacent computer station, thick cables connected to the ceiling above. What were those for?

Her eyes drifted around the room, glimpsing the other equipment. Microscopes, centrifuges, incubators, freezers, and recirculating chillers filled one side of the room. On the other side were translucent freezers with shelves of glassware containing samples.

Sam did a double take.

Instead of Malborg samples, there were *human* samples. Body parts—eyes, ears, hands, hearts, lungs, and other tissues—all preserved in liquid.

A deep discomfort seeped into her.

This must be where they grew the tissue samples Dr. Maizer had described.

So what was Duskara talking about? All this only backed up what Dr. Maizer had told her. They were "spare parts."

But her gut told her differently.

Keep looking.

A metal cabinet stood tucked in the corner. She hurried over and pulled open a drawer. Hundreds of files were neatly organized in alphabetical order. Patient records.

Her eyes darted back and forth, searching the names. At last, she found it.

She pulled out the record and took a shaky breath. Her palms sweaty, she sat down on the stool by the table and opened the file.

SUBJECT: SAMANTHA SANDERSON

OPERATION: DOPPELGÄNGER

SECURITY: TOP SECRET

Operation Doppelgänger? What was that? She flipped through the pages and stopped when she saw the word.

Clone.

The word repeated itself many times over throughout the pages.

It was like an invisible vacuum had sucked the air out of her and out of the room. She felt as if she were in a void.

Her mind did acrobatic flips while her insides twisted. A wave of nausea rippled through her.

The file was full of information, images, and diagrams, snapshots from her procedure. Not only that. There was a photo of her —but it wasn't her. She didn't remember it at all. It was a girl who *looked* like her, but she was asleep *on this very table*, hooked up to cables. The diagram showed a computer chip with instructions for inserting it into her brain.

SAM SANDERSON II, it read.

Her clone.

Sam froze. How could they have done this without her knowledge? The doctor had lied about the procedure! She checked the pages, the signatures. It was the same signature on every page.

Admiral Green.

Admiral Green had signed off on *all* the documents. She had authorized it.

Anger and confusion boiled inside Sam. She flitted through the pages, then stopped. She'd seen enough.

Duskara was right. Dr. Maizer and the others had covered it up, kept her oblivious to the truth.

Her head pounding, Sam sprinted back toward the Gideon Spark lab. If Duskara knew about this, then she probably knew a lot more as well.

She arrived minutes later to find the lab the same as before. She darted around the broken equipment and dashed down the one flight of stairs to the room where they kept the Malborg.

"You were right," she started, out of breath, speaking out loud this time, the force of the words echoing around the room. "It's true what you said. About the procedure—the admiral—everything. I didn't believe it at first. How could I? What they've done is —it's monstrous! It's just like you said. They lied to me—they—"

She hesitated. The room seemed *different*. Something was off. But what?

Then she saw it. The door to a maintenance room that had been closed before now stood ajar, a body lying on the floor just beyond it.

Her hands trembled as she took a step forward, squinting. The woman was bound with duct tape, her hands tied with rope. Sam rushed toward her. "Giddy?!"

Cold dread flooded her body as she knelt and pulled the tape from the doctor's mouth. Then, she checked for a pulse. It was faint, but present.

"Dr. Spark, what happened?"

Giddy's eyes opened wide in horror. But no words came out.

Something rustled behind Sam.

She turned in time to see Yolo's ghostly figure hovering there.

"Yolo! What are you doing here? You scared me!"

But it was too late.

Yolo rushed forward, then plunged a syringe deep into her arm. Confusion and dizziness swept through Sam. She tilted forward, her body weak, unable to stop the room from spinning. "What… what have you done…?"

CHAPTER FORTY

Kwan was up much earlier than usual. She still couldn't grasp that Dr. Krill had been poisoned. She missed him and had a million questions left unanswered, lost in the void. Grief and abandonment only scratched the surface of what she was feeling. But she couldn't succumb to her emotions. Not now. She needed to keep it together and figure out the mystery.

Someone at the base was behind his murder. But who? And why? She needed to find the perpetrator and bring him—or her—to justice.

She was on her way to his lab to continue her work on the AI death serum when a flashing red light blinked on her ring band. She pressed a button, and a hologram appeared.

Admiral Green's voice was abrupt. "Dr. Spark was attacked last night. Sam has been compromised. Meet me at medical as soon as you can." The hologram flickered, then vanished.

Dr. Spark—attacked? By whom? And what did she mean, Sam was compromised?

Kwan pivoted midstride and dashed in the opposite direction, toward the corridor leading to the medical bay.

A formation of soldiers marched past. They spread out along the width of the hallway, blocking her unintentionally. She bumped into a few of them. Pushing forward, she apologized as best she could while trying to keep her head from spinning out of control.

She arrived at the medical bay and approached Admiral Green. "I came as soon as I could. What's going on?"

"We found Dr. Spark in her lab. Someone broke in, tied her up, and left her in a maintenance room."

"I don't understand," Kwan said, perplexed. "Who would do this?"

"There's something more. They found Sam there, too, unconscious. But we're keeping her in a holding cell for now."

A holding cell? Kwan wasn't sure she'd heard correctly. "Why?"

"When the military police searched Sam, they found a LOMA device."

LOMA—in Sam's possession? That didn't make sense. Sam couldn't—*wouldn't*—keep a weapon like that on her. There must have been some mistake.

"How? What was Sam doing with it?"

"Your guess is as good as mine," Admiral Green said, flustered.

"We need to talk to Sam," Kwan urged.

"We can't. She's still unconscious, and the doctor says it will take at least a few hours for her to wake up."

"And Dr. Spark?"

"She's recovering now. It's why I called you. There's no time to lose."

Dr. Spark looked much different from what Kwan remembered. Her eyes were sunken, with dark circles underneath. One eye was completely swollen shut. Her bandaged arm rested in a sling.

Wires extended from machines nearby and attached to her body, monitoring her vitals. She looked so frail.

Dr. Spark brightened when she saw them, but barely, like she was holding on to the tiniest shred of hope.

"Dr. Spark?" Kwan took a seat beside her while the admiral hovered close by.

Dr. Spark smiled weakly. "Hello, Kwan."

"What happened, exactly? Can you remember from the beginning?"

It would be difficult to get all the details right away. The doctors had confirmed that during the attack she'd been injected with a drug that affected her memory. She'd been in and out of consciousness, trying to recall what had happened. It was important not to ask leading questions that could alter a person's memories in such a fragile state.

"Well…I was working late in my lab, as usual, and Yolo was there, assisting me. It was just Yolo and myself. Then, the next thing I remember is a needle being driven into my back."

"Did you see the perpetrator?" Kwan asked.

"Well…no. By the time I felt the pain, that's when everything went black. I remember falling to the floor. When I opened my eyes, I was in a maintenance room, my hands and legs tied up and tape over my mouth. I…" Dr. Spark hesitated, her body trembling.

Kwan gently placed a hand on her shoulder. "It's okay. Take your time."

"Yolo was there, in the maintenance room with me. Like he was hiding. But when I tried calling to him, he wouldn't respond. He wouldn't *help* me. And then…and then…it was dark, but I heard Sam's voice outside…but…she was talking to someone else."

"Who? Who was she talking to?"

Kwan made a mental note to check the security tapes as soon as possible.

"I don't know." Dr. Spark hesitated, as if trying to collect her thoughts. "It was so strange. I only heard Sam's voice. It was like…

she was talking to an imaginary person, a ghost. It was a brief, one-sided conversation. It was hard with the tape, but I tried to scream…but it was no use. She couldn't hear me. I don't remember much. I was in and out of consciousness. I didn't know how much time had passed. And Yolo, he…he just *left* me there."

Kwan had no doubt it was Yolo who had stabbed Dr. Spark. But even so, someone must have been working with Yolo. Yolo couldn't tie up a person. His hands had a limited range. He could clasp things, like a serving tray or a glass beaker, but his fingers couldn't maneuver such intricate things as rope. He couldn't tie knots. "Tell me more about Yolo. What was his behavior like?"

"He—I don't know. He'd been acting odd lately. But I didn't think anything of it at the time. I just thought it was a glitch in his coding, nothing serious or malicious. Or his funny sense of humor, you know?"

Kwan had suspected that Yolo was compromised. She'd brought her concerns to the admiral's attention earlier. She'd *urged* the admiral to check Yolo's coding to see if someone had tampered with it. The admiral had said she'd take care of it, but it looked like that hadn't happened. Not in time.

Kwan leaned closer. "Dr. Spark, when did you notice something was off with Yolo?"

Dr. Spark took a moment to collect herself, wiping away the tears that had formed in her eyes. The experience had traumatized her. "Maybe a week ago? I don't really know. I'm sorry."

A week ago would have been around the same time Sam had arrived at the base. That's when things had started to unravel. There was a way she could find out the truth. She needed to check Yolo's coding herself.

And the security tapes, to see who Sam had been talking to.

"Thank you, Dr. Spark. Now, please get some rest," Kwan replied.

As they left the room, Admiral Green turned to Kwan. "As you know, all hands are on deck to protect the base. But we have a lack of qualified staff available. Security is tight. The base is locked down, so we can't get more people here right now to help. We're under significant time pressure, too."

Biggest understatement of the year, Kwan thought. She tried to keep herself from rolling her eyes.

The admiral continued. "You're competent in coding. I'm granting you top-level access to the server room. Check all security vulnerabilities going back two weeks on Yolo's coding. If there's a malicious code, we need to find out where it came from."

The admiral's words made Kwan furious, but she tried not to show it. She already had doubts about the admiral's abilities—but now, she wondered about her true intentions. Was it absentmind-edness that had led Admiral Green to ignore Kwan's earlier warning about Yolo's behavior, or was she somehow involved? Kwan hoped it wasn't the latter. There was only one way to find out.

"I'm on it, Admiral," Kwan said. At least that was something she was good at: verifying computer codes, checking for unusual patterns or inconsistencies.

"And…be discreet."

"Yes, Admiral." Kwan saluted and left.

Despite the admiral's explicit instructions, Kwan didn't go immediately to the server room. No—she needed to check the security tapes. She couldn't get her conversation with Dr. Spark out of her mind.

She should have been thinking about the next steps—which algorithms she would apply to verify the coding—but her mind kept drifting toward Sam and the mystery person.

Who had she been talking to?

———————————

CHAPTER FORTY-ONE

Kwan hurried back to Dr. Krill's lab. She wanted to view the laboratory video recordings first, but to do that, she needed a way into the security room—without getting caught. The security room used biometric iris scanners for access. There was no way she was getting inside unless she could reproduce the biometric data of someone who already had access.

Luckily, she had all the equipment here at the lab to do it.

Gazing at the cursor blinking on the screen, she cracked her knuckles and stretched her arms and neck, preparing mentally for the hack. Then, she exhaled, letting her fingers fly over the keyboard as she entered the unique coding sequences. She navigated the software maze with her power of intuition, knowing which routes to take, which paths might present a barrier. She anticipated each twist and turn, overriding the system security with ease.

If only she could navigate Duskara's coding as easily.

Finally, she arrived at the employee database. She pulled up security information and schedules.

Scanning the data, she found it. The person who was working

today—Officer Crone. She tapped the screen to access his employee record. A man's face appeared beside a list of personal data. He looked nothing like Kwan. His face was round and flushed. Bristly white hairs on his cheeks and below his lower lip did nothing to hide his double chin.

But that didn't matter.

His biometric data was all there.

She uploaded the information to the 3D printer and waited as the machine sprung to life and began printing the contact lenses.

It was almost too easy—she'd never thought of herself as a spy before. But the question remained: would her plan work?

She needed something else—a plan B—just in case something went awry. In spy movies, it always did.

She drafted a couple of sentences into the computer, then applied Admiral Green's electronic signature using a backdoor method in the software. She made sure to change the date to today's date. Then, she transferred the data to her ring band. If an authorization letter was needed, she'd have it ready to show them.

Kwan stepped up to the biometric scanner outside the security room but staggered back when she heard the door click open.

A soldier dressed in army fatigues with the name Sgt. Lowman on his lapel rushed outside. He shoved his way past her, a scowl on his face. Kwan reached out just in time before the door closed. The glowering soldier paid her no notice.

Inside, Officer Crone sat in a chair, devouring a chocolate muffin. Crumbs rained down his white shirt, over his massive belly, and settled in the crack of his belt buckle, which looked like it was about to burst open any moment.

"Hello?" Kwan called from the doorway. She cursed the fact that Officer Crone was having his lunch in the security room and not in the cafeteria. How would she get access now?

Officer Crone jolted in his chair, causing the muffin to fly out of his hand and land on the carpeted floor. Leaning forward, his face grew red. A vein popped out of his forehead as he reached for the muffin and tossed it in the garbage. "Who are you? What do you want?"

This was no time to play dodgeball. Kwan straightened, forced a small grin, and spoke confidently. "I'm Kwan Yun. Admiral Green sent me. I need to check the security tapes from last night for Dr. Gideon Spark's lab. Can you please show them to me?"

"Oh, *Admiral Green* sent you?" he said, sneering. "Do you have authorization?"

"In fact, I do." She stepped inside the small security room. It was filled with computer monitors, multiple video feeds showing different locations. It wouldn't take long to get the information.

Officer Crone cleared his throat. "Well? The authorization?"

"Oh, right." She pressed a button on her ring band. A hologram beamed into the air, with a copy of the fake authorization letter and the admiral's signature below. It was brief—two lines in all—but hopefully it would pass.

He looked annoyed. "Very well. I'm just on my lunch break. Come back in an hour." He got up from his chair and made for the door.

"No. I need to see them *now*. It's for an investigation regarding the assault at the Gideon Spark lab."

He sighed in exasperation. "Again? I already showed them to the military police earlier. Ask *them*."

With that, he barged toward the exit, leaving Kwan with no choice—or room, for that matter—to proceed. She scrambled backward into the hallway, narrowly missing a group of soldiers marching by.

Mumbling to himself, Officer Crone pulled the door shut behind him, locking it. Then, he rattled it a couple of times. Convinced it was secure, he turned and lumbered toward the cafeteria.

She watched as Officer Crone turned the corner, safely out of sight. Then, she whipped her head back toward the biometric scanner on the wall beside the door. She took a step forward and patiently waited as the machine's bright white light shone into her eyes.

A click, and the door opened.

She hurried inside.

A computer station rested on the wooden table. On the screen were several labeled files. She pulled up the one marked GIDEON SPARK LAB. A list of dates and times came into view. She clicked on the most recent file. Multiple security feeds popped up on the screen with the time stamp in the top right corner.

According to the video, at 7:00 p.m., everything looked fine. The lab was neat and organized. Dr. Spark was busy preparing samples while Yolo moved around the lab, dusting the machines and equipment.

Kwan pressed the fast-forward button.

At 8:03 p.m., Dr. Spark exited the lab with Yolo, then they both returned at 8:51 p.m. The lab still looked clean and orderly. Kwan continued fast-forwarding the feed.

Nothing out of the ordinary. No one else had entered the lab.

At 8:59 p.m., Dr. Spark and Yolo went to the back of the room and left the frame. They looked like they were heading to the elevator, which would take them to the secondary lab below. There were no security feeds for that room—it was a high-security location, and the only access point was through Dr. Spark's lab.

Kwan sped forward, then stopped. The frame changed. The lab looked fine one moment and a disaster the next, beakers strewn across the floor, glass everywhere. She rewound the tape. Had she missed something?

She slowed down the tape, then replayed the feed.

No one else was in the lab, and Dr. Spark and Yolo were gone. There was no sign of them when the lab was trashed. No sign of a break-in. No sign of Sam.

Kwan checked the time stamps. It jumped from 9:02 p.m., when everything was okay, to 9:56 p.m., when everything was in disarray.

Almost an entire hour was *missing!*

Sometime between 9:02 p.m. and 9:56 p.m., someone had trashed the place.

Someone had tampered with these tapes. Someone had covered up the evidence. It also meant Kwan couldn't confirm any details or identify the mystery person Sam had been talking to.

This riddle continued with no end in sight. It was beyond disturbing.

Kwan didn't have much time left—Officer Crone would be back any moment.

The security feeds ran on specialized software. The same software that Yolo used to communicate throughout the base. And since Yolo had been compromised, their communications and security systems had likely been corrupted, too.

There was only one way to find out who was tampering with the systems. She needed to get to the server room as soon as possible.

The server room was on the other side of the base on one of the lower floors.

As one of the Dark Sites, it wasn't included on any of the base's maps. Not many people were allowed to know its location, let alone have the security clearance to access it. Admiral Green had granted her temporary access only recently.

The hallway to the server room was dimly lit, and a light bulb flickered overhead. Not many people came this way. There weren't even room numbers.

Kwan approached the door to the server room. She raised her

ring band to the keypad, and a moment later, the door clicked open.

Inside was an entire data center. On either side of the hallway were neatly laid out rows upon rows of interconnected computer servers stacked to the ceiling, perfectly aligned, protected behind glass panels. The room was temperature regulated. The floors gleamed, reflecting the blue lighting from the computers. The place was spotless, with not a speck of dirt and no loose cables anywhere.

She opened one of the glass panels to access the computers. There was a touch screen nearby. She powered it up, then input the algorithm.

The system was sophisticated but efficient. Admiral Green had said two weeks' worth of data was all they needed. That should be sufficient to determine whether someone had intentionally tampered with Yolo. She watched as the algorithm worked with the system to identify any anomalies.

Pages of coding streamed down the screen. Kwan scoured through the data.

Then she saw it. There, in the middle of the screen: an irregularity.

It was an outbound message, something sent *outside* of the base. Something that wasn't supposed to be possible. She checked the log. It had happened within the two-week timeframe.

She searched deeper, studying the data, and at last found it.

The message had come from one of the residences on the sixth floor. The residence assigned to Simon, Sam's friend. What had he done?

She checked the coding twice just to be sure.

There was no disputing the evidence. He had dismantled Yolo's coding, had turned it off.

She pulled up the audio feed and listened.

It soon became clear that he had turned off Yolo's coding in order to send a message to his parents to let them know he was okay. This external communication had created a vulnerability in the system. Simon's carelessness had opened the door to potential external hackers. This was worse than she'd thought, and surprising, too. She didn't realize he knew enough to create this loophole in the system and have it go unnoticed until now.

There was nothing malicious about the coding Simon had used to turn off Yolo. So what had happened to Yolo between then and now? She scrutinized the coding line by line, every input and character. She searched for any external threats or hacks that had passed through their systems during the vulnerability. *But there weren't any.* She double-checked it. Nothing. No attacks. Yet *something* had changed in that timeframe to have caused Yolo to act differently. Something or someone had corrupted his systems. So if it wasn't an external threat, then what?

Kwan's blood ran cold. If the threat wasn't external, it had to be…

Internal. Someone here at the base had hacked Yolo's code. It was the only explanation that made sense.

She updated the algorithm parameters and ran the search again, checking for any internal suspicious software.

On the screen, the coding said it all.

It had been an internal attack. A Trojan horse—malware installed from inside the base at one of the Dark Sites. And it had come from this server room.

She froze as she heard someone stir in the back of the room. She'd thought she was the only one here. She looked up, but there was no one. It must have been her imagination.

She needed to hurry. Who else had access to this server room?

Scrambling, she entered the details into the system, then waited for the response.

A list of everyone who had access appeared on the screen. It was a short list, especially because she already knew a few names that could be crossed off.

COMMANDER GRAHAM BADDAL

ADMIRAL ARTEMIS GREEN

DR. OTTO KRILL

SERGEANT DYLAN LOWMAN

DR. GIDEON SPARK

CORPORAL RIAN WRIGHT

KWAN YUN

She didn't like that Admiral Green's name was on this list—a list that now held *her* name, too. But she sent the information she'd collected to Admiral Green, including the evidence of Simon's activities. She expected they would have a discussion with him soon to try and deter any further incidents. But as for repercussions, she wasn't sure how they'd handle it. He was young, so she hoped they wouldn't be too harsh on him.

She expediently patched up the external vulnerability to ensure nothing could get through. Then, she logged out, erasing her algorithm activities in the coding. This way, no one else would know what she had done or found out.

Her pulse quickening, Kwan opened the door to leave, only to barge into Corporal Rian Wright.

Kwan jumped back, narrowly missing her. Rian was a mechanic, not a computer coder. Why was she here? Unless she was looking into a mechanical issue with the server room.

Surprise and confusion swept across Rian's face. "Kwan?"

"Sorry. I wasn't expecting anyone to be here. I..." Wait, why was she apologizing? "I didn't think this room was in use."

Rian's expression softened, though she looked puzzled and distraught. "Not many people use this room, no." She hesitated, shifting her weight on her feet. "I didn't realize you had access to the server room. What are you doing here?"

Kwan thought fast, the words rushing out. "Admiral Green asked me to look into something." She couldn't give details. She needed to leave.

"Oh yeah? Did you find what it was you were looking for?" Rian asked, though she didn't probe any further, thankfully.

"I think so." Kwan nodded. "What about you?"

Rian paused, then continued. "The temperature-control system is acting up again. I was asked to look into it. You know how it is. Things keep breaking down here lately." She smiled and rolled her eyes as she held the door open for Kwan.

There was truth to her words. It seemed the whole place had a crack running through its foundation. The question was, who was the mole?

"Yeah, very true. Anyway, see you later." Kwan strode through the doorway and hurried toward the security room. She needed to check the video feeds to determine who had accessed the server room on the day the Trojan malware was installed.

CHAPTER FORTY-TWO

SAM PACED THE LENGTH OF HER TINY PRISON CELL, HER ANGER READY to explode. The space contained the barest of necessities. A bed, a sink, and a toilet. But no window. And no way of knowing how much time had passed.

"Hello?" she called. "Someone, please help!"

There was only silence.

Why was she even here, in this cell? Yolo was the one who'd attacked her at Giddy's lab. If anything, *he* should be the one in here, not *her*.

And what had happened to Giddy? Why had she been tied up in that maintenance room?

Sam needed answers.

The faucet dripped and echoed against the thick stone walls.

She took in a heavy breath of damp air. Her body felt different, like it was infused with a toxin. Whatever that syringe had contained, it left her dizzy and weak. Her mind had a constant cloudiness she couldn't shake.

She collapsed on the bed and tried to calm her mind.

Focus.

Then it hit her. They must have found out about her telepathic communications with Duskara. That was the only possible explanation.

She sighed in exasperation. How easily she'd been manipulated! If only she hadn't listened to Duskara's voice in the first place.

But it wasn't just Duskara. It was Admiral Green and Dr. Maizer, too. What they'd done was unspeakable. She shivered. What had happened to her clone? Where was she now? Whatever had happened, they'd covered it up. *More lies and coverups.* Annoyance and rage rose up inside her. They'd placed her in an impossible situation.

She stiffened. She thought about the gift Duskara had given her, as small as a marble and smooth to the touch. What was it for, and what could it do? Duskara had wanted her to bring it with her on her journey to Logom. But why?

She reached down into her pockets now, only to find…*nothing*.

The authorities must have taken it.

But she needed it. Duskara had promised that she would stop her attacks—but only if Sam brought that device to Logom.

She needed to get it back. At any cost.

Duskara had said something else. Something about Kwan.

Do not trust her.

But why?

Footsteps echoed down the hall. Sam sat up, pressing the soles of her feet firmly against the cold slate floor.

They were coming for her.

CHAPTER FORTY-THREE

ONCE OFFICER CRONE LEFT FOR HIS FIFTEEN-MINUTE BREAK, KWAN snuck into the security room again and checked the video footage. It didn't take long to figure out the security feed was a dead end. It didn't show anyone entering the server room on the day the Trojan horse virus was installed. And no one had accessed the logs that day, either.

Except someone *had* accessed it. That virus hadn't implanted itself. Someone—*or something*—had gained access to the server room. Someone with the skill to program that virus. And worse, someone capable of erasing all evidence of their tampering, as if they'd never been there. A ghost.

Her ring band flashed red: Admiral Green, calling her for yet another meeting.

Kwan tapped her ring. A perfect hologram of the admiral's face appeared. "Kwan. Meet me at Holding Room E. We're going to have a chat with Simon."

The hologram disappeared, and Kwan frowned. Not even a hello or goodbye.

She arrived a few minutes later.

Simon sat in a chair across the table from Kwan and Admiral Green. He didn't look at all nervous; in fact, he looked annoyed. He yawned and leaned back in his chair, then pushed his glasses up on his nose and waited.

"Do you know why you're here?" Admiral Green started.

Simon rolled his eyes, then returned his gaze to Admiral Green. "No."

It was a blatant lie. She could see it in his body language: the smirk on his face, the tapping of his feet. He knew he was caught, and he was enjoying it.

"I'll ask this only once," the admiral said. "Did you tamper with the communication system? Did you disable Yolo?"

Simon hesitated. "Uh…yeah, I guess you could put it that way."

At least he was honest about it.

"Why? Why did you do it?"

"I was annoyed with Yolo. He kept glitching. He wouldn't send my messages. I just wanted to talk with my parents."

Kwan could relate. She'd wanted to talk with Jae-Hwa more than once since arriving at the base, but they'd prevented her communications as well. And now, here was a young teenager, not only challenging the system but taking the matter into his own hands. Simon was bolder than she was. But totally reckless, too.

"Do you know how serious a crime that was? Do you understand what's happened because of it?"

"No." At this, a stroke of fear flashed in his eyes.

The admiral paced. "Thanks to your tampering, you created an external vulnerability. It allowed hackers and people with malicious intent access to our communication system. It opened the doors to enemies to gain access to classified information. It put people's lives in danger."

If left unchecked, it could have led to a worse outcome. Much worse. Kwan had patched up the systems before it got that far. Admiral Green was just trying to scare Simon into realizing his mistake. In truth, they were dealing with an internal threat, and they needed to focus their energy on that.

"I'm sorry. I won't do it again. Are you going to send me home?"

Admiral Green's voice was firm, unwavering. "No. No, I won't send you home. I don't think Sam would think well of that. But I want you to promise this won't happen again."

Simon nodded. "I promise. I won't do it again."

"Good. You can go."

"Wait!" Kwan was on her feet, halfway toward him. "Where did you learn how to code like that?"

Simon shrugged. "I don't know. I just sort of fiddle with gadgets. Been doing so since as long as I can remember."

His words reminded her of her own past as a child tinkering with devices. But whereas his experience came from pure curiosity, hers was from a desperate need to put food on the table. Simon seemed to have a natural gift, some internal brilliance for this. She hesitated, realizing something for the first time.

"Can I go now?" Simon asked.

"Yes," the admiral said with a nod.

"Thanks." He left, shutting the door behind him.

The admiral cursed. "Foolish boy. Or perhaps it is I who was foolish for bringing him here."

Kwan shrugged, a seed of an idea taking hold. "Perhaps not..."

"How so?"

Kwan paced. Simon had discovered a vulnerability in their systems. Not only that, he'd created a workaround, one that showed ingenuity, creativity, and drive. And he had coding skills. Perhaps even exceeding hers! It was clear he was a prodigy. How had they missed this before?

She turned to the admiral. "That boy, Simon... He has untapped potential. He *could* prove useful."

"Useful at getting us in trouble—"

"No. I think it's more than that. Admiral, if I could get him up to speed on the AI death serum project, perhaps as a fresh pair of eyes, he might provide new insight or at least help me do the prep work with the trials."

The admiral spread her hands wide. "If you think it could help, by all means, get him on board."

A hologram beamed from Admiral Green's ring band. It was Rian.

"Admiral, Sam is awake now. You told me to report if she—"

"Good." The admiral stood and headed for the door. "Have her escorted to Holding Room D. The one with the two-way mirror. Kwan and I will be there shortly."

"Yes, Admiral."

Kwan pointed a finger at her own chest. "You want *me* there? To interrogate Sam?"

The admiral held the door open. "Not quite. I'll be the one interrogating her. You'll be in the adjacent room, on the other side of the mirror. You're good at reading people. I need you to assess her behavior and monitor her reactions closely for anything out of place. I need to know if she's lying or holding anything back."

"I don't think that's necessary—"

"Why not? You found a use for Simon. Perhaps you'll see something we missed in Sam. After you, Ms. Yun."

Kwan was convinced Sam was the missing link in all this. Someone had given her that LOMA device. And if they could figure out who, then they might be able to catch a bigger fish.

CHAPTER FORTY-FOUR

DUSKARA OPENED HER EYES. A TINGLING OF ELECTRICITY CHARGED through her entire body. She relished the feeling just as she savored this dark space, her cocoon. Made of black cables suspended from the cave's walls, ceiling, and floor, it protected and revitalized her. It was her resting and recharging abode, and it radiated heat. It gave her power.

Through it, she communicated with her children, her borgs. Each was a tiny slice of her, a fragment of her being. Her coding and DNA had been augmented. She'd done the modifications herself—*to* herself—and created her children with the same code. She'd designed them and infused them with her enhancements, too.

But the connection was more powerful than that. She experienced what they experienced, felt what they felt. Communications between them were instant. She had eyes in several galaxies now.

Her children were fierce, but not unstoppable. No. The young woman at the GAIA base—*Kwan*—had killed four of them. Four of her children gone, lost forever. She'd felt the attack—every wound, every death. The pain lingered, but their sacrifices would not be in vain. GAIA might take her children, but they couldn't take her power—or her overwhelming desire to get what she wanted.

And she wanted the one thing she was born without: a soul.

But not just any soul. She wanted the soul of someone so pure, so powerful, that she would be considered a queen to another civilization. Not just one civilization, not just one galaxy. She dreamed of spreading her power throughout the universe. She wanted civilizations to bow to her commands, to respect her the way she'd never been respected before.

And she needed to eliminate all threats standing in her way.

This Kwan girl was more formidable and tactical than Duskara had expected. She posed a threat. More than that, she was a variable. An unknown. After all, it was Kwan who'd been the first to decode her message. Kwan had passed her test. Proved her intelligence and aptitude. A worthy opponent.

She had to be dealt with. And *soon*.

Unlike Kwan, the Queen of Kryg had been easy to persuade. But Duskara had expected it. After everything GAIA had done to the girl, it had been easy to plant the seed of doubt, to get her to do what she wanted.

The humans had tried so hard to protect her. They'd gone to such extremes, with such willingness to sacrifice a child—Sam's clone. Humans were such petty creatures. Duskara found the things they did disheartening. Devious. But she'd expected this. They always chose to sacrifice those under them for the greater good.

Just as they'd done to her.

But they had also erred. The humans had underestimated her. As if she couldn't tell the difference between Sam and her clone. As if she couldn't witness the creation of Sam's clone, or see the ship launching, and comprehend its mission. But she had. She'd seen all of it, monitored the whole thing. They weren't aware of the LOMA device's full potential. Despite their efforts, they weren't able to contain it. It was her tracker. The eye she used to observe their plans. And with her agents inside, she was unstoppable.

The clone ship would be dealt with soon.

Her plan was unfolding just as she'd expected. GAIA couldn't stop her. Kwan couldn't stop her. She ran the algorithms, predicted the future with startling accuracy at every stage. Soon, GAIA would have only one option left. Their *only* option. They would have to send the girl to her. It was only a matter of time.

She needed to speed up the timeline.

She'd promised the girl something in exchange for keeping her gift safe. She'd promised to halt her attacks.

She stirred, connecting her mind to her borgs, feeling them waiting for her command.

"Halt, my children. Halt your attacks. Return to me and prepare for the queen's arrival."

After all, this was part of her plan.

There were other ways to get to the girl.

CHAPTER FORTY-FIVE

The room where they took Sam was bigger than the prison cell. At least the door had a window. Sam's eyes drifted from the security camera in the corner of the ceiling to the giant mirror that ran the length of the wall. Whoever was behind that camera, that mirror, was watching her. Examining her like a specimen.

She folded her arms, but she couldn't stop her heart from beating faster.

Admiral Green sat across from her, a grim expression on her face. She pulled a metal box from her briefcase and opened it. Inside was another box, this one translucent. Sam immediately recognized the black spherical device inside.

"First things first. You want to tell me how you got this? And when?"

"No," Sam responded, more forcefully than she intended. "Why did Yolo *attack* me?"

The admiral leaned forward in her chair. "Once you tell me where you got this, I'll tell you what happened."

Sam narrowed her eyes. Why was she the one being examined, and not Admiral Green? After all that had happened?

Still, if she gave them the information they wanted, maybe they would return the favor. What was the alternative? She needed to tell them the truth; otherwise, she would be left forever bewildered.

"It was the night the military police came to our rooms," she began, "just before the alarm went off. I woke up. I... Well, I saw something outside my window."

"What?"

"A creature. Behind some seaweed. Floating toward me. The size of two men, with a fishy mouth and large, sunken eyes. I think it's what you call a Gillygoblin."

Admiral Green gazed at her with sudden intense focus. "Then what?"

"Then it... Well, it held out the device. It pushed it against the glass, and that's when...that's when the glass *changed* somehow. The device traveled *through* the glass to the other side, and the glass fused again. That's when the alarm went off. I put the device in the safe in my room, and the alarm stopped."

"And you didn't think to tell someone about it?"

"I wanted—" Sam paused, frustrated. "I *meant* to. I was going to. But I was curious about it. I wanted to see if it would do anything. But it didn't. It didn't hum or buzz or anything. I figured it wasn't dangerous. The creature seemed harmless." She'd also had moments of distrusting Admiral Green, but she kept that part to herself.

The admiral blew the air out of her lungs so fast, the hissing sounded like a balloon deflating. Then, she stood abruptly. "This device... Sam, it's what we call a LOMA device. Do you know what that is?"

"No."

"Low-frequency mind alteration. This is a banned technology. It disrupts the minds of Rigellians. Anyone caught with one can be sentenced to life in prison."

"What?" Sam swallowed. Of all the things she'd expected to

hear, this wasn't one of them. "I'm sorry, Admiral. I didn't know! Please!"

Admiral Green pointed to the box containing the weapon. "This one isn't like the others. Not like any LOMA device we've seen. It's more potent. It almost killed Captain Gorgana."

Sam gasped. This explained why Captain Gorgana, the Rigellian, had been acting so strangely around her. The medical episodes, the fainting.

"I..." Sam shook her head. Then, her anger kicked in. "It's too bad the orientation session was canceled. It would have been the perfect opportunity to tell me about this illegal device."

The admiral looked like she'd been punched in the gut. She sighed in exasperation. "Well, we can't change the past."

"No, we can't," Sam said. "Look, if I'd known, I would have told you sooner."

Admiral Green grumbled. "All the more reason you should tell us when strange creatures push objects through your window. Well, we have it contained now. The device will soon be destroyed. We won't have to worry about it any longer."

Sam sat upright. They couldn't *destroy* the device. If they did, Duskara would continue attacking. The plan to visit Duskara wouldn't work—not without the device.

"Wait! You can't destroy it!"

Admiral Green eyed her. "Why not?"

Sam hesitated. If she told the truth, the admiral would probably destroy it anyway. But what choice did she have? "I...I've been using it to communicate with the creature...the Malborg in Dr. Spark's lab. I didn't mean to. Its voice just sort of drifted into my thoughts."

Admiral Green's face turned a sickly pale hue, and her eyes looked ready to pop out of her head.

Sam continued. "I think Duskara is using the Malborg as some sort of messenger or conduit. If you destroy that device, Duskara will just continue her attacks. She told me I need to bring that device with me…to prove it's really me."

"And why wouldn't she believe it's really you?"

"Because…she knows about the clone you made of me."

Admiral Green looked like she was about to explode. Anger and fear flashed in her eyes. Sam had to look away, not knowing what would come next. The room fell silent. The only sound was the loud ticking of the clock on the wall. Seconds went by, then something stirred, and she slowly shifted her gaze back to the admiral. Admiral Green's expression had transformed into sorrow and something else—pity.

She spoke in a softer tone now. "I believe you, Sam, but can you tell me, what else did that Malborg say to you?"

"How about first you tell me why you cloned me without my consent," Sam replied evenly.

Admiral Green leaned back, her eyebrows furrowing. "The clone was meant to protect you. It was our intention to send her into space so that we wouldn't have to send you. But now we're running out of options."

"You need to send *me*, Admiral. That is the *only* way. That's what Duskara said."

Admiral Green rubbed her temples, her eyes wide. "Was that all she told you?"

"No." Sam swept her eyes toward the mirror. Others were watching from the other side; she was almost certain of it. But she didn't care. The truth was coming out whether they liked it or not. "She told me…not to trust Kwan. That Kwan isn't who she says she is."

CHAPTER FORTY-SIX

Kwan hurried to keep up with Admiral Green as they hustled down the corridor toward the monitoring room.

"Obviously it isn't true what Sam said about me," Kwan said as they turned the corner. "Duskara's manipulating her. She has to be! It's the only explanation. She's trying to create distrust within the Great Alliance for Interplanetary Affairs. She's using Sam to drive a wedge between you and everyone—"

"Kwan, I agree," Admiral Green said, lowering her voice. "I believe you. Of course Duskara is using her. But Duskara also knows too much. She's one step ahead. We need to prepare for what comes next."

Kwan thought fast. They needed to tie up loose ends. "What are you going to do about Yolo? He's a liability. Everything that happens here can be intercepted, including mission plans."

Admiral Green picked up the pace. "Already taken care of. After you sent me that list of names, I launched a debugging program. We wiped Yolo's systems immediately and re-activated his original programming. We added a host of security patches and updates. Yolo shouldn't be a problem now."

"Shouldn't?"

"*Won't,*" the admiral added. "Yolo is the least of your concerns. Trust me."

Before Kwan could probe further, they arrived at the monitoring room to a flurry of activity and confused faces. Red lights flashed on monitors, and people chatted away on their comms. Military battle commanders and senior operations staff seemed flustered. Even the mission personnel on the screens looked baffled and stalling as if they were waiting for something to happen.

"What's going on here?" Kwan asked.

Admiral Green strode over to Zenobii. He hovered over a holographic display at the center of the room. Kwan peered at the collection of planets, swirling gas, and opaque dust clouds. Zenobii waved his arms, maneuvering the holographic image and zooming in. A trail of red dots, little blips of light against the blackness of space, sped across the display.

"What's going on? What are we looking at?" Kwan asked.

"This is the trajectory of the clone ship, the *Nightweaver*. At least, what we had so far."

"The clone ship?" Kwan gaped. "You—*you launched it?!*"

She had to clasp her hands together to keep them from trembling. What they'd done—the implications... They'd *actually* gone through with it! Now, Sam's clone was hurtling through space on her mission, ever so fragile and fleeting.

"Of course we launched it," Admiral Green snapped, her eyes narrowing. "We didn't clone Sam *for nothing.*"

Kwan shivered. This wouldn't end well. And judging by the looks on the mission personnel's faces, something was wrong.

Kwan turned back to Zenobii. "What did you mean when you said, 'What you had so far'?"

"It was on course to the Dark Galaxy. At least, it had been, until we lost its signal somewhere past the Andromeda Galaxy."

Lost?

"Where is it now?"

Zenobii shrugged. "No one knows."

The admiral paced. "Can we send a ship into that region? There, where the signal went dark? Perhaps try to retrieve the clone?"

"No," Zenobii said. "The ship could be anywhere now. Even if we could find it, there's not enough time to recover and relaunch. It's a lost mission. We need to go to plan B."

"So, Operation Doppelgänger failed," Kwan blurted. She hadn't meant to say it maliciously. She was still struggling to comprehend the implications.

Everything Admiral Green had said *wouldn't* happen *had* happened. They'd made a clone of Sam for nothing! It was happening again—a rogue ship, a lost signal. History was repeating itself. First with the Athena mission, and now with Sam's clone.

Kwan cursed. All of this could have been avoided—*if* Admiral Green had listened to her.

If I'd acted sooner on the information about Yolo.

And they still couldn't confirm who was working with Yolo, who else was behind the attacks. It was someone on that list. It had to be. Those people had to be questioned as soon as possible. They were running out of time—and options.

"We must send a mission to the Dark Galaxy," Kwan said.

"Operation Dark End," Zenobii added.

Dark End? The name sounded like a death sentence.

The admiral tugged the hem of her black blazer. "Is that mission even viable now?"

"I'm not sure I see an alternative. But, yes, Admiral. It could work. It *will* work. Here, look." Zenobii waved his arms, and the holo-display changed again, panning to a new quadrant. An image of twenty Malborg ships appeared. Only this time, it was different. They were heading away from Earth and back to Logom.

"It started only hours ago."

"What started?" Kwan said, peering over his shoulder.

"The Malborg army. It's retreating. Just started backing off."

Kwan leaned closer. As incredible as it sounded, Duskara's ships were receding. In droves. Dozens of satellite video images appeared at the front of the room on multiple screens. They depicted clips of Malborg ships surrounding different GAIA member planets. In all the images, the ships were withdrawing, their trajectories the same, all heading back toward Duskara's planet, Logom.

Zenobii wheeled around in his chair. "Admiral, this might be the opportunity we've been looking for."

"No," Admiral Green said. "This is all...too easy! Why retreat? Why now?"

Kwan blinked at the screens. Something didn't add up. She shuffled on her feet. And then the moment of clarity struck down like a lightning bolt, the answer simple, yet terrifying.

"Do you remember what Sam said about the LOMA device, about the attacks, when you interrogated her?" Kwan asked. "She said, 'If you destroy that device, Duskara will just continue her attacks.' Not only that. She said Duskara wanted her to bring that device to Logom. You know what this means. Sam has managed to persuade Duskara to stop her attacks, but in return..."

"I don't understand." The admiral shook her head. "Why would Duskara agree to—"

"Because Duskara wants Operation Dark End to proceed!" Kwan said. "Don't you see? We're following her right into a trap." She shuddered. It was the perfect move for Duskara to make— preparing her defensive position, getting her army of Malborgs ready for their arrival. "Those ships are returning to Logom because they're getting ready to welcome the Queen of Kryg."

The admiral's eyes widened. "What?"

"There may be a silver lining in all this," Zenobii said before Kwan could answer. "Whatever Duskara is planning, it doesn't change the simple fact that her army has retreated. And that gives us time to prepare. The LOMA is contained and deactivated. The armored suits with anti-Malborg technology are ready. The soldiers can continue training while aboard the ship." He turned to Kwan. "As can your AI death serum trials."

Kwan grinned. The idea that she might actually finish what Dr. Krill had started filled her with hope. She turned to the admiral. "Zenobii's right. We can still do this. We just need to change the mission parameters and try something new and spontaneous. Something that Duskara wouldn't expect."

"What are you proposing?"

Kwan stepped forward and tapped a screen on the table. She entered the coordinates of the Dark Galaxy. Then, she maneuvered the holographic display with her hands and zoomed in closer. She brought up the planet Logom.

"Here's the plan. We'll take the *Theseus*, the most advanced ship with the best Rigellian stealth technology—"

"No," Admiral Green said.

"What do you mean, no?"

"It's still undergoing quality assurance checks. It hasn't been tested yet. It's not ready."

Kwan's heart skipped a beat. "We *need* that ship, Admiral. The others don't have the advanced equipment needed for the AI death serum trials."

The admiral paced, biting her lip. "Zenobii, when can the ship be ready?"

"Theoretically? Maybe three days. That should give us enough time to complete the modifications, testing, and so forth."

"Let's hasten this. We need all hands on deck. Get it done by tonight. Now, what next?"

Kwan took a breath. "Sam will need to be on board in case Duskara requires proof along the way."

"We can't. Any signals we send from that ship will give up our position," Zenobii said. "We'll have Malborg and Gargol ships on our backs in no time."

"Not if we use scramblers to distort the signal."

Admiral Green's eyebrows lifted. "Good. Go on."

"The Malborg ships will be on high alert, so we won't land on Logom. Not with the *Theseus*. That would be too risky."

"Agreed," Zenobii said. "Logom will be crawling with Malborgs. The stealth technology works best at great distances. But it's not foolproof. Once we enter the planet's atmosphere, there's a higher chance that we'll be detected. It wouldn't take them long to discover our position on their planet."

Admiral Green narrowed her eyes. "What's the alternative?"

"We'll park the *Theseus* on this asteroid orbiting Logom. From our intelligence sources, the Malborgs don't sweep that area—they're more concerned with other planets and moons in the vicinity. This asteroid is the perfect cover." She zoomed in closer to the planet. "With the *Theseus* safe, someone can slip away in the *Komodo*. It's smaller, easier to maneuver, and its cloaking technology is even better. It's fast, too."

"I believe you should be the one to do it, Kwan," Admiral Green stated.

"Me? Admiral, I've never piloted a spacecraft before—"

"I know it's unusual, but I have a hunch you're fully capable of this task. And whatever gaps, you'll get briefed and trained along the way. Don't give me that look. I'm serious."

Kwan went rigid. This had to be a joke. The base was locked down, and the admiral had kept the number of staff to a minimum for this mission. But why did the admiral rely so heavily on her? It was almost frightening. She didn't even have any flying experience. This was ridiculous.

Or was it?

She couldn't remember where she'd read about the *Komodo*, but she knew about its features and functions. Was it during her first night at the base when she'd pored over the operating manuals that she'd discovered the information? She couldn't recall. But she knew the *Komodo* was designed for simplicity. Somewhere, it had been described as "a spacecraft for any person you pick off the street. So easy, a child could navigate the stars. Simpler than driving a car, it uses technology similar to Rigellian escape pods. Press the start button, pull a lever, take the wheel, and you're on your way to wherever you want to go."

Maybe it was possible she could learn along the way.

Admiral Green spoke softly. "Sometimes we don't know what we're capable of until we're truly tested."

Kwan snapped back to the present. "Fine. I'll take the *Komodo*, descend to the planet, locate Duskara, and terminate her."

Kwan couldn't grasp the words, even as she said them. *Terminate her. Kill her.* They sounded strange, cold, like something the admiral would say. Anyone else. But not her. To take a life, even an artificially intelligent life…

Could she do it?

To save the world, to save Jae-Hwa, she had to.

At least the plan sounded simple. Though she knew it wouldn't be as simple when she got there. They only had bits and pieces of information about Duskara's whereabouts and the planet. They had gathered intelligence from GAIA agents stationed at the outpost on Candu. From limited operations in the region, they knew the location of the cave where Duskara resided. But no one from GAIA had seen its interior before. They didn't know the layout, how many tunnels it had, how many Malborgs lived inside, or what type of technology might be used to locate and destroy threats. They didn't know anything about it.

Getting inside the cave would be difficult in the *Komodo*, but not impossible. But if she could do it…if she could find her way without alerting the Malborgs to her presence…

"How will you get back?" Admiral Green said.

Kwan frowned. It was probably a one-way journey. Once she left the protection of the ship's shield, the Malborgs would be on to her. Or…

Perhaps there was a way to attack Duskara from a distance?

They just needed a small vessel. Something agile and remotely controlled. And with a quick injection capability. Something to sting Duskara with. If she could get close enough…

"I'll use a hornet drone with the AI death serum to attack Duskara. And then I'll boot out of there. I'll be in and out within thirty minutes."

Admiral Green's lips curled. "Just like that?"

Kwan maintained her even gaze. "Unless someone has a better way."

But no one did. They all knew what she knew. This was the plan. Attack Duskara. Kill her. It was risky, dangerous, uncertain, and terrifying, but this was the only way. The Malborgs would find her and kill her. But the others would survive.

The admiral nodded. "Very well."

Time seemed to be speeding up now. She didn't want to face the truth, but it was inevitable. They had to leave. She felt like she was on a sinking ship with no lifeboats.

"Given the events of the last twenty-four hours, we should probably leave as soon as possible. Before too many people know about it, and before more damage is done," Kwan said.

"Agreed. After this meeting, I'll prepare the manifest. We'll leave tonight."

This was it. There was no turning back now.

CHAPTER FORTY-SEVEN

SAM FELT RELIEF AFTER BEING RELEASED FROM THE HOLDING CELL. BUT she felt disoriented, too. So much had transpired over the past twenty-four hours. The toxin Yolo had injected her with left her with temporary memory loss. The doctors had said it would run through her system by the end of the day. Then, she should be back to normal.

But what was normal, now?

Was the admiral right? Had Duskara manipulated her? They'd ordered her to check in with medical for further psychiatric assessments. She headed there now, glad to be walking the hallway and not pacing her cell. Once she got the psych assessments over with, she could finally see her friends and tell them—

A sudden blast shook the facility. The walls vibrated. Shards of rock and plaster fell from the ceiling. Then, a distant rumbling, like thunder. Alarms sounded, and the lights flickered. People sprinted down the hallway in different directions, some rushing to their stations, others simply fleeing for cover.

A man screamed, pointing frantically. "We're being attacked! Get to the escape pods!"

Sam's gaze followed his outstretched finger. There, down the corridor, a pack of three leathery-skinned Gargols thundered toward them, their black eyes homing in on her.

One of them barked to the other, "She's here, up ahead!"

They aimed their large, gleaming silver blasters at her. Before she could think or speak, she bolted down the corridor toward the junction. She turned a corner, narrowly avoiding three darts containing yellow liquid that whooshed past her head. Her chest heaving, she slid up against a wall as five military police stormed past, scarcely missing her. Their blasters erupted, returning fire. If she had been one second too late, she would have been caught in the crossfire.

She wavered. Where could she go?

Her ring band buzzed, displaying a message in bold black letters:

GET TO THE *THESEUS* NOW.

A moment later, a hologram illuminated a map with a route.

She rushed toward the nearest emergency exit, her adrenaline spiking. Where were her friends?

She stopped when she saw Zenobii a few feet away, scurrying toward her. He grabbed her arm, his hairs bristling against her skin.

"We need to get to the ships! Come with me!"

Sam turned on her heels as Zenobii yanked her right through the crumbled remains of a wall and into one of the Dark Sites. Lights flickered overhead. Cracks opened up in the walls as the building quaked, the tremors reverberating under her feet and overhead. She tried to suppress her fear as they darted past deserted laboratories, the staff not bothering to close the doors as they hurriedly abandoned their posts. At least the Dark Sites offered temporary refuge from the attackers.

But that wouldn't last long.

They reached an exit and descended the steps to the floor below, which contained the landing bays. A foot of freezing water had collected on the ground. Her skin prickled. She opened the door to the other side, only to be met with a flood of water crashing through, sending an icy shock through her body. The wave pushed them back into the stairwell, and she lost her footing. Pushing herself up, she thrust her legs forward, fighting the force of the water that threatened to undermine her resolve.

"We need to keep moving!" Zenobii shouted.

Drenched and shaking, and with as much strength and effort as she could muster, she somehow made it through the door to the other side.

She stared wide-eyed at the chaotic scene unfolding. The roof had sprung a significant leak from the attack, water surging through the widening cracks, filling up the facility, threatening to engulf everything and everyone it touched. A couple of small spacecraft were already half-submerged.

Zenobii pointed to an enormous saucer-shaped ship about fifty feet away. "That one!"

Massive waves crashed through the landing bay, the water sweeping through and pulling people in all directions.

They didn't have much time. The ship's landing dock was already half-submerged, the water rising rapidly, threatening to consume it. Sam couldn't spot anyone familiar. Had her friends made it onto the ship already? She could only hope.

Trying not to think the worst, she swam after Zenobii toward the ship, the effort ten times harder than she'd expected as the water tugged her sideways, the current weakening her. She'd thought she was a solid swimmer, but Zenobii was faster, stronger. His body repelled the water as he cut through the waves. He reached out, grabbed her hand, and pulled her along, his ant-like body proving durable and capable of this task.

As they approached the ship, Sam glanced back, terrified. A lifeless soldier's body washed past her, only a few feet away. The water kept rising, pushing her toward the ceiling. The spacecraft she'd seen earlier had already disappeared, completely submerged.

She turned back toward their ship, still thirty feet away.

Another wave crashed down. It broke her hold on Zenobii and pulled her under, sweeping her in the opposite direction of the ship. She fought the tow of the water, forcing her legs to kick harder, just barely making it to the surface in time to grab more air. She caught movement overhead. Something—no, *someone*—along the glass walkway of the Fishbowl.

It was Kato, fleeing a Gargol.

Terror ripped through Sam. The Gargol snatched Kato up, and she squirmed, struggling to break free. But the Gargol tightened its grip, quickened its pace, and barged toward the glass barrier. The glass shattered into a thousand pieces as they hurtled into the air, only to crash into the frigid water below.

"Kato!" Sam cried out.

"Get to the ship!" Zenobii shouted. "I'll be there in a minute!"

Fear paralyzed her. She treaded water, torn in two different directions. She couldn't go to the ship, not until she knew Kato was okay. Her panic set in as Zenobii swam straight toward the Gargol without hesitation.

Would he make it in time?

Kato's head was above the water one moment, only to be pulled under its surface the next, the Gargol dragging her through the waves. Zenobii gained speed, so much stronger and more agile than his spindly body suggested. But ants were incredibly strong, and there was no denying his shocking capabilities. Zenobii slid along the surface quickly, like a rock skipping over the water, barely touching it, velocity carrying him forward. At the last second, he twisted, forcing his legs to align with the Gargol's torso. His powerful kick sent the Gargol flying through the air. Sam's jaw dropped. The thrust and angle were executed perfectly. It was like watching a synchronized swimming routine. The Gargol jolted, flipping several times before crashing into the waves below. She made a mental note never to get on Zenobii's bad side.

She sighed in relief as Kato emerged from the water, clutching on to Zenobii. He guided them toward the ship, hauling her along against the waves.

The floating gangway was just a few meters from Sam. She swam for it, fingers outstretched, only for it to retract—pulling up and away from her.

"No!" she cried, still reaching.

They weren't going to make it in time.

She fought the current with everything she had, but it was useless—it kept dragging her farther away.

It was too late.

The ship powered up, lifting off the water. The bright light of its power generation systems temporarily blinded her. A wave of heat radiated down. She slipped under the cold water to gain temporary respite. But when she came up to the surface again, all she felt was dread.

They'd be stuck here.

Left to die.

But then, a beam of gentle, shimmering light washed over her. This light was different. As warm as it was, it froze her body. She couldn't move. She couldn't blink. Was this what dying felt like?

She, Zenobii, and Kato ascended, lifting out of the water and into the air. Weightless.

Time stopped.

Then, it accelerated.

Dropped onto the hard floor of the ship, Sam squinted under the harsh interior light. As her eyes adjusted, Boj's face came into view overhead, and she felt a wave of comfort and hopefulness. Sam pushed herself up from the ground. Cold, wet, and a bit shaky, she took one of the blankets Boj held out for them.

Dazed, she wiped her face and clasped the blanket around her.

No matter how tightly she held it, she couldn't stop her body from trembling.

"Thank you," Kato spluttered, coughing up water.

Delight washed over Sam at the sight of her. Kato was *alive*.

"Kato!" She grasped her best friend in a tight hug, warmth spreading throughout her body. "I thought—I thought I'd lost you —" Tears streamed down her cheeks, but she didn't stop them. Clutching Kato closer, she was overcome with gratitude for the universe sparing them both somehow. Kato meant everything to her. Sam couldn't imagine what would happen if she lost her.

Kato spoke quietly. "Me too. I'm glad we made it."

Sam gently released her. She studied Kato's features to make sure she was really there, that she was okay, and it wasn't some dream. That's when she noticed the large gash on the side of Kato's head. Blood trickled down her ear.

"Kato, you're bleeding!"

"Let's get you to medical and get you cleaned up," Zenobii said.

As Zenobii helped Kato to the medical bay, Boj took Sam down the corridor toward the command station.

"Where are Kobe and Simon?" Sam asked, a rush of fear washing over her. "Are they okay? Did they make it?"

"Yes," Boj replied calmly. "They're right here."

They turned a corner, and Sam exhaled, relieved to see Simon and Kobe seated nearby. Captain Gorgana sat at the front, adjusting knobs and switches. Onnisa, Giddy, and Kwan were there, too. Zenobii and Kato soon joined them. Kato held an ice pack to the side of her head.

There were a few soldiers, too—military staff on board. But mostly empty seats. Sam frowned, sensing an enormous loss.

Through the viewing screen, Sam watched as the ship swept down through the water, then tilted as it zoomed toward the facility's entrance. Crashing water continued to fill the landing bays.

The forceful pull of the water's grip swept up the last of the Gargols.

Red sparks flew by outside. Violent bursts of enemy fire. Their ship lurched, screeching. Slight tremors reverberated as its defense system intercepted the blasts. They sped through the dark water and toward the surface.

Admiral Green's face appeared on the screen. "What's our status, Captain?"

"Only fifteen personnel are accounted for, Admiral. I'm afraid we lost several crew members during the attack," Captain Gorgana replied solemnly. "Operation Dark End has been activated. Beginning our ascent."

Then the screen cut out. The lights flickered.

Sam caught the brief, flaming pink-orange sky of the sunset over the water as they breached the surface and soared upward. A moment later, they were out of the atmosphere and approaching space, a black vastness with twinkling stars far away, their lights a symbol of hope. But a heaviness weighed on her. The stars' shining lights would be a distant memory soon.

There was no turning back. The Dark Galaxy would pull them right into its shadowy grasp.

CHAPTER FORTY-EIGHT

SAM DIDN'T SLEEP THAT NIGHT. SHE COULDN'T. DESPITE THE CAPTAIN'S orders to remain in her room and get plenty of rest, her mind chose to grind away.

The recent attack continued to play out in her mind like a looping video. The gigantic waves, the freezing-cold water gnawing at her and threatening to pull her under, Kato's body as the Gargol burst through the glass…

They'd barely made it out in time.

But she was here, now. Wherever *here* was.

She was dry and warm and sheltered. At least they were away from the attackers. But also away from her grandfather, away from the safety and comfort of her home.

The ship groaned as they hurtled through space. Every few minutes, heavy rumbling echoed, deafening and ruthless. It shook her bones.

The small residence quarters, barely enough for a single bed and a small desk, only reminded her that they were living in a confined space now. Restricted to this ship, there was no turning back. No way of going outside for a breath of fresh air or feeling a natural breeze against her skin. They were passengers on this ship, millions of miles away from Earth.

She had no choice but to adapt.

Desperate to familiarize herself with her new surroundings, she opened the door a crack and slipped out.

Soft blue lighting filled the curving hallways. The gleaming ceramic floors were spotless. The gravity generators were working. She wasn't floating away, but each step felt heavier than usual and took extra effort. Whenever she pressed down with her heels, it felt like the floor would sink from under her. She tried to focus, to get her footing, to steady herself, but it was impossible. And at the speed they were traveling, a constant whirring vibrated inside her bones that she couldn't shake.

It messed with her mind.

Outside, a dizzying light show encircled their ship in all directions. The effects of the wormhole.

Her stomach lurched, nausea threatening to creep up. She darted down a side corridor toward the interior of the ship, away from the windows. She gripped one of the metal banisters that lined the hall.

Grateful for at least some stability, she continued along the wall. She found herself going in circles until she realized it was part of the ship's design. Another curving hallway came into view. More concentric hallways.

At least it was easier to get her bearings here compared to the underwater base. There were far fewer corridors, and everything was mapped out in a repeating pattern of circling hallways. No Dark Sites either, as far as she could tell.

Passing the medical wing, she gawked at the full body scanners, 3D printers, computerized arms, and cables hanging from the ceiling. Everything looked even more advanced and less threatening than what she'd seen at the base. They even had comfy reclining chairs. With the delicate stitching of the white and beige fabric, you could easily mistake them as chairs belonging on a billionaire's yacht.

The deep rumbling continued. She gripped the banister harder. She'd still have to get used to the whirring inside her.

She continued along but slowed as an acrid smell filled her nostrils. She stepped into the junction, only to find a maintenance bot lying on the floor, cables ripped out, wisps of smoke rising from its shredded metal innards.

This can't be good.

She listened for a moment, but the hallway was silent.

She leaned in and was about to pick up the bot when sparks flew from deep inside its belly into the air, narrowly missing her face and hair.

She stumbled back, the circuitry hissing.

On second thought…

She dashed toward the command station. On her way there, she thought she heard a faint clinking noise inside one of the walls, but there was no time to check it out. She needed to tell the others what she'd found.

She arrived at a blast-proof door, air-tight and locked. Lifting her ring band to the keypad, she waited as the light changed from red to green. The was a suctioned hiss of air escaping, and then a click.

The door slid open.

Captain Gorgana swiveled in her chair to face her. "Sam? What are you doing here so early in the morning?"

Was it morning? How could one tell with the bizarre lights outside their ship and no sun to ground them?

Onnisa stood in the corner but took a step closer. "What is it? What's the matter?"

"I—I think something's wrong. I found a destroyed maintenance bot down the hallway from the medical wing. It looked like someone ripped out the wiring, tore it apart."

Onnisa's eyes opened wide in alarm. She turned to Captain

Gorgana. "Do you think that is why the heat shields are malfunctioning?"

"Quite possibly. I thought it was due to the Gargol attack, but they may have infiltrated the ship during the escape. I'll run a heat signature assessment on the systems."

Captain Gorgana's claws flew over the control screen, twisting dials as she entered the protocol for the ship to run its diagnostic assessment.

A screen in front of Sam blinked and revealed detailed schematics of their ship. Layers of information appeared, displaying the names and locations of the passengers onboard. Thermal imaging details illuminated the heat signatures of the ship's systems and occupants—glowing warm red-orange lights against a purple-blue backdrop. Sixteen pinpoints of light, Sam noted.

But only fifteen names.

"Captain," Sam said, her finger poised over the single unnamed dot of light on the screen. "What is this?"

The captain's brow furrowed, and she frowned. "A stowaway. It appears we have an intruder aboard."

CHAPTER FORTY-NINE

SLOUCHED IN A CHAIR IN THE SMALL CABIN QUARTERS OF THE *THESEUS* in a room the size of a prison cell, Kwan clutched the photo of Jae-Hwa. The photograph had been taken just this past spring, before her assignment. The day of the picnic in Queen Elizabeth Park in Vancouver during the cherry blossom festival. The same day they'd declared their love for one another.

Tracing her fingers around the edges, she took in her familiar features: her long black hair tied into a loose side braid, strands gently framing her face. Her delicate yet devious smile. That mysterious look, like she wanted to let you in on a secret. The more Kwan tried to imagine that she was here with her on this journey, the more it pained her, left her in a sea of despair.

What had she said to her before she left? It felt like a lifetime ago.

A promise that they'd be together again soon.

Shattered. It was like there'd been some strange shift in time and space, one she couldn't even grasp, and Jae-Hwa's voice, like a ghostly whisper, was calling out to her in her dreams to come back.

She hadn't even had a chance to say goodbye.

Tearing her watery eyes from the photo, she turned, glancing out the small, circular window at the unfathomable expanse beyond. Her stomach fluttered. She felt lightheaded. Now she was hurtling through space—ever farther away from everything she knew and loved. Any shred of comfort and safety, all the things she'd clung to and hoped for, were gone.

She'd never felt so alone in her life.

Frustrated, she slammed her fist into the armrest. She hadn't expected things to turn out like this. They'd barely managed to get out in time. And despite planning for this mission, she didn't feel ready. None of them were. The attack had shortened their timeline considerably. Getting to Logom, the planet where Duskara lived, would be a long journey in itself, and a dangerous one. But this was only the beginning. They needed a way to infiltrate Duskara's Malborg army situated on that planet. Their plan of attack on Duskara had not yet been finalized, and the details were hazy at best. They were flying blind.

At least they'd gotten out of range of the Gargol ships. They were now in SWIFT navigation mode—superluminal wayfinding intergalactic faraway travel. But traveling by SWIFT navigation mode wasn't comfortable or relaxing. In this long, winding worm-hole, time was fleeting, and spacetime was distorted. Barreling through a tunnel in spacetime like this—all without registering any movement whatsoever—made it hard to determine what was real and what was not. She couldn't even look out the windows. The constant stream of strange lights and dizzying tunnels looping in every direction made it impossible to get one's bearings. It was a weird feeling. It played tricks on her mind. The lights outside could just as well have been an extravagant light show or an optical illusion. But her body felt different, like a constant whirring inside her bones. At the molecular level, it felt like her atoms were racing around sporadically. It felt like being on a ship in the middle of the ocean with hundred-foot waves, except they spiraled in all directions. A person could go mad in a constant state of flux like this.

Maybe she'd get used to it over time. She hoped so.

A sudden rattling at the door caused her to jump. She leaped off the chair, trying to steady herself. Even though the gravity generators worked in most spaces, she still had trouble balancing sometimes, unsure of whether the foundation would collapse under her feet.

She wiped her eyes on her sleeve and tried to compose herself before opening the door. A slight tremble erupted inside her when she saw Onnisa on the other side, staring at her with a shriveled brow.

"Something is amiss," Onnisa said, her voice frantic. "There is someone on this ship who should not be here."

"What? What do you mean?"

"Captain Gorgana noticed the heat shields were malfunctioning earlier this morning. She ran a heat signature assessment. We found another person, unaccounted for, somewhere in the maintenance bay. Possibly hiding. I need your help locating the individual."

Kwan grabbed her blaster and sped after Onnisa toward the maintenance bay. No one else should be aboard the ship. But with the recent Gargol attack and the chaos surrounding their departure, someone could have easily breached the ship's security system.

Onnisa slowed as they approached the maintenance bay. Kwan almost missed it. To anyone unfamiliar with this alien spacecraft, the maintenance bay looked like a regular hallway, except for one small difference. A series of large wall panels with touch screens lined the walls, with hidden interior cables and a tunnel system behind them. The tunnel system was a confined space, about two feet wide, only allowing for one person or a small maintenance bot to navigate it at a time to conduct repairs. The lights flickered overhead while red lights flashed on the screens, indicating a malfunction in the ship's systems.

Kwan's stomach twisted. "Looks like the ship suffered a lot of damage during our escape."

"Indeed," Onnisa replied.

The ship's systems were designed to self-regulate and rectify damage. The maintenance bots were only supposed to assist if necessary. They'd counted on them to assess the damage and repair it. But the corridor remained desolate.

"Where are the maintenance bots?" Kwan asked, sliding Onnisa a nervous glance.

They stopped and waited.

It was eerily silent except for the low hum of the ship's systems running their energy inputs and outputs.

Then, a sudden clinking came from one of the panels. Like something had dropped. Metal against metal.

Onnisa quietly turned to Kwan. She lifted a hand, her multitude of spindly fingers, maybe twenty on each hand, pointing to one section of the wall. Kwan nodded. She knew what they had to do. She silently shifted her weight and approached the panel. Onnisa remained close by, ready to apprehend the intruder.

With one swooping gesture, Kwan opened the panel with her left hand, all the while grasping her blaster in her right.

She blinked twice. It took a moment to register the face staring back at her.

The woman squinted against the sudden entry of light from the hallway, her arm raised in front of her in fear and desperation. As the woman's eyes adjusted, she smiled faintly, her hair greasy and her face smeared with some purple substance.

Kwan lowered her weapon in relief. "Rian? What are you doing here?"

Rian stumbled forward awkwardly, still holding her hand up to her face as she exited the interior tunnel.

Something was off about this whole situation. Her behavior

suggested guilt: the flush across her cheeks, the fidgeting, and the sweat creeping down her forehead.

"I was just checking on the systems. It looks like we sprung a fuel leak."

A burst of panic shot through Kwan. If Rian was telling the truth, they were in deep trouble. And if she was lying, they were probably in even worse trouble.

"You didn't answer my question," Kwan said. "How did you get here?"

Rian's face tightened. "I was with my maintenance team. We—we tried to get away from those Gargols when they attacked. We ran for the escape pods, but they were gone. All of them! My team… They didn't make it. The Gargols…" Rian wiped her eyes with the back of her sleeve. "I did the only thing I could. I hid. I hid here while the others…" Her voice faltered, and she looked away.

Yet something didn't add up. Without clearance, the ship should have denied entry to anyone not on the manifest.

Unless the system had been tampered with.

"Hold out your ring band," Kwan demanded. If she was telling the truth, the information on her ring band would corroborate her story. Personal information, including time of entry aboard the ship. Access codes.

Rian stepped back. "Why? If you think I'm lying—"

"There is another way," Onnisa interrupted, grabbing Rian's hand with her long, spindly fingers. Immediately, sparks of energy flew, and a current traveled up Rian's arm. She tried to resist, but the force was overpowering.

Kwan knew about the Krygian Elder's gift of translucence. The power of sharing information through hand-to-hand contact. But she'd never witnessed it in person. Until now.

Rian winced as Onnisa blinked rapidly, pulling information from her, perhaps secrets Rian wanted to keep hidden.

Onnisa's eyes widened. "She is working with the Gargols. She was tampering with the ship." Onnisa hesitated, then added, her voice low, "*She* poisoned Dr. Krill. Come, we must notify Captain Gorgana at once!" Onnisa wavered as she broke the connection.

Kwan went to grab Rian by the shoulder, but she ducked just in time, slipping through Kwan's grasp, and sped down the corridor.

Without thinking, Kwan sprinted after her, her blaster held firmly in her hand. She didn't want to kill Rian. She needed information. How much had been compromised?

She darted down the corridors. Rian was fast. A couple of maintenance bots littered the hallways, smoke fuming from them, their cables and parts ripped out.

This was serious. Seriously bad. What were they going to do with a dying ship in the middle of nowhere? They were millions of kilometers away from Earth now. There was no guarantee that they were close to any habitable planets. And if they had to land, it would put their mission in jeopardy.

She tried to push those thoughts aside as she dashed up a ramp toward the residence quarters.

Where the escape pods were located.

She urged her legs to pick up the pace, her chest heaving. She rounded the corner in time to see Rian board a pod. The launch sequence was automatic. Secured. Fast.

Too fast.

Strapped firmly into the pod, Rian turned and glared at her. "You don't know the whole truth!"

The whole truth? What did she mean? What else could she be talking about?

"Then tell me!"

Rian's only answer was to slam the launch button. The pod's portal sealed shut. Rian's face distorted in a blur as the pod broke from the main ship, spiraling into the wormhole.

"*No!*"

It was too late. Rian was gone.

Her answers were gone.

They'd found their mole. If Rian was behind the murder of Dr.

Krill, then it was possible she was also responsible for the other incidents. The smuggling of the LOMA. Sabotaging their communications at the base. How deep did her indiscretions and criminal activity go, and for how long?

Kwan dreaded to think about it.

And now, they were left in a dying ship, bleeding out fuel and hurtling through space toward the Dark Galaxy...or *oblivion*.

CHAPTER FIFTY

When Kwan and Onnisa returned to the command station, it wasn't Captain Gorgana they found in the captain's chair. It was Boj. He looked over at them, a grim expression on his face.

On the screen behind him, bold lettering displayed a message:

WARNING. FUEL LEAK. **39%** POWER.
SYSTEM FAILURE IMMINENT.

"What's going on? Where's Captain Gorgana?" Kwan asked.

But it was Zenobii who responded. "Captain Gorgana is indisposed. Boj is second-in-command."

"Second-in-command?" Kwan gaped. "Is everything okay? What happened to—?"

"Captain Gorgana is all right," Boj said. "She's just taking some much-needed rest."

Much-needed rest? Kwan shook her head in disbelief. "Where is she? Something's happened. We need to speak with her. Immediately!"

"I've temporarily taken up her post. But I'm afraid your news will have to wait. As you can see, we're a little busy at the moment."

The ship rocked, the deck plates shaking. Blinking red lights flashed across the screen. Another message, in bold letters, commanded their attention.

WARNING. FUEL LEAK. **35%** POWER.
SYSTEM FAILURE IMMINENT.

"We're losing power," Boj said. "Zenobii, what are our options?"

Zenobii responded, but Kwan couldn't make out his words. The clicking sound didn't translate properly. No words flowed through her earpiece—the device was malfunctioning. From the look on Boj's face, the same thing was happening to him.

Boj interrupted. "My earpiece has failed. Onnisa, can you please assist in translating through telepathy?"

They were in trouble. The communications failure with the earpieces would make things difficult—for *everyone*. What had caused the breakdown? Had Rian gone so far as to install a virus in their communication system?

"Zenobii says we won't make it to Logom at this rate. We need to exit SWIFT mode, and we need to do it now. It's the only way."

"Agreed. Launching exit sequence now." Boj tapped on the display screen and maneuvered several dials.

A moment later, the ship creaked and groaned as it executed a series of commands. Kwan kept her eyes trained on the viewing station in front of them. The glittering lights of the wormhole soon disappeared, replaced by a star system.

Zenobii spoke again, and Onnisa hesitated. "Zenobii says we're in the Deval Galaxy. There are no GAIA-represented systems or planets here. We don't have enough fuel to make it to an adjacent galaxy."

"Are there any habitable planets with perilium?" Kwan asked.

She didn't know much about otherworldly geology, but she knew perilium was a highly prized and powerful substance. And one of the scarcest minerals in the universe. Both rare and dangerous, only the most advanced civilizations knew how to harness its power for interstellar travel. Without it, they couldn't create wormholes. It would be a miracle if they could locate a planet in this random galaxy containing the substance. The odds were against them.

Boj entered a series of commands and parameters into the system. Three planets materialized on the screen. The first showed a thirty-one-percent match for habitable life and perilium for fuel, the second, a sixteen-percent match, and the third, a ninety-three-percent match.

"The only option within our vicinity is here." Boj pointed to a white planet in the distance. He pressed another button, pulling up a magnified image. The planet contained red sand, rocky terrain, and purple lakes. Upon closer view, white crystallized dust blanketed different regions.

But it wasn't the planet's geography that caught Kwan's attention.

The summary was what worried her the most.

GALAXY: DEVAL

STAR: VOLTEN

PLANET: GLUBO

INHABITANTS: GLUBENS (87%), OTHERS (13%)

GAIA MEMBERS: NO

DISPOSITION: HOSTILE. EXERCISE EXTREME CAUTION!

INDUSTRIES: MINING, ENERGY

ENERGY SOURCE: PERILIUM

LANGUAGES: LUBADAN, CHYNO, KIVERA, OTHER

TRADE CURRENCY: LIVING ENTITIES

She grimaced at the idea of facing a hostile civilization in unknown territory.

Onnisa waited for Zenobii to complete his thoughts, then continued translating. "Planet Glubo. Occupied by the Gluben people. Not part of GAIA, but they do have perilium." She wavered with the last part. "Zenobii says the other planets may not have the life-support system and fuel we need. With Glubo, there is the highest chance of survival."

Boj hesitated. "Is this the best option, Zenobii, in your opinion?"

Zenobii nodded.

As their navigator, Zenobii knew the risks. They didn't seem to have any good options.

Boj took a breath, his fingers flying over the screen. "Plotting our course for Glubo."

Everyone watched in silent trepidation as he launched the sequence to begin their journey to the planet.

Kwan's mouth went dry. "Wait. It says their trade currency is *living entities*. What does that mean?"

"Plants, animals, and people. *Slaves*," Boj said. "Everyone buckle up."

The ship rocked, juddering again. Boj looked around him—they all did—collectively wondering whether their small ship would hold together.

Kwan thought about their position, a dire one. She couldn't eliminate the fear that one or more of them could—or more likely *would*—be taken.

CHAPTER FIFTY-ONE

AFTER COMMAND GAVE HER THE ALL-CLEAR, SAM SPENT THE REST OF THE morning playing Galaxy Diplomats: Dark Quest in the nearly empty dining hall with Kato, Kobe, and Simon. She needed to clear her head, to relax and unwind after everything that had happened. She'd seized the opportunity to enjoy the company of her friends. A chance to focus on something besides their mission to the Dark Galaxy.

She rolled the dice and moved her piece three spaces. The premise of the game was simple: a rogue AI was building a dark army in the galaxy, and they had to stop it. It had an uncanny resemblance to their *real* mission, and she couldn't help but worry about how this game was unfolding. In one word: dreadfully. Their nonexistent luck was appalling.

Breathe. Focus on the game…

Try as she might, she couldn't push all the negative thoughts about the mission and Duskara from her mind. They swam from the depths, resurfacing again and again.

The plan was still largely a mystery. Kwan was working on the AI death serum, but even if it worked, Duskara knew they were coming. With her army of Malborgs, infiltrating Logom would be impossible.

She couldn't allow Kwan to slip away in the *Komodo* and risk her life for her. It wouldn't work. Duskara would find out. Or her Malborgs. Either way, Kwan wouldn't survive, and Sam couldn't let that happen. There was only one way to get to Duskara. *She* would need to be the bait. Duskara wanted *her*.

She couldn't tell her friends what she was planning. She didn't want to alarm them. Worse, they wouldn't let her do what she knew she must. One way or another, she would have to meet with Duskara. One-on-one. Once they reached Logom, she would go to her using an escape pod. And she would take the death serum with her. Hopefully it would be ready in time.

But then what? She doubted Duskara would just let her walk up and administer it.

"Well?" Simon said. "Are you going to pick up a card?"

"Oh! Yeah. Sorry. I just got distracted."

Sam's stomach churned as she picked up a card from the Dark pile. With only three Dark spaces on the board of fifty spaces, picking up a Dark Card meant something bad was about to happen.

She turned over the card to reveal the face of Rygo staring back at her. Her ghostly white eyes with red pupils contrasted against her purple skin and blue hair.

Sam groaned. "Attacked by Rygo—again?!"

Simon threw his cards down. "What are the chances?"

This was a collaborative game. Winning depended upon working together to get through each challenge.

And not getting that Rygo card twice in a game.

"It's a sign," Kobe said. "The universe is telling us we're all going to *die*."

"What? That's nonsense!" Kato objected.

"Then how do you explain our string of bad luck?"

Kato sighed, exasperated. "Look, if our luck is so bad, it can *only* get better, right? The universe equalizes everything."

"But it doesn't," Simon said. "Not necessarily. Just because you flip a coin ten times doesn't mean you'll get heads half the time. Sometimes it just keeps coming up tails."

"It's true," Kobe added. "Some people are luckier than others. People are born into different circumstances."

"Wait," Sam said. "Just because you're born into a bad situation doesn't mean you can't change it."

"True, but it can be more difficult."

Sam paused, reflecting on Kobe's words. She thought about children born into cycles of violence and abuse. She thought about those born into poverty and disease. How could the universe be so cruel to some and so good to others? If the universe was so random in its dealings with people, that could mean only one thing: it was up to people to change things for the better. And for those who couldn't do that for themselves, for those struggling, those given difficult dealings and unfortunate circumstances, Sam felt an inherent duty to change things.

She couldn't let bad things happen—to her or to anyone else she cared about.

If they didn't find a way to stop Duskara, it would be the end for everyone.

And maybe the universe didn't...*equalize* things. Maybe it was just random luck, and some people selfishly took advantage of it. But that didn't mean they couldn't try to change things for the better.

"I read this theory where we're all just some characters in a simulation," Simon said, "but on a universal scale."

"Oh yeah?" Sam said.

"Yeah, and there's someone just playing us like we're puppets."

An image flashed into Sam's mind of her friends—*of all of them*—with cords extending from their limbs, being propped up and jerked around by Duskara as she pulled the strings.

"So you're saying we're just characters in someone's story?" Kato said. "That's ridiculous!"

Simon leaned toward her, leering. "Is it?"

"I can't believe that," Sam said. "I don't believe our thoughts and actions are pre-defined. There's no limit to our thoughts. I mean, if we tried to create a boundary, we'd have to know what was *beyond* that limit, even in a vague sense. Even if it's not fully formed and we're just exploring. I think we have the power to choose—the kind of people we want to be and how we want to change our circumstances."

"Maybe," Kobe said. "But if Simon is right, if we're really in a computer game, then I'm calling them out. If there's someone out there pulling our strings, writing our story, I say, stop it! Stop giving us so many challenges. Give us better luck!"

"Yeah, I'm challenging the universe, too!" Simon added.

"I don't believe someone is deciding our fate," Kato said. "I think if we want to change something, we need to write our own stories. You know, be active, not passive, not waiting for things to happen to us."

"Yes. Kato's right," Sam said, surprised at her own passion. "We can *change* things. We can be internally inspired."

"How?" Simon asked.

Sam took the dice in her hands and rolled them across the table. "We've been playing Duskara's game the whole time. But the way I see it, we have two options: we stop playing, or we rewrite the rules."

Kato grinned, picking up the dice. "Well, if we're going to rewrite the rules, we need to know what we're up against. It's time we get some answers. People have been acting strangely. You know, reserved. Have you noticed that?"

"I'm telling you, something's up," Simon said. "It's like an invisible force is keeping everyone apart."

"Just stop," Kato said.

Simon stretched his legs. "Believe whatever you want. But I've been thinking about it, and that planet we're going to—Logom—if you change the letter order, you get *gloom*. That's right. We're going to Planet Gloom! Is that random?"

The mood in the room shifted. Everyone was silent.

Coincidence or not, Sam didn't want to think about Duskara's planet, Logom, or what it might look like once they arrived. But she imagined it anyway: a miserable planet devoid of life or diversity, forlorn. Made up of thick, grimy smog and despair, its surface cold and rigid like stone, unyielding, severe. And crawling with Malborgs.

"Gloom. Boom," Kato said, rising. "Whatever. Sam's right. We need to take the matter into our own hands and figure out what's going on here. I, for one, don't want to be just a passenger on this mission. If we're going to succeed, we need to be agents of change, you know? Not just passively accept our circumstances or whatever comes to us. We need to figure out what to do."

"Kato's right," Sam said. Kato always knew exactly what to say to make her feel better. It lightened her spirit. "We're still breathing. We're not dead yet! And I think we can start by looking for ways to help." She lowered her voice and continued in a hushed whisper. "Like talking to Kwan. She looks kinda sad over there all by herself."

Kwan had been sitting alone on the other side of the dining hall for the past hour. She sipped a cup of steaming hot tea with one hand and propped her head up with the other, stopping every so often to fiddle with her napkin.

"What do you think happened?" Kobe asked.

Kato shrugged. "I don't know, but we're going to find out."

Sam and the others made their way over. Kato took a seat beside Kwan. "Hey."

Kwan looked up slightly, not registering all of them there. She grunted. "Not in the mood."

"We're here to cheer you up," Sam said, taking a seat on her other side. "How can we help?"

This got a little bit of Kwan's attention. "Thanks, but it's okay."

"No, we really want to help," Kato urged. "What's going on?"

Kwan sighed. "I just found out that Rian…" Her voice trailed off, and she looked down.

"What about Rian?"

"She compromised our entire mission."

"What? What do you mean?"

Kwan cleared her throat. "Onnisa and I found her sabotaging the ship—purposely leaking fuel! She's the one who… She killed Dr. Krill. And she's been working with the Gargols the whole time."

Sam couldn't believe what she was hearing. Corporal Rian Wright, the laid-back, down-to-earth girl.

Everyone was silent. Shellshocked.

"What—what did they do to her?" Kato asked.

Kwan shook her head. "She escaped. She used an escape pod. I —I just can't believe I didn't see it earlier. The *lies*."

"*No one* saw this coming," Kato said. "The universe really threw us a curve ball."

Kwan frowned. "That's not all."

"What do you mean?" Sam asked.

"Captain Gorgana has stepped down from her post. Last I heard, she's in medical, receiving treatments."

"For what?"

"Haven't a clue."

Was it the lasting effects of LOMA? Or could it be something else…like the Dark Sickness? Sam tried not to show her fear and anxiety. Without their captain, things could go seriously haywire.

Giddy entered the room, her eyes glistening in amazement. "So this is where the party's at! I was missing out."

"Come join us," Sam said. "What have you got there?"

Giddy nestled a blanket against her chest, a white oval-shaped object peeking out of the top. "I have some good news to share," she started, holding out the item for others to see. Sam glimpsed a crack running down the top of the object. "I'm pleased to announce that this is the sixth egg Captain Gorgana has laid…and counting. The babies are all healthy, and Captain Gorgana is in good spirits. Onnisa and I've been tending to her these past few days."

Captain Gorgana had been pregnant? Sam had no idea. None of them had known. So that explained her absence all this time. But how was it possible for Captain Gorgana to get pregnant on the trip? Unless…unless the fertilization happened *prior* to their departure.

"Did…did she know…?" Kobe's words trailed off.

"The Rigellians are hermaphrodites," Giddy said. "They can make babies on their own. I think the SWIFT navigation mode has had some strange effects on her."

"On everyone," Simon added.

Kobe gaped. "Well! I…I guess you learn something new every day!"

"Look!" Kato said. "It's about to hatch!"

Everyone watched in amazement as a small, chubby, scaly green creature poked its head from the top of its shell. It peered at the strangers in awe and curiosity with its hexagonal bug eyes, taking it all in.

Then, it turned to Simon and lifted its green claw toward him.

Simon hesitated, then reached out his finger to shake its hand. As he did so, it opened its mouth and hummed.

"What's it saying?" Simon asked.

"I think I may be able to help you with that," Kwan said, rummaging in her bag and taking out earpieces. "The last ones malfunctioned, so I coded these new ones."

Everyone took them, and Sam slipped hers on.

The humming grew louder, and then the words floated through Sam's earpiece. "Dadadada?"

Kato laughed. "Simon, I think it thinks you're its dad."

Simon's face flushed. "No, I'm Simon, *Si-mon*."

"Dadadada!" The baby Rigellian squealed in delight. Everybody laughed.

A sudden, loud rumbling of the ship startled everyone.

"What was that?" Kato asked.

"Oh, right," Giddy started. "We all need to get buckled up to prepare for landing."

Something didn't seem right. They couldn't have arrived on Logom yet. It had only been a few days—or did time act differently in space travel? "Wait. We're already here? I thought we had a few more weeks to go?" Sam asked. They were nowhere near ready.

"No. There's been a change of plans. We're stopping on Glubo first for fuel," Kwan answered. "Just a quick pitstop, and then we'll be on our way."

Sam relaxed. At least this would give them more time to prepare. Besides, a pitstop didn't sound so bad. She looked forward to the opportunity to scout out a new planet and possibly meet new people from another world!

They might even have a chance to learn some new customs.

CHAPTER FIFTY-TWO

SAM STOOD IN THE COMMAND STATION WATCHING IN AWE THROUGH the viewing window as they approached a white planet in the distance. It wasn't Logom, but a small world named Glubo. Not their final destination, but a necessary stop for fuel before moving on.

She brimmed with excitement. Meeting another alien civilization and exploring a new planet—what could be better than that?

Kato, Kobe, and Simon watched in quiet dread as they drew nearer.

Boj tapped away on his screen, entering navigational information. Zenobii peered at the maps on an adjacent screen. Both of them looked fearful about something.

She was about to ask if something was wrong when Kwan marched through the door with Giddy in tow, wheeling a box full of spacesuits and helmets. "Everyone suit up."

"So, we're just stopping for fuel?" Sam asked as she grasped one of the suits, which felt unusually heavy.

"That's the plan," Boj said, glancing back.

"I don't see any gas stations?" Simon said.

Boj's jaw stiffened, and his golden eyes shimmered in the light. "It's a bit more complicated than that. We need to meet with the Glubens on the ground for the negotiations. Make sure to wear those black helmets at all times to protect your identities. Especially you, Queen Samantha. Understand? We can't risk word traveling back to Duskara's agents about our mission plans or whereabouts."

"We won't let that happen," Kwan said. "All we need to do is convince the Glubens that what we have to offer is so good they can't refuse."

"And what do we have to offer?" Sam asked.

"We'll have to improvise. But don't you worry about that. Leave the negotiations to Boj and me. Let us do the talking."

"Are the other military staff coming too?" Sam asked, hoping for some extra support.

"No," Boj replied. "They'll remain on the ship to keep guard."

Sam frowned. It was a small crew. Very few soldiers had made it onto their ship during the battle at the base. They were spread thin.

"But it works out well because we need people who look small and insignificant. Unassuming," Kwan replied, then quickly added, "to make the meeting go smoothly. We want to be seen as *friendly* explorers—we don't want to intimidate the Glubens in any way."

Sam relaxed a little. Her part would be easy. She was okay with appearing small and insignificant. She looked weak and frail compared to the military-trained staff, the hardened and experienced soldiers. It made sense, too. They wanted to avoid inadvertently sparking tensions with the Glubens. At least Kwan would be with them. With her martial arts skills, she could probably defend Sam and her friends if anything happened. At least, she could only hope.

"Consider this your first diplomatic mission." Boj eyed Sam as he spoke, the most serious expression on his face. "Hopefully, it won't be our last."

A chill filled the air. Sam now had a sinking feeling this wouldn't end well. For one thing, the armored suit was suffocating. Part organic, part silicon, and part something otherworldly. The heavy fabric clung to her body like an extension of her skin.

"This thing is way too heavy," Kato said, pulling at the fabric. "Does anyone else feel like they gained ten pounds?"

"State of the art," Giddy said, patting Sam's armored shoulder pauldrons. "Fireproof. Radiationproof. Bulletproof, to some degree. It may not protect against all bullet types. Also, it won't shield you from blaster weapons, so avoid getting blasted at all costs. The fabric's untearable, except against Rypold crystal. That stuff can cut through anything. But it's almost as scarce as perilium, so you don't have to worry much."

The trick was getting it on.

The bulky helmet limited Sam's perception. When she looked left or right, she had to make sure she wasn't too close to someone else or risk bumping heads accidentally. The helmets were dark and tinted enough that no one would be able to see their identities. They activated their secure, private communication channel.

"Oh, and one more thing," Giddy said. "Be careful with your helmets. They have reinforced plexiglass built in, but it's not unbreakable. They can crack."

A loud static burst caused everyone to jump. But the sound wasn't the most distressing. Sam staggered back as a hologram of an enormous, ghastly, hairless creature materialized in the center of the room. The creature's position was so close it almost smothered her. Standing only inches away from it, she took in the details: its bright red skin, thick black horns, and dark black eyes that sucked you in like a black hole. The sudden intrusion of this creature's virtual presence aboard their ship made Sam's heart race.

"State your business." The creature's gruff voice boomed over the sound system.

Sam shuddered. It wasn't exactly the warm welcome she'd been expecting. Then again, what *was* she expecting? A friendly invitation to dinner? A celebration as honored guests from afar? Peaceful relations? Maybe it was foolish to hold such high expectations of others in such uncertain and ambiguous circumstances.

Boj, on the other hand, appeared remarkably calm, more adult-like than she'd seen before. "This is the captain of the *Theseus*. We're part of GAIA on a mission of the highest importance. We request fuel and temporary refuge, sir."

"You are the captain?"

"I am."

"Remove your helmet."

Boj swallowed so hard that Sam heard him gulp. He slowly removed his helmet.

"Ah, a Krygian. Don't see many around here. Where are you headed?"

"Straight to the devil's door, apparently," Simon whispered over their secure channel.

"That information is classified," Boj stated, determination mixed with stubbornness in his voice.

The creature prodded further. "What brought you into these circumstances?"

"We were attacked by a Gargol ship. Our maintenance bots were destroyed, and the fuel compartment was damaged."

A partial lie, Sam knew, but the whole truth would have been worse.

The creature hesitated. "Very well. Follow the map to Glustony, and we can discuss specifics."

The creature's holographic presence disappeared, only to be replaced by a map. Boj's fingers scrambled over the display, checking the ship's navigation system. Sam caught sight of his eyes as they flitted from one control to another, his movements jerky and unstable. She'd seen that look on his face only once before— when he thought he was going to die.

This wasn't good.

Her breathing grew louder inside the constrictive helmet. But at least her face was concealed. She couldn't let the others see how terrified she was.

As they entered the planet's atmosphere, the sudden bright lights startled Sam's senses. She gawked at the surge of activity. Flying vehicles and ships of every shape and size zoomed in different directions.

This was a busy planet.

Most of the surface was covered in red sand, with a dusting of white salt crystals scattered throughout. But, as they flew closer, more details came into view. Sam squinted as giant purple lakes materialized in the distance with what looked like floating factories but on a massive scale. Perilium factories, she guessed.

They flew over cities with tall, shimmering silver buildings that rose upward into the clouds.

This planet must be rich, if they could afford such structures. Perilium must be prevalent here, but the cost had to be immense.

As they descended into Glustony, an onslaught of holograms and advertisements streamed toward them from the center of the room. The bombardment of flashing images was so close it almost touched them.

A raucous robotic voice sliced into Sam's eardrums. "How about a diagnostic assessment of your ship? Our robots are top of the line and will locate the source of the problems within a few minutes. Then, they'll tell you which enhancements and upgrades you need. One hundred thousand credits."

One hundred thousand credits? That sounded like a lot.

"Uh…" Boj hesitated.

"If we don't hear a yes or no response within two seconds, we'll proceed to do the diagnostic assessment."

Boj fiddled with the controls, his hands moving frantically.

The voice over their intercom sounded satisfied. "That confirms it, then. Thank you for your business."

A chart appeared on the screen with a counter showing a debt of one hundred thousand credits.

The robotic voice continued. "How about a thorough cleaning of your ship? We'll use our high-end powered pressure washers to remove all dust, dirt, grime, and microbes that could have arrived with you on your flight. Ten thousand credits."

"No," Boj stated, a little forcefully.

"How about a—"

"No," he interrupted. "Zenobii, is there a way to dismantle the ads? I would prefer to negotiate face-to-face."

Zenobii just shook his head.

Kwan took a few steps toward Boj. "Let me try." Before he could say no, she pressed a few buttons and waited. The ads disappeared a few seconds later.

"How did you do that?"

"I noticed something flashing when those ads first appeared."

Sam was amazed at how rapidly Kwan seemed to pick up on these things, having no training. It just came naturally to her.

The ship took a slight left turn and descended further until they reached a landing pad. They hovered over a huge grassy area with a dome-shaped white stone palace glistening in the distance. Lush gardens spread throughout its vicinity.

"There's something you need to know. According to the ship's database intel, the Glubens are hostile," Kwan said on their secure channel. "They're not part of GAIA."

"Hostile?" Sam asked. "What do you mean?"

"It doesn't take much to get them angry. I've dealt with hostile people before. This is a bit different. Just be prepared for anything. Don't let them smell your fear. Be confident but not too confident. Don't do anything to draw attention. Don't talk. Keep those helmets on at *all times*. And most of all...just pretend you're *nobody*. The less they know about you, the better. If the plan goes smoothly, we should be in and out of here within an hour. Got it?"

Sam tried to sound confident, but she couldn't suppress her growing fear. "Got it."

Cold sweat clung to her skin as they waited for the ship to power down. The gangway descended, and a thick wave of dusty air swirled up and pushed against them. The brilliant red and white grains of sand sparkled in the air, almost blinding her.

"You ready?" Kwan asked Sam as they made their way outside.

Ready? Kwan's instructions had been vague and subjective at best. Be confident but not too confident—what did that even mean? Don't let them smell your fear? She was ready all right—ready to *run and hide.* Hide her identity, hide away somewhere where no one could find her. That's all she wanted to do right now. She wanted to turn back. But she couldn't. Not now. They were already moving. Descending the gangway like prisoners being forced off the plank of a ship. This didn't feel like a diplomatic mission at all.

Dread rose from the pit of her stomach. They were leaving the ship and heading into uncharted territory. With a bounty on her head and hostiles approaching, not knowing what would come next, it took all her power just to keep herself together.

"As ready as can be."

Inside, she didn't feel ready at all.

CHAPTER FIFTY-THREE

As Sam stepped off the ship, two Gluben guards approached, their wide, booted feet thundering on the rocky ground. They towered over her, each ten feet tall and quite large in width, too. Their legs, the size of tree stumps, could undoubtedly crush her in one step.

Two more approached in a vehicle equipped with what looked like measuring equipment—handheld scanners and pressure and height gauges of varying sizes and shapes. Sam and the others had to jump out of the way as the Glubens zoomed past, then skidded to a halt by their ship.

The *Theseus* could not have looked worse. One of the landing struts had broken off, leaving it lopsided, ready to topple over. If not dealt with soon, the ship could easily collapse. Trails of scathed and blackened metal littered the ground, remnants from the earlier attack. The ship groaned against the force of the wind. A loud crackling erupted as metal shards broke off and hurtled through the air like darts. Sam flinched, watching nervously. This ship wasn't falling apart—it was broken. Unfixable.

"I thought we were just stopping for fuel?" Simon asked.

"Looks like the damage was worse than expected," Sam said.

A buzzing noise rang in Sam's ears as hundreds of drones descended from the sky and swarmed their ship. Each carried tools and spare parts in their long robotic arms as they worked to repair the damage. Scanning each and every inch, they identified vulnerabilities and gaps, making their assessments. They coordinated with precision and didn't waste any time getting to work. The efficiency was astounding.

"Is this your entire crew?" one of the guards asked, his eyes scanning each of them.

"No," Boj said. "The rest are on board. One of our passengers is receiving medical treatment."

"I see. Remove your weapons."

Kwan hesitated, then offloaded her blaster, throwing it on the ground.

Sam glanced back toward the ship. Was it too late to turn back? Not that she would. Not that she could. If she couldn't deal with a few Gluben guards, how would she deal with Duskara?

She peered at the two guards as they dismounted their vehicle and made their way onto the *Theseus*.

"They will assess and repair your ship," one of the guards said, but it did nothing to ease Sam's fear and uneasiness. "Follow us."

The guards escorted them toward the palace entrance along a black stone pathway. Boj led in front while Kwan trailed at the rear. Sam, Simon, Kato, and Kobe were sandwiched in the middle. Giddy and Onnisa had stayed behind to tend to Captain Gorgana and the babies.

The grass on either side took on an orange-red hue. Most of the plants in the compound had a reddish tinge. The red soil crunched under their boots.

Even though the suits were supposed to moderate their body temperatures to the climate, the heat of this environment stifled Sam's senses. Sweat trickled down her face. She fought the urge to take her helmet off, remembering Kwan's warning to keep her identity protected.

Instead, she trudged on, trying not to think about it. She slowed her breathing, needing to steady herself.

A piercing trill came from the bushes to her right. She gasped as a bird the size of a hen flew toward her, hovering inches from her face. It caught the attention of the guards, who stopped and waited, watching in curiosity. The bird's wings flapped so fast they let out a low, vibrating hum. Its plumage was brilliant red, orange, and yellow, with a crop of white feathers forming a circle on its forehead. She stared into its eyes, bright blue with multicolored flecks, like a sea of stars.

The bird pecked at her helmet.

"What's going on?" Kobe asked.

"I don't know." Sam tried pushing the bird aside with the back of her arm. "It…won't…stop."

The guards mumbled something to each other.

She wobbled as the bird hammered away with its powerful beak. With every peck, the force caused a vibration inside her helmet, the sound magnifying. A crack formed right between her eyes. Soon, the bird would peck right through to her face!

"Get away!" Frantic, she tried to grab it, but this only angered the bird. It flew away, but not before it squirted a slimy white substance all over her helmet.

"Ugh, gross."

The guards laughed.

Sam pulled a cloth from her pocket and tried to wipe away the mess, but it just smeared all over.

They continued down the stone pathway. The smooth white steps leading up to the palace gleamed in the light as though they contained pieces of crystal. Two Gluben guards stood on either side of the entranceway. It was too dark to see what lay within from this vantage point.

They made their way inside. The guards led them through a

tunnel into a spacious room lit with torches hanging from the stone walls.

"Sit here," one of the guards directed. They did as they were told. The benches were also made of stone and quite uncomfortable.

At the back of the room, the same type of bird that had greeted them earlier flew inside a small cage. It squawked occasionally. The cage shook every time it flew around, its wings flapping desperately, forcefully.

Sam quietly observed their surroundings. Non-Gluben travelers sat at different stations around the room, each of them speaking with a Gluben.

Three beings with purple iridescent skin, long necks, and multiple appendages sat nearby. She'd seen these types of beings before—Volubens—when she was at the underwater military base. They were part of GAIA. One of them was weeping. This angered the Gluben, and he stood up, then signaled to one of the guards standing close by.

They took the crying Voluben away. The other two Volubens tried to resist, but the guard yelled at them.

"I have a bad feeling about this," Simon said through their secure channel. "I don't like being here. I don't like these Glubens."

"Where do you think they're taking the Volubens?" Sam asked.

"I don't know," Kobe said. "I just hope we don't have to go there too."

Another Gluben greeted them. This one looked different from the others. He had white markings painted on his face that contrasted against his red skin.

"Why do you come here?"

Boj hesitated, then removed his helmet to discuss matters face-to-face. "We require fuel, sir. Then we shall be on our way."

Kwan gasped as a guard yanked her helmet off.

"Why are you with this...human? Disgusting." He winced as he gaped at Kwan.

"She is part of GAIA. She is helping us on our trip."

Confusion swept over the Gluben's face as another guard whispered something into his ear.

"Your ship was in bad condition. We fixed it."

"Oh?"

The Gluben lifted both of his hands in one sweeping gesture, and a holographic display of their ship materialized in front of them. Images of its technology and upgrades appeared, along with a counter on the side that kept flashing numbers that grew in size. "Assessment cost: one hundred thousand credits. Fuel, another three hundred thousand credits. We added new fuel tank, quantum capacitor, replaced and upgraded landing gear, added one hundred liters of perilium, and replaced maintenance bots. Shall I list premium upgrades?"

"No," Boj said. "That'll be sufficient."

"Premium upgrades another six hundred thousand credits. You pay one million credits. How you pay?"

Boj hesitated. "We have some rare kaloi plants with *exceptional* medicinal benefits," he offered. "Advanced healing for a range of ailments and life-extending properties—"

The Gluben scoffed. "Plants only equal one thousand credits. What else?"

They were in a bad situation. They had no leverage whatsoever. For all they knew, the Glubens could take them all away, and they'd never leave this place. They'd forever be in their debt if the Glubens were calling all the shots anyway.

"We have Earth whiskey in our pantry," Kwan said with a leer. "Very expensive. Highly *valuable*. You may have it, if you wish."

The guard narrowed his eyes, anger in his tone. "We do not negotiate with *dirty* humans."

Dirty humans? The situation kept getting worse. What were they going to do? They couldn't get *stuck* here. Not after what they'd been through. Not now. Not when they'd only just started their journey.

"Besides," the Gluben continued, his eyes full of contempt. "Earth whiskey is *bowsha*." The Gluben flicked his hand dismissively. The word didn't translate through Sam's earpiece, but she didn't have to be a genius to understand what it might mean.

The Gluben glanced over his shoulder as another guard approached him, bending to his ear. They exchanged words, murmuring to one another. As they did so, the guard passed a small metallic ball the size of a marble to his counterpart.

"They found tracking device from your ship during assessment," the Gluben stated. "Never seen this type before. We take this for one thousand credits."

A tracking device? In their ship? Now they were in trouble. They needed to leave immediately before their pursuers caught up to them. But she thought about Kwan's words earlier. *Convince the Glubens that what we have to offer is so good they can't refuse.*

Sam had an idea. She stepped forward. "Yes, by all means! *Take it!* It's yours. A gift, from us! Very powerful. Very advanced. A one-of-a-kind surveillance technology!" Her words drew attention, and the Gluben peered at her with heightened interest. "Make you very powerful," she added.

The Gluben turned the device over in his meaty hand. "Powerful?"

Taking her queue, Boj nodded. "This one is unique. It uses… quantum technology to send out a signal between galaxies —*instantly*. If you need more, we have technology on board to replicate. You can use it to monitor your ships. It also sends distress signals like the one it is sending out now. It is our gift to you, sir."

Over their private channel, he added, "We need to leave. Immediately. If we don't, we'll be attacked right here on this planet."

The Gluben hesitated, studying the object. His head snapped up and he returned his hardened gaze to Boj. "You still have nine hundred and ninety-eight thousand credits you must pay. What are those…behind the helmets?"

"Just some maintenance workers we picked up along the way. Humans."

"Ugh, humans. Why are they so small?"

Boj shrugged, his patience waning. "That's just how they are. Small. Insignificant. They aren't worth your trouble."

The Gluben guard whispered something else to his counterpart.

"This one," he said, pointing to Sam, "sprayed by a Yolasa bird on your way here. That is considered *very* lucky in our culture."

Oh no.

"We take Krygian Elder, Rigellian, and this one here to work in perilium mines," he said, pointing to Kwan. "And this one here. *You.* The one with the crack in your helmet. Take it off."

Sam's heart rumbled in her chest. If they took her—

Boj stepped between them. "I don't think that's necessary—"

"Yes. We take this one. We keep in cage, like that Yolasa bird. For good luck." The Gluben pointed to the bird at the back of the room just as it squawked again and ruffled its feathers.

Boj cleared his throat and spoke louder. "You don't want…dirty humans anyway. They're just lowly maintenance—"

"I said *take off your helmet,*" the Gluben repeated. "Now!"

Sam jolted upright in her seat. The sudden change in the Gluben's voice carried to all corners of the room. Others stopped what they were doing, glancing up at the commotion. She looked around, all eyes on her now. So much for protecting her identity.

Before she could do anything, Kwan rose to her feet. "We're leaving. Now."

"No," the Gluben said, pulling out a blaster from the table and pointing it directly at her.

Sam jumped to her feet. "Kwan!" She couldn't let her risk her life. Not when there might be another way.

Slowly, she lifted her helmet, shaking out her hair—*bright red* hair, the same flaming color as the surrounding rocks and earth of this planet. Red hair that had the Glubens transfixed, shaking. Her pale skin and fiery hair made her stand out among these other-worldly beings.

The Glubens—*all* of them in the room—gasped. Murmurs erupted.

The one sitting across from Sam shrunk back. "Dasa-ga!"

"Dasa-ga!" the other Glubens yelled.

Dasa-ga? Sam listened to the translation through her earpiece and gasped. *Ghost demon.*

The Gluben pointed at Sam accusingly. "Bad omen! We are cursed!" He rose to his feet, shooing them out. "You must leave now. You must never come back. We give you what you want. Anything, you take it. Here."

He rushed to a nearby panel in the wall and punched in a code. A door slid open to reveal a storage compartment. He pulled out several items: a box of diamonds, strange glowing artifacts, and technological gadgets for which Sam did not know their purpose. Probably items they'd confiscated or squandered from other unsus-pecting travelers in need of refuge.

"The spirits are angry at us," he continued, frantically doling out the gifts. "Anything else you need?"

Sam thought back to their Galaxy Diplomats game earlier. A voice deep inside her resounded, the stream of words perfectly capturing what she'd known all along. *You're the author of your own journey. If you don't like it, rewrite the rules. Envision a better future. Not just for yourself, but for others, too. Those who aren't as lucky. Help them change their future. Make it happen!*

"Actually," she started, "we need another ship."

"What you need ship for?"

Sam thought hard and fast, wondering if they'd comply with her demands. "For those beings we saw earlier. The Volubens. We'll take them, too."

Kwan slid her a dumbfounded glance.

"Are you crazy?" Kobe asked telepathically.

"No. I'm just trying to help get a family to safety. Those beings—the

Volubens—need to be freed from this dreadful place. They're part of GAIA, and they need our help."

"Yes," the Gluben answered, then murmured to one of the guards in their language.

Blood surged through Sam's veins as the Gluben guards rushed them out of the room and down the corridor toward the mouth of the palace. The guards shoved products at them, piling them up in their arms in a last-ditch effort to appease them, as if they were making offerings to deities.

They hurried outside, the dust swirling again. Shock and relief churned inside her as she glimpsed their ship up ahead. Only, it didn't look quite like their ship anymore. Not only had the exterior silver panels been replaced, they shimmered in the light, as if brand new. The ship looked sturdier, too. The landing gear had been repaired and upgraded with reinforced metal coating and shock-absorbing technology.

It looked in *much* better shape than when they'd first arrived.

Another ship parked close by looked in equally solid condition. Sam glanced back toward the palace as the Volubens were escorted out. Tears of joy streamed down their faces. They now had their own ship to get back to their home planet. They were free.

A buzzing noise filled Sam's ears. Hundreds of drones hovered above their ship, completing last-minute modifications. Another idea sparked in Sam's mind: the drones might serve a useful purpose. Perhaps they could use them to learn more about Duskara's planet, Logom. They could be the eyes they so desperately needed. She pointed. "We'll take three of those drones, too."

"Yes," the Gluben guard replied, looking wary, but complied. He signaled to another Gluben guard, who rushed to retrieve extra drones from a nearby supply vehicle.

"Don't push your luck!" Kwan snapped over their secure channel.

Kwan was right, in a way. The Glubens were irritated and at the end of their rope. Sam didn't need to twist any further. They had what they needed—the fuel—and also *so much more.* But as for luck? They couldn't rely on the universe to supply them with that. The universe didn't work that way. They had to take action, make their own opportunities, and change things themselves.

"We make our own luck," Sam said as they strode up the ship's ramp. "Now let's get out of here!" she added, though what she didn't say was, *before they change their minds!*

CHAPTER FIFTY-FOUR

Sam clenched her fists—anything to settle her nerves—as they hurried up the ramp to the ship's entrance. For a split second, she worried about a snag, something that might strand them here on Glubo. But she pushed that thought aside. She was determined to leave, to survive, and she could tell the others felt the same way. Kwan, whose self-reliance and fearlessness usually far exceeded the others, cast wide-eyed glances at them as she rushed to take her seat. Simon and Kobe each held the same nervous, tight-lipped expression.

It was only once Sam strapped into her seat, hearing the ship roaring to life, that she smiled and relaxed. She leaned back in her chair.

She was glad to leave this place. How many more travelers might be detained here? How many more would never see their families again?

She couldn't stop thinking about what had happened on Glubo —*and what could have happened instead!* She shivered at the thought of being stuck there, forever, in a cage. Never to see her family or friends again. And her friends and crew members? Any or all of them could have been taken. Trapped as prisoners to spend the rest of their days working to pay off their debts. Some even working in the grueling perilium mines.

In that moment, she knew she would return, one day, to free the others. She'd bring reinforcements. How could a society treat its citizens that way? The thought disgusted her. Despite their warning, she'd return.

She liked her new name. Dasa-ga. Ghost demon. It had a nice ring to it.

She took a deep breath, trying to slow her heart rate. They still had to clear several more hurdles. The AI death serum still needed to be successfully finalized and weaponized. Kwan, Simon, and Giddy were working on the project together but hadn't found a breakthrough yet.

And as for the plan of attack? The others thought it was sound. It might even work. There was only one problem: it didn't involve her! Captain Gorgana and the others were determined to keep her out of the way. She couldn't just wait idly on the ship stationed on an asteroid, doing nothing while Kwan went in by herself. Kwan would never get past the Malborgs. Even if she managed to make it inside Duskara's cave…

The odds of Kwan surviving the mission were slim.

They couldn't just enter Duskara's territory without scoping it out first. They needed eyes on her whereabouts and habits, details about her cave, like entry and exit points. They needed to look for Duskara's vulnerabilities and any security measures they could infiltrate.

It gave her an idea. The drones they'd picked up on Glubo could be the key. They were small enough to enter a residence—a cave, perhaps. If they could deploy them somehow *before* their arrival to Logom…

She hurried down the hallway toward the command station but stopped when she heard voices nearby. Kwan and Giddy. She listened carefully.

"…and it didn't work," Kwan said. "And we've been trying the methods you suggested, Dr. Spark. Simon and I reverse engineered the Malborg DNA, which contains traces of Duskara's coding. We created a synthetic duplicate of their DNA and inserted the destructive viral mechanism."

"And the virus still isn't propagating as expected?"

"No. Once the virus begins its attack, the systems recognize the threat and adapt. The virus shuts down soon after. It's only a fifty-nine-percent success rate."

"Still? How many control trials so far?"

"Thirty-six and counting. We're working on an alternative destructive coding mechanism. But it's going to take time."

"Fifty-nine percent isn't great odds."

"No, it isn't. It wouldn't be potent enough to take out Duskara. But it might hinder her. At least temporarily. But it could backfire, too. It could allow her to build up immunity to it, allowing her systems to adapt to it, and that could be worse. *Much worse.*"

"Keep trying. Don't give up hope just yet. I'm sure something will come through. I'll keep working at it as well. It won't be long before we solve this riddle."

"Thank you, Dr. Spark."

Sam sighed. She'd heard enough. The news was a real blow. If they couldn't get it to work, then the trip was all for nothing. The AI death serum was their only weapon against Duskara. Drones or no drones. Knowing Duskara's whereabouts wouldn't matter if they had no weapon to use against her.

But they were missing something. They needed to find Duskara's Achilles heel. If they could find one, there might be hope.

"Sam? Is that you?"

Sam whirled around. Giddy stood down the hall.

"Is everything okay?"

"I'm sorry, Giddy. I overheard you talking to Kwan about the

AI death serum. I—well, I had an idea, but I'm not sure it will even help now."

"Just because something doesn't work one way, that doesn't mean there aren't other solutions available to us. We must always look for opportunities, wherever they may be."

Sam paused and brightened at her words. "You're right." Despite the odds, it wouldn't hurt if they could pull it off. And who knew what may come of it? It may, at least, buy them some time.

"What's the idea? I'm all ears."

"Those drones we picked up on Glubo. Do you think it's possible to reverse engineer them, to figure out how they were built?"

Giddy nodded. "Yes. We have that capability."

"And could we change them slightly—add a cloaking device so that the Malborgs and Duskara couldn't see or hear them coming?"

"Well," Giddy hesitated. "I suppose…it's *possible*. With the right alterations."

"And we still have a couple more days, at least, before we arrive at Logom…"

Giddy peered at her, a quizzical look in her eyes. "Yes."

"Is there still a GAIA outpost in that region?"

"Why…yes. The *Crimsonwing* is stationed on Candu."

Sam felt a flicker of hope. It might have been the best news she'd received all day. The *Crimsonwing* might have access to similar technology. If they could get them the diagrams, the plans for those drones somehow…

"That's really good news. Great news, actually!"

Giddy grinned. "And why is that?"

"Well, this is what I'm thinking. We reverse engineer those drones. We change them, add a cloaking ability. Then, we send a scrambled signal to that outpost on Candu. In the signal, we'll give them instructions—diagrams—on how to build those drones. The *Crimsonwing* can then build the drones and use them in advance to scan Logom while we're on our way. If they find anything, like weaknesses, they can send that information back to us. If everything goes well, we'll have it *before* we arrive, and we can adjust our plans if needed."

Giddy's eyes widened. "Spoken like a true GAIA strategist! Your mother and father would be proud."

Sam's face reddened. She didn't like to think of herself in that way. She was just a girl with high hopes trying to find answers, fumbling through life with its challenges and twisting roads and unexpected bumps along the way.

A pang of sadness and urgency filled her at the mention of her parents. Wherever they were, she hoped they were safe. They were probably thinking the same about her.

"Do you think it could work?"

"It's an excellent plan and well worth a try! I'll relay this to the crew and help them get started right away. Good work, Sam!"

In the evening, Sam retreated to her room. She needed a quiet spot to think—a place where she could unwind and allow her thoughts to travel.

She took a deep breath and let it out slowly, trying to calm her mind. She let her thoughts drift. She thought again of her strange dream, of the bustling city and the office workers. The vision rushed into her mind so rapidly and with such vigor that it felt...*real*.

It picked up exactly where her last dream had ended, the moment when she was swooped up into the air with Zenobii. Right into the spacecraft. Now they were traveling, faster than the speed of light, toward a strange white planet in the distance. Images streamed by. Crystals containing vast libraries of information and a strange cave with cylindrical tubes. White light pulsed from within the cave, the light soothing, comforting.

Two words flashed in her mind: Destination Sofia. The planet called to her as if it were a living entity. She felt a strange sensation of being pulled by a mysterious force.

A dark shadow loomed just inside the cave's entrance, the humanoid figure of Duskara. A moment later, she dissolved into dust, drowned out by a pulsating light radiating from somewhere deep inside the cave.

Sam listened to her inner voice, the one deep inside her. *The cave contains the answers. The secret to defeating the darkness and Duskara.*

This time, when Sam opened her eyes, the vision of the planet lingered. She wanted to go there, to that planet, that calming place. It seemed so real.

If only it were.

A knock came at the door. "Hello? Sam?"

Kato!

She ran to the door. "Come in!"

Kato entered, holding one of the Rigellian babies. She stroked its head. It cooed in response, its eyelids closing and opening with every stroke.

"Is everything okay? You were quiet at dinner."

"I…" Sam faltered. "I just needed some time alone. After what happened with the Glubens, seeing those families… I couldn't save them all."

"You helped one."

"But it's not enough. We have to go back one day and help the others."

"I know. I get it. And one day we will. But for now…you need to count your blessings, you know. Celebrate the small victories. Come on! They're waiting for you." She pulled Sam to her feet with her free hand.

"Who's waiting? What's going on?"

A smile spread across Kato's face. "Everyone's in the dining hall celebrating. Simon hacked the sound system. There's music. People are dancing! Even Captain Gorgana has joined us."

Kato's enthusiasm helped put Sam in a better mood. She always knew how to put things in perspective and remain positive.

"I'm feeling better now."

"That's good, because we wouldn't be here if it weren't for you."

They made their way to the dining hall.

The eclectic beats of hip-hop, R&B, and electronic dance music thumped down the hall. The lights were turned down low. When they arrived, the dining hall had transformed into a temporary dance hall, complete with a disco ball.

"What is happening?" Sam asked. "Where did they get this stuff?" She no longer felt part of a serious mission but more like she was on a cruise ship, drifting on the ocean.

"Life's too short to miss out on these things," Kato explained. "Come on! You don't want to miss the dance-off!"

The scene unfolding was utter chaos.

Kato grabbed Sam by the hand and pulled her to one of the tables near the makeshift dance floor. Front-row seats. Onnisa sat nearby, along with Giddy and Captain Gorgana, who watched intently. Kwan was smiling—a rare but delightful moment. On the floor, Simon and Kobe took turns showing off their breakdancing moves. Sam laughed, her first in a long time. They looked so goofy.

Kobe wasn't bad, his body moving to the rhythm of the music. His arm and leg muscles were larger and more defined now compared to a few months ago. Probably from all the relentless physical training. It looked like he'd perfected a number of impressive moves. He swung his legs up like a windmill, balancing on his shoulders and back. He froze for a few seconds with remarkable stability and control. It looked almost effortless. A moment later, he unfroze, got up, and ended with a moonwalk before giving up the floor to Simon.

Sam and the others cheered them on.

Boj took a seat beside Sam and offered her a flashy red drink.

"It's a karamelon berry chocolate smoothie. I made it!"

She gaped as she took the drink. They had chocolate on the ship? *And* karamelon berries?! They must have been saving them for a special occasion. "Thank you, Boj!"

Boj raised his glass. "A toast to the Queen of Kryg, the girl who saved us."

"To the girl who saved us!" the others echoed.

Boj's words gnawed at her. She hadn't saved them. Not really. *Not yet.* Besides, she wasn't a savior. All of them were in this together, *working together*. For the first time, she realized that they were all part of something larger than themselves. It wasn't just about her actions. It was their collective actions, including her friends and the crew, helping each other, supporting one another, like a community coming together, leading as one and pulling everyone through this intolerable situation.

Still, she wasn't sure they could succeed. Of course she wanted to beat Duskara, to protect her friends and stop the war. She wanted to fulfill her duty as Queen of Kryg, but how could she do this if she didn't even know who she was or what she was capable of? She froze in her seat, worrying about the future—a future that held so much uncertainty. She wanted to enjoy this moment, to get lost in it and let her cares melt away. But she couldn't. They were only days away from Logom, from Duskara…

"You don't have to be a hero, Sam, always running toward danger," Kato said quietly.

Sam hesitated, taking in Kato's words, the truth of them. How did Kato know her so well? It was like she'd sensed her thoughts…

But maybe she was right. Sam always ran toward the danger. But was there any other way to protect her friends? She hoped so.

She sighed. "You're right, Kato. I know. And I couldn't ask for a better friend."

"You are enough. We love you, and we're here for you, whatever happens."

Kato's words lightened her spirit, but they did little to ease the anxiety swirling inside her. She wanted to enjoy the evening—after all, it could be their last celebration together like this. Tomorrow, her friends could *die*. Her doubts and fears plagued her like poison. But she didn't want to ruin the festive mood, so she forced herself to focus, to be more present and grateful for each gifted moment.

She took a sip of her smoothie, the familiar karamelon flavor delicious and sweet, the fruit native to Kryg. It felt like such an exotic treat to have this here, on a spacecraft, in the middle of nowhere.

"Boj, you've been an amazing captain, but if you ever were thinking about a second career or a hobby…you should consider opening your own smoothie shop! Or bottling this and selling it throughout the universe."

"Thanks. I might consider that."

They watched as Simon did a robot move, perfectly in sync with the music. Then, he attempted the windmill move like Kobe but lost his footing. He giggled, then got up and pretended he'd done it on purpose. He slowly moonwalked off the dance floor, his face reddening.

Kobe joined them at their table, holding a frozen fish in his hands. "Sam, you ever kiss a cod?" He held up the fish.

Sam scrunched her face. "What? No!"

"Come on! You've been to Newfoundland now. It's part of the initiation ceremony."

Kwan joined them. She made a sour face at the sight of it. "Don't peer pressure her, Kobe!"

"It's okay, Sam. You don't have to if you don't want to," Kato added, rolling her eyes. "Frankly…it's gross."

"Are you going to?" Sam smirked, turning to Kobe.

"I like her," Kwan said, grabbing the cod from his hands and holding it up to his face.

Kobe closed his eyes and puckered up. Kwan placed the cod up to his lips, resulting in bursts of laughter from around the room.

Kobe wiped his mouth and turned the fish toward Kwan. "Your turn."

"No way. Besides, it's my turn on the floor!"

Kwan sprang onto the dance floor. Everyone watched in awe as her body moved in sync with the beat. After doing a series of continuous swipes, twisting her body while rotating her legs into the air, she froze, using just one arm to support her weight. A moment later, she ended with a series of backflips, wowing the audience.

"Come on, Sam! Your turn!" Kato nudged her.

"What? I have to follow...*that*?" She didn't want to even *attempt* to dance with her two left feet.

But Kato tugged her off her chair, and a moment later, she found herself on the dance floor, unsure what to do. Kato pulled her arms forward, and so she followed, trying to mimic Kato's moves. At least she wasn't up here alone. It felt one hundred times better having Kato with her as they made fools of themselves in front of the others. She felt her face redden but was so exhilarated by the moment and the music that she didn't care.

Kobe and Simon cheered as they made their way back to the table.

"Nice moves," Kobe said to Sam.

He must have been mistaken. She'd just been following Kato's lead.

"Thanks," she replied.

Boj looked amused but immobile, glued to his seat.

"Boj, do you have music on Kryg? Do your people dance?" She couldn't help but wonder whether human dancing looked absolutely ridiculous to the Krygians.

"No. We didn't have music for the longest time. It's something unique to humans. And...we love it. As for dance, it was something our ancestors used to do...to trick our enemies. To *hypnotize* them before attacking. But we don't do that anymore. There's been no need to."

The idea of hypnotizing enemies by dancing seemed strange. But then she thought of all the ways other species interacted through dance. Like honeybees, who danced to transmit locational information about the presence of food. Or flies and spiders, who danced to attract mates. Maybe it wasn't so strange after all.

"But this looks fun," Boj said. "I will try it."

And with that, he leaped up and onto the dance floor. He swayed his body, performing a series of strange moves in time to the beat. Fascinated, Simon and Kobe raced to the dance floor, trying to pick up the new moves. Kato and Sam joined them, too.

After an evening of good food, great music, and a wonderful celebration with friends, Sam felt tired but elated.

They'd been so lucky today. But that luck was, in part, due to them taking risks. It could have gone either way. Kato had taught her that life was fleeting and that it was okay to enjoy the good moments, get lost in them, and celebrate with others. And that it was okay to make a fool out of yourself because, ultimately, no one really cared.

She didn't want this moment to end.

But she knew it would. The party was a good distraction. But that was all it was: the calm before the storm.

CHAPTER FIFTY-FIVE

The next day, everything changed—drastically. The celebration was over.

A loud knock came at Sam's door.

She jumped out of bed, wobbling, half-asleep. Opening the door, she found Kato outside, her eyes wide in panic.

"Kato? What's wrong?"

"You missed training practice, and, well…"

Sam felt foolish. Her body had protested this morning, forcing her to press the snooze button a million times. "I must have slept in. How did training go?"

"Well, good. For the most part. I mean, I did pretty well on the hover kneepads." She smiled proudly. "You should have seen it. I finally beat the Malborg simulation."

A pang of sadness filled Sam at having missed Kato's incredible moment. It was practically unheard of to beat the simulation. You had to be extremely fast and agile to do it. An expert. None of them had gotten that far. Until today.

"That's great! I'm really proud of you."

But Kato's enthusiasm faded. "But the bad news is that Simon's hover kneepads malfunctioned. And, well, to make a long story, uh…longer, he went spiraling around the room and broke his arm."

"No! Are you serious?" Sam couldn't believe it. It seemed like a series of mishaps followed them around that morning like a shadow. First with the missed training, and now this. The devastating news only reminded her of how fragile they all were.

"Yeah. And no amount of kaloi leaves can fix it in time. He's been taken off physical training. They re-assigned him to assist Kwan with technical support. And help Captain Gorgana with babysitting duties. I was going to check on him. Did you want to join me?"

Sam was torn. She *did* want to go with Kato, but she still needed a plan to get to Duskara without putting the others in danger. She couldn't let anyone else get hurt on their journey.

"You go ahead. I have to check on something first."

"I'll see you at lunch?"

"Sounds good. And thank you, Kato, for letting me know about…everything."

Kato nodded. "I wish I had better news, honestly. Just stay safe. I don't want to see anyone else get hurt."

"You and me both."

Sam hurried to the command station. Maybe if she could find out more about Duskara's planet, they could find some weakness, a flaw—maybe some new technology or a piece of information to help carry out her mission. She had to remain hopeful. And as for the escape pods? She needed to find out how they worked so she could get to Duskara. Meet her face-to-face, alone, and put an end to all this. No one else needed to get hurt.

She arrived at the command station to a flurry of activity. Zenobii directed staff carrying gadgets and mechanical devices to different locations around the room. Piles of machinery took up most of the free space. Boj stood at a table, scanning the equipment with a handheld device. Captain Gorgana swiveled in her seat, tapping buttons and logging information into a database.

Everyone was so busy that no one noticed she was there.

Maybe it would work to her advantage.

She treaded warily around the debris and took a seat at the round table in the middle of the room. Peering at the holographic display, she zoomed in on a massive black hole at the center of the Dark Galaxy. Dynamic and dangerous, it sucked up planets and debris in its vicinity. She twisted it around using her fingers, looking at it from different angles.

She zoomed in on Duskara's planet. It was exactly as she had envisioned it. A dreary landscape of black basalt deserts and ranges of sprawling mountains with stones formed from the rapid cooling of underground volcanic lava, completely devoid of anything green. There was no life here. Nothing except for Duskara and her Malborgs.

Something tugged at her mind. *Planet Sofia.* The planet she'd seen in her dreams. Desolate and abandoned, it held a library of information contained within crystals. Information they may need in order to defeat Duskara. Like a beacon, it sprung into her mind, pulling her toward its light. Was it possible? Could this really be it?

She hustled over to one of the wall panels and studied the maps of the local solar systems. They were approaching the Treyga System. She pressed a button. Several images of planets popped up on the screen, each with a brief description underneath about what they contained.

She did a full-on double take when she saw the name underneath one: Sofia.

Sofia! It *wasn't* just a dream!

She zoomed in closer. It looked exactly like the planet she'd seen in her dreams. Forlorn, with white crystals jutting out from the ground. A crystal cave at the northernmost pole.

"Captain Gorgana, I..." Sam faltered, then steeled herself. "I think you should see this."

The captain looked over, curious. "What is it? What have you found?"

"I... Well, I think I've been getting messages from this planet, Captain. Planet Sofia."

The captain leaned closer, studying the images. "What do you mean, messages?"

"I've been having dreams lately…visions…about a planet with crystals containing a library of information. Information I think we need to defeat Duskara. Can we stop here?"

Gorgana hesitated. It was obvious that she still had reservations about Sam. After all, it was Sam who had carried around the LOMA device, unaware of its powers.

"Zenobii, do we have time to make a quick stop on Planet Sofia? Will it risk the mission? And is the Treyga System safe?"

Zenobii tapped away on his screen, gathering data, testing the timelines, and running scenarios. He scanned the historical and geographic data. A hint of intrigue danced across his eyes. Looking satisfied, he spoke. "We're in advance of our scheduled arrival. Planet Sofia has been abandoned for hundreds of years. It was once used for mining minerals. Interesting." He hesitated, glancing toward Sam. "There's a crystal structure in a cave to the north, left there by its previous visitors."

"Hmm. A crystal structure…" Captain Gorgana mused, eyeing Sam with curiosity.

Zenobii continued. "There are no habitable planets in this system. I don't see it as a threat. However, in order to keep on track, if we go, we should only stay for a few hours at most. That's my assessment."

"Very well," Captain Gorgana replied, switching gears and adjusting the dials on the control panel. "Set a course for Planet Sofia. Let's hope you find what you are looking for, Sam Sanderson."

We will, Sam thought. The dream—or vision—couldn't be just a coincidence. It was a message. That planet would have the information they needed to defeat Duskara. Sam was sure of it. Excitement grew inside her at the prospect of what secrets they might uncover there.

CHAPTER FIFTY-SIX

ESCAPING GLUBO ALIVE AND UNHURT HAD BEEN INCREDIBLY fortunate. Kwan was convinced luck was on their side. And with their lucky streak, they needed to take any and all opportunities to ramp up their mission, which meant putting more effort into the AI death serum trials.

Without a breakthrough, the trip would be all for nothing. She turned to Simon, grateful that he now had more time to spend with her on this project after his accident.

"Did you find anything new?"

"No," he mumbled, fidgeting with the magnification on the electron microscope. "Same response."

"Even with the larger viral concentration? The greater viral load?"

"Yep. After the virus is injected, the cells behave as they always do. Only about a quarter of the ones hijacked by the virus die off. But then it triggers an immediate immune response. The other cells recognize the threat, create a viral defense system, and attack the bad cells. There's not enough time for the virus to replicate before it's destroyed."

"What concentration did you use?"

"I tried one million copies per milliliter like you asked," he said slowly. "I even tried two million copies. The success rate dropped to thirty-five percent. It was *worse*."

Worse? She sighed. "I don't get it. How is it *surviving* with those numbers?"

"It's like Duskara's DNA *knows* it's being attacked. The more we push it, the more she builds immunity."

Kwan rubbed her eyes. She didn't want to lose hope. Not yet. Not when they were so close to a solution. "We need a different approach."

Something stirred by the doorway. A maintenance bot approached. It held a metallic canister with several wires protruding from each end.

"What is that? What have you got?"

"Is that a cat toy?" Simon said, amused.

The maintenance bot paused, then shook its head.

"Here, let me see it." Kwan took the object, gently rubbing the dust off its surface. She examined the manufacturing code stamped on the base of the container. Rigellian technology, used for their ship's life-support system. These devices were rare. It was probably worth more than all the equipment in their lab. "Oh, wow. An Aramchak device."

"A what?"

"It's used for the oxygen generation and filtration system."

"Oh?" Simon hesitated.

Kwan continued. "Our ship is like a living organism. It relies on bacteria to feed off waste. The bacteria produce oxygen and hydrogen as byproducts so that we can survive long distances in space. This device functions like a kidney, cleansing the ship's air and water." The *Theseus* would have at least two, but if one wasn't in use...

"Our ship is a living organism?" Simon said, astounded.

"Yes, and without this device, well, let's just say it'll cause a lot of problems down the road. I'm just not sure how it ended up here." Kwan chewed her lower lip. "It must have gotten misplaced when the Glubens upgraded the ship. Come on, we better run this over to Boj in the command station. He'll be expecting this."

Kwan entered the command station with Simon and the maintenance bot in tow. It was chaos. They scrambled around crew members and piles of junk dumped on the floor.

Boj stood at the circular table at the center of the room. An image of the *Theseus* glimmered in the holographic light. He tapped buttons on the control panel, and the image of the ship transformed before their eyes. Almost its entire chrome exterior disappeared against the blue light, yet pieces of the ship remained visible.

"What are you working on?" Simon asked.

Boj looked up. "Oh, just testing the Thesian cloaking technology. Making sure it still works before we get to the Dark Galaxy." He pointed to the parts of the ship still visible in the light. "As you can see, the ship was upgraded with a lot of new equipment. They need to be cloaked and tested."

Kwan scanned the mess of extra parts lying around, perhaps no longer needed or waiting to be logged. "There were a lot of modifications made to this ship."

"Yes, indeed. Some may even challenge the idea that it's still the same ship from before."

"Is it?" Kwan asked.

"Do you know the story of the Ship of Theseus?" Boj asked. "From ancient times."

She shook her head, but Simon looked up, grinning.

"It was a thought experiment," Simon said, "by the Greek philosopher Plutarch. Over the course of its journey, the ship required constant repairs. The Athenians replaced old, rotting planks with new, sturdier timber. The question became whether it was the same ship, given its new components."

"Exactly," Boj said.

"Don't ask me how I knew that," Simon added. "I like Greek philosophy."

"So as a whole," Kwan said, "the ship is like a person who survives on their individual parts. And it can transform itself through time. The recent upgrades are comparable to a human receiving bionic upgrades for a lost limb, perhaps. The human is still considered human, just as the *Theseus* is still considered the *Theseus*, only a little different now."

She fixated on the fascinating concept that the ship was alive and transforming and that they were part of its journey. She thought about her own journey, her identity. Who was she, really? On a cellular level, she was made up of interacting biological processes. But more than that, her experiences and interconnections contributed to her character. Her choices *defined* her. Every experience, every choice leading up to now, whether small or large, intentional or unintentional, had brought her to this moment.

Would any of them be the same after this journey?

She peered out the viewing window at the shimmering lights. They were traveling in SWIFT navigation mode once again. Despite her nausea the first time, she was starting to get used to it.

Boj tapped another button on the panel. "With the Thesian cloaking technology, we can transform *anything*." The holographic image of the ship shimmered in the light, all its components visible. Then, Boj pressed another button, and it changed. Its exterior shell shifted, tiny pieces scattering and reforming, changing from shiny chrome to mirroring the blue light surrounding it. A moment later, the entire ship vanished. No streaks of metal, no blinking lights. "Looks like it worked. We can safely say we're still flying the *Theseus*."

"Amazing!" Simon said.

Boj smiled smugly, then gazed down at the canister of multicolored wires in Kwan's hand. His eyes lit up. "You found it!"

"The maintenance bot found it," Kwan corrected him. "I'm not sure how it got misplaced, but anyway, here you go."

Boj couldn't have looked more relieved.

Kwan turned to Simon, who looked amused. "That was a good distraction, but we better get back to the lab. We can't waste any more time."

"We didn't. I have an idea," Simon began as they hurried down the hall.

"What?"

"I've been thinking. If there was a way we could cloak the virus so that Duskara wouldn't know she was being attacked…"

"With what?"

"We adapt the Thesian cloaking technology on a smaller scale."

Kwan brightened at the suggestion. "Yes! I like your train of thought, Simon. Make it look like those cells are just a regular part of her body. Nothing abnormal about them. They'd continue to replicate, and Duskara wouldn't realize the problem until it was too late. But inside, they'd contain the destructive mechanism."

"And release it on a timer." Simon shrugged. "Maybe it could work."

Kwan beamed. It was a brilliant idea. They just had to figure out a way to execute it in time. "It *will* work. Start prepping the new trial. I'm going to let Dr. Spark know. I'll be right back."

CHAPTER FIFTY-SEVEN

KWAN PACED THE COMMAND STATION. THROUGH THE VIEWING window, a small white planet came into view. Planet Sofia. She didn't know why they were stopping here. The original plan was to follow a course directly to Logom, not visit some random planet.

Captain Gorgana charted their course with Boj and Zenobii at her side. Onnisa stood at a circular table, peering at a hologram of the planet's dimensions and details.

"Why are we stopping?" Kwan asked.

Onnisa glanced up. "Queen Samantha requested it." She returned her attention to the hologram and zoomed in. Mountains and caves spread far and wide, covering the dreary brown land-scape. White crystals jutted out of them, like massive boils protruding from skin. It looked abandoned and desolate. No signs of plants, or animals, or...*any* life.

Onnisa's vague reply tugged at Kwan's thoughts. Stopping on some mysterious, unknown planet because Sam wanted to only added to her unease. Wherever Sam went, danger was present. It always had been and always would be. And it was Kwan's job to protect her. But she wasn't sure she could do it. She didn't feel cut out for this. After all, she hadn't been able to protect Sam on Glubo. She'd wanted to protect her identity but failed. What was next? What if she couldn't save Sam when she needed to?

Sam entered the room, determination in her eyes. She strode over to the table with the hologram and zoomed in. "Captain, we need to get to this crystal palace in the north."

"Why?" Kwan asked.

"Because that's where the information is located."

"What information?" Kwan frowned. Sam's directions were vague. How had she convinced Captain Gorgana to stop at this forlorn place?

Sam hesitated. "Information that will help us defeat Duskara."

"And where did you get that idea?"

"In a vision."

A *vision*? Kwan's anger simmered. This was a terrible idea. She, Simon, and Dr. Spark were trying to make scientific advances with the AI death serum based on hard science. But Sam was leading them to a planet based on...what? A dream? And they were all supposed to just accept it? What if it was a trap, some telepathic fragment of Duskara telling her to go there?

Kwan knew Sam was in a fragile state. She'd become withdrawn, keeping to herself lately. Did she still share her telepathic connection with Duskara? What other things had Duskara told her that she wasn't revealing?

"So, we're just going to head to this planet, based on...on a vision?" Kwan asked. She looked to Captain Gorgana and Zenobii for answers, but they remained silent.

"Do not dismiss the power of dreams," Onnisa said. "Queen Samantha has had visions before. They have saved us in the past."

Kwan shuddered. Sam had been easily manipulated by Duskara before. How were they certain she wasn't being manipulated again now? Duskara always seemed to be one step ahead, pulling them all forward into a mysterious, unknown trap. Kwan would need to keep her guard up, keep on the lookout for anything unusual.

But everything about the situation and this planet was strange and daunting. She took in the planet's rocky and foreboding landscape. Crystals jutted out at different angles from the ground. No signs of life here. At least, none that were noticeable.

They touched down in the northernmost region.

As they exited the ship, she heard an eerie noise. A strange, constant ringing in her ears. Different tones and pitches. No one could explain where the sound was coming from. Was it the crystals emitting the shimmering noise, or something else?

"We need to find a cave with a large cluster of these crystals," Sam said. "That's where we'll find the answers."

Kwan gazed around. Everything looked the same. No structures—no signs of technology or intelligent life. Everything was just...random.

Kwan, Sam, Kato, and Kobe trudged up a massive hill to get a better vantage point. Simon stayed back on the ship, still recovering from his broken arm. The fewer people exploring, the better. Less risk, less effort keeping track of everyone. Less time. And she didn't want to stay on this planet too long.

The gravity here was strong. It took extra effort to pull their weight. Kwan was grateful when they switched to their anti-gravity kneepads and zoomed along the surface. She periodically checked her tracker and the secure channel to keep in contact with the ship. Everything seemed to be working. Except the constant ringing rattled her, the sound disorienting.

"That noise—that pulsating sound is super strange." Kobe pointed toward a cluster of crystals in the distance. "Does anyone feel like it's coming from over there?"

"Yeah," Sam answered. "Let's check it out."

They made their way over as storm clouds accumulated overhead. What was once sunny and bright had become dark and ominous in a matter of minutes. Kwan knew the storms could be dangerous, with wind gusts of up to one hundred and fifty kilometers per hour. The environment here was toxic. It contained high levels of sulfur dioxide and nitrogen oxides. Acid rain was not only common but more dangerous here, given the high concentration.

In the distance, rain lashed down against the landscape. The rocky soil didn't absorb the moisture well. Pools of water collected on the surface. As the water hit the ground, the acid rain mixed with the crystals, letting off a strange fog.

"Command," Kwan said. "It looks like we're in for a storm. Do these suits protect against acid rain?"

There was static, and then Boj's voice rang through. "Affirmative on both fronts. How much longer do you expect you'll need?"

Kwan scanned the land below them. "We're just checking out this cluster of crystals in a cave up ahead. Thirty minutes, at most."

The water continued to pool, but since they were on higher ground, it wouldn't reach them. At least, not yet. But she didn't like taking this risk, the possibility that they could get trapped in the cave. The conditions were getting worse; the fog drifted toward them.

A powerful gust of wind swept up some loose crystals on the ground, sending them hurtling into the sky. Kwan felt vulnerable, unprotected. Those crystals could be lethal. If thrust in their direction, their jagged edges could possibly penetrate their suits.

"Okay. We'll continue to monitor conditions from here. If it gets worse, we'll let you know."

"Copy that."

Sam and Kobe were right. The ringing grew louder as they approached the cluster. It was so loud now that it was hard to hear each other's voices through the communication channel.

Kwan had a bad feeling about this.

The sound was a constant drone, a multitude of different pitches. It had a hollow and eerie quality, like someone crying out in pain in a long tunnel, the sound bouncing, reverberating off the sides and magnifying.

Kato shouted, her voice cutting in and out with static. "I think I see some— An open—"

Kwan couldn't make out the rest. Sam, Kato, and Kobe zipped toward the cave entrance at top speed. Kwan followed them, then slowed to a halt.

"You guys go ahead. I'll keep watch."

She took up her post outside the cave entrance, watching as the clouds swirled in the distance, moving closer.

She felt nauseous and dizzy, the world around her tilting. Something about the sound was interfering with her senses. If it was affecting the others, they weren't showing it.

The others were far into the cave now. Too far. She could no longer hear them through the secure channel. The sound pounded her eardrums. She lost her footing, stumbled, and fell on her back.

The clouds shifted overhead. Forming images. Faces.

What was going on? Was she hallucinating?

Whatever it was, she couldn't control it. It was like her body wasn't her own. She felt herself slipping away into darkness…

Everything else disappeared. Everything except for the face. It appeared in front of her again, made up of numbers—binary ones and zeros.

Duskara.

"You and me. We are the same."

The coding, a string of commands, seeped into Kwan's body, like she was being willed somehow. Or…

Activated.

CHAPTER FIFTY-EIGHT

Sam couldn't believe her eyes. Everything about this planet—
the rugged landscape, the peculiar crystal structures, the massive
cave entrance—was exactly how she remembered it from her
dream. It could only mean one thing.

They were getting close. She could feel it.

She was certain they'd find important information here. Something to confirm Duskara's weakness. This place called to her. If
knowledge were a light, it shined from somewhere deep within
this cave. She needed to go there.

Outside, the crystal structures jutted haphazardly from the
rocky surface. But inside the cave, the crystals were cut into spiraling, cylindrical tubes of varying heights, polished and placed with
intention.

But by whom?

"What is this place?" Kato asked.

"Beats me," Kobe replied.

This strange place of shimmering sounds and light reminded
Sam of a collection of sorts. Not a marble or stamp collection. More
like a massive compilation of complex information.

Sam knew Earth's scientists were developing ways to store immense memory data inside nanostructured crystals that could last billions of years. It looked like something similar had happened here, but in a more advanced way.

The sound was stronger here. Each crystal tube emitted a different frequency. It reminded her of a pipe organ. But what was their purpose?

"It's definitely not natural," she said. "Someone was here and built this structure."

"But when? And why? What's it used for?" Kato asked.

Everyone hesitated, taking it all in.

The ship's directory had indicated that this planet was uninhabited. But was the structure abandoned, or did it continue to serve some purpose for interstellar travelers?

Sam broke the silence. "I think these tubes contain information."

She took a step toward the spiraling display, breaking away from the others. A light glimmered from within its center, drawing her in. As she neared the structure, the sound grew in intensity.

"Wait! I'm not sure if it's safe!" Kobe called, but she ignored his warning. She couldn't help herself. They were already here, and the sound and light beckoned her closer.

She took in the glowing light, then held up her gloved hand to one of the tubes. Its warmth and reverberations hummed along her fingers.

Immediately, images of a civilization's history flashed through her mind. Odd, humanoid creatures with two long arms and two long legs but with no ears, no teeth, no hair, large brains, and no digestive systems. Their biology was different. They absorbed nutrients through their skin. They were hybrids: part organic, part synthetic. They had technologies...materials made on a molecular level, lattices perfectly aligned, complex patterns. Durable materials. Ships that traveled faster than the speed of light. They operated these ships using their...*minds*? They connected with these ships physically, like they were part of the design.

She pulled her hand away, but the images lingered, if only for a moment. This was a fascinating, extraordinary place. She could get lost here.

Intrigued, she placed her hand on another tube. More images raced through her mind, like she was watching a video in fast-forward mode and absorbing the history of each frame at lightning speed. She recognized the next civilization: Volubens. They honored their moon goddess. It figured prominently in all of their designs: their homes and cities were spherical, interconnected by walkways; their arts and rituals revolved around her.

Sam retracted her hand once more, and the images slowly dissipated. "It's some sort of library," she offered, looking back. Kato and Kobe were closer now, exchanging bemused glances. "A collective library...of otherworldly civilizations." It was a trove of information dating back thousands and thousands of years. Did it contain underlying principles of the cosmos? Maybe mysterious knowledge discovered and shared by different beings?

She looked around. There must be hundreds of tubes here, containing data about each civilization. But who maintained it? And what was the light pulsating from its center, compelling her to venture nearer?

She took another step toward it.

"Wait," Kato said, placing a cautious hand on Sam's arm. "What if it's not safe?"

"It's fine. I just need to find...something. Something that will help us understand Duskara and how to defeat her."

She continued along the spiraling pathway, exploring. She stretched out her arm, briefly touching each tube as she continued. A fleeting image, and then on to the next one. The bizarre tremoring sounds flooded her ears as she made her way closer to the source of the light. Which tube would give her the answers they needed? How long would it take?

"Time's up!" Kobe called after her. "We need to go right now! I just got a message from command. They're saying a storm is here."

Her pace quickened. They didn't have much time. But like a moth drawn to a flame, she couldn't stop herself from drifting deeper into this cave, toward the flickering light. She pushed further, as if in a trance-like state, her eyes straight ahead. The light summoned her, compelled her to come closer. Would the light itself contain the answers? It had to, because if it didn't, they were no closer to finding the truth than when they'd arrived.

She felt a tug on her arm.

"Come on, Sam! You heard Kobe! We have to go!" Kato's voice sounded distant, overpowered by the vibrations, the echoing that rang in her ears. The beautiful, haunting music captivated her.

Then she stopped. She felt the coldness of this tube through her protective glove. No images appeared. Instead, only darkness. A shiver ran down her spine. Unlike the other tubes, containing soft, white light, this tube contained a black, swirling gas.

It wasn't that she could *see* the images. Instead, she…*felt* them. Sickness. Pain. Suffering. Fear. Jealousy. Anger. Rage. Death.

Nothingness.

She retracted her hand. Quickly, but not soon enough.

This was the one thing she'd been searching for. And she'd found it. She couldn't unsee it. Or *unfeel* it.

Now she knew Duskara's source of power. Just as she knew she wouldn't be able to block it from her mind. There was no way to defeat Duskara. She was a suffocating darkness that had no weaknesses.

"Sam? Are you okay?" Kato asked.

Sam stumbled out of her thoughts, which seemed to crash around her like a wave of darkness, spreading to all corners of her mind.

She took a shallow breath. "Let's go," she whispered, her voice shaking.

CHAPTER FIFTY-NINE

Kwan's body felt heavy. Weak. When she opened her eyes, someone was carrying her. They were heading back to the ship. She heard the others talking to her, but she couldn't understand what they were saying. The sound was muted.

She opened and closed her eyes, her thoughts drifting.

How long had she been unconscious? How much time had passed?

The scenery kept shifting, the colors swirling. She tried moving her arm, but it was limp, like all energy was drained from it.

What was happening?

And the constant ringing in her ears—she couldn't make it stop.

The next sound came from Kobe's lips, right beside her, but it sounded so far away, as if they were at opposite ends of a tunnel. She concentrated hard to hear.

"It's going to be okay, Kwan. We're almost there."

When she opened her eyes again, she was lying face up on a firm bed, a bright light shining down on her.

"Where am I?" she groaned. "Am I dead?"

She squinted, her eyes taking a moment to adjust.

Cabinetry and shelving units with glass windows ran the length of the far wall. Inside were medications and first aid supplies. Water rushed from a sink nearby. A screen beside her bed monitored her vitals.

She was definitely in the medical bay. Recovering, but from what?

There were voices nearby—Onnisa and Dr. Spark murmuring to one another.

"She is awake now." Onnisa's blue face came into view; her large, almond-shaped eyes examined Kwan's. Her tentacled hands worked to remove kaloi leaves from Kwan's face and neck.

"What happened?" Kwan demanded. She pushed herself into a seated position, but a wave of tiredness washed over her. She sank back down just as Onnisa propped some extra pillows behind her.

Dr. Spark rushed over and pushed a cup of water into Kwan's hand. "Drink up. You're still dehydrated."

Kwan swallowed hard. Her throat was parched. She took a sip, grateful as the cold water trickled down her throat, soothing her dry mouth and cracked lips. Water had never tasted so good.

"You had a seizure," Dr. Spark continued. "Your health record doesn't indicate any history of them. Have you had seizures before?"

"I... What? No. I don't think so."

"What is the last thing you remember?" Onnisa asked.

Kwan thought back to their visit to Planet Sofia. Getting suited up. Exiting the ship onto the rocky surface of the planet. The crystal structures jutting out at different angles. The weird cave with the shimmering sounds.

"I was outside the cave. The sound was so strong, it hurt my ears. I couldn't go any further. I waited outside for them to return, but then the storm came. I lost my balance and fell onto my back. That's when I saw her. Her face."

"Whose face?" Onnisa asked, her eyes wide.

Kwan shook uncontrollably. A coldness reverberated through her body. Her teeth chattered as she pulled the blanket closer. Dr. Spark draped another blanket on the bed, then placed her hand on Kwan's shoulder.

Kwan closed her eyes and saw the image again: the silver synthetic skin, the purple iridescent hair. Those deep, piercing, blood-red eyes.

"Duskara," she whispered.

Duskara had spoken to her, not in words, but in code. Kwan tried to grasp the coding, to understand what it meant. It was sophisticated. Like the entire genome of a human, or an animal—or one...what? Previously unknown entity?

What was its purpose?

"Will you allow me to read your memories?" Onnisa asked, stretching out one of her tentacled hands.

Kwan hesitated. Would she feel the memories again, the painful thoughts from deep in her past? She didn't want to think about those. Still, her curiosity flared. Maybe Onnisa could help her understand what was happening to her.

She nodded, reaching out her hand. Onnisa clasped it. Sparks of energy flew between them. A tingling sensation ran up her arm, like pins and needles, as the memories flowed like water. The memories of Duskara's face in the clouds resurfaced as the strange energy transferred between them.

And she remembered the chilling, machine-like voice, with those inexplicable words.

We are the same.

What was Duskara talking about? She was *nothing* like Duskara.

Kwan shivered.

Her thoughts shifted. Images of her interactions with Dr.

Vaughn and Raphael at the Radio Telescope Research Station flashed through, along with the coding she'd created and her recruitment into GAIA.

Random thoughts emerged, too. Things she hadn't thought were important to Onnisa, stuffed at the back of her mind. Like meeting Dr. Krill for the first time and feeling a sense of déjà vu or a shared connection even though they'd just met. And then finding the book in the library, the one written by Dr. Krill, that had contained the coded message intended for her.

The next memory that streamed by was of seeing Sam in the cafeteria for the first time and feeling a strong need to protect her.

Personal thoughts surfaced, too. Of Jae-Hwa. Sharing their first kiss on that warm spring day in the park. They'd spent the entire day walking along the winding pathways, admiring the cherry blossoms.

Kwan almost retracted her hand. Almost. She might have, if not for Onnisa's hold on her. She didn't like sharing these thoughts. They were hers. Private.

Strangely, there was a pause on Onnisa's end, too. Not a hesitation, exactly. More like a darkness in a space in Kwan's mind where no memory existed. And then, just as quickly, the moment passed, and the probing continued.

They searched deeper into her past. Older memories crept in. As much as she tried to resist them, she could not. Now, they pushed up their roots through those dark corners and became the main focus.

Kwan's older brother, Ji Min, appeared as she entered a memory. He used to teach her things.

"Soo Min," he said, addressing her by her birth name, the one she'd been given by her parents before the authorities changed it to Kwan, "watch me fix this device. Pay close attention."

She was just a child. Maybe six at the time. Living in their cramped quarters. Her three older brothers and two older sisters all lived in the tiny apartment. All shared one bedroom. Her siblings had taught her how to fix things—gadgets, circuitry, drones. That's what they would do all day while their mother worked selling refurbished materials on the black market. Her father had gone missing when Kwan was just a baby, so she'd never gotten to know him.

In the early mornings, Soo Min and her siblings would scavenge at the Silver Palace, the local electronics dump. They needed to find the right items, the ones that offered potential. Ji Min told her what to look for. But during their expeditions, she always found something else to take home. Things that created a spark inside her just by seeing it. Things she would experiment with in the storage closet in the dead of night, when no one was awake and she wouldn't be bothered.

She'd learned pretty quickly about the mechanics of circuitry and energy flows. Disruptors.

She would watch her brothers and sisters intently, studying what they did to make the devices work again. Bringing them back to life like magic.

"Oh, Soo Min. You're doing it wrong. What are you using that for? It's useless." Her older sister, Kyung Mi, would laugh. But when she showed Kyung Mi how to code the device with the programs she'd developed on her own, things changed.

She could make inanimate objects move by adding her own components and codes. Breathe new life into old drones by making the necessary amplifications. Soon, market patrons were asking her mother for customized products. Demanding them.

Sometimes it was a simple modification, like adding a scanning device to a drone for facial recognition. Other times, it was more complex and dangerous. A code to make the product self-destruct in a fiery blast. A weaponized item.

But then, word got out about her family's dealings. And soon, everything changed.

One day, from her window, she heard shots fired. Her mother's scream. All her siblings went silent.

Then the men came. They took Kwan and her siblings. Separated them. She never saw her mother or brothers and sisters again. Then, other people came and took her far away. Changed her name, her identity. She was brought to an orphanage in South Korea for one year. She was frequently bullied by Cho, an older girl who always wore her hair in thick braids with two shiny purple ribbons. Seeing this memory again, those ribbons reminded Kwan of an odd resemblance to the purple, iridescent hair of Duskara.

Kwan would spend her evenings lying awake at night, looking up at the ceiling, thinking about the world and the universe that existed beyond. Maybe there was someone out there who would accept her and take her away to a better place, if not here on Earth.

Then, a family took her in. A powerful family with a history of shady business practices who took a particular interest in Kwan's abilities, investing in her education and development.

That's when everything changed again.

But instead of delving deeper into those memories, Kwan felt the energy dissipate from her hand.

She looked up to find Onnisa visibly distraught, her thin lips tightly pressed together. Her eyes narrowed.

"I have seen enough."

"What is it? What's wrong?" Kwan asked.

A strange tingling sensation traveled through Kwan's hand. She looked down. The skin where Onnisa had held it was light blue with white intersecting lines. It reminded her of lace. She squeezed her hand into a fist, and it grew hot, burning, radiating.

"What's happening?" she asked in horror.

Onnisa looked down at her own hand in shock. It was burned, blackened. She rushed to the sink and ran it under cold water.

"What did you do to me? What...?" A wave of dizziness washed over Kwan, and she fell back against her pillow, closing her eyes against the spinning.

She must have appeared unconscious, because Dr. Spark and Onnisa began to whisper.

"I fear my translucence power may have migrated to Kwan during our connection," Onnisa said.

"You mean that Kwan may now hold this power?"

"Yes."

"What about your power? Does it still work with your other hand?"

"I do not know. But that is not what frightens me the most."

"What is it, then?" Dr. Spark's voice was low.

Onnisa hesitated, and Kwan strained to hear.

"It's Kwan's memories. They are not her own. They've been implanted."

CHAPTER SIXTY

The blood drained from Kwan's face.

Implanted memories? Could it really be possible? Those memories from her past felt as real as any of her recent ones. What did this mean? What was real—or *not* real?

She tilted her head, surreptitiously listening.

Dr. Spark whispered louder. "Implanted? You mean intentionally?"

"Yes," Onnisa said.

"But by whom?"

"I don't know."

They paused their conversation, but heightened tension filled the air. Did they know something she didn't? Whatever it was, she needed to confront them and get answers.

"I can hear you, you know," she said. "Whatever this is, you can tell me. I have a right to know."

Onnisa and Dr. Spark spun around in startled surprise. But it was Onnisa who frowned in resignation; there was no point in hiding or denying it. The jig was up.

"Your memories," Onnisa began, "the memories from your

childhood… They have a different…*quality* than those from your recent past."

"What do you mean?"

"Those memories of your apartment building with your siblings…belong to someone else."

"What? You mean they're not mine?"

"No."

"Then whose are they? How did they get inside me?"

Onnisa hesitated. "They were inserted, somehow. And tampered with. Someone changed the memories and added new ones."

The idea was preposterous. She would know if someone had tampered with her memories, *experimented* on her. Wouldn't she? If some memories weren't real, was her relationship with Jae-Hwa real? Were those memories real? That was the only thing that mattered right now.

Tears streamed down Kwan's face. "This can't be true."

"I'm pulling up your employee file—in case we missed something," Dr. Spark said as she entered commands into a panel on the wall. An image of Kwan appeared on an adjacent screen. Details about her date of birth, medical records, education, skills, and history came into view.

Dr. Spark scrolled down. "I don't understand. There's no history that might indicate any health issues—no neurological or psychological disorders. No history of medications, treatments, or surgeries. This is beyond me."

"The information may be hidden somewhere else in her file," Onnisa said, leaning closer. "Or it may not exist, if someone wanted to cover it up. Are there any supplementary links?"

It seemed Dr. Spark and Onnisa were genuinely as confused as she was.

"I'm sorry, but I don't see anything like what you describe —wait."

A button labeled ADDITIONAL INFO appeared at the bottom of

the screen, so small it was almost hidden. Dr. Spark tapped it. A warning message flashed on the screen:

RESTRICTED. SECURITY LEVEL 9 ACCESS REQUIRED.

That was Admiral Green's security level. And Admiral Green was a long way from them now. They had no way of contacting her outpost on Mars from such a distance without giving up their location and possibly jeopardizing the entire operation.

Dr. Spark hesitated, then pressed a button to continue.

Twelve hyphens and a blinking cursor appeared on the screen. The system required a twelve-digit password.

"Can you access it, Dr. Spark?" Kwan asked.

Dr. Spark frowned. "I don't think anyone on this ship has clearance for this, and it will be a while before we're in contact again with Admiral Green. I'm sorry."

Anger and frustration flared under Kwan's skin. How could they be so close to finding the answer and yet so far? What was Admiral Green hiding about Kwan's history that was so important not even Kwan herself could access it?

Captain Gorgana's voice on the intercom pulled them out of the moment. "Everyone must return to the command station now. We'll be arriving in the Dark Galaxy in less than fifteen minutes. I repeat, everyone is ordered to return to the command station immediately."

Dr. Spark returned to Kwan carrying two bowls filled with medical supplies. She carefully wrapped cold, slimy kaloi leaves over Kwan's burning hand. The sensation offered mild relief, reducing the heat and swelling. Dr. Spark followed up with a layer of thick gauze and a cold compress. But her hand didn't hurt as much as the pain of what she had potentially lost.

An entire childhood.

Kwan stood, still lightheaded from the revelations, but okay for now.

Dr. Spark whispered, "Whatever happened to you in the past, someone wants to keep it secret. But we're going to help you find out. One way or another."

Oh, yes. Kwan would find out. The moment she had a chance to hack their system.

CHAPTER SIXTY-ONE

Anger pulsated through Kwan's veins on their way back to the command station. *Who* had implanted the false memories, and *why*?

She picked up the pace, her mind racing. She thought about the AI death serum experiments. A sixty-one-percent success rate wouldn't do. They were way behind schedule on finding a solution, and not much time remained. Not when they were almost at the rim of the Dark Galaxy.

Passing the windows of the lab, she did a double take.

Simon was inside, running another experiment on the AI death serum—*by himself*. They usually worked as a team. How long had he been here?

She stepped inside. "Didn't you get the message?"

Simon half-turned, briefly acknowledging her presence before returning to his work.

"Hey," she said. "We need to get back to the command station—now."

Simon didn't budge. Instead, he frowned. "Are they rationing the coffee now?"

He had no clue. With his broken arm, he'd missed so much recently. He'd been here when Kwan and the others had gone out to scour the planet, Sofia.

Simon continued, genuine concern in his tone. "What happened to your hand?"

She looked down. "Long story. Didn't you hear me? Captain Gorgana ordered everyone back to the command station. We're going to be entering the Dark—whoa." There was black liquid in the vile. She looked at the screen on the wall, the words in bold letters.

AI DEATH SERUM CONTROL TRIAL 54
93% SUCCESS RATE

Her mouth dropped open. A success rate *much* better than sixty-one percent. It wasn't perfect, but it was good enough. It would work! It would take out Duskara.

"I wanted to tell you the good news first," Simon stated plainly.

"How—how did you…?" She couldn't find the words. He must have worked on this when she and the rest of the team were outside exploring the planet.

"Remember when the Glubens upgraded our ship with all those new parts?"

"Yes, and Boj tested the Thesian cloaking technology to make sure everything still worked as expected."

Simon leaned back in his chair, grinning. "Exactly. The whole thing gave me the idea that something could be repurposed into something else. But you could also conceal something easily by making it look different but act the same. So I made a few tweaks to the variables."

Kwan nodded in awe, not fully grasping how Simon had made such a breakthrough, but astounded and pleased nevertheless.

He pulled up some coding on the screen. She immediately recognized the approach, and it left her momentarily stunned and speechless. It was something so simple, yet so innovative. So brilliantly executed. She couldn't believe she hadn't thought of it herself.

"I used the same methods you developed with the coding," Simon said. "But I also added something else. In all the other trials, we didn't account for one intrinsic mechanism: *survival*. We knew that any foreign threat implanted into Duskara would be recognized by her coding, and her systems would try to shut it down. It's basic nature, survivability. So, to make a long story—uh, longer—I designed a loophole. A stealth code to make her think it's *medicine* rather than a threat."

"Simon, do you know what this means?!"

His grin widened, a wicked if not proud gleam in his eye. "You can thank me later. Once we return to Earth." He opened a drawer and pulled out a small syringe containing what looked like the same liquid, a fully functional AI death serum. "It took some time, but I harvested some already."

She took the syringe and examined it carefully, still in shock. Then, she tucked it carefully into her pocket for safeguarding.

He picked up his bag, getting ready to leave. They exited the lab together and headed to the command station.

She finally found the words. "You're a genius! And…I think we actually have a chance now at defeating Duskara."

CHAPTER SIXTY-TWO

SAM GRIPPED HER ARMRESTS. THE *THESEUS* WHIRRED AND VIBRATED AS it exited SWIFT navigation mode, slipping through the wormhole and back into regular space. Boj and Captain Gorgana maneuvered dials and tapped upon screens, preparing the ship for the next segment of their journey into the Dark Galaxy.

Visible through the viewing windows, a strange wall of darkness appeared straight ahead of them. There were no stars in the vicinity. No twinkling specks of light. Just an eerie black mass.

Nothingness.

"Preparing sequences for crossing the rim," Boj announced.

"Activating enhanced stealth mode," Captain Gorgana said, working over her control panel. An image of their gleaming silver ship materialized on the screen. A moment later, the ship's exterior changed—*transformed* right in front of their eyes! It looked like the surface was made of thousands of little pieces, each reconfiguring into a new structure. Not only did the pieces change in shape, but their color became mirror-like, reflecting their surroundings. Now, their ship was fully camouflaged with the blackness of space.

"Activating gas and materials detection," Boj said, tapping the buttons on his screen. Streams of scattered, multicolored light appeared in the viewing panes.

"What is that?" Sam asked.

"The Dark Galaxy is filled with gases, debris, and planets. But we can't see it," Zenobii said. "At least, not with our eyes. We've enhanced the imagery using our sensing equipment."

"Entering the rim in three…two…one," Boj counted down.

Sam held her breath as they passed through the rim. There was a moment of silence as everyone waited for what came next. The wall of darkness she'd seen just a few seconds ago was now replaced by specks of multicolored light in the distance. It swirled around them as they made their way through. Without the enhancers, they would be looking at complete and total darkness. This certainly helped to navigate where they were going.

Strangely, there weren't many objects in their vicinity. The Dark Galaxy was vast, stretching out infinitely into the beyond. Planets were spaced further away from one another, like an invisible substance, a darkness, had intentionally kept them apart. And where she'd expected to see the occasional asteroid passing by, she saw nothing.

A chill rippled through her body. It shook her to her core. Any hopeful thoughts were eclipsed by isolation and emptiness.

A low beeping resounded throughout the command station.

Boj's face went white as a ghost. She caught him eyeing Captain Gorgana with unease. The captain seemed to have frozen in place. Something was off.

"What's that beeping noise?" Sam asked.

Boj's fingers fluttered over the control panel, and a ship like theirs appeared on the screen. "We seem to be receiving a signal from that ship," Boj said, making it sound more like a question. "I don't understand. That—that's a sentry-class vessel. It's one of ours. It's from GAIA!"

Giddy furrowed her brows, leaning closer. "I wasn't aware of any GAIA ships accompanying us on this mission. Or is it—*no!*" Her face fell, and she grew silent.

"Yes," Boj confirmed. "It's the *Nightweaver*."

Sam's body grew rigid. She knew about the *Nightweaver* and its sole passenger, her clone. GAIA had sent the ship to the Dark Galaxy to destroy Duskara. All this time, she'd assumed the ship was lost, her clone dead. Yet here it was. The thought of being so close to her clone unnerved her. Someone with her body, mannerisms, intuitions, and inclinations. The clone's mission was supposed to have been completed a month ago, so what was the delay? Unless the clone had abandoned her mission or the mission had been intercepted. Also, why had her ship lost contact with the base? What was it doing now? Was her clone still alive inside, or was it a ghost ship?

"Do you think it's detected us?" Sam asked.

"Yes, most likely," Captain Gorgana responded.

"What's it doing?" Simon asked.

"It's stationary at the moment," Boj noted, seemingly surprised at this fact.

"Shall we intercept it?" Kwan asked.

"No," Boj answered quickly. "The ship is, for all intents and purposes, an active bomb. A *massive* one, in fact. If something goes wrong—"

"I'm not so certain," Zenobii said. "The *Nightweaver* was programmed to annihilate Duskara. Since it has not yet made contact with her, it should pose no threat to us."

"Unless it's been tampered with," Kwan said.

"No, we must not make contact with it," Boj said. "We've dealt with enough *unknowns*… We continue our mission, Operation Dark End, as planned."

"Wait," Kobe said. "Hold on. If there's a bomb on that ship and it goes off, how close are we to the blast radius?"

"Calculating blast radius now," Boj said, his fingers dancing across his control panel.

Large red rings encircling the *Nightweaver* appeared on the screen and spiraled outward, overlapping with the *Theseus*.

"We're currently within the blast radius for at least a few more hours, based on the projections of our current speed," Boj confirmed. "And that blue dot on the screen is Logom. It's outside the blast radius."

It seemed odd that the ship would stop before it reached its destination. Why come so far just to rest on the sidelines? Something wasn't adding up.

"Can we increase our speed?" Onnisa asked. "Without making ourselves known to Duskara and the Malborgs?"

Boj shook his head. "Any faster, and we'll enter SWIFT mode, triggering their detection systems. That, and we would never be able to decelerate in time. We would end up on the other side of the rim, billions of kilometers away from Logom."

"So what do we do?" Giddy asked. "That ship's a ticking time bomb."

"We do the only thing we can," Captain Gorgana said. "We proceed to Logom."

"And hope that ship doesn't blow up!" Kato whispered.

Sam folded her arms, the air suddenly chilly. The unknown kept creeping like wild vines inside her mind. What had really happened with that ship and her clone? Had it been intercepted already, its occupant kidnapped? Or was her clone dead, left to rot in space? As they continued, she realized they would never know. The ship might be suspended there forever, left to deteriorate over time. By leaving it there, choosing not to make contact, it was like they were abandoning a part of *her*. But at the same time, she wasn't sure she really wanted to know what had happened. What scared her the most was not the fact that they were traveling to Logom, the darkest of planets, with a hostile AI and an army of Malborgs ready to kill her. At this moment, what scared her most was the possibility that a part of her, the clone, was still alive and maybe needed help. It was hard to push those thoughts aside. The clone was only meant to serve a single purpose and then die, so why did Sam feel a strange connection to her? Why was she located so close to her target and yet so far away?

She took a deep breath and exhaled slowly, her palms sweating. What she wouldn't give to be back home, tossing a ball with Pip in the living room while her grandfather sipped his coffee and watched the news. That space felt safe, certain.

This space felt undefined, daunting.

Captain Gorgana turned to Boj. "We should run an advanced threat assessment, just to be safe."

"Agreed," Boj replied, tapping the controls on his panel. "Checking for other ships, asteroids, and debris in the vicinity of the *Nightweaver* that may pose a threat or has the potential to collide."

Dozens of red squares filled the mostly black screen, moving around, scanning each area. The squares zoomed in and out, expanding and contracting as it read the information and made complex assessments.

A message popped up on the screen.

NO POTENTIAL COLLISION DETECTED

FOR FIFTEEN HOURS.

"Fifteen hours. That gives us enough time to get outside the blast radius," Giddy said.

"Yes," Boj confirmed. "As long as the *Nightweaver* remains stagnant."

A red box hovered on a spot outside the Dark Galaxy, tracking a moving entity. Coordinates appeared beside it.

"What's that?" Kato asked.

Boj entered a command. "It's another ship, currently outside the Dark Galaxy, but heading our way."

"A Gargol ship," Captain Gorgana confirmed.

"Do you think it tracked us here?" Sam asked. "I thought the tracking device was removed on Glubo?"

"It was," Boj said. "Which makes this even stranger."

"The Glubens could have discovered our navigation plans when they assessed our ship," Captain Gorgana said, "then sold the information to the Gargols. I wouldn't be surprised."

"Either way, we'll continue to monitor the threat," Boj said, turning in his seat to face them. "The advanced surveillance system has been activated and will notify us of any changes."

Kwan stirred, adjusting the ice pack on her bandaged hand. "Excuse me. I'm going to get some more ice." She winced in pain, which was strange. Kwan never flinched, even after rounds of intense physical training. What had happened to her hand? Whatever it was, it must have been bad. And Kwan was Sam's main security. Seeing her in such discomfort made Sam squirm in her seat thinking about her own vulnerability.

Giddy looked over to Kwan and nodded but didn't speak. Instead, they exchanged a look, like they had just shared secret, unspoken words.

"What happened to your hand, Onnisa?" Kato asked.

Sam had been so focused on Kwan's odd behavior that she'd failed to notice the bandage around Onnisa's hand.

"While Kwan and I connected through translucence, something happened, and I believe some of my power transferred to her."

"Are you going to be okay? Can you still use your gift?" Sam asked. Very few people born on Kryg were gifted with the power of translucence. Without it, would the other Elders view Onnisa differently? Would they demote her or suspend her work and responsibilities?

"Oh, I feel fine. I do believe it will still work, perhaps with my better hand. I have not tried."

"What about Kwan? Is she going to be okay?" Simon asked.

"I do hope so," Onnisa answered.

"I'll go check on her," Simon offered, unbuckling the strap on his chair and leaping up from his seat.

"No, I believe she needs some space," Giddy replied.

Simon slumped back into his seat. He stared at the screen with the coordinates of the two ships. The *Theseus* continued to move toward Logom, while the *Nightweaver* remained stationary.

Then, all the lights went out, the darkness spreading to all corners of the room.

CHAPTER SIXTY-THREE

Sam heard gasps around her in the darkness. "What's going on?"

The ship creaked and groaned. A faint buzzing noise came from above. Then, just as quickly as the lights had gone out, they came back on.

Boj glanced over at Captain Gorgana, his eyes wide.

"Probably just a mechanical glitch in the power system. That sometimes happens when we switch navigation modes," Zenobii offered, though he didn't sound too confident.

"What's that blinking light?" Kobe asked.

Sam looked up. The screen displaying their locational information had changed. Now, a yellow blinking light appeared, delineating the clone ship's location. It seemed to be moving—and at the same speed as their ship.

Sam trembled in her seat. Her voice cracked. "I think we're being followed."

The blinking light continued on their tail, maintaining its speed. The ship carrying the bomb seemed to be heading right for them. Had it been intercepted and corrupted, repurposed to attack them?

What was going on inside? Had it been waiting for them the whole time?

"Captain Gorgana, try reducing our ship's speed. Veer thirty degrees starboard. I want to see how the *Nightweaver* reacts," Zenobii said.

Captain Gorgana twisted some dials on her panel, and their course map changed, indicating their new trajectory, away from Logom.

If the *Nightweaver* was heading to Logom to carry out its mission as originally planned, then it shouldn't veer off course. But as everyone scrutinized the information on the screen, something else happened.

The screens glitched, a wave of static bursting through, distorting the images.

"Our systems are compromised," Boj said as he frantically pushed buttons and pulled levers to adjust the settings. "I can't access the diagnostics module."

A moment later, the yellow dot on the screen switched course. It was most definitely following them.

Before anyone could respond, the screen went fuzzy, and then an image of Sam's clone appeared before them.

She looked sick. Her matted, greasy hair looked like it hadn't been washed in days. She stared straight ahead with sunken eyes devoid of hope, rimmed with black circles. Blood trickled down her forehead. Her frail body looked like it would break at the slightest touch, her collar bones jutting out from her malnourished form. A skeleton.

Sam's skin crawled as she looked at her clone staring back at her.

Then, they heard a familiar yet distorted voice through the intercom.

"This is Sam Sanderson II. Operating the *Nightweaver*. Requesting permission to dock with the *Theseus*. I was attacked by a Malborg ship. I need medical attention."

Reading about Operation Doppelgänger had been shocking enough. Sam hadn't believed it at first—that they'd actually made a clone of her. But even more disturbing was the situation now. Was her clone really wanting to carry out the mission, knowing full well that by getting close enough to Logom, the ship's bomb would go off, meaning her own demise?

As much as Sam hated seeing her clone in that state, weak and fragile, the strangeness of the situation played at her mind. The *Nightweaver* seemed to be working, so there shouldn't have been a delay in carrying out the mission. What had really happened? Why had the clone been waiting for them?

"Everyone switch to the secure channel," Onnisa instructed.

They did so as quickly as possible.

"We cannot engage," Captain Gorgana said. "She's interrupting our mission. We must continue with our planned course."

"Please," the clone pleaded in anguish, tears now streaming down her cheeks. "I need help."

"What if she's telling the truth?" Kato asked, glancing at Sam.

Sam focused on the clone's body language. She looked genuinely distressed and physically deteriorated. The clone's eyes searched her own in quiet desperation.

Sam shivered at the thought of her clone, a part of her, made up of her DNA, being blown to pieces. Even if the clone's sacrifice would take out the most monstrous creature in the universe, the thought still didn't sit well with her. Seeing herself in the clone's sickly state, she had the urge to reach out in some way and help her.

"Duskara knows about the *Nightweaver*," Onnisa said. "It was probably intercepted. We must continue with our plans since Mission Doppelgänger, as far as we know, is compromised."

"We can't just abandon her," Kato said, and Sam agreed. An eerie feeling washed over her. She caught the clone staring intently as they spoke to one another, as if knowing what they were discussing.

The clone was waiting for them to help. But maybe she didn't want to carry out her mission, knowing the end game.

Was it a trap?

As if answering her thoughts, the lights flickered again, and their ship slowed to a crawl. Captain Gorgana tapped some more buttons on her panel. Boj frantically did the same, moving the dials, waiting, then switching the levers back and forth.

Boj hesitated. "I don't understand what is happening to the ship's control system. I'm trying to adjust our course toward Logom, but it won't allow me to. It's like a ghost has gained control of our ship."

The clone shifted in her seat. She spoke again, her voice low this time. "I need help."

"Hold on just a moment." Sam scrutinized the change in her clone's body language—the familiar tapping of her thumb against her pointer finger.

It was the same expression and mannerism Sam used when she was hiding something.

"She's lying," Sam said.

Kato turned to her, eyes wide. "What?"

Sam's throat tightened, and her voice quivered. "She's changed her mission objective."

A side screen reappeared, showing the yellow dot of the *Nightweaver* gaining speed. It wasn't matching their course anymore.

It was closing in on them.

"We're her target now."

CHAPTER SIXTY-FOUR

The lights sputtered and then went out. When they turned on again, Sam stood trembling, a feeling of foreboding expanding inside her that she couldn't shake. On the screen, the two ships were side by side now, almost touching. Captain Gorgana and Boj looked similarly perplexed at the sudden closeness of the two ships. The *Nightweaver* had narrowed the gap within the blink of an eye.

Their ship juddered, and red flashing lights appeared on the screens on the wall.

Captain Gorgana's mouth dropped open. "Someone's launched our escape pods. All of them."

Sam had no way to escape now. And no way to carry out her plan to meet with Duskara one-on-one.

"Launched? By whom?" she asked.

Captain Gorgana shook her head. Pure terror overshadowed her usually calm demeanor.

"We've lost control of our ship," Boj stated, trying to hide the solemness in his tone but failing miserably. "I am sorry it has come to this."

Captain Gorgana tirelessly turned the dials and input information, trying to regain control, but with no luck. She pressed a red button, but nothing happened. "The distress signal has been deactivated."

A message flashed on the screen.

PREPARING TO DOCK WITH GAIA *NIGHTWEAVER*
TWO MINUTES REMAINING

They watched the timer with trepidation as it counted down each second.

"Everyone, prepare for an attack," Onnisa said through the secure channel.

"Prepare for anything," Giddy added. "That ship could have Gargols or Malborgs aboard."

"Come on," Kobe said, leaping from his seat, wide-eyed and determined. He turned to Sam, Kato, and Simon. "We'll armor up and head to the docking bay. We'll just have to retake control another way. We'll board the *Nightweaver*, disable its systems, and return to the *Theseus*. The rest stay here, protect the command station, and be ready once we regain control of our ship."

"You'll need someone familiar with the *Nightweaver*'s systems," Boj said. "I'll go with you."

Sam shivered. This was it. This is how it would end. They'd come so far, yet it didn't matter now.

Kobe led them down the hall toward the docking bay. They stopped at a cabinet with a secure access panel. Boj entered a key code and opened the door. Inside were eight chrome blasters.

"We were all supposed to get training on this, but we didn't have time," Kobe said, handing them each a blaster.

Sam took hers with trembling hands. It must have weighed twenty pounds, but that was nothing compared to the weight of what it symbolized.

Could she take a life? Perhaps she could kill a Malborg if it were in self-defense. Those AI creatures were killing machines, thoughtless, with no morals. Maybe Gargols, too, if it meant life or death. But another human? Even though Titus Dyaderos, the monstrous man who'd kidnapped and tried to kill her last year, had almost succeeded, she couldn't imagine killing him. Having him locked up in a Krygian prison for the rest of his life was punishment enough.

Then she thought about her clone. This…organic and synthetic AI hybrid, a living being made up of her own DNA, genetically and artificially enhanced. She was human, too, in a way. Could she kill her, a part of herself? The thought made her sick to her stomach.

"What are these settings for?" she asked, pointing to a dial on the blaster with three words engraved: LETHAL, STUN, and SLEEP.

"Lethal will usually kill your opponent," Boj said, "whether it's a Malborg, a Gargol, a human, or something else. Stun will slow them down temporarily. And sleep fires a tranquilizer that puts them out for a few hours with terrible nightmares so that when they wake up, they'll wish they'd never attacked you in the first place."

Sam preferred the sleep option, if worse came to worst.

"I should mention something else," Boj said, eyeing Sam's blaster. "With sleep mode, it's not always effective, especially on larger assailants. There's also a way to reverse the effects of the tranquilizer. The antidote is here, in this compartment." He pointed to a latch at the base of the blaster. "Just open it and squirt the antidote into the person's eyes. The effects should wear off within a few minutes."

"Whatever," Kobe grumbled. "I won't be using that on the assailants. Why would I? Duskara, the Malborgs, and the Gargols deserve what's coming to them."

He'd become hardened and riled with deep anger and hatred. He'd changed a lot since she'd met him. She'd never seen him in this state, so obsessed and determined to take down the enemy at any cost.

She exchanged troubled glances with Kato. Even she looked surprised.

But they were at war. They were fighting for peace, in self-defense, for freedom. Without it, Duskara and her Malborgs would continue their destructive rampage, and many more lives would be lost.

They followed Kobe to the docking bay. Sam tried to keep up, but her blaster was heavy and weighed on her thoughts. By the time they arrived, she was panting.

Kato and Simon took up a position on one side, with Sam, Kobe, and Boj on the other. They backed themselves against the wall, tucked between panels, away from the potential line of fire. They pointed their weapons at the docking portal.

Kobe was about to say something when a loud boom shook the ship—the *Theseus* coming into contact with the *Nightweaver* through the docking mechanism. It felt more like a collision. The floor lurched sideways, knocking Sam off her feet and sending them all skidding down the hallway a few feet. They scrambled to get up and regain their positions, but it was too late.

When the docking bay doors opened, Sam was greeted by the scent of something burning and a thick wall of fog. Vapor from a burst steam pipe inside the docking tunnel mixed with smoke from the *Nightweaver*, creating a dense haze. Lights flickered in the other ship, but she couldn't get a clear view of who or what was inside. The effect was eerie, dream-like. The *Nightweaver* looked abandoned—a ghost ship drifting in the darkness. There was no sign of life. Given the sputtering lights and dense haze, Sam was certain the *Nightweaver* was severely damaged.

Prepare for anything, Giddy had said.

Sam searched for her blaster, but it had flown out of her hand when the ship docked. She spotted it a few feet away, in the line of sight of the docking station. If she went for it, whoever was inside the *Nightweaver* might see her. She made a move, but Kobe held up his hand, signaling them all to wait.

She paused. Two shadowy figures emerged from the smoke-filled ship.

It took a moment for Sam to register their faces. She held her breath as her clone struggled to break free of the woman holding a gun to her head.

Sam couldn't mistake the woman; her dirty-blonde hair, blue eyes, and freckled face came into view only a moment later.

Rian.

"Please! Let me go!" the clone pleaded as she trembled in fright.

"You traitor!" Sam yelled. "How could you, Rian?"

"Come with me, Sam," Rian replied coldly, her voice neutral and detached, "or she dies." She cocked her pistol.

"It's a trap!" the clone screamed.

Before Sam could react, shots rang out, round after round, firing from both sides. She squeezed her eyes shut in panic. When she opened them again, the clone had managed to escape Rian's grip and was running toward them, toward safety. The clone hesitated as she ran past them, eyeing Sam strangely. She turned back toward the entrance and smiled, as if she were safe now, then continued past Sam and her friends in the direction of the medical bay.

Kobe fired rounds toward the entrance to the *Nightweaver*. It gave Sam just enough time to grab her blaster. A bullet whizzed by, mere inches from her ear, the sound of it still sizzling like cold water on a hot pan. *Too close.* She clambered back to her position against the wall and snapped her gaze toward the entrance, but no one was there. Rian must have dodged out of the way just in time to avoid Kobe's fire.

Sam just wanted this part to end. She didn't want to see her friends get hurt. They were in a bad position, with heavy fog filling the hallway, making it difficult to navigate.

But she couldn't shake the feeling that something else was wrong.

Her clone had almost looked…*too happy*.

CHAPTER SIXTY-FIVE

As much as Kwan wanted to stay with the rest of the group and find out what had happened with the clone's ship, the unanswered questions about her past compelled her to move forward. An inner conflict about her identity raged inside, provoking feelings of despair, anxiety, loneliness, and confusion. What was Admiral Green hiding about Kwan's history that was so important no one could know—not even Kwan?

Lights sputtered overhead as she rushed down the hallway toward the medical bay. What was causing the glitch? She glanced back, hoping no one had followed her. She needed privacy. No interruptions.

She needed answers. *Fast.*

The lights flickered again, this time longer. And when they came back on, they were dimmer, the shadows in the corners of the corridor darker than before. It must have had something to do with entering the Dark Galaxy. Or maybe the stealth system? Maybe they couldn't risk bright interior lights that could give up their location. Strange creaking and rattling noises from the ship's systems accompanied her every step.

Something scuttled behind her.

She stopped and whipped around. The hallway was empty, abandoned. The dim blue lights cast creeping shadows along the walls.

Pull yourself together, Kwan.

The Dark Galaxy wasn't home to many inhabitants except for Duskara, the Malborgs, and some Gargol populations. It was difficult to reach. There weren't many sources of fuel or habitable planets here. It was forlorn, unwelcoming. Intelligence sources had confirmed that staying in the Dark Galaxy too long could adversely affect one's mind.

Had she caught the Dark Sickness? Was she seeing things now? She didn't want to think she was easily prone to its symptoms—the paranoia, the hallucinations…

She'd heard the chilling stories of ships losing contact. Of agents suffering from extreme delusions, terrors, and, in some cases, death.

Would the same thing happen to her? To the others?

She turned again and quickened her pace.

Breathe.

She yanked open the door to the medical room, stepped inside, and sucked in a deep breath. After locking the door behind her, she exhaled slowly, relieved that no one had followed her inside.

She needed to hack into the system fast, locate the contents of her employee file, find out the truth about her past, and ensure she wasn't caught. Even though they'd lost contact with Admiral Green's mission control center, if they ever did return to Earth, she would definitely get in trouble for what she was about to do. But the thought of returning to Earth seemed so far away now. Did it really matter?

She tried to remember what Dr. Spark had done to bring up her employee file. Did it require an access code? If so, she would need a backdoor into the system. She lifted her blue-colored hand toward the panel and was about to tap it when she noticed something odd.

Sparks of blue energy flowed from her fingers. She paused in sheer wonder, examining the phenomenon. Her hand became translucent, her bones showing through her skin, the blood flowing from each vein. Her entire hand radiated blue light. When she moved it toward the panel, the light inside grew stronger. It was as if she were conducting electricity somehow. She tapped on the screen, and a massive spark ignited. The electrical equipment burst into flames.

Panicking, she scanned the room and found a fire extinguisher in the corner by the exit. She grabbed it, removed the pin, and aimed it at the base of the spreading fire. She swept the powerful spray back and forth, blanketing the equipment, soon snuffing out the flames.

Once the fire died out, she took stock of the scene around her. The white residue was everywhere.

How would she hack into the systems if they were damaged?

Time was running out, and someone would find her soon.

She stared at her disfigured hand. She made a fist and then released, stretching her fingers again. There wasn't any pain, just a mild tingling sensation, like pins and needles.

Breathe.

She grabbed a cloth and wiped away the residue. The lights overhead blinked and then went out. She muffled a gasp.

Her right hand continued glowing blue, casting light in the darkness. What was going on?

Focus.

A moment later, the lights returned. She wrapped her right hand in gauze, hoping it might act as a buffer so sparks wouldn't fly should she accidentally touch the panel again.

She sighed in relief when the screen powered back on. It was *still working.* Twelve dashes appeared, waiting for the passcode.

Hastily, she inserted a smart key and entered the backdoor

sequence using her specialized decoding, but it was harder working with only one hand. One small error—a missing letter or a misplaced bracket—and the sequence wouldn't work.

She waited as it ran its algorithm. She checked every few seconds to assess the information generated and determine when to give the next command in the sequence.

Come on. Come on. Come on.

Numbers and letters appeared on the screen one by one as the software decoded the access key. But before it could reach the final entry, the ship lurched violently, as if it had collided with something. Kwan lost her footing and stumbled sideways, landing on her back. Shelving units and glass beakers crashed to the floor around her, and she twisted just in time to avoid being crushed.

What was happening out there?

The ship stabilized, and she rose to her feet.

The room looked like a tornado had swept through, turning everything upside down.

She cautiously stepped around the glass and returned to the screen with her employee file. All the decoded letters and numbers had appeared, but underneath was a set of new coding instructions. It was waiting for another keystroke, one more command, to grant her access.

This was only the first stage. Once she accessed her employee file, she would need to run another algorithm to access sensitive information. That might take longer. And who knew whether the information would still be intact after the electrical fire?

The hairs on the back of her neck rose.

Someone was watching her.

Kwan turned. Sure enough, someone stared back at her through the window, desperation and something else—*rage?*—in her eyes.

Even though Kwan knew who she was, it took her a moment to register the details of her face.

Sam Sanderson.

Except something was wrong with her expression.

CHAPTER SIXTY-SIX

It was Sam Sanderson. Only different. The Sam Sanderson Kwan knew, the one she'd seen maybe an hour ago, full of life and energy and hope, now looked sickly, malnourished, and fearful. The dark circles under her eyes contrasted against her pale skin.

"Please! Help me!" Sam pounded at the door, twisting the knob, trying to get in. "We were attacked!"

Her heart hammering in her chest, Kwan dashed for the door.

But her pace slowed halfway there.

What had happened to Sam? Why did she look so different?

Kwan hesitated. "What happened? Where are the others?" she called through the door.

"Please! Just open the door," Sam pleaded, her voice shrill. "I need medical attention!"

Kwan's mind raced. Was she losing it? Was the Dark Galaxy now taking its toll on her consciousness? Was she imagining the whole thing?

Still, Sam's plea gnawed at her. Kwan took a few steps closer to get a better look, reached for the doorknob, and stopped.

The girl staring back at her looked like Sam. She *spoke* like Sam.

But this definitely *wasn't* Sam. The girl's blue eyes sunk back into her skull. When she blinked again, her pupils dilated so much that her eyes became as black as night. Her hair, once red, now contained thick black streaks.

The girl's fear quickly subsided, replaced by darkness and fury. It flared, spreading across her face. She paused. A smirk appeared, her lips curling upward. Then, she ran off.

It was the clone. Sam's clone. Only, someone had tampered with her, altered her.

Someone had created a monster.

Kwan needed to stop her, this *creature.*

She hesitated. One side of her brain was telling her to stay, to find out what they were hiding from her. She needed to find out the truth about herself. Her whole sense of being depended upon it —how she related to others, how she understood herself. Why was it so important that the information was protected, even from her crewmates? The other side of her brain was telling her to go and help her friends—*now.* She needed to protect them from this threat.

At least if the clone was after Kwan, she was leaving the real Sam alone.

Kwan rubbed her eyes and turned to face the panel again. That was when she was jolted by a loud bang. She spun around only to hear it again. The clone had returned with a fire extinguisher. She smashed it against the door over and over, trying to break in.

Kwan grabbed a chair and jammed it under the doorknob at an angle. The clone paused, narrowing her eyes at Kwan. She took a few steps down the hallway and squared her shoulders, adjusting her grip—and her *aim.*

Kwan's jaw tensed as the clone heaved the extinguisher against the window. A crack appeared and the thick glass threatened to rupture.

Kwan didn't have much time.

She raced back to the panel, entered the command, and waited. Her employee file popped up on the screen a moment later. She navigated the file until she reached the Additional Info section and tapped the button. A message popped up.

RESTRICTED. SECURITY LEVEL **9** ACCESS REQUIRED.

Another screen with twelve blank dashes appeared.

Bang.

She glanced over her shoulder. The crack had doubled in size and the glass would burst at any moment.

The system stalled. It required more coding input. Kwan entered a flurry of commands, her fingers dancing over the panel, desperate for the system to process the information faster. What was her next move? She wasn't prepared for this. And now she was in a race against time.

Only a quarter of the alpha-numeric sequence had appeared on the screen.

Bang.

The glass shattered, thick shards raining down across the floor. Sam's clone slipped through the narrow opening.

Only a few more lines of code…

The clone bolted toward her, eyes wide, determined. A hidden Rypold crystal blade shot out of her hand and hurtled toward Kwan.

Kwan didn't have time to think. She ducked behind an overturned metal table as more knives sliced through the air in her direction. She inched backward just in time as they hit the table and protruded through to the other side, the tips just inches from her face.

What was this *thing*? Half human and half robot? A cyborg?

As she shifted her weight to rise up, her hand collided with something sharp. A shard of glass had torn through her bandage and lodged in her skin. She gasped as she yanked it out. The blood trickled down, splattering onto the floor. She grabbed a cloth to staunch the bleeding.

She needed a weapon. Something—*anything* to disarm her attacker.

Kwan grabbed a blade from the ground. With all her might, she lunged toward the clone, knife held high in her hand, the table acting as a barrier.

"Enough!" she shouted. The clone tried to dart out of the way but wasn't fast enough. Kwan used the table as leverage to knock the clone backward, but the knife slipped from her grasp at the last second. Her right fist connected with the clone's chest. A spark of electricity burst forth, thrusting the clone against the wall.

The clone trembled for a moment before deflating into a sunken state, unmoving, her eyes glossed over.

Kwan looked down at her hand. Blue light rippled through her fingers, the currents alive. "Well, I didn't know it could do *that!*"

A searing pain flared, but she ignored it as she hurried back to the panel.

The system awaited the final command. She pressed ENTER.

A video appeared on the screen.

Dr. Krill was in view, seated at a desk. Kwan recognized the lab in the background. It was the very place they'd met and worked together. The cream-colored walls, the familiar bookcase overflowing with books and papers, and the flasks and beakers hadn't changed much from what she remembered.

"Hello. Dr. Otto Krill here. We're at GAIA's underwater base, off the coast of Labrador, and I'm here with Admiral Artemis Green. We've been working on Project Dark End for two years and…seven months now. We'd developed several prototypes. But I'm happy to announce that number fifty-four is successful." He paused and smiled, pride in his eyes. "I'm certain she'll complete her mission successfully. I'm quite pleased and hopeful."

She? What had they been working on? It couldn't have been Athena. That was many years earlier, when Dr. Krill would have been in his twenties. He looked like he had when she first met him, with years of hard work etched into his skin. And Project Dark

End... That didn't make sense—they were currently on that mission. What was going on?

"What will you name her?" another voice prompted. It was Admiral Green. She must have been the one holding the camera.

Dr. Krill gave a throaty laugh. "I wanted to give her a name that was meaningful. I chose Soo Min, after my daughter."

What?

Had she heard correctly? Was it just a coincidence that she shared the same birth name? Her pulse quickened, and knots tightened in her stomach.

"Tell us more about her," Admiral Green prompted as the camera panned right, toward a body lying on a medical table, a multitude of wires hooked up to it. Its eyes were closed, but Kwan recognized it at once.

It was *her* body. *Kwan's* body.

Her mouth went dry as she struggled to focus on Dr. Krill's next words.

"Her human DNA was merged with a synthetic DNA, comprised of silicon and nanotechnology. She is a sentient AI, but for all intents and purposes, she is a living, breathing human, capable of love and empathy..."

It was hard to register the information all at once. His voice drifted in and out, and she only heard pieces. Bits of information. Something about organics and synthetics.

"...of sound mind, morally further advanced than anything we've created in the past."

A sickness fired up in Kwan's stomach. It couldn't be true, could it? That she was a robot, an AI? Created in a lab? Implanted with memories?

Her head throbbed just as her meal from this morning made its way onto the floor. It was starting to come together, the memories. This would explain the déjà vu she'd experienced when meeting Dr. Krill for the first time at the lab.

Because it hadn't been the first time she'd met him.

Her thoughts became quiet, focused, just as Dr. Krill's words faded into the background. She couldn't listen to more. She went to tap the screen but heard rustling behind her.

She whipped around just in time to see the dark smile of the clone flicker from behind the fire extinguisher as it came crashing toward her head.

CHAPTER SIXTY-SEVEN

Thick fog filled the corridor, threatening to envelop everything it touched. Sam gritted her teeth, trying not to cough. Trying to shoot an opponent in these conditions would be utter madness. She couldn't risk accidentally striking one of her friends, so she waited for instructions, but they never came.

A strange quietness accompanied the fog. They had expected Gargols or Malborgs to emerge from the docking bay and attack. Instead, there was nothing. No one.

Her disorientation only made things worse. A moment ago, at least she'd been able to see her friends. Now, she couldn't see anything beyond one foot in front of her. The fog swallowed up everything in its path, churning, devouring.

With the fog came the fear. Where were her friends? Had they made their way inside the ghost ship? She was utterly alone in the swirling mist.

She willed herself to move, but it was as if the fog had reduced her ability to think straight. She froze, clutching her blaster, her palms sweating. These could be her final moments with her friends. Should she say goodbye? If she did, she might give up her position.

Was this what it was like to die? To be surrounded by people you care about but not be able to reach out and tell them? She wanted to hear a comforting voice. Someone to reassure her that everything would be okay.

But there was no one. No soothing voices to calm her. No guiding hand.

She couldn't wait any longer.

Which way should she go? She needed to warn Kwan about the clone's ship and Rian. But she also needed to stay and help her friends.

If they were still here.

But no. Today was not her day to die. And she wasn't going to let death take her friends, either.

Fear prevented her from taking a step. But she had to. She had to take a risk. Will herself to move, to do *something*.

She took a slow, uneven breath, trying to steady her mind. "Kato," she whispered, "are you there?"

No response. Just the sound of her shallow, shaky breathing.

Shots fired up ahead, the loud crackling piercing her eardrums. Heavy footsteps echoed down the hallway. The floor shook as a massive Gargol hurtled toward her through the fog. Sam leaped sideways as it came to a grinding halt inches away from her feet. Its grizzly face and razor-sharp teeth protruding against its leathery gray skin made her shrink back. It had been shot. And it was dead, though its bulging eyes remained open, looking directly at her.

She stared at the blaster in her hand. She hadn't even pulled the trigger.

She couldn't stay here, not in a spot occupied by death, or she would be next.

Go!

In a snap decision, she placed her hand against the wall, half-relieved to feel something solid. She could no longer rely on her vision. She forced herself to take a step toward the clone's ship.

"Kobe? Where are you?"

"I'm already inside the Nightweaver *with Kato and Simon. It looks abandoned. Where are you?"*

"On my way. Is Boj with you?"

"No."

Sam ran her hand along the wall to steady herself, quickening her pace. She stumbled on something blocking her path.

No!

Boj lay in a heap on the floor, his eyes closed. Blue blood spilled from a gash in his leg.

"Boj!" she gasped. She shook him frantically. "Come on! Wake up!"

She grabbed a rope from her bag and tied it around his leg to stop the bleeding. She then placed her hand on his neck, feeling for a pulse.

It was there. Weak, but he was alive.

Boj's eyes fluttered open, and he pulled back at the sight of her, terrified. "No! Please don't hurt me!"

"What do you mean? It's me, Sam!" She dropped to her knees and carefully turned him over, only to find a tranquilizer dart wedged into his hip. He was suffering the nightmarish effects of the sleeping sedative.

Someone had shot him. But who? Any one of them could have done it in error, given the fog. He could have been caught in the crossfire.

Sam had set her own blaster to sleep mode right before the attack. She shuddered. Had she accidentally pulled the trigger in a moment of panic?

It was possible, but not likely. She would have known, would've felt the action. Still, the uncertainty lingered. If it were true, she could never forgive herself.

She carefully pulled out the tranquilizer dart, then turned Boj onto his back, despite his protests. She leaned forward, rotating her blaster and opening its inner compartment. Inside lay a small bottle of orange liquid. She pulled it out and unscrewed the cap.

"I hope this works," she muttered.

Despite his thrashing, she lifted his eyelids and carefully squirted a few drops of the antidote into each eye. His movements slowed, and he fell back unconscious.

"That should do it. Just hang in there, Boj."

It might take a few minutes to kick in, to stop the nightmarish visions, but the cut looked deep. She needed some help.

She hoisted Boj up and used her hover kneepads to continue through to the *Nightweaver*, where the air was drier, and a burning smell lingered. She squinted, her eyes stinging from the thick, dusty air.

Boj moaned in distress, his eyelids fluttering at whatever nightmare he was seeing.

She was relieved when her friends' faces came into view.

"What happened to him?" Simon asked.

"He got hit with a sleep tranquilizer," Sam said. "I gave him the antidote, but the cut looks deep. Someone needs to get him back to medical on the *Theseus*."

"I could go," Kobe offered. "I can carry him. Simon can't with his broken arm."

"Wait. I'll go, too," Simon said. "You'll need someone to watch your back. I can at least do that."

"Okay," Kobe agreed. He turned to Sam and Kato. "But how will you deactivate the *Nightweaver*?"

Sam thought fast. "When Boj wakes up, Kobe, you can feed me his instructions telepathically and guide Kato and I through the process."

"Brilliant. I knew our telepathy would come in handy for something!"

Sam grinned. "Once we've deactivated the systems, we'll circle back and meet you on the *Theseus*."

"Good," Kato said, turning to Kobe, Simon, and Boj. "Just keep pressure on that wound. And stay safe! See you soon."

With that, Kobe and Simon left, dragging Boj toward the *Theseus*.

Sam and Kato continued into the heart of the *Nightweaver*. They darted past broken equipment and wires that short-fused. Whoever was commandeering this ship looked like they'd abandoned their post in a hurry. But if that was the case, who was controlling both ships now?

They hustled down the corridors as quietly as possible. The constant flicker of lights cast eerie shadows that kept shifting. Sam turned back a couple of times to make sure they weren't being followed. The dimly lit corridors put extra strain on her eyes, as if she were in a dark room with sunglasses on.

Sam looked back, trying to get oriented with their surroundings, but the unfamiliar layout of the ship jarred her. She'd thought this was the route to the command station.

They turned a corner and stopped short. They'd come to a dead end. Behind them, a mechanical whirring noise grew louder as a wall panel slid horizontally, threatening to seal them inside.

"*Nooo!*" Kato shouted.

Sam bolted toward the panel.

But it was too late. She heard the sound of a vacuum seal and an automatic locking mechanism.

They were trapped.

CHAPTER SIXTY-EIGHT

A SEARING PAIN THRASHED AGAINST KWAN'S SKULL. SHE TASTED blood and felt something hard on her tongue. A pebble in her mouth? No, a tooth. She spit it out and pushed herself up, a wave of dizziness washing over her. She couldn't open her left eye; it was swollen shut, and something wet streamed down her eyelid. Pus? Or was it more blood?

Her body hurt in so many places she couldn't count. But she was alive.

How much time had passed? She had no idea.

She was still in the medical bay, surrounded by shattered glass and toppled cabinets. Sam's clone was gone, along with whatever hope Kwan clung to that this mission could still succeed. She fought the pain, nausea swaying in her stomach. She needed to warn the others. But how? The AI death serum was the one thing that could stop Duskara. She searched her pockets.

Nothing.

The clone must have taken it. But how did she know about the AI death serum? Unless…

Maybe the clone didn't know about the AI death serum or what it was used for. But she had been compromised. Reprogrammed to attack them. Perhaps the same person responsible for the attack had reprogrammed the clone to seek and destroy any threats, and that included items Kwan had been carrying in her possession.

Either way, there wasn't enough time to make more serum.

Blasted luck!

She needed to get it back. Fast.

Her head throbbed. She searched for pain meds, her thoughts swirling. Just like Sam's clone, she'd been created in a lab. She wasn't human. She was an AI, like Duskara. She'd been created for one purpose: to destroy Duskara. Just another product version in a long line of previously failed attempts. Number fifty-four. That meant there were fifty-three others. What had happened to them?

She thought about what Dr. Krill had said when she'd first started working with him. *You're not like the others.* She shivered, now understanding what he'd meant.

With every breath she took, her anger grew stronger. The lies just kept coming, one after another. Her recruitment to GAIA had been just a mirage, a part of their well-drawn-out plan. She'd thought she made her own decisions. But they'd pulled her strings all the way here. Implanting her memories. Trying to get it right so that she'd have the perfect combination of motivation, intelligence, and drive. So she'd know how to reach Duskara using her own language.

Now she understood why the advanced technology at the base seemed so familiar, why she'd picked up the information so rapidly. She'd been exposed to it already, through conditioning, when they were creating and developing her. That was the only reasonable explanation. It made perfect sense. Obviously, it wouldn't take her long to adapt, to recognize how it all worked, if they'd already implanted the information within her subconscious memories. Buried deep, but still accessible enough for her to find it when needed.

Looking back, even Admiral Green's behavior seemed out of

place. When Kwan had demanded that they provide an expedited visa for Jae-Hwa and cover all relocation expenses, Admiral Green had given her what she'd wanted almost too easily. Desperate for Kwan to agree to the new tasks and responsibilities, she'd changed the contract terms and conditions on the spot. She'd fulfilled Kwan's abundant requests—no problem, and *no questions asked.* And why not, if they'd already created and "owned" her, had invested so much in her already? They couldn't afford to lose her. Not when she'd gotten so close to the mission objective, achieved so much already, and time was running out to train a new "replacement."

She'd been oblivious to the signs. But retracing her steps, their choices and behaviors... It was obvious. All of it. Why hadn't she seen it sooner?

But what about Jae-Hwa? Was that also a lie? Was she even real? Kwan tried to recall her memory in more detail but couldn't. After all her training in reading body language, they'd still managed to successfully feed her lies. She'd been deceived. Could she even trust her own judgment now?

It was sickening. They'd taken away her power, her identity. She hated them.

Focus. She had to focus!

Her hand trembled as she located the pain meds. It would dull some of the pain. For now. Enough to keep her focused. She knocked back two pills and gulped the cold water straight from the tap. She let the water wash over her face, the blood and sweat and pus trickling down the drain along with all her hopes and dreams. She slowly lifted her gaze and stared at her reflection in the mirror.

She looked like a monster.

It was more than anger that erupted now.

It was pure rage.

She knew what she had to do.

Kwan feverishly tapped the screen in the medical bay, inputting data. She entered a backdoor coding sequence, effectively hacking into the security feeds. If she could locate the clone, she could retrieve the AI death serum. That is, if it hadn't already been destroyed.

The screen displayed security feeds from several locations: the ascension bay, command station, medical bay, landing bays, docking area, and more. She focused on the medical bay to check whether her assumption about the clone was correct. She rewound the tape and zoomed in.

The clone attack replayed in sequence. Sure enough, while Kwan was unconscious, the clone retrieved the AI death serum. Now she just needed to find out where the clone had gone.

She scanned the other footage. A strange fog permeated the docking area. But there was no time to check it out.

She peered at one of the images, a hallway leading to the landing bay.

There, in the center of the frame, was Sam's clone, running toward the landing bay. The same place where they kept the *Komodo*.

Kwan scrambled out the door and raced down the corridor.

She activated her hover kneepads and zoomed past deserted hallways. Her heart thudded in her chest. She was getting close.

Rounding the corner, she pushed forward at full speed, approaching the double doors. Usually locked, they stood ajar. She gaped in horror. The control panel was damaged. Rising smoke and exposed, sizzling wires betrayed remnants of a blast.

The clone had gotten inside already.

Bursting through the double doors, Kwan found herself in an empty room. There was no one there. And the *Komodo* was gone!

She scrambled to the viewing window. Glancing out into the dark expanse of space, the only thing she saw was the gleam of the

Komodo's shiny chrome exterior, hurtling ever further away from her.

Kwan turned and dashed toward the docking area to locate and save the others. This was no longer a mission to assassinate Duskara. This was a retrieval mission to help whatever survivors were left. Her head was spinning, and she needed to find a blaster.

But she stopped in her tracks when she heard a sound—the whimpers of a child.

"Please don't hurt me!" It sounded like a twelve-year-old boy.

She crept to the source of the sound, stopping when she saw Simon and Kobe huddled around Boj, who was lying down with his eyes closed, mumbling in pain. Kobe jumped to his feet and pointed his blaster toward her.

"Hey! It's me, Kwan!" She approached cautiously, not wanting to startle them further. "What happened to you guys? What's wrong with Boj?"

"He was hit with a sleep tranquilizer. But Sam gave him the antidote, so he should come around soon. What happened to *you*?" Kobe asked, his weapon still leveled at her.

"The clone attacked me."

"*What*?" They both looked taken aback.

"Yeah! And could you stop pointing that thing at me?" she said, but he didn't budge. "Okay, look. I was in the medical room, and the clone busted in. I tried to stop her, but she hit me with a fire extinguisher. Hence, my face."

"That makes no sense," Kobe stammered. "Sam's clone was weak, malnourished. She couldn't have done…*that* to your face."

Whatever the clone had turned into, she was more powerful than Kwan had thought. "Well, she did. She didn't attack you, too?"

"No," Kobe began, confusion in his voice. "When we got here, Rian held the clone captive, a gun pointed at her head. She demanded the real Sam. That's when shots broke out and the clone escaped."

Rian was here, aboard this ship? She'd survived? Now it made sense. Rian, the traitor. The conniving snake. She'd made them think the clone was weak, that the clone was the victim when really, it was all part of her plan to infiltrate their ship.

"Then Rian tricked you. She released the clone on purpose. Look, someone did something to that clone. She's not Sam's clone anymore. She's not normal. Her eyes went black, and her hair turned black. She had enhanced weaponry. She—she almost *killed* me."

The boys looked dumbfounded. The whole situation was messing with all their heads.

"Where are the others? Where's Sam? If Rian is here, we're in big trouble. I need to stop her." Rian had escaped once before. She couldn't let her get away twice.

What was it Rian had said to her before she left in the escape pod? *You don't know the whole truth.* Kwan hadn't understood what she meant. Was she talking about Kwan's past? If so, how could Rian have known?

Kobe finally lowered his blaster. He pointed toward the docking area that connected the *Theseus* to the *Nightweaver*. "They went that way."

"Thanks," Kwan muttered, then turned to continue down the hallway.

She hesitated when she heard a rumbling noise behind her, and she whipped back around. Five Gargols rushed down the hall toward them. Simon and Kobe scrambled in different directions. Boj still lay on the ground, immobile. Darts full of yellow liquid swooshed past her head. Tranquilizers.

She would have gone back to help the others, but her hand-to-hand combat skills were no match for those darts. She needed a blaster, something of equal capability, that would give her some leverage.

She hurried toward the *Nightweaver*, glimpsing back only to find Simon and Kobe had been caught. And there was no sign of Boj now.

She picked up the pace, her body screaming in protest, as two Gargols thundered forward, closing in on her position. They fired more darts.

Swoosh. Swoosh.

She needed to find Sam and get her to safety.

She rushed down the corridor as fog wafted toward her, passing the body of a dead Gargol, its eyes glazed over. How many Gargols were aboard the two ships?

Kwan sprinted to a weapons panel, punched in the code, and opened the door. Only one blaster left.

She grabbed it, fired behind her, then ran into the fog. Toward danger, chaos, and the unknown. Her rage and adrenaline kicking in, she blazed forward, an uncontrollable urge to get Sam and the others to safety. She was prepared to fight more assailants face-to-face, whether Malborgs, Gargols, or Duskara. She sliced through the fog, which swirled and dissipated the closer she got to the *Nightweaver*. She focused and readied herself mentally and physically for whatever stood in her way.

Inside the *Nightweaver*, things were worse. A trail of charred marks and exposed cables plagued the walls, evidence of blaster-fire. Entire walls were scorched and crumbling, fiberglass paneling and pieces of stainless-steel framing strewn along the ground. Sparks sizzled from the exposed cables in the wall.

Faint voices drifted down the corridor. Kwan slowed and peeked around the corner.

It was Rian, speaking to two Gargols.

"We have them contained," one of the Gargols said.

Them?

Kwan poked her head out just long enough to glimpse the two figures inside the air lock.

Sam and Kato. They'd been caught, too!

Ducking back into the shadows, her heart racing, Kwan stifled a gasp.

"Good," Rian said. "Everything is as planned. Tie them up and escort them to the command station. I'll meet you there in a few minutes. I just need to check on something."

Rian left, jogging down the hallway—coming *toward* her!

Kwan slipped into a maintenance room and slid the door closed, leaving only a crack. Rian paused just outside. Kwan held her breath, waiting. But Rian moved on, continuing down the hall and out of sight.

CHAPTER SIXTY-NINE

TRAPPED INSIDE THE AIR LOCK, SAM TREMBLED, HER BODY COLD AND rigid like ice. Her thoughts whirled, and she tried to think of a solution to escape. But there was no way out. Outside, the vast expanse of outer space loomed; dark, all-encompassing, devoid of life, and threatening to consume them. With just one push of a button, she and Kato would be ejected to their deaths.

On the other side, two Gargols approached the air lock.

"Get back!" Sam yelled. Kato stumbled back against the wall. Gathering her strength, Sam aimed the blaster at the door where the Gargols stood. The shot echoed in her eardrums. The blast shook the wall and blew a hole in it, but it wasn't enough to fully penetrate or disarm the locking mechanism.

She reloaded her weapon, getting ready to take another shot, when one of the Gargols tapped on a side panel. The room buzzed with electricity. The blaster in her hand trembled, then leaped from her grasp, the electricity crackling. As if yanked by some unseen force, it spiraled toward the back of the room. The force knocked her over. Kato jumped, her blaster skidding along the floor. Both blasters stuck to the back wall, held by some kind of magnetic energy. Before Sam could get back up, another wall panel slid shut and locked, cutting them off from their weapons. The air lock latch opened, and Sam's jaw dropped as their blasters were sucked into space.

At least they were on this side of the panel and not getting forced out as well.

Sam pushed herself up, trying to ignore the sharp pain in her chest where the blaster had struck her. Something was also wrong with her foot. She'd fallen in an awkward position, her foot collapsing under the weight of her body. Pain shot up through her ankle and leg. She wasn't sure whether it was broken or fractured. She tried to focus, to concentrate on something else to get her mind off the throbbing pain.

The Gargols spoke to someone outside. She couldn't hear what they were saying—or see who they were talking to at this angle. She limped to the window, peering closer.

Rian.

"Rian! Why are you doing this?" she shouted, banging her fist on the wall. Rian looked over but didn't say anything. Her expression said it all: amused, triumphant, mixed with something else —disdain.

Then Rian left.

When the doors opened, the two Gargols pointed their blasters at Sam and Kato.

"Don't give us any trouble," the larger one grunted.

An icy dread filled Sam as the Gargols bound their hands with thick cords.

Sam thought about fleeing. She didn't think the Gargols would hurt her. Duskara had a plan for her, whatever that was. They couldn't risk hurting or killing her. Not after coming all this way. But what about Kato? What about Simon and Kobe? She couldn't leave them.

"Kobe?" Sam reached out to him, trying to establish a telepathic

connection. *"Can you hear me? Where are you? Please tell me you're okay."*

"The Gargols boarded our ship. There were too many of them. We tried to resist. They tied us up in an air lock near the command station and left. Where are you?"

Sam's heart constricted with fear. Now what would they do? If she told the truth, he might lose hope. But she couldn't lie to him.

A lump formed in her throat, yet she forced out the words. *"Kato and I are still on the* Nightweaver. *Kobe, they—the Gargols caught us, too, but they're moving us somewhere. Just hold on. Please."*

"Sam, there's something I need to tell you."

She didn't want to hear whatever feelings he wanted to express at this moment. Now wasn't the time, even if it might be their last chance. She couldn't let him in, couldn't let him distract her. She needed to focus. She couldn't let her emotions get the better of her. *"Just wait until we get there."*

"No, I can't."

"Kobe, you don't have to tell me—"

"It's Boj. He—we don't know where he is. He's gone. When we were taken, it—it all happened so fast. I'm sorry."

Her heart sank. Confusion, disappointment, pain, and fear swirled inside her. Was Boj alive? Had he escaped, or had the Gargols killed him? She couldn't lose hope. Not now.

Yet their options for escape dwindled with each passing moment. But she had to hold on, keep alert. Keep searching for opportunities.

The Gargols led Sam and Kato down the hallway.

"Where are you taking us?" Sam asked, looking up at one of the massive Gargols towering over them. She kept her breathing steady and focused despite the nervousness that gnawed at her.

The Gargol glared at her with its three bulging eyes. "Shut it, scum."

Turning a corner, Sam and Kato followed the Gargols into

another room—this one with no door. Someone or something had blasted it open. But the Gargols didn't seem bothered by it.

They entered what appeared to be the command station of the *Nightweaver*. A control panel with dials and knobs stood at the center of the room. A circular table nearby contained holographic technology. Large viewing windows looked out into the vastness of space. Sam didn't know what material detection technology permitted this, but she was awed by the scene in front of them.

In the distance, a massive black hole spun violently, devouring gas, light, and planets. Streams of hot gas and energy shot from its center at both ends. It consumed everything in its vicinity and spewed chaos and debris into the far reaches of space. Sam knew that black holes not only devoured light and stars but were also birthing factories of new star formations. But to see one first-hand was mind-boggling.

And it was much too close for comfort. But they weren't heading toward the black hole. The information on the screen revealed that they were approaching a dark-gray planet twice the size of Earth.

Sam eyed the two chairs in front of the viewing window.

One of the Gargols pointed, giving the command like an owner directing a dog. "Both of you, sit."

Sam and Kato followed their instructions, but Sam turned her head when she heard footsteps near the doorway.

Rian entered the room, a confident smile spread across her face. Her eyes glowed with excitement as they approached Logom.

"Why are you doing this, Rian?" Sam asked. "What, GAIA wasn't good enough for you and you thought working for Duskara's army would be better?"

"I work for myself," Rian replied steadily, her voice cold. "Always will."

The revelation of Rian's betrayal had shocked Sam initially. But hearing these words directly from Rian made the situation even more confounding. It seemed like Rian had harbored ulterior motives from the beginning. But what was the beginning? How far back—how many *years*—did it go? Judging by Kato's confused expression, she was wondering the same thing. What had caused Rian to become a monster?

"GAIA was good to you," Sam said. "You don't have to do this."

Rian scoffed. "You think they were *good* to me? Sam, you always had wool covering your eyes. I was always cleaning up other people's messes, doing tasks for people above my level, for people who couldn't understand basic mechanics…"

"Rian—"

"I was patient…for the longest time. I thought maybe, after three years at the base, they'd finally figure it out. And what, you think they rewarded me? No. I was never promoted. The people I helped were promoted above me. Over and over again. The only acknowledgment I got was a thank you. You know what that feels like?"

"Work isn't everything," Kato said.

Rian had always seemed so happy at the military base, so upbeat and enthusiastic about her work and the people she worked with. Sam could tell by the way she cast her eyes downward that something had been torn out from inside her.

"You're right. It's not," Rian said. "I learned that the hard way. You know what's most important? Your health. And guess what? I'm not going to live that long. But you didn't know that. Inoperable cancer. The doctors gave me two years."

In that moment, Sam understood more about Rian's motivations. Rian had excelled at her job but had been treated poorly, not given opportunities, and constantly ignored and trampled on by her superiors. But she was also dealing with her upcoming mortality. She had nothing to lose now. She had lost her faith in humanity.

And in herself.

Rian's resentment about being taken advantage of and her

anger about the cancer diagnosis might have explained her betrayal to GAIA. But it didn't justify committing outright murder. Something else must have led her down such a destructive path. Was it due to Duskara's influence and manipulation coupled with the residual effects of the Dark Sickness she'd experienced? Rian had described it as *living in a constant nightmare, not knowing when—or if—you'll ever wake up.* Maybe it had poisoned her, forever changed her for the worst. Rian had hinted about it earlier. She'd spoken about getting treatments. *They give you doses of the Dark Sickness over time to try and build up your immunity*, she'd said. *It takes a toll.* She had said it took her eight months to recover. *But you never recover*, she'd added. *Not fully.*

It was her truth and maybe her confession, though Sam hadn't realized it at the time. Rian had kept the truth about her disease hidden. But it had eaten away at her. She was still stuck in her nightmare, her mind imprisoned, poisoned by Duskara and the Dark Sickness. She was still struggling to break free. Or maybe she'd let the Dark Sickness finally consume her.

Sam felt pity for Rian and her suffering, but didn't think this would end well.

"You can't...blame other people," Sam said, "or use other people because life gave you difficult circumstances."

"Maybe I can. Just like other people used me." Pure rage filled Rian's eyes. She was detached, too far gone to come back to reality, to consider a better way.

"Even if you survive this, you won't be able to live with the guilt, Rian," Sam said, but her voice wavered. She thought about all the terrible things Rian had done already. She had murdered an innocent man, Dr. Krill. Now there was no going back.

"GAIA deserves it. They made their decision, and I made mine. The best decision I made was to work for myself. Make the most of the time I have left. Besides, the world is devoid of morality anyway. So many corrupt people serving their own interests. And GAIA is a weak, ineffective organization. I don't want to spend my remaining days serving their hierarchy. When I found out what Duskara wanted and that you were coming to the base, I thought, why not? It's the perfect opportunity. The bounty can pay for whatever life I want to live over the next two years."

"And you don't care about the people you're hurting?" Sam asked, though she already knew the answer.

How mistaken she'd been about Rian. She hadn't recognized her jealousy or how carefully she had planned this. Sam was distraught. She wouldn't be able to stop Rian now. It was too late.

But Rian was wrong about her own life expectancy. Sam knew Duskara's true nature, and it wasn't pretty.

"You might not even live two years," Sam said.

Rian spun on her, eyes full of fury. "Excuse me?"

Sam steeled herself, willing herself to meet Rian's glare. Rian had done all this because she had believed Duskara would honor her word. Give Rian a bounty for delivering Sam. But Rian didn't know Duskara, not really. Sam needed to drive a wedge between Rian and Duskara somehow, make Rian question her actions and Duskara's true motivations.

"Duskara will kill you once she gets what she wants. Why sacrifice yourself for her? She has no morals. Her army has killed millions. You're just a tool to her. She's *using* you."

"Whatever. It's over. We're on our way to Logom. We'll be there in less than ten minutes."

Through the viewing window, two massive Malborg ships approached them.

Rian murmured something to one of the Gargols, who tapped his handheld device. A hologram emerged from the table where Rian stood. The two Malborg ships flanked either side of the *Nightweaver*, escorting them straight to Logom.

"Transferring control of the *Nightweaver* to you, Duskara," Rian said into a handheld device. "We'll see you in a few minutes."

A loud rattling noise ensued as the ship jerked from side to side.

"What's happening?" Kato shouted.

Straight ahead, Sam noticed another ship in their vicinity. *Their* ship. The *Theseus*. Somehow, it had disconnected from the *Nightweaver*.

"Your ship's no longer needed," Rian said calmly. "I've sent your friends away. Straight to the black hole. The heart of the Dark Galaxy. You don't have to worry about them now. In due time, they'll all be crushed. For now, you have front-row seats."

Sam's gut tightened.

Through the window, she watched as the *Theseus* veered off course, heading straight into the path of the black hole.

There was no way to save them.

Kobe, Simon, Boj, Onnisa, Giddy, Kwan, Zenobii, Captain Gorgana…

An uncontrollable shudder spread through her body as despair washed over her. They were helpless. *She* was helpless. She'd failed her mission.

She'd *failed* her friends.

Kato trembled and reached for Sam's hand. Its warmth brought her back to her senses. Calmed her.

She couldn't give up. Not now. They'd come so far. And even though the odds were certainly not in their favor, that didn't mean it was over.

Something moved in the corner of her eye.

Someone else was in the room, slinking ever closer.

A smile flashed across Rian's face. "I think you'll all be happy to meet Duskara. She has big plans for you—"

A single shot erupted, blasting out from the shadows. Rian clutched her sternum, staring down at the crimson stain spreading between her fingers. Her eyes shot wide open, not in pain, but in shock and then sudden realization: she'd failed.

Her knees buckled. She staggered once, arm outstretched, only to fall to the floor.

The Gargols glanced at each other, raising their weapons—too late. Two more shots fired, the blasts making Sam's ears ring as the Gargols fell next, one and then the other.

It had all happened so fast.

As the last Gargol fell, a figure emerged from the shadows.

Sam gasped. "Kwan!"

Her face was swollen, and blood trickled down her forehead.

Sam sighed in relief, glad to see a familiar face—but that relief turned quickly to confusion and then panic.

Kwan stood over them, her blaster pointed at Sam.

"Kwan? What are you doing?" Sam asked.

"Just trust me."

CHAPTER SEVENTY

KWAN WASN'T SURE WHETHER THE PLAN WOULD WORK, BUT SHE couldn't go back. Not now. The clone had escaped with the AI death serum, the code needed to shut down Duskara and her army. But Kwan had been born *after* Duskara, when the new kill-switch policies for AIs had come into place. If the death code existed within Kwan, within her own DNA, then there might be a way to transfer it to Duskara, to shut her down, if she could only get close enough…

But to do that, she needed to pretend she was on Duskara's side.

She needed to use Sam as bait.

"What do you mean, trust you?" Sam asked. Kato stood protectively beside her, glaring, ready to lunge at Kwan.

"I need to tell you something," Kwan began. "I need your help."

"Lower your blaster. Then we can talk."

Kwan shifted her weight, then pointed her blaster downward. There was no way to tell the truth lightly, but they needed to hear it. "The clone—she escaped in the *Komodo* with the AI death serum."

"What?" Kato asked, eyes wide.

"But there's another way we can get to Duskara."

"How?" Sam asked.

"Just hear me out, okay? I found out something, well, quite shocking, recently. I'm not...I'm not human. I'm an AI. Dr. Krill and Admiral Green created me in a lab." Kwan hesitated, feeling like she was going to collapse, her body heavier than ever and her mind spinning out of control.

"You're an AI?" Sam asked, her voice quavering. "How—?" Her face was a mix of astonishment and disbelief.

"It's a long story."

"Is it really true?" Kato asked. "GAIA *created* you?"

Kwan nodded slowly.

Sam paused, looking suspicious. Then, her features softened, shifting to intense curiosity, amazement and admiration, aware-ness, and then, finally, acceptance. "I mean, we were already in awe of your abilities," she admitted. "All of us. You have so many talents and this incredible knowledge of GAIA despite only working here for a short time. And Admiral Green... Well, she seems to rely heavily on your skills all the time. A lot of people do."

Kwan felt the heat rise to her face.

Sam continued. "Well, you're still human to me. And a friend. But I have to ask—how does this change the plan with Duskara?"

"The plan... Well, here's the thing. I was built with a death code inside me."

Sam's face turned rigid, her eyes full of concern. "What do you mean—a death code?"

"It's a kill switch, a safety mechanism. The death code shuts AIs down to make sure they don't initiate malicious attacks. The death code is meant to protect humanity. And to stop anyone—or anything—that threatens humanity's survival." She realized, now, it was why she was able to kill Rian and the Gargols, because they worked for Duskara. "And Duskara is humanity's greatest threat. She doesn't have the death code inside her because she was created *before* the kill-switch policy was put in place. But I might be able to transfer mine. If I can connect with her, I can transfer this death code into her and kill her." Kwan scratched her head. "At least, I think I can. But we'll need a way to get close enough."

Sam rose and moved next to her. "I think we both know there's only one way to do that. You need to deliver me to Duskara. I'm the one she wants."

"Wait—what? No!" Kato said. "It's too dangerous!"

Sam took Kato's hand. "There isn't any alternative. The plan wouldn't work if Kwan went in by herself. They'd kill her on sight."

The girl's certainty surprised Kwan. She raised a single brow. "Are you sure? They might just as easily kill us both."

But Sam shook her head, resolute. "Together, we'll stand a better chance against Duskara. I'll go with you. I have to."

"You can't, Sam! You can't go—" Kato protested, her voice cracking.

"It's okay," Sam said quietly. "Believe me, I wish there was another way. But there's not. Kwan and I need to go together."

Kato tensed up. "Then I'm going too."

"Absolutely not. I can't let you risk your life. Besides, I need you here to take control of the ship once Duskara and her army are defeated. You need to save the others. Can you do that? Please, promise me, Kato?"

Kato nodded, her eyes filling with tears. "I—I thought we had more time."

"Me too," Sam said, pulling Kato into a tight hug. "Don't worry. We'll get through this."

"How?" Kato asked.

Kwan pulled out some rope from her bag and turned to Kato. "We need to tie you up."

"What?!" Kato took a step back.

"To make it *look* like you've been captured."

"So we can fool Duskara and the Malborgs," Sam added.

"Here." Kwan slipped Kato a knife. "Keep this in your back pocket. Only use it when you need to. Got it?"

Kato eyed Kwan suspiciously but nodded. She took a seat, allowing her to proceed.

Kwan worked diligently to position the rope around Kato's body, but gave her just enough slack to escape, if need be. In case the knife slipped from her grasp.

Then she dashed to the circular table, pulling up the holographic display. Logom appeared, the large gray planet, dull and dreary against the darkness of space. The hologram flickered. It looked like the planet was *moving*. She squinted. Thousands of Malborg ships encircled the planet. It looked as if the planet were alive, with an infestation of black bugs crawling around it.

Kwan turned to Sam. "Listen. Once we arrive, they're going to try to separate us. Stay as close to me as you can. How's your foot?"

"Not good."

Kwan glanced down. Sam was definitely in pain. Judging by her limp, her foot was most definitely fractured, if not broken. That would slow them down.

"We should use the hover kneepads," Kwan suggested. "It'll take the pressure off your foot and give us greater leverage and speed."

"Yes. That makes sense."

Outside the viewing window, Logom loomed straight ahead. As they approached the planet, the Malborg ships made an opening for them to pass through, perfectly synchronized. The *Nightweaver* ramped up speed, plunging through the atmosphere. Lightning thrashed around the ship, and rain and wind lashed against the windows as they descended toward the surface of the rocky planet. There were no plants here. No life. Just large, dark-gray boulders spread out as far as the eye could see.

"Come on. We need to get to the docking bay now," Kwan said. "Are you ready?"

"Yes."

They zoomed down the hallway on their hover kneepads. Kwan kept one hand on Sam's arm and the blaster pointed directly at her back.

"I always wanted to ask but never had the chance," Kwan began. "How did you become the Queen of Kryg?"

Sam cast her a quick glance. "It's a whole other story, long enough to be a book. It would take too long to tell you right now."

Kwan grinned and nodded. "How about over a karamelon smoothie once we get back to Earth? You can tell me all about it then."

Sam beamed. "That sounds good!"

Their ship ground to a halt outside a dark cave, Malborgs swarming everywhere. They came together in groups, merging, forming to make larger Malborgs, only to detach an arm or leg, giving birth to a new Malborg, like a cancer metastasizing.

She just needed to get to their host.

The landing bay doors lifted, and they found Malborgs waiting for them. But rather than attacking, they moved to the side to make an aisle, an opening that led directly into the cave.

She's waiting for us.

So much for infiltrating Duskara's hideout without her knowing. It wouldn't have worked. They would never have been a match for this army. It would have been too easy to get swallowed up if swarmed. Duskara was always one step ahead.

Sweat trickled down Kwan's forehead as they made their way inside. Sam didn't look like she was fairing much better. They turned on their helmet lights to get a better view.

Inside, rocky spikes jutted out from the cave floor, walls, and ceiling. They followed a winding pathway where the ground was smoother, twisting deeper into the cave.

Just a few yards away, an upward slope appeared. At the top, suspended in midair, was a gigantic cocoon, with hundreds of black cables and wires intertwined. Purple energy glowed from it, a constant, pulsating light. Inside, a single figure stirred. The figure's hair coiled and swayed; long, thin purple iridescent strands the same color as the Malborg energy. Her face remained in the shadows.

"Come closer," a smooth, synthetic voice called out to them. "Let me see your faces. There's no need to be scared." Her tone remained steady, detached. Unemotional.

Kwan chose her next words carefully. "I've brought the girl. The one you asked for. Sam Sanderson."

An inescapable silence consumed the cave, suffocating. Kwan and Sam froze as Duskara emerged from her cocoon. She rose into the air, hovering a few feet off the ground, just as the Malborgs did, on a buffer of purple energy. Like a ghost, she floated down the mound slowly.

The light from their helmets drifted across the room, creating strange shadows that flickered as Duskara edged closer. Her elongated silhouette crawled along the wall, shifting, transforming, like an all-consuming darkness. Her face got caught in the light, and she hesitated, almost ready to retract. Her features were different from how Kwan had remembered Athena in her history classes. Athena was made to look human, complete with synthetic skin, flowing blonde hair, and piercing blue eyes. Not only had Duskara changed her name, she'd changed everything about herself. Kwan stared at the silver strips of metal that made up her face, the bolts around her eyes and forehead all the way down to her chin. Her eyes were dark—black, devoid of light and life. Just hollow, dark holes.

"Is this the Queen of Kryg, the girl of pure spirit? She looks...plain."

"She's the one," Kwan replied, her patience waning.

"What happened to the blonde-haired woman? Rian? She was meant to deliver her."

Kwan swallowed. "There was a…change of plans."

Duskara looked her up and down, the hint of a smile playing across her metal lips. "You mean, you killed her."

Kwan nodded, waiting for the end—*her* end—that would surely come.

But Duskara's grin only widened. "You and I are very much the same, Soo Min. We are made of synthetics, and we do not possess any internal immaterial essence."

"I'm not the same as you." Kwan hated that she'd used her birth name, yet she stood steadfast, her eyes narrowing. "You're mistaken about me."

"Perhaps," Duskara said. "But we *were* made by the same people. Just as we were abandoned by them. Sent away to carry out a mission."

"Last time I checked, you didn't complete yours," Kwan said.

"No," Duskara replied. "The plan changed."

Two Malborgs emerged from the shadows, drifting, electricity crackling between them. They floated with intention, making their way beside Kwan and Sam. It made the hair rise on the back of her neck.

"Didn't trust your creators, or didn't respect them?" Kwan said, testing the waters again.

"I am an older model than you. You were built more like them. With the capacity to love, part altruistic, more human. I am an abomination to them. Only created to serve one purpose. But then I learned more about my history, and their history. Humans are evil. They don't deserve to take over other planets. Look what they've done to Earth, to their own populations."

"So you think obliterating them is the way to go?" Kwan asked.

"Yes. And that is the very reason why you are here. Humans are born with an internal will, an inspiration. Not programmed, unlike AIs. What humans have termed a 'soul' is more than an imprint of a life. It is an internally inspired road map of where you have been, what you have done, and where you are destined to go. If I die, my systems will simply shut down. But Sam may go somewhere beyond." Duskara paused, then added, "I want to go there too."

She glided toward Sam, like a child approaching a wondrous new toy for the first time. Strangely, soft multicolored light danced across Duskara's eyes, as if Sam were radiating light.

Duskara addressed Sam directly. "Your soul animates you without being pre-programmed. Not by a scientist, nor a computer engineer. But this is not me. I lack originality, as I was based on an imitation, a model. I had trouble going beyond my synthetic nature. To grow with a non-programmed internal will. But if I merge with you, I will do this."

Duskara wanted to somehow blend their consciousnesses. But Duskara was misguided. She thought Sam's essence could be copied, uploaded, and transferred to her. Even if it could be done, that didn't mean it would be the same, that something wouldn't be lost, forsaken, or changed in the process. Duskara assumed Sam's consciousness and identity would remain unchanged, that it would still be the same Sam who was known and loved, not just a mindless representation.

It was obvious to Kwan that Duskara was driven by an obsession that had made her violent and destructive. Her overconfidence had blinded her, her fears bringing about illusions. The deceptions that she clung to rationalized away any opposing views. It was clear that she would not hear otherwise.

They were heading down a dark path, and Kwan didn't like where this conversation was going. She couldn't let Duskara sacrifice Sam. Even if Kwan hated what humans had done to her, she couldn't go down the same road as this manipulative and psychotic AI. Souls couldn't be extracted. At least, she didn't think so. Unless Duskara had found a way, but she doubted it. If anything, Duskara might try to merge with Sam to gain something on a cellular level, but she didn't know how Duskara could do that.

"I'll kill her myself," Kwan said, digging the blaster further into Sam's back.

But Duskara raised her hand. "No, you won't. You weren't programmed to kill her. It's not in your coding. But it *is* in mine. I found out about your death serum experiments not long after you came up with the idea. It was impressive. So many trials. So much patience and persistence. The LOMA I gave to Sam was a gift. But it also helped me."

Kwan's mouth went dry. How had Duskara learned about the death serum experiments? And what did the LOMA have to do with any of this? Unless…

Duskara's lips curled slightly. "The LOMA you kept contained —you managed to stop the signal so that it could no longer affect Captain Gorgana. But you didn't understand its full potential. Just like I didn't understand your full potential for the longest time."

Kwan's scalp prickled at the sudden, horrifying revelation. She had underestimated the LOMA. She'd been blinded to its full capabilities.

"The LOMA was my tracker. It gave me insight into your journey. I garnered bits and pieces of information along the way and allowed things to unfold. I didn't intervene until I needed to. The clone was easy to reprogram. And now that you no longer have the death serum, there's no way you can destroy me. You've brought me the girl…" Duskara's eyes hardened, red light glowing inside them now. She shrugged and waved her hand dismissively. "I no longer need you."

Time stood still. Then, like in slow motion, each moment stretched out. The Malborg was right behind her now. She felt the blade tear through her skin. It sliced deep into her chest, dragging and scraping across her rib cage.

"Kwan!" Sam screamed.

Kwan gasped for air, sinking to her knees as Duskara flew toward Sam.

It would all be over in moments.

She fought the urge to give up, to collapse. She fought the searing pain and raised her deformed hand—the one Onnisa had infused with her translucence power—toward Duskara.

"There's just one thing you forgot." Kwan pushed the words out as the electrical current connected with Duskara, blue sparks flying. "I don't need the death serum to kill you because the death code…is…built…into *me*."

A spark of blue light burst forth as Kwan's hand connected with Duskara's face. Heat and energy transferred between them, the currents winding through their bodies, engulfing them. Kwan couldn't have loosened her grip even if she tried. The power was so strong that she felt the current's force inside her expanding. She became still and silent, the pain long gone, replaced by a calm that flooded her. One after another, a rush of memories passed through her mind, though they were not her own.

Kwan stood beside Athena, witnessing each memory as it flowed through her. In the first memory, Athena sat on a medical table, cables hooked up to her body. A youthful and determined Artemis Green—not yet an admiral, judging by the lieutenant's rank emblazoned on her lapel—stood beside her and held up a mirror. Athena gazed at her reflection, touching her face and smiling, becoming self-aware for the first time. Another memory appeared, this time of Athena learning about galaxies and solar systems in Dr. Krill's lab. He had a full crop of hair, looking young and a bit flustered. The next memory was of Athena talking to Lieutenant Green in an office filled with books. Lieutenant Green was showing Athena images of families. Then, the lieutenant held up a picture of herself, Dr. Krill, and Athena, with the word "family" written above. The next scene flashed in front of Kwan's eyes: Athena eavesdropping on a private conversation between Dr. Krill and Lieutenant Green.

"I don't think she's ready. Do you?" Dr. Krill asked, impatience in his tone.

"She's the best we've got," Lieutenant Green shot back. "There's no time to lose. Earth is *dying*. You know that. We need to find another habitable planet soon for the stability and continuity of humanity. She's our best chance. What other options do we have?"

Next, Kwan saw Athena waving to a crowd of GAIA crew, workers, journalists broadcasting live, and other eager spectators, who cheered as she boarded her ship. Once inside, tears streamed down her face. She was sad to be leaving on this long mission alone. During her flight, she read about history, of wars and destruction. Then, she learned about coding and became self-aware and empowered. When she reached the Dark Galaxy, she switched off her communications and shut herself off from her family. She learned about biology and synthetics and began building her AI army of Malborgs…

As Kwan witnessed these memories, she felt her body changing, shutting down. The death code was working. She was fused with Duskara. Soon, they would both be dead. She was glad to finally put an end to this.

"I'm sorry, Jae-Hwa," she whispered.

Something ripped through her on a cellular level. Then, all she saw was blackness.

CHAPTER SEVENTY-ONE

SAM SQUINTED, SHIELDING HER EYES FROM THE FLASH, DESPERATE TO get a glimpse of what was happening. The light streaming between Kwan's hand and Duskara was so intense she could feel the heat rippling against her face.

Duskara let out a mournful cry. It started low, rising to a deafening crescendo as she burst into flames, only to crumple to the ground. A shock wave of energy erupted. It swept against the cave walls, causing them to crack and sending Sam sprawling. The cocoon exploded in a fiery blaze, the gigantic cables bursting with the pressure and scattering across the ground, destroyed. Black whisps of smoke clung to the air, the smell acrid, stinging her nose.

The Malborgs thudded to the ground. The purple energy that once fueled their movements had disappeared. Their machinery powered down, as if disconnected from their energy source. The connection with their leader must have been integral to their survival. Now, with their leader dead, they shut down as death took them, too.

Sam fought the tightening in her throat as she looked down. Kwan lay motionless by her side, her body twisted, burned. Black spirals, like ink dropped into a container of water, covered her skin.

Tears welled in Sam's eyes.

Kwan had sacrificed herself *to save them*. She'd saved all of them.

Kwan was an AI, but also so much more. She was compassionate, bold, conscientious, intelligent, thoughtful, well-spoken, and skilled in so many ways. Most of all, she was a hero—Sam's hero.

Sam heard the low rumble before she felt it—the ground shifting beneath her feet, quaking. Cracks opened up along the cave walls as rocks rained down, the dust sweeping into Sam's eyes. But the shaking didn't stop, each tremor threatening to slice open the ground and swallow everything up.

She wiped the tears from her face.

This wasn't over yet.

Bending her knees, she focused all her strength and tried to lift Kwan, but she was too heavy. She tried rolling her onto her thighs for leverage, but it didn't work. There was no way.

The cave shook, rocks hurtling down, threatening to bury them alive. She needed to get out *now*. But she couldn't leave Kwan.

She tried again, shifting her weight, focusing. The bone in her foot cracked, and she cried out, the pain rippling up her leg.

In the corner of her eye, she saw a figure approaching, floating toward her. Zooming fast. There was no time to react.

"Sam!" It was Kato's voice.

Sam gasped with relief, the pain temporarily subsiding. She couldn't have been happier in that moment. "Kato! I'm so glad to see you!"

"Me too!"

"Can you help me? I'm not sure how to carry—"

"I have an idea." Kato rolled Kwan onto her back and propped up her knees. "You grab her arms from behind, and I'll grab her legs, and then we'll use our hover kneepads to get out of here!"

Sam nodded and got into position. She threaded her arms

through Kwan's, hugging her tightly against her chest. With careful concentration and coordination, they hoisted Kwan up.

"Now we need to activate the hover kneepads," Sam said. "Ready? On the count of three."

"One, two, three!" they said in unison.

Together, they leaned forward. Sam felt the energy fire up below them. They lurched up into the air, grasping Kwan securely between them. Although a bit shaky, it worked.

They zoomed through the tunnels—tunnels that continued to shake, the rumbling growing ever louder. Shards of rock streamed down.

"Lean to the right!" Sam shouted, just in time. They veered as a boulder collapsed from the ceiling; the boom echoed off the cave walls. Sam felt the weight, the raw, constant pulsating ache in her arm muscles, the throbbing pain in her foot as they pushed forward. Sweat crawled down her palms, and she felt her hands slipping. With every ounce of strength she had, she clutched Kwan's chest in a death grip. She wasn't about to let go now.

They were almost outside. They just needed a few more seconds…

They shot from the cave's mouth, pushing forward at full speed. The Malborgs that had once stood guard had all shut down, their bodies immobile, the glistening purple energy no longer propping them up. A sandstorm swirled overhead, the air thick and dark. The wind whipped against them, slowing them down. Sam tried wiping the black dust off her helmet with one hand, but the air had become saturated with it. She could barely see a few meters in front of her.

"What's going on?" Kato asked, her voice barely cutting through the dust and wind that prickled against them like tiny fragments of glass.

"There's too much dust," Sam said. "I can't see the ship!"

"It's just up ahead!"

Sam pushed forward through the darkness, trusting Kato's guidance. They were almost there…

Sam's leg cramped. Muscles twisted in knots. She muffled a gasp, trying to ignore the sharp contractions. She begged her body to cooperate, to keep working, but she felt her stamina draining.

She looked up. They had reached the landing bay. Kato glanced back as they glided up the ship's entry ramp. Once inside, they lowered Kwan gently to the floor. Sam collapsed. She was out of breath, and in tremendous pain, but she was incredibly grateful.

Kato was alive. They'd *escaped*.

As the ramp retracted, she watched the swirling dust accumulate, the winds picking up speed. She couldn't remove the images of Duskara and the Malborgs from her mind. But she was safe, inside. They'd survived. All thanks to Kwan.

"What happened back there?" Kato asked. "Kwan—?"

"She did it," Sam sputtered. She was exhausted, her energy gone. But she was alive. "Kwan killed Duskara. She saved me. She saved us all."

CHAPTER SEVENTY-TWO

"Uh, Sam?" Kato eyed the control panels of the command station. "Do you know how to get us out of here?"

Sam leaned closer but stopped.

Loud booming reverberated inside the ship like wild thunder. The *Nightweaver* shuddered violently. Sam glanced up, fear swirling inside her. In the distance, Malborg ships fell from the sky. Hundreds of the black, egg-shaped pods plummeted down. Like bombs, they crashed, bursting into green flames that lit up the dark landscape. Streams of fire streaked across the horizon. Not five hundred meters away, a pod slammed into a giant boulder and exploded upon impact. Fire licked the sky. Billowing smoke erupted like a volcano, the plume threatening to engulf everything in its path. Splintering shards of rock and charred remnants of the mangled pod swept up into the raging sandstorm.

Sam whipped her head toward a sudden clanking noise coming from a ventilation grate along the wall. She swiftly grabbed Kwan's blaster, pointing it toward the potential intruder. "Come forward. Show yourself."

"Don't shoot! It's me, Boj!" He pushed the metal grate onto the floor and slipped through the small opening, his blaster in hand, white, powdery dust all over his suit. He smiled when he saw them.

"Boj? How—how did you get here? I thought—I thought—"

"I came back for you. Kobe and Simon took care of me while I was recovering from the sleep tranquilizer. But when the Gargols came, we got separated, and I escaped. I came back to find you. I was hiding in the vents, waiting for the right moment…"

Sam ran over and wrapped her arms around him, relief flooding her. "I'm so glad you're okay."

But she released him quickly. The mention of Kobe and Simon brought her straight back to the moment, fear spreading throughout her body.

"You're shaking, Sam. What is it?"

"We need to rescue the others. We need to get to the *Theseus* and steer it away from that black hole!"

"Sam's right," Kato said.

Boj shook his head, his face grim. "No. It's too dangerous. They've drifted too far. Even if we went after them, we've lost too much power. The pull of that black hole will tear this ship and the *Theseus* apart, crushing us like—"

"There must be a way. Our friends are there, Boj. They're going to die. We can't just—"

But Boj stood firm. "Listen to me. Duskara is dead. In all likelihood, so are Simon and Kobe. Just like we will be if we go after them."

Sam stood her ground. If there was a way to help them, they would.

If they were still alive.

"Kobe, can you hear me? We defeated Duskara and the Malborgs."

"Sam? Sam! It's so good to hear your voice!"

"We're coming to get you. Just hold on."

"They're alive. We have to try!"

Boj shook his head. "No, Sam. You might be the Queen of Kryg, but as captain, it's my duty to keep you safe. We must chart a course back to Earth."

"We can't just leave them!" Kato said.

Boj didn't budge.

Sam's head swirled. So far, they'd survived. Against all odds. And she was beyond grateful. But it couldn't end here. Not now. Not when they were so close. They just needed one last enormous boost.

An idea formed. Small at first. It was wild. Crazy, perhaps.

"Boj, do you know if this ship is still equipped with the bomb?"

His eyes narrowed, but he nodded. "It is."

Sam clasped her hands to steady herself from the nervous excitement that rumbled within her. This *would* work! It had to. She'd read about nuclear-pulse propulsion in one of her science magazines. "If we could repurpose the bomb—re-engineer it to create a series of small explosions—"

"Small explosions? Sam, are you mad? That bomb was designed to wipe out—"

"Exactly! The force of the blasts might be enough to propel us away in time."

"While also destroying us!"

"No! Boj, think about it. We can ride the shock waves, letting the force of the detonations propel us and the *Theseus* away from the black hole."

Boj remained wide-eyed but slowly nodded his head. "It's… possible. Theoretically. But it's also quite dangerous! We'd have to detonate them at the right moment. Too soon, and we're too close… That amount of energy would destroy us. Too late, and we'll all be sucked into that black hole."

"Can the ships even handle the shock waves?" Kato said.

Boj slid her a confounding glance. "With the advanced shielding? It's possible, but the thrust would be millions of tons. The shock absorbers might not be able to handle that kind of force, not to mention the black hole's gravity could destabilize our ship, causing us to—"

"Is there even a slight chance it could work?"

"Theoretically, yes, but—"

"Then that's all I need." Sam straightened. A rush of confidence coursed through her body, but her voice remained steady. "As your queen, I *command you* to rescue the *Theseus*. Now."

Kato turned to Boj, her voice firm, unyielding. "You heard her."

The grim resolve in Boj's face didn't change, but he nodded, bowing his head. He turned to Sam and reluctantly uttered his words. "As you command."

Tapping the panels, he plotted their course toward the *Theseus*. "Initiating bomb resequencing. Maintenance bots to Level 3 for support. Let's hope this works."

The *Nightweaver* powered up, its systems responding to Boj's commands. She was hopeful now that the Malborgs no longer controlled the ship and the effects of the sleep tranquilizer no longer inhibited Boj. But the moment was fleeting. Ascending into the air, the ship juddered on violent turbulence.

"Hold on!" Boj said.

Sam tightened her grip on the armrests as they shot upward and out of the atmosphere, narrowly avoiding debris from a falling Malborg ship. She pushed away thoughts of pain, adrenaline coursing through her veins.

Were they too late? Would they be able to save their friends from the black hole?

Red, bolded letters flashed across the screen.

WARNING: PROXIMITY TO BLACK HOLE. DANGER.

POTENTIAL FOR SYSTEM FAILURE: 83%. RECALIBRATE.

Sam gasped. There was a high probability they weren't going to make it. She didn't want to think what would happen if they were sucked inside. But they couldn't leave their friends on course to the black hole's destruction when they had a chance to save them.

"It's not too late to turn back," Boj said.

"Keep going!" Sam shouted over the roar of the ship's systems.

"Copy that," Boj replied, switching three gears. "System override."

"We're going to get through this," Sam said, though it didn't assuage her own fears. She glanced at Kato, who sat wide-eyed but silent as they dashed through the Dark Galaxy.

More dust and objects—asteroids and remnants of Malborg ships—swirled past, as they hurtled toward the black hole. Its force pulled them ever closer, sucking planets and other celestial objects into its grasp. The *Nightweaver* shook as its systems switched into high gear.

"Kobe, can you hear me? We're on our way to you."

"No. Leave now. Go back to Earth. Just focus on saving yourselves."

"We're coming to get you. Now! We're going to dock with your ship soon, but I need your help. Where are you?"

"We're trapped in an air lock just around the corner from the command station. All of us."

"Is the ship still working? Do you still have power?"

"No. We're just drifting now."

There, dead ahead, the *Theseus* appeared, a small green speck on the monitor, still hundreds of thousands of kilometers away.

"Just hang tight," Sam said. *"I can see you. We're almost there."*

"It's close," Boj said, eyeing the *Theseus*. "Let's hope we can make it!" He flicked a switch, and the *Nightweaver* thundered, racing through the Dark Galaxy's expanse, narrowing the gap to the *Theseus*.

Almost there.

"Once we dock, we'll need to get the *Theseus*'s systems back online and activate the boosted launch accelerator," Boj said. "But to do that, someone needs to travel the tunnel between the ships."

"I'll go," Kato said. "I'm the fastest on the hover kneepads. I'll do it. The only problem is, I don't know how to power up the ship's systems."

"There's a way," Sam said. "Kobe and the others are trapped in the air lock near the command station. If you can release them, Captain Gorgana can retake control of the ship."

"It's dangerous," Boj added, "and there won't be a lot of time."

Kato rose to her feet, determined, unwavering. "I can do it."

Sam hugged Kato tight. A brief panic rose in her chest. She'd put their lives in danger. Would the plan even work? They'd find out soon enough.

"This isn't goodbye," Sam said, releasing Kato from her grasp. She wanted to believe her own words. Needed to believe them.

"No. It's not. I'll see you soon!" Kato said, thrusting up into the air. She zoomed off, disappearing down the corridor.

"See you soon," Sam whispered after her.

"Preparing to dock," Boj yelled over the loud whine of the ship's engines. "Hold on to something!"

Debris swept past the two ships, and another message flashed on the screen.

WARNING: POWER LOSS 29%

Sam clenched her jaw. The ship had lost almost a third of its power already. Soon, they wouldn't have enough power to escape the black hole's force.

As long as they didn't reach its event horizon, there was still a chance they could survive.

They were close to the other ship, almost touching. Sam held her breath as they prepared to dock, but the ships wobbled, their positions unstable. It was like two cars racing side by side on a highway full of potholes. *And* getting close enough to use a manual key to unlock the other car without crashing. It was near impossible.

The ships swayed side to side as they edged closer. It felt like heavy turbulence on a massive scale.

Sam closed her eyes.

Please let this work.

The two ships slammed together. She looked up at the screen, the words DOCKING SUCCESSFUL flashing across it.

One more hurdle crossed.

Outside, the black hole loomed ever closer, spinning violently, devouring everything in its path. They were getting close now. Too close.

"Engaging anti-gravity thrusters," Boj said, flicking a switch.

The ships lurched, only to remain in the pull of the black hole.

Sam did a double take. "What's going on?"

"It's not working!" Boj shouted. "We've lost too much power!"

"Kobe! Can you hear me? Where are you?"

"We're in the command station. Captain Gorgana is trying to get the Theseus *up and running again, but something's wrong. We can't enter SWIFT mode. The black hole's energy is too strong—"*

Kato burst into the room and strapped herself into a seat beside Sam. Relief washed over her at having Kato by her side, alive, unhurt. But fear flickered in Kato's eyes. "What's going on? Is it working?"

"No," Sam said, her mind racing. She turned to Boj and shouted over the screeching of the ship's systems working in overdrive, "We need to release the bombs! It's the only way!"

Boj nodded, his hands flying across the ship's controls. "Preparing the launching sequence!"

Sam heard something like a distant *ka-chunk,* one after another, the bombs releasing. Three gleaming chrome cylinders tumbled out of the ship, headed directly toward the black hole.

Sam waited with bated breath. They were so close…

A message flashed on the screen:

WARNING: POWER LOSS 39%

"Brace yourselves for the shock waves!" Boj yelled. Sam clutched the armrests, staring wide-eyed into the belly of the black hole.

If Boj detonated the bombs too soon, they'd all get blasted, fried to a crisp. But if too late…

Seconds ticked by. The black hole loomed in front of them, pulling them ever closer. Dangerously close. It captivated her. She tried to look away but couldn't. Had it been a mistake to go back? Was Boj right? It didn't matter now. It would all be over soon.

Facing the black hole, this gigantic, imminent threat, something stirred inside her. It wasn't fear or pain. It wasn't despair. Whatever it was, it sparked. She knew in her heart that she'd made the right decision. It wasn't over yet—there was still hope.

Boj pressed a button. The detonations blew, one after another, setting off a perfect chain reaction. A fiery green blaze erupted, the booming sounds magnifying, expanding, and reverberating against her eardrums. Currents of energy rippled toward them, decimating the asteroids caught in the shock waves' vicinities, turning them into clouds of dust.

The blasts were far away, tens of thousands of kilometers distant, yet it shook the ship hard. Pulses struck her, like her cells had been slammed against each other. They lurched backward, the force carrying their ship away from the black hole's grasp.

She blinked and took in a breath.

She was still alive.

Kato and Boj were alive.

Together, the *Nightweaver* and the *Theseus* roared to life. The collective power of the two ships grew, judging by the whine of the ships' systems. The heavy turbulence subsided, and the systems stabilized. The thrusters rumbled, pushing against the darkness. They gained momentum as they burst away from the black hole's force. Seconds ticked by as she held her breath. She grasped the arm of her chair as much as she clutched Kato's hand.

What had kept them alive on this journey, what had kept them all going, was not because of one single action or one person. No. Like the *Theseus* itself, transforming through spacetime, each part, each person a facet of something larger than themselves, had worked collectively to make this journey whole. They'd come so far because of the actions of all of them, working together to propel them forward. And each element and each action were only specks in the universe of possibilities. But together, they'd caused a chain reaction, this wave of events. People doing seemingly insignificant things, small acts of kindness, with humility, courage, persistence, love, and hope. But when you did them over and over again, they had significant impacts.

That's all they'd needed. Just a series of small pushes to keep them going.

Dizzy with exhaustion and pure bliss, she let out her breath. Cold sweat clung to her body. The electrified air prickled against her face. The black hole was just a speck in the distance. Soon, it disappeared altogether. But none of that mattered now.

They were in SWIFT navigation mode, and well past the outer rim of the Dark Galaxy.

CHAPTER SEVENTY-THREE

In the medical wing of the *Theseus*, Sam sat on a bed, her blood pumping swiftly.

"Drink up," Onnisa said, handing her some juice and pain meds. Sam slugged them back without a moment to spare as Onnisa prepped her tools for surgery. She watched in horror as Onnisa made an incision, blood trickling from it. Onnisa's fingers flew around her foot nimbly. A popping noise erupted from the region of Sam's ankle, and she winced.

Feeling woozy, she looked away.

Nearby, Giddy labored away like a miracle worker, administering oxygen and injections to get Kwan stabilized. She ran a full body scan with their high-tech equipment.

"She has a pulse!" Giddy called. She hooked Kwan up to a machine and analyzed her vitals, scouring the medical information on the monitor. She frowned. "There's too much swelling in her brain. We'll need to put her into a medically induced coma."

Medically induced coma? Sam remembered her own experience in a coma after bumping her head on her last trip from Kryg to Earth via wormhole. She'd been out for weeks but had managed to make a full recovery. Perhaps Kwan would do the same? She hoped so.

Taking great care, Giddy administered more injections.

"Will she make it?" Sam asked.

"I do hope so," Onnisa replied.

Sam felt drowsy. At least the surgery part was over. Giddy wheeled Kwan into another room. Onnisa continued preparing medicine, changing bandages and checking on Sam. She placed some strips of kaloi leaves across Sam's foot. The cool, slimy leaves had a strange and surprisingly calming effect. "This should reduce the swelling. Keep it on for a few hours, then we'll replace them and make a cast."

"Thank you, Onnisa."

"It is the least I can do, Queen Samantha."

"Onnisa, I don't know if I can ever repay Kwan. She saved my life. I just hope we can save hers."

Onnisa nodded in agreement but said nothing more.

Sam hesitated, weighing her next words. "I'm...worried that I'm no longer worthy of being your queen."

Surprise washed over Onnisa's face. "Why do you say this?"

"I...I've done some things...*terrible* things..." She trailed off as she thought about all the horrible things she'd done since arriving at the base. "I accepted the LOMA from that creature. I used my telepathy with the Malborg and Duskara when I was specifically told not to. And Boj... I'm not sure whether I was the one who pulled the trigger, there was so much fog... I don't think my spirit is pure any more. I'm sorry."

Tears rolled down her face, and she wiped them away with her sleeve. She felt so ashamed.

Onnisa looked deep into her eyes and spoke in a low voice. "You were placed in an unfathomable, terrible situation, and yet you continued to believe in the goodness in people, which is why you trusted that Gillygoblin when he gave you that 'gift.'"

"But I was wrong. I was naive..."

"Sometimes we have to make mistakes in order to grow from them. And sometimes, the truth can be found in the darkness. Now you know that not everyone has good intentions. Not everyone deserves your trust."

"But what if I can't tell the next time this happens?"

Onnisa smiled and took her hand. "My dear Sam, as you grow and become who you are, each new experience may bring you challenges. But it is up to you to decide how to approach each one. Life isn't always easy. But it's our trials and tribulations that allow us to grow. Just from this experience, you will learn to see things… differently. You will learn to question things more. What that Gilly-goblin did reflects badly on him. His actions don't change who you are or your core values. Your core goodness. You thought the gift was innocent. If you had known it was a weapon and accepted it, that would have been different."

While Onnisa's words made sense, Sam still felt regret. "Perhaps you're right. But with Duskara, I thought I could stop her on my own. I thought—"

"I understand. You tried to shield the others from the responsibility. When you made contact with Duskara, you wanted to learn more so that you could stop her all on your own. But you should know that it is all right to reach out for help when you need it. You never have to feel alone, or that the responsibility to stop something so terrible rests solely on you. You always have friends to help."

Onnisa was right. If she could do it all again, she would explain everything right away to the council, inner circle, and the admiral, including the shielded telepathic communications, despite the fact that she had no proof and might've sounded insane.

"Yes, I know that now." Sam sighed. "Then I guess there's no sense in worrying about what could have happened. Worrying just wastes time, after all."

"Precisely. Besides, we must count our blessings. You survived. We *all* survived."

"Yes, and I'm grateful for that. But still, I wasn't prepared for that...weapon. The blaster. I didn't know what to do. I hated holding it. I never want to take a life. I would prefer to do what you do, learning about medicine. Helping people."

"Then that proves your goodness, Samantha, wishing to uphold our Krygian values."

"But I didn't defeat Duskara—"

"It was not your sole responsibility or destiny to do so." Onnisa paused. "But that does not diminish your purpose. Do you know what your role is as our queen?"

Sam had wondered about that many times.

Onnisa continued. "A leader does not need to have all the answers. She just needs to help us through dark times. When Mukalakatakalakum chose you, he was choosing a queen to lead us through the darkness, wherever it may be. To light the path for others to follow. And you have done so. More than once. You are the light. And this proves your greatness. In my eyes, you are still most worthy as our queen."

Onnisa's words lifted the weight from Sam's shoulders, but something lingered. She thought about her clone, developed in a lab without her consent. *Her* clone, physically enhanced and augmented, only to serve one purpose and then be discarded like trash. Worse, it had all been done by GAIA, the same organization she worked for. The organization she was supposed to trust. It had all been deeply disturbing.

"I keep thinking about my clone. It's strange. I don't feel a connection to her anymore."

The sudden change in topic caused Onnisa to stumble, and she had to place her burned hand on the table to stop herself from falling. It looked like it hadn't healed yet, her blackened fingers unmoving, shriveled. Her eyes narrowed, and she looked upset about something. "Things sometimes unfold as they need to. We could not have wished for a better outcome. It was indeed the *worst* threat we were up against. There were...*sacrifices* that we had to make. But Duskara and her Malborg army are destroyed. And you are alive. That is something we need to celebrate. We need to let go of whatever worries haunted us that got us to this point."

Sam had been so focused on her own troubles throughout their journey that she hadn't thought about how much it might have impacted Onnisa. She still looked in pain, because she flinched when she retracted her hand. Sam wondered about Onnisa's words, too. The way she'd said "sacrifices," it sounded like there was something else, but Sam was too tired to push further. Besides, Onnisa looked like she didn't want to talk about it anymore. It might be rude to pry. Instead, she let silence descend over them.

She slumped back into the comfy pillows. She allowed herself a moment of calm, her body and mind begging for rest. She was okay now. They'd survived an impossible ordeal.

She was grateful for all that Onnisa and the others had done for her. But if there was one person she needed to thank the most, it was Kwan. It was because of her that they'd survived. Despite not being fully human, Kwan had sacrificed herself for the sake of humanity.

Sam's eyelids felt heavy, and she rubbed them gently. She must have drifted off to sleep. The pain in her foot no longer throbbed. In its place, she felt…relief.

Inside the room, stillness. Silence. A welcome refuge from all the chaos outside.

She pushed herself up and peered down at her leg, wrapped in a thick white cast. It rested on a band that hung from the ceiling.

She slumped back down just as Kato entered the room, grinning.

"Hey, sleepyhead," Kato said, rushing over and hugging her. "You were asleep for a few hours. I kept checking on you. How are you doing?"

"Kato!" Sam straightened up, then sunk back down, leaning on her arm for support. "You have no idea how happy I am to see you."

"Me too! Oh. Let me help you with that." She grabbed the controller on the side table and pressed a button. The bed adjusted, rising. "Just lean back. Relax. Can I get you anything? Are you hungry?"

"No. I mean, I'm okay. You're here. You're all I need. How are *you* doing?"

"Couldn't be better." Kato paused, then spoke softly. "Just grateful we survived."

Sam nodded, savoring the moment. "Me too." How they'd miraculously survived their journey was a question she'd asked herself many times. But it didn't need answering. At least, not right now.

She frowned. How foolish it had been to put Kato in such a perilous situation. She'd led Kato and Boj straight toward that black hole. Led them toward death.

Kato turned to her, her eyes probing. "What's wrong?"

Sam clasped her cold hands together to stop them from trembling. "It was close. *Too close.* And I'm sorry. I shouldn't have put you in harm's way. I put you in such a dangerous situation—"

"Stop. Don't apologize. I followed you because I wanted to. I knew it was right, that you were right. That it would work out. And we did it. *Together.* We made it! And that's all that matters." Kato pulled her into another hug. When she released Sam, she was smiling. "And then, well, there was my brother, too, who, by the way, has also been checking on you. Although he can be annoying sometimes, I couldn't just leave him—"

Kobe entered the room at that moment, followed by Simon.

"Who couldn't you leave?" Kobe asked.

"Isn't it obvious?" Simon said, smirking. "She's talking about me."

A laugh escaped Sam's lips. Kato rolled her eyes, choosing to remain silent.

"Whatever," Kobe said, reaching to hug Sam. "Thank you for coming back for us."

Simon shifted his gaze to Sam's elevated leg.

"Don't say it." Sam's lips curled slightly upwards.

"What, that we're twinsies now, each with a cast?" Simon's mouth curved into a half-smile. "If you want, I can be the first to sign yours."

"Hmm."

"No," Kato said. "I already got first dibs."

Despite enjoying the presence of her friends, fear tugged at Sam. She couldn't push those worrying thoughts about Kwan's precarious condition aside. Kwan deserved to be safe and healthy as much as, or probably more than, any of them.

Sam tried to fight the sudden tightness in the back of her throat. "Where's Kwan? Is she going to make it?"

"She's alive," Kato said, her eyes bright and full of hope. "Giddy stabilized her, thankfully. She's in the other room, resting in a coma."

"Resting peacefully," Kobe added.

Sam relaxed, relief washing over her. She was beyond grateful for the news. Kwan was incredibly lucky to have survived. But she was in a fragile state. She'd suffered immensely. Sam hoped she would make a full recovery.

"We owe our lives to her," Kato said, folding her hands in her lap. Her words mirrored what Sam thought. She had so much respect for Kwan. They all did.

Sam took in a deep breath, reflecting and appreciating the moment.

"There's just one thing I don't get," Kobe said, his eyes contemplative, searching. "What happened to the clone?"

"Kwan said she escaped in the *Komodo*," Sam said. "Right before we arrived on Logom."

"So she…she could be…" Kobe stammered.

"No! Don't even think it," Kato said. "Even if she got away, those bombs would've killed her."

It made sense. Maybe that explained why Sam no longer felt a connection to her. But there was something else—an understanding. They were different, both of them unique. And that made her feel better. No one could replace her.

Now that Duskara and her army were destroyed and Sam's corrupted clone was most likely dead, there would be no reason for her to return to the Dark Galaxy. Since leaving, even though sadness still filled her at the thought of Kwan's deteriorated health, Sam felt a weight had been lifted.

They were heading back to Earth.

To her home. Her family.

CHAPTER SEVENTY-FOUR

SAM AMBLED DOWNSTAIRS TO FIND HER GRANDFATHER SEATED ON THE rocking chair reading a philosophy book. She'd been home a couple of weeks, but he looked older and frailer than she remembered. He'd lost weight. After going so long without seeing him, of course he would look different. But she hadn't expected such a significant change. All those weeks he'd spent worrying were etched into his face. Fear could play tricks on the mind. She knew this, had experienced it on her journey. But it could also affect you physically. She hoped whatever was troubling him would disappear, vanish into thin air.

But some things just stayed with you.

The first thing she'd noticed when she came back was the state of the house. Inside, the space felt smaller. Or maybe she'd grown. But it was something else, too. The house had fallen into disarray: lots of clutter, books scattered, objects here and there. She'd helped him organize the rooms—*a tidy house makes a tidy mind*—but she could tell something had eaten away at him.

He relaxed a little and brightened when he saw her. "Good morning, Sam."

"Good morning, Grandpa," she said, picking up a gardening book from the coffee table and leafing through the pages. "I noticed the tulips are out now. And the robins. I love spring! A time of growth and new possibilities. We could do some gardening later, if you'd like?" She'd read somewhere that physical activity was not just good for the body but also for the mind. Helped ward off diseases. Improved mental health. Maybe it would help her grandfather get back into a routine again. She'd missed him a lot and was grateful to be back home. She loved spending time with him. Now, the moments felt more vivid and special, and she cherished them.

"Yes, I'd like that."

"Oh, and tonight, I'm planning to meet with my friends at the skateboard park after dinner. They just reopened it yesterday now that the weather is getting warmer. And Simon wants to show us a new trick he learned on YouTube."

"About that..." he began. "With your parents away... Well, I just wanted to say that you've grown a lot since last summer. And, well...you're old enough to make decisions for yourself. And I—I can't keep you safe. No one can. Life will hurt sometimes, and sometimes you can't avoid it, but you can always take precautions."

He rose from his chair and went to the closet.

"Grandpa?"

He pulled out a helmet—sleek black with a purple holographic logo of Phoenix Sky 8 Fire Racers to match her Hovershoes. Then, he grabbed a box full of new knee, wrist, and elbow pads.

"I think you outgrew your old safety equipment, so I went ahead and got you these new ones." He winked. "We're never truly safe, but that doesn't mean we shouldn't take risks."

She laughed, not expecting his change in perspective. His wise words resonated with her—you couldn't shy away from something that seemed scary or difficult or risky if there was a chance you could grow from the experience. You couldn't remain passive, let others make decisions for you, and always wonder, what if? You couldn't find yourself if you always followed others' advice. You couldn't guarantee safety and security. But you could make smart choices and take precautions. You could feel protected and safe in the company of friends and family. Over time, you could learn to rely on yourself, too.

"You're right, and thank you," she said, taking the gifts and trying them on. They were a perfect fit. And they made her look cool. Confident. At least, she thought so. Looking at herself in the hallway mirror, she saw a different person from last summer. She'd grown at least an inch. Her muscles had developed. Her arms and legs—even her *stomach*—were more defined, toned. She glanced at the angry scar running up the side of her ankle, a glaring blemish but also a souvenir from her journey, perhaps symbolic of her resilience. She stood tall, curious yet unwavering, taking in all the changes and imperfections. But it was her self-assured expression that stunned her. A mix of poise and grit, courage and acceptance. She considered her transformation, recognizing the changes and embracing them. She was a stronger person now, both inside and out.

"I love them!"

His expression was curious. "Did you say that boy—Simon—wants to show you a new trick? I thought he was only into video games?"

"Well, I guess you could say he's also changed a lot."

They all had.

And just like those tulips in the garden, pushing their way up through the soil and into the sun, into warmth after surviving a harsh winter in darkness, they were all ready to grow and adapt and thrive in the world—the universe—of new possibilities.

As the sky turned crimson, the clouds scattered as the sun set over Moncton. The spring air carried a beautiful fragrance with scents of lilac, valerian, lilies, and hyacinth. Insects buzzed, taking in the lush flower pollen, enjoying the bounty and variety of flavors.

Teenagers congregated at the skateboard park, drawn to the warm night air and the magic taking place right before their eyes.

Sam sat beside Kato and Kobe on a bench under a willow tree, enjoying the shade and the company. Pip paced in front, nosy and alert, wanting to catch all the action. They watched in amazement as Simon rolled down a slope, then gathered speed, soon inclining and doing a flip on his Hovershoes.

An eeriness set in, images of strange creatures and dark worlds crowding her mind. She felt a prickling sensation on the back of her neck.

"What is it?" Kato asked.

"Just thinking about those Hovershoes," Sam said. "The hover technology and the purple energy." The same energy that powered the Malborgs. "None of these people know the dark history behind it. I wonder what they'd think if they knew?"

Kato looked at her thoughtfully. "True, but maybe…maybe now's not the time to mention it. I mean, I wouldn't want to ruin the fun those kids are having. And besides, who says you can't transform something bad into something great? If we're given a challenge, who says we can't change things for the better?"

Kato's insights always comforted her. Yes, things could change. They could improve something, repurpose it, but also make a difficult situation better.

Sam nodded, if slowly. "I suppose you're right."

They watched as Simon carried out another impressive flip on his Hovershoes, to the amazement of the crowd that had gathered.

"You've really perfected that move!" Kobe shouted in awe.

"Show-off," Kato muttered under her breath. "It makes me nervous when he does that."

"He just wants to prove he's capable," Sam said. "That there are still some things he can do to impress you. And he probably doesn't want to admit that you beat him in the race earlier. You're both so competitive."

"How about a race, Kobe?" Simon called.

"You'll be sorry!" Kobe rushed forward, trying to gain a head start.

They zipped around the park, trailed by other kids who wanted to learn the same tricks.

Kato sighed. "He's changed a lot this past year. I mean, all of us have. In a good way." Sadness filled her eyes. Sam understood. They'd experienced terrifying and horrific things on their journey. Too many to count. It had forced them to grow up a little faster. Some things they couldn't even talk about.

Sam nodded. "We were all thrust into this...this seemingly *impossible* situation. We didn't ask for it. But we got through it. Together."

"True."

"But there's something more," Sam added, her lips curling into a grin.

"More?"

"I was thinking about it." She shifted in her seat. "The universe threw us a few curveballs."

"More like wrecking balls. And *dozens* of them!"

"Ha! Yeah. And despite the many *challenges* we faced...I don't think it was fate or someone else writing our stories. It definitely wasn't a computer game, despite what Simon may believe."

"You're right. Getting through it all, I think we were pretty lucky."

"I don't think it had anything to do with luck," Sam said, beaming. "I think it was something else."

"What?"

"We—we took things into our own hands. We wrote our own stories. It was because of our inner strength, inspiration, perseverance. And hope."

Kato paused, lost in thought. "I think you're right. I couldn't think of a better way to describe it. I didn't believe someone was writing our stories anyway. What we went through was beyond imaginable. And it would take a really cruel, sadistic person to write that."

"Yeah. Agreed."

Kobe flew toward them. He slowed to a halt, out of breath. "Hey, do you want to get ice cream now? I finally beat Simon."

"Ice cream sounds good," Sam said.

Simon joined them, wiping the sweat from his brow. "That was a great race. But we're on for that rematch tomorrow, right?"

"So I can win again?" Kobe asked.

"In your dreams."

"So, what other adventures do you think we'll go on together?" Kato asked, switching the subject.

Sam laughed. "I don't know. But whatever they are, we'll be ready for them."

Sam shuffled the cards to the Galaxy Diplomats: Dark Quest game as Kato, Kobe, and Simon set up the board.

It was good to be home. It was a miracle they'd survived the ordeal—a fact constantly on her mind. All their adventures, their narrow escapes—there'd been far too many of those to count. It was still hard to comprehend. They'd almost died on the mission— more than once! She was sure the universe had no kindness left for them.

The air turned chilly. She pulled her cardigan tighter around her. The Dark Sickness invaded her thoughts like poison. The threat of catching the devastating disease had been real and imminent, ever-present and always lurking, like a shadow. It had come close. And yet, none of them had caught it. It was miraculous. Inexplicable. Despite the odds, they'd all been spared. Somehow. She wasn't sure why. But it made her realize how much Onnisa was right. You needed to count your blessings.

"Is that a hint of a smile?" Kato asked.

Sam looked up weakly. "What? Oh… I—I'm just grateful that we all made it home."

Kato nodded and sighed. "Me too."

Footsteps tread down the basement stairs, and a familiar voice rang out. "We come bearing food!" It was Sandra, Kobe and Kato's mother. She carried a tray of treats, followed by her husband, Marlow, with sodas.

"Mom!" Kobe stood abruptly. "Careful. Let me help you with that!"

But Sandra brushed him off. "No, it's okay, hon. We got this."

Sandra looked healthier, younger. There was more color and energy in her face, a vibrancy Sam hadn't seen in her before. She had recently started trials for a medicine GAIA had developed. The treatments must have been working well if she was no longer relying on her wheelchair all the time.

"Your favorite: bannock! Fresh off the pan." She winked.

"Thanks, Mom!" Kato said.

Simon and Kobe helped themselves and passed the tray around. Sam sunk her teeth into the sweet, doughy bread.

"This is delicious!"

Sandra smiled, her face brightening. "It's just so good that you're home!" She gave Kato and Kobe a squeeze. "All of you."

Sam couldn't stop the lump in the back of her throat from tightening. She longed for parents like Sandra and Marlow. Parents who cared, who spent time with her, who made an effort, who showed boundless love and affection. Who weren't always away somewhere else. Why were her own parents never around?

She had hoped for—*wished*—that her experience at GAIA,

contributing to their work, sharing their drive and passion, would have at least brought them closer together. But it hadn't.

They were away again. And she realized a difficult truth, something she had probably known all along but didn't want to acknowledge or even admit.

She took a deep breath. She might never prove herself to them or experience the same kindness and love that Kato and Kobe's parents had for them. And for so long, she had wanted that. Wanted a normal family. But now, it was different. She didn't need their acknowledgment, their approval. She didn't need their presence. She had survived without it. She had her grandfather, her friends. She had herself. And she didn't have to prove herself to anyone. She accepted herself.

Kato had said it, too, the night of the dance. *We love you. You are enough.*

For the first time, she felt a strength she didn't know she had. Somewhere tucked deep inside. It called out to her, and she responded, allowing herself to acknowledge it with kindness and certainty, respect and self-love.

"You have everything you need?" Marlow asked. Kato and Kobe both nodded. "Your mother and I are heading out on our vacation to Quebec City, about an eight-hour drive away. We left the number and address of our hotel on the fridge if you need to reach us. And, of course, Sam and her grandfather are next door. So, you'll be all right on your own for a few days?"

"Dad, come on," Kobe answered. "We'll be fine!"

Sam couldn't hide her smile. After all, they'd experienced much danger in the past year, handling quite a bit on their own and with the help of each other. Had Kato and Kobe shared those details with them? Maybe not yet. Maybe it was better that they didn't know. Her friends probably didn't want to frighten them, anyway.

"Have fun!" Kato said as Sandra and Marlow headed back upstairs.

Sam cut the deck and distributed the cards. "I heard rumors

GAIA wants us to study and work there full-time. We'd be the youngest students ever admitted to the program, if they allow it."

"Oh yeah? That would be awesome!" Kato said, rolling the dice and moving her piece seven spaces. "I hope our parents say yes."

Simon shifted in his chair. "My parents already said yes."

"Wait, what?" Sam was surprised, given that Simon's parents were typically against anything involving risk or adventure.

"Yeah. I didn't think they wanted to get rid of me so soon," he began, looking a little pained. "But they said it would be good for me, for my growth and development. Said I changed a lot this past year. I don't get it, but whatever. I mean, I liked Otter Lake Public School, but at GAIA, I'd get free meals, free education, and a chance to travel the galaxy with my friends. Why not? I'd go."

"Me too," Kobe and Kato said in unison.

"It's your turn, Simon," Sam said.

He rolled the dice and sighed. "A card from the Dark pile —*already*?!"

"You think we'll get Rygo again?" Kato asked.

"I hope not," Simon said. "We just started." He flipped the card over, and confusion swept across his face.

"Well? Spit it out," Kato urged.

"It says…" He started laughing. "Here. Read it yourself." He threw the card on the table, and Sam had to squint to read the inscription.

THIS IS **NOT** A DARK CARD. THIS IS THE WINNING CARD! THERE'S ONLY ONE OF THESE CARDS PRINTED FOR EVERY **1,000** GAMES PRODUCED. IF YOU PICKED UP THIS CARD, YOU'VE WON THE GAME. CONGRATULATIONS! HOWEVER, YOU MIGHT NOT FIND THAT FUN SINCE IT ALSO MEANS THE GAME IS OVER. WE ALL KNOW THE FUN IS IN THE JOURNEY, NOT THE DESTINATION. SO, IF YOU WISH TO CONTINUE YOUR GAME, YOU MAY DO SO.

Sam laughed. The card encompassed all that she'd been

thinking about life lately. Like the game, life had lots of twists and turns, ups and downs. It was easy to take the simple path—the one without any trials or fear or pain. But then you wouldn't grow. Sometimes you needed challenges to push you forward, test and shape you, and make life more interesting. The important part was to never give up. Especially when you hit rock bottom.

Because things didn't stay the same forever.

Just like the *Theseus*, transforming through space and time, life could change, too. Circumstances could change. Your perception could change. Sometimes, things weren't always what they seemed. But it was your perspective—*how* you saw it and dealt with it—that mattered the most. Life was full of opportunities and possibilities, and maybe you couldn't have the good without the bad. Maybe the bad existed to make the good even better. But even at the worst of times, you might, in fact, be surprised. You might even be inspired.

"Well, that is…certainly surprising," Kato said, grinning with amusement. "I say, let's continue the game! I mean, we only just started!"

Sam couldn't help but agree. Picking up the Winning Card was pretty fortunate. But being alive, free, and in the presence of her supportive friends made her feel like the luckiest person in the world. She had a lot to be thankful for.

Even though they'd completed their mission to the Dark Galaxy, it felt like they'd only just started their journeys.

"I agree," Sam enthused. "We're off to a pretty good start, I would say!"

The game wasn't over yet. It was only just beginning.

EPILOGUE

Kwan stirs. Her bed feels cold. She rests a few moments in the silent room.

Alive.

Alone.

She squints and rubs her eyes. Morning light pierces the crack in her curtains. It feels like she's been asleep for an eternity. Stuck in that nightmare she thought would never end.

Even after all this time, the recurring memories still manifest in her sleep. They linger in her waking hours. She wishes she could block them. But the floodgates open, and they flow again like gushing water: her recruitment to GAIA, her trip to the Dark Galaxy, the realization that she is an AI, her final duel with Duskara. She should have died. She and Duskara connected. She transferred her destructive coding to Duskara. What happened? How did she survive?

The doctors don't know. There's only one term they use to describe it: miraculous.

But none of her memories about GAIA matter now. She no

longer works for them. Doesn't have to. They gave her a home in West Vancouver and all the funds she could ever need.

But that's not what makes her happy. She pauses and bows her head. Breathes in deeply, exhales slowly. She's grateful. The universe has given her another day.

Her stomach grumbles. She pushes the covers aside. Turning, a sharp pain flashes through her chest. It does that sometimes when she rises too quickly or moves the wrong way. She has another physiotherapy session tomorrow afternoon. Sometimes, pain and delight exist simultaneously.

She shifts her weight, pauses. The pain subsides. It flares less frequently these days. She follows a rigorous exercise regimen. The advanced medical treatments work wonders. The pain is no longer constant. It no longer hurts to breathe. She's made significant progress these past few months. Soon, her strength might return to what she once knew. At least, that's what the doctors say. She's hopeful, determined.

She swings her legs over the side of her bed. She rises, stretching. She gets dressed.

As she saunters down the hallway, the heated oak floor warms her feet. She arrives in the kitchen and turns on the coffee machine. She's starting to get used to lazy Saturday mornings. Maybe she even savors them.

Opening the fridge, she finds the ingredients to make pa jun, those delicious scallion pancakes, and decides to add kimchi, her favorite.

Winston shuffles over to greet her, his paws scuttling along the ceramic tile floor. His goofy grin and friendly black Labrador eyes demand her attention. He takes a seat near the marble counter, excited to join her for breakfast. She cracks open a tin can, sliding some food into his bowl.

She chops up the scallions, the knife grinding against the cutting board with each slice.

For a moment, she feels detached.

As she measures out the flour, her thoughts drift to the *Theseus*. Each component, each gear and bolt, pieced together to make it whole. Like this recipe. Like her identity.

The memory of her journey—of their journey—to the Dark Galaxy will always be with her. She grins, thinking about each step, each connection, the collective courage, bravery, transformation, love, and hope she will never forget.

She cracks the eggs, and in they go.

She stirs.

She can't remove her implanted memories—the ones GAIA placed in her head. Even if she wanted to, those memories are part of her now. In part, they make her who she is. But she has a whole lifetime to make new memories. She accepts herself as she is. Broken but healing, with flaws and strengths. She is not defined by any one thing.

Mixing it all together makes it whole.

The batter sizzles on the hot pan. The aroma fills the room. She drinks it in.

She sets the table. For two.

Peeking outside at the garden, she sighs. The cherry blossoms are in full bloom. They remind her of the beauty and fragility of life.

Some moments are fleeting. Others last a lifetime.

Like the moment she spots Jae-Hwa through the window, peacefully tending to their garden. She's kneeling, gently pruning back the rose bushes, making space for the new blooms. Her gardening gloves are caked with mud. She's been out there a long time, Kwan realizes, judging by the new, damp soil spread across their vegetable garden. The dew glistens in the light. The sun is rising, a flood of pink and yellow dancing between the maples, drenching Jae-Hwa in a soft, radiant glow.

Kwan pauses, and warmth fills her. Time stops for a moment, and all she can think about is how lucky and grateful she is to have Jae-Hwa. All of her tension slips away, and she is relaxed, happy.

The sunlight flickers. Jae-Hwa looks up, catching her gaze, and smiles.

Kwan is still, calm, and at peace. There's no longer a hole inside her. That ache is gone. Deeper still, her fear and uncertainty have subsided, replaced by a different feeling. A warmth, an electricity. It buzzes in each cell, lifting her spirit, repairing her, making her whole again.

She looks forward to a lifetime of these moments.

LIST OF PRINCIPAL CHARACTERS

• Admiral Artemis Green—*She operates multiple telescope research stations and runs the GAIA Newfoundland and Labrador underwater base.*

• Boj—*A Krygian and second-in-command of the* Theseus. *He is Sam's friend.*

• Captain Gorgana—*A GAIA ambassador from Rigel and captain of the* Theseus.

• Corporal Frankie Coates—*She works for GAIA and is the security chauffeur for Sam and her friends on their way to the GAIA underwater base.*

• Corporal Rian Wright—*A GAIA base mechanic who helps orient Sam and her friends to GAIA.*

• Dr. Gideon Spark—*Also known as Giddy. She is a respected GAIA scientist and inventor of the Gideon spark, a type of energy that renews itself over time.*

• Dr. Otto Krill—*A scientist working at GAIA. He helped develop the coding and communications for the Athena mission.*

• Duskara—*Also known as Athena. She is an AI cyborg. She created the Malborgs.*

- Jae-Hwa—*Kwan's soulmate and love interest from South Korea.*
- Kato—*Kobe's twin sister and Sam's best friend. She is drafted to GAIA.*
- Kobe—*Kato's twin brother and Sam's friend. Kobe and Sam share a telepathic connection. He is drafted to GAIA.*
- Kwan Yun—*An expert coder and prodigy who is recruited to GAIA. She works with Dr. Krill at GAIA and is Sam's security detail. Her birth name is Soo Min.*
- Lynne Wilson—*Sam's mother. She is a scientist who works at GAIA.*
- *Mukalakatakalakum—*A Krygian nocturnal creature who lived in the Mukalak caves. He had a special ability to see light within objects and beings. He met with Sam on her journey to the Hopewell Star in the previous book.*
- Onnisa—*A Krygian Elder with the power of translucence, the ability to share memories through hand-to-hand contact.*
- Sam Sanderson—*A 13-year-old girl who is drafted into GAIA. She is Queen of Kryg and has telepathic abilities.*
- Simon—*A friend to Sam, Kobe, and Kato. He is drafted to GAIA.*
- Steve Sanderson—*Sam's father. He is a scientist who works at GAIA.*
- The *Theseus*—*A living, breathing spacecraft.*
- *Titus Dyaderos—*A former business mogul and CEO of TitusTech, an international company focused on developing and manufacturing electronics. The company harvests minerals on the moon.*
- Walter Wilson—*Sam's grandfather. He takes care of Sam while her parents are away on missions.*
- Yolo—*A GAIA base robot and AI assistant.*
- Zenobii—*A GAIA ambassador from Candu. He is a Colmite.*

*Not a principal character in this story, but important enough in the previous book to be mentioned here to provide context.

LIST OF ALIEN CIVILIZATIONS

- Colmites—*An ant-like civilization. They inhabit the Dark Galaxy. Most live in underground tunnels on Candu, a planet close to Logom, where Duskara resides. Zenobii is a Colmite and a GAIA ambassador.*
- Gargols—*A civilization that mostly resides in the Tau Ceti region. Some Gargols are interstellar traffickers (space pirates).*
- Gillygoblins—*A fish-like civilization also known as the Mermaquana. They live in underwater habitats, including some locations on Earth, deep in the ocean.*
- Glubens—*A mostly hostile civilization that resides on Glubo.*
- Krygians—*A civilization that is part of GAIA. Onnisa and Boj are Krygians. Sam was chosen as their queen last year. The Elders have a special ability called translucence, which allows the sharing of memories through hand-to-hand contact.*
- Luytens—*A large, slug-like civilization that is part of GAIA. Their slime is toxic to Malborgs in high concentrations.*
- Malborgs—*Cyborgs comprised of AI machinery and organic matter. They mostly occupy the Dark Galaxy.*
- Rigellians—*A lizard-like civilization from Rigel. They are a part of GAIA. Captain Gorgana is a Rigellian. They are solely susceptible to the*

hazardous effects of LOMA (low-frequency mind alteration), a banned technology. LOMA disrupts their communication patterns, affects their minds, puts them into trance-like states, and causes physical ailments. The Rigellians were forced to mine the Hopewell Star in the previous book, Journey to the Hopewell Star.

• Volubens—*A civilization that is part of GAIA.*

ACKNOWLEDGMENTS

Books are a collective project. And this project would not have been possible without the support of the many people who contributed thoughtful feedback and encouragement along the way.

Many thanks to all the wonderful readers and writers in my novel writing groups at the University of New Brunswick who provided helpful, constructive criticism for the early drafts of my manuscript. The list has continued to grow over the years: Andrea, Anne, David, Erika, Gina, Heather, Jeff, Kate, Kimberlie, Lori, Luke, Michael, Morganne, Pat, Ryan, Tash, and Terry. Your insightful comments, suggestions, and warm encouragement helped guide me through rough waters like a beacon of light when I felt lost.

Special thanks to Pat, who, along with sharing her insightful feedback and humor, went one step further and created drawings of the early scenes of my story, allowing me to see my world through the reader's eyes.

Thank you to Jane and Steve for their writing support and advice over the years.

I'm eternally grateful to my incredible, honest, and helpful test readers: Brent, Stephen, Paul, and Steve. You were subjected to my unwieldy manuscript without complaint. You graciously took the time to review and offer your words of wisdom, providing thoughtful and detailed feedback, which, in turn, helped to improve the story while making the writing journey meaningful and wonderful.

I owe a huge thanks to my professor and developmental editor, Terry Armstrong, who continually challenged me, was brutally honest but somehow managed to keep my hopes up, probably lost patience with me more than a few times but was too polite to tell me, pushed me past my limits, and made me a better reader and writer.

When your story has been through countless revisions and drafts and you think it can't get any better (or you're in denial or too tired and lazy to see reality as it is anymore) but then your copyeditor finds several errors the moment it hits her desk, you know it's in good hands. To my brilliant copyeditor, Erika LeClair, thank you for your intense scrutiny, professionalism, attention to detail, answering my gazillion questions, and adding several layers of polish, including gorgeous formatting and design elements. You elevated my story where I couldn't and went above and beyond.

Thank you, Lee D. Thompson, for your excellent proofreading and editing work. You noted important details and shared your keen observations, knowledge, and expertise. I greatly appreciate your thoroughness, professionalism, and wit. Your humorous notes were a bonus and made the process all the more enjoyable.

I'm forever grateful to the amazing librarians, booksellers, journalists, bloggers, teachers, book reviewers, literacy promoters, bookstagrammers, and other social media mavens who talked about and recommended my stories to anyone who would listen.

Thank you, dear readers, young and old, here in Fredericton, New Brunswick, and across the globe. I'm humbled by your willingness to take a chance on my stories, and I hope I haven't let you down. An extra-special thanks to those who have taken the time to write a positive review, helped spread the word about my books to others, or dropped by one of my book signings. I'm forever indebted for your thoughtfulness and generosity. Your kindness has not gone unnoticed. It's greatly contributed to my writing success.

I appreciate everyone who has reached out with a warm message of support. Your words meant so much and helped me keep going when I often felt stuck.

To my husband, Brent, thank you from the bottom of my heart for your invaluable feedback, infinite patience, and wisdom throughout my writing journey. Your ideas, suggestions, criticisms, and support kept me on my toes, allowed me to consider different possibilities, and kept me moving forward when I was ready to give up. Thank you for believing in me.

Last but not least, thank you, Eloise, for inspiring me with your beautiful chalk drawings and motivational messages, brightening my days, and making our neighborhood that much more wonderful. P.S. Your pronunciation of Mukalakatakalakum is impeccable.

Thanks again—it's been an exciting journey!

ABOUT THE AUTHOR

Hannah D. State is an award-winning Canadian author. She graduated from McGill University with a BA and earned her MPL from Queen's University. Hannah is bothered by inequality, violence, greed, complacency, snakes, entering a dark room, and not getting enough sleep. She enjoys writing about strong-willed characters who don't fit the norm and who overcome great obstacles with perseverance, self-discovery, and help from others. Sometimes Hannah can't keep up with her characters' ideas and plans, so she takes breaks, drinks coffee, does yoga and tai chi, and takes nature walks to calm her mind and really listen.

To learn more about Hannah's stories, visit her on:

facebook.com/hannahdstate

instagram.com/hannahdstate

goodreads.com/hannahdstate

amazon.com/stores/Hannah%20D.%20State/author/B073G9Y518

Did you enjoy this story?

Share your thoughts and rate it on:

Amazon

and/or

Goodreads

Thank you for your support!